Walking
Shadows

Moon Music

Jupiter's Bones

Stalker

The Forgotten

Stone Kiss

Street Dreams

Straight into Darkness

The Garden of Eden and
Other Criminal Delights: A Book of Short Stories

WITH JONATHAN KELLERMAN

Double Homicide

Capital Crimes

WITH ALIZA KELLERMAN

Prism

Walking Shadows

A Decker/Lazarus Novel

Faye Kellerman

HARPER LUXE

An Imprint of HarperCollinsPublishers

WALKING SHADOWS. Copyright © 2018 by Plot Line, Inc. All rights reserved. Printed in the United States of America. No part of this book may be used or reproduced in any manner whatsoever without written permission except in the case of brief quotations embodied in critical articles and reviews. For information address HarperCollins Publishers, 195 Broadway, New York, NY 10007.

HarperCollins books may be purchased for educational, business, or sales promotional use. For information please e-mail the Special Markets Department at SPsales@harpercollins.com.

FIRST HARPERLUXE EDITION

ISBN: 978-0-06-286779-7

HarperLuxe™ is a trademark of HarperCollins Publishers.

Library of Congress Cataloging-in-Publication Data is available upon request.

18 19 20 21 22   ID/LSC   10 9 8 7 6 5 4 3 2 1

To Jonathan
And to Lila, Oscar, Eva, Judah, Masha, and Zoe—
with love from Nana

Walking
Shadows

Chapter 1

It was a mob, but not yet a full-fledged riot. Over a dozen retirees, dressed in housecoats and robes, had taken to the streets, demanding action at eight in the morning. The call had come through twenty minutes earlier, just as Decker was knotting his blue tie, putting the finishing touches on his typical uniform: a dark suit over a white shirt. He skipped checking in at the station house, going immediately to the crime scene—seven smashed mailboxes, metal poles uprooted, letters and flyers strewn into the street.

White-haired Floyd Krasner led the charge. "It's the third time in what . . . three months?"

"Less than that," Annie Morris chimed in. She was in her seventies and wore a terry-cloth robe over floral pajamas. "Third time in two months. Not a good way to start the summer."

"I'll say," Floyd added.

Janice Darwin tightened her own coral robe and added, "I didn't give up my life in the city just to find crime here, you know."

Decker wasn't sure what city she was from. Not that it mattered. He smoothed his mustache—silver with hints to its once red color. It matched the hair on his head. "I know you're frustrated—"

"Y'think?" Floyd blurted out.

Grumbling from the masses.

Decker looked at the old man—stoop shouldered with angry eyes. He and Floyd were around the same age. Decker had the advantage of a strong back and broad shoulders, although he suspected that gravity had shoved his spine down an inch or so. Still, he had plenty to spare, always the tallest kid in the crowd. People often asked if he had played basketball.

Nope. Too much weight and too slow.

He said, "Anyone hear anything last night? This much damage must have made noise."

No response. That was expected, since half of them wore hearing aids that they took out at night. Decker's eyes drifted upward to the roofline, then back at Floyd. "What happened to the CCTV camera that we installed on your property?"

Krasner bit his lip. "I took it down."

"*Why?*" Decker asked.

A pause. "It was interfering with my gutter."

"Floyd, I installed that myself. It was nowhere near your gutter. I made sure of that."

The man looked down. "The missus didn't like it. She said it made the place look like a fortress." His eyes flashed. "Who cares? You know who these punks are anyway."

"Probably, but without evidence, I can't arrest them, right?" Decker shook his head. "That camera cost over two hundred dollars. What did you do with it?"

"It's in the garage."

"It still works?"

"Yeah, it still works."

"Could you get it for me?" Decker turned to Anne, who lived next door to Floyd. "Do you mind if I install it on your roof?"

"Be my guest. You could have asked me in the beginning."

"Floyd volunteered. I didn't know he took it down."

"It was interfering with the gutters," Floyd said again.

"No, it wasn't." Decker looked at the sea of faces. "Everyone, go home. I'll take pictures of the mess, and we'll get someone out here to reinstall the mailboxes."

Karl Berry spoke up. "Wouldn't it be easier just to get us all PO boxes?"

Janice said, "I don't want a PO box. I like having a mailbox."

"Why? All I ever get is junk."

Decker said, "Karl, you'll have to take that up with the city council. I just do crime."

"And not very well," Floyd said.

"That was uncalled for," Annie said. "If you hadn't taken off the camera, we might have caught them in the act."

Floyd muttered under his breath. Then he said, "I'll get the damn camera."

Decker said, "Go home, people. I'll start at the end of the block and work my way up."

As people slowly started filing back into their houses, Decker walked down the street. Greenbury was a rural eastern upstate town, but some places were more rural than others. This particular road—Canterbury Lane— backed up into woodlands, now green and leafy with the advent of summer. The days were longer, the sun was brighter, the sky was brilliant, and despite the up- rising, Decker was in a good mood.

The warmer nights also brought out the local teen- aged punks. They loitered in the streets, smoked weed in the back alleys, and when they really wanted privacy, they met up in the forest to get high, have sex, and do whatever crazy rituals underdeveloped frontal lobes do. Decker figured the kids entered the street through the woodlands, full of meth and Satan, and decided to vandalize for fun.

The last house on the block—surrounded by the wilds on two sides—belonged to Jeb Farris, a retired money manager who usually summered in Greenbury. He had yet to arrive, so Decker didn't have his permission to tromp around the yard, but he figured Jeb wouldn't mind. He was looking for evidence of teenage delinquency—cellophane wrappers with white powder, pills, ashes from crack pipes, marijuana butts. He didn't find that, but what he did find took him aback.

It took Decker a few moments to regroup his thoughts. Then he took out his phone. The first call was to McAdams, who said, "How's the walker brigade doing?"

"Harvard, I just found a body."

"*What?*"

"At the mouth of the forest where Greenbury bleeds into Hamilton. The north side of Jeb Farris's place. I need two uniforms with tape to cordon off the area, the Scientific Investigative Division, and a coroner. His head was bashed in on the right side, and next to him there's a bloody bat."

"How old?"

"Early to midtwenties. A male with facial hair, although not much of it. Send out Kevin Butterfield if he's available. He can direct the procedure."

"Any ideas who the victim is?"

"No. He's lying on his side, face partially hidden, and I'm not touching him until the coroner gets here. Call up Hamilton. They should have someone qualified in their ME's office. Are you writing this down?"

"Every word."

"After you get the cops, Kevin, and the SID guys, I need you to round up the following dickheads: Riley Summers, Noah Grand, Chris Gingold, Erik Menetti, and Dash Harden. I want to know where each and every one of them was last night and what they were doing."

"Don't those guys live in Hamilton?"

"The body is in Greenbury." Decker thought a moment. "I'll run it by Radar. Let him handle Hamilton PD. But we need to talk to them."

"The dickheads."

"Yes. How are you doing, by the way?"

"What?"

"How are you settling in? Everything okay?"

"I'd prefer to stay with Rina and you."

"Not happening."

"It's just for the summer, Old Man."

"Still not happening. But you can have dinner with us tonight . . . if we're done by then. And even if we're not, Rina can make us sandwiches."

"Okay. It sounds better than what I had in mind."

"Which was?"

"Canned tuna served on a bed of self-pity."

The bigger municipality of Hamilton abutted the college town of Greenbury, but the two places had entirely different demographics. Hamilton had the big box stores, the supermarkets, the fast-food chains, and a real city government with real problems and real crime. Greenbury and its university village was a town filled with boutiques, farmers' markets, cafés, gastropubs, and a quaint little city hall—a Beaux-Arts wannabe—around a hundred years old. The station house sat in the center of the village—a rectangular brick building as modern as a one-room schoolhouse. But it did have Wi-Fi, and the HVAC had been recently renovated, so it was comfortable in all seasons.

Decker looked up the names on the computer. The Hamilton boys had multiple citations for tagging and vandalism, but none had ever been charged with a violent felony, let alone murder. The boys' MO seemed to be to create as much havoc as they could in Green-bury, then run back to the safety of their own city. Decker had every right to haul them in, but it would be much easier to get to the little buggers if he greased the skids. If he wanted full access to Hamilton PD files, he needed Hamilton PD cooperation, and that was always a delicate dance. Mike Radar could help, and Decker pleaded his case to the captain.

Decker said, "Certainly Hamilton hasn't been very successful at curbing their activities."

"I'm sure Hamilton would love hearing that." Radar was nearing his second retirement. His first was leaving the big city to take on the captain's job in Greenbury. Decker had echoed his path, leaving Los Angeles for something quieter and less time consuming. But in the past three years, he had dealt with three very unusual homicides. Like the noir title, trouble followed him.

Decker said, "I don't want to walk in and make demands. I wouldn't want that done to me, but I need those boys."

Radar was wiry with thinning gray hair. He was sharp and insightful, but sometimes a little too cautious. He looked at his watch. It was a little after nine in the morning. "Who's at the scene right now?"

"Kevin Butterfield. Maybe McAdams. We're waiting on the coroner."

"Do you have any officers from Hamilton?"

"The crime was in Greenbury. It's our territory. It has the earmarks of these punks, and all I want is a little interdepartmental cooperation."

"What makes you think that any of the boys committed the murder? You told me that none of them have violence in their criminal histories."

"Vandalized mailboxes are their signature."

"They could have done the vandalizing without doing the murder."

"If they found the body, they didn't call it in."

"Maybe the murder happened after the mailboxes?"

"Or maybe one of them did it. Or maybe they didn't do it, but they saw who did. The smartest thing would be to call them in as witnesses and see what they have to say."

Radar agreed. "I'll make a couple of phone calls. But without proof of what and who was involved, it gets sticky."

"Like you said, the body may not have anything to do with the teens."

"And we don't know who it is?"

"The body? No idea. I'm waiting for McAdams or Butterfield to call me."

"Maybe we should wait for an identity before I made the calls."

"Tell Hamilton I just want to find out if the boys *saw* anything. Keep it simple."

"And when it gets more complicated?"

"Not a problem." Decker grinned. "I do complicated very well."

Chapter 2

Greenbury in June was a month of seesaw weather from cool to warm and muggy and back to cool again. The Five Colleges of Upstate had just started summer sessions, and there was life on the streets. Graduation had been a couple of weeks ago and every inn and B and B had been booked, meaning that lots of seniors on Social Security had rented out a room for a little extra cash. Neither Decker nor his wife, Rina, wanted strangers paddling around the house in a bathrobe and slippers. Paddling was strictly his domain.

He had dashed out of the house earlier than usual. When he did that, he often came home for a morning coffee break, especially if Rina wasn't working. Today he went home and found her out in the garden planting pots of mums, delphiniums, sunflowers, and gladioli bulbs that would make up her cutting garden. Next week would be the vegetables.

She looked up and then got up, brushing dirt off her denim skirt. Rina was five five and slim. She was now in her fifties. Life had softened her once angular face and features. She had small wavy lines on her forehead and laugh lines around her radiant jewel-blue eyes. Her hair was still thick and, for the most part, it was still dark. "Hey."

"Hey," Decker answered. "Time for a cup of coffee?"

"Sure. Everything okay?"

"Fine. Why do you ask?"

"You look like something unexpected happened and you're waiting for the right moment to tell me."

"Found a body. Male. Young. Don't know who it is."

"Ugh! The handiwork of the boys from Hamilton?"

"Don't know. Am I interrupting you?"

"I've got all day. Let's go inside. You can make the coffee while I wash up."

Once seated with a caffeine fix a sip away, Decker described the scene in detail.

Rina said, "If the victim caught the boys vandalizing the mailboxes, don't you think that murder would be an extreme reaction?"

"I've seen odder things."

"Yes, but more likely, they'd just take off. And if

they murdered the victim first, why bother knocking down the mailboxes afterward?"

"I don't know who the victim is. I'm just wondering if it's one of the boys, in which case I'd need to talk to the others anyway—" His cell rang. He glanced at it as he extracted it from his pocket. "It's Tyler."

"Go take it."

"Thanks." He walked into the living room and depressed the button. "Yo."

"We've got a wallet and a driver's license. Brady Neil. Twenty-six, five eight, one hundred fifty-five pounds."

"A little guy."

"Everyone to you is a little guy."

"Address?"

"It's in Hamilton." McAdams gave him the street and the numbers.

"Okay. Does the face look like the picture on the license?"

"Do you ever look like your picture on your driver's license?"

"McAdams—"

"His face was distorted by the blow, but it's him. I'll take a picture of his face and of the license and text them both to you."

"Good. If there are parents in the picture, they can

ID him from pictures. Save them a trip to the morgue. What did the coroner say about the time and cause of death?"

"Last night around blah to blah."

"That specific, huh. What about the cause? Anything other than what I saw with the naked eye?"

"His skull was bashed in, but she wouldn't commit to a cause until she's done an autopsy."

"Who is she?"

"Fiona Baldwin. Do you know her?"

"No."

"That makes two of us. Let me text you those pictures. I can't do it and talk at the same time."

McAdams hung up. A moment later, Radar had buzzed in.

"Where are you?"

"Home having a cup of coffee before I head out to the scene."

"Come to the station house. We need to talk."

"This doesn't sound good."

"See you in five." Radar hung up.

Decker sighed, came back into the kitchen. "The captain wants to talk."

"About what?"

"Probably about me not getting what I asked for."

"Permission to round up the boys and look at their files?"

"On the money."

"Well, there are plenty of cats in trees and little old ladies and gents crossing streets to keep you busy." When Decker bit his lip, Rina stood up and kissed him. "Radar is a good guy. If he doesn't want to confront Hamilton, I'm sure he has a good reason. Go. I'll see you tonight. Or maybe I won't if you get what you want for this case. Either way, it's a win-win for you."

"Victor Baccus is a reasonable guy," Radar told Decker. "I think he's more than happy to have an experienced homicide detective take over."

Decker paused. "Obviously you could have told me that over the phone. What's the catch?"

"He has a daughter on the force—"

"No way. I'm not babysitting someone until I know what's going on."

"She was with Philadelphia PD for five years, two of them as a detective."

Decker made a face. "She goes from a major city to Hamilton? She screwed up something."

"Well, she's coming over, so you can ask her yourself."

"Mike!"

"Look, Baccus is a good man, Pete. His wife has been sick for a while, so maybe that's why the daughter came back. Don't prejudge until you know what's going on."

"It sounds like I don't have any choice."

"You don't if you want the case."

Decker's phone rang. "It's McAdams."

"Take it."

Decker said, "What's going on?"

"Put it on speaker," Radar said.

Decker complied. "Go ahead, Tyler. Captain is listening."

"Hi, sir."

"Good morning, Tyler," Radar said. "I know you found a wallet. Brady Neil. He's twenty-six and lives in Hamilton."

"Do you know him, boss?"

"No, I don't."

"Do we know if the kid has a record?"

Decker said, "We do, and he doesn't. But I still want to talk to those boys."

"Are we getting cooperation with Hamilton?" McAdams asked.

"This is the deal," Radar said. "Chief Baccus wants full cooperation between the two police departments.

No one has any problem with that. But Baccus wants us working with his daughter, Lenora: Lennie Baccus. She's twenty-seven and was with Philadelphia PD for five years, including two as a detective, where she broke a very sophisticated GTA ring."

Decker said, "What GTA ring was that?"

"I don't know," Radar answered. "If you and McAdams take her on, it will definitely grease the skids. And you both know that the murder could have happened in Hamilton and the dump was here. If they find a crime scene, it isn't going to be our case anyway."

"Sounds reasonable," McAdams said. "We have an address from his license."

"I've already looked it up. It seems that Brady lives—or lived—with his mother," Decker said. "I'll do the death notification after I'm done talking to this person."

"Officer Baccus, Decker."

"Officer Baccus, excuse me." Decker took the phone off speaker.

McAdams said, "What do you need from me?"

"You can stay at the scene and help Kevin direct. Unless you want to do the notification."

"You're much more adroit with these things, boss. As hard as I try, I just don't have the soul sensitivity."

"McAdams, only you could saddle me with an onerous chore and make it sound like a compliment."

"That's me in a nutshell. I'm terrible at feelings but good with words."

She was a beautiful woman with short blond hair surrounding a serene face. Her features were strong—defined chin, full lips, and almond-shaped, bright blue eyes. She appeared to be around five ten but more lanky than muscular. Dressed in a black suit and white shirt, she looked more executive than cop. Decker found her to be self-effacing, but not shy. They were talking in one of Greenbury's four interview rooms because the detectives' squad area was a big room of open desks and everyone could hear everyone else's business. It was a good layout insofar as information sharing, but not so good for privacy.

About ten minutes into the conversation, Decker said, "I heard that you broke a very sophisticated GTA ring in Philadelphia."

"My dad told you that?" Her laugh was nervous. Lennie had long red nails. She clicked them against one another before she spoke. "He exaggerates. More to make himself feel good, I think. He always wanted boys."

"Tell me about the operation."

"First of all, I was one of four. But we were all women, including the sergeant who led the operation. We worked really well as a team. The sergeant was a tough taskmaster, but she was fair. We got results. It turned out well for all of us."

"Why'd you leave Philly, then?"

"Philly?" She smiled. "Are you a native?"

"No, but I know a few people there. Why'd you leave?"

A pained look came across her face. *Click, click* went the nails. A nervous habit.

She said, "This is going to sound very bad, but the truth is, I was smart enough but not mentally strong enough. I couldn't stand the harassment from the guys."

"Did you file suit?"

"I thought about it. I talked to my sergeant, and she said she'd support me. But we all know the drill. Once you file, you're finished. Word gets around that you're not a team player and no one wants to work with you anymore." She shook her head. "I should have powered through it. But then Dad offered me a position here—more money, less stress." She shook her head again. "I suppose I took the easy way out."

"It's good to know your limits." He regarded her face. "I was told that your mother is ill. Not that I'm getting personal, but was that also a factor in your returning to Hamilton?"

"Mom has multiple sclerosis. She's been ill for a long time. And I suppose maybe I considered her illness when I came back. I'm certainly helping Dad out with the care." A pause. "I would love to work on a real homicide. The cases I've been getting aren't very challenging."

"You want big-city cases, you have to work in a big city. Most of what I do is routine and not interesting. And that's why I came here. You can't have it both ways."

"Of course, you're right," Lenora said. "When you're part of a team, nothing is too little or too menial." Decker was quiet. She smiled and looked down. "I'd be happy getting the coffee and doughnuts."

"I don't like doughnuts," Decker answered. "Look, Officer Baccus, Homicide is nasty. We deal with the worst parts of humanity, and it stays with you for a long, long time. I have no idea if you're up for the job, and nothing you've told me convinces me one way or the other."

"Call up my former sergeant. She'll tell you that I really am very good at my job. Her name is Sergeant Cynthia Kutiel. If you give me your cell number, I'll text you her number right now."

"Do that." When he heard the text beep on his phone, Decker said, "I'll give her a call. I'll also want you to talk to Detective McAdams and Detective Kevin Butterfield. They'll be working with me. We all have to get along for this to be successful."

"Of course."

"Anything you'd like to ask me?"

"Nothing right now. I'm sure I'll ask you lots of questions when we work together." She made a face. "I mean if we work together."

Decker regarded her again. "You know, it's good to show confidence even if you don't feel it. Nobody likes people who feel sorry for themselves."

Instead of wilting, she said, "Point taken. I really want to learn, and I'm a workhorse. I'll be a good asset to you."

"Good. Detectives McAdams and Butterfield are with SID at the crime scene." Decker gave her the address. "Go out there and have a look-see. I'll tell McAdams that you're coming."

"Absolutely." She stood and offered a hand. "Thank you very much."

"This is a trial period, you know."

"I understand."

"Good." Decker paused. "McAdams is studying to be a lawyer—at Harvard. He's a good detective, but he's young and brash. He doesn't choose his words carefully. He can be very rude, but he thinks on his feet, and that's important. You've got to be able to deal with that. The good news is he won't come on to you, Lenora. That's not him."

"Then we'll absolutely have no problem. And you can call me Lennie, by the way."

"Fine, Lennie. And you can call me boss."

Chapter 3

"So now I have to babysit a spoiled brat!"

"Ahem. Pot . . . kettle."

"Spoiled I will agree to, but you can't be a brat if you've been shot in the line of duty. That is just not right."

"She worked five years with Philadelphia PD. She was in GTA as a detective."

"GTA Philadelphia? As in your daughter?"

"The very same city. Cindy was her detective sergeant."

"Wow. Did you tell her?"

"Baccus? Of course not. But I will call up Cindy after I get the death notification done. I just wanted to give you a heads-up about Baccus. She should be with you shortly."

"Did she tell you why she quit Philadelphia PD?"

"Sexual harassment."

"Ah, c'mon! You can't be serious!"

"She's beautiful, Harvard. I can completely believe it, but I'll ask Cindy about it. At least, in Hamilton, no one is going to mess with the chief's daughter."

"But it does show a certain lack of resilience."

"Yes, it does. She's on her way. Be nice, Harvard. We need her on the team to get into Hamilton's files."

"If I'm too nice, then she'll think I'm coming on to her."

"Hmm, a valid point," Decker admitted. "You're right. Don't be nice. Just be your usual obnoxious self."

Jennifer Neil identified her son, Brady, from one of the photographs taken by the police photographer, saving her the agony of coming down and seeing the body in person. She was five foot two and thin as a reed. A little thing with a weathered face, making her look older than her forty-nine years. Her thin lips could have passed for another crease in her wrinkled face. Blue wet eyes were rimmed in red. She wore baggy jeans and a Guns N' Roses T-shirt with a concert tour dated twenty years ago.

The woman looked utterly lost.

"Do you have someone I can call to be with you?"

When she didn't answer, Decker said, "A relative or friend?"

Slowly she shook her head. "When can I see him?"

"You don't have to see him, Mrs. Neil. It's best to remember him as he was." She didn't speak. "Are you sure there's no one I can call?"

"No husband, if that's what you mean."

"Do you have other children?"

Her lip quivered. "A daughter. We don't talk." A pause. "I suppose I should call her."

"I can do that for you if you want me to."

She nodded.

"What's her name?"

"Brandy."

Decker thought, *Brandy and Brady.* Or maybe it was Brady and Brandy. "How old is she?"

"Thirty."

Brandy and Brady. Jennifer had been just nineteen when she had her first child. "Do you have a phone number?"

"Gotta look it up. I don't know if it's current or not." She left the living room. It was a small house, neat and clean but unadorned. The faux-leather furniture matched, the end tables were dusted, and the brown carpet was vacuumed though thin in some parts and stained in others. A moment later, Jennifer came back with a slip of paper and a number. Decker pocketed the paper and took out his notebook. "I know this is a horrible time to ask you questions, but it would be helpful if I knew a little bit about Brady."

She said nothing. Just wiped her eyes.

"Brady was twenty-six?"

"Yes."

"Did he live with you?"

"Yes."

"Did Brady work or go to school?"

"Both."

"Where is work and where is school?"

"He worked at Bigstore in the electronics department."

"He's good with computers?"

"No idea."

Her apathy took Decker aback. "No idea?"

"No. He was secretive about his life."

"Okay. Secretive as in . . ."

"We just didn't talk about anything personal. Truth be told, we hardly talked at all. He's a single male in his twenties. We don't have anything in common."

"Got it. Do you know how long he worked at Bigstore?"

"About a couple of years. He must have gotten a promotion because Brady always had money."

"He had money?"

"Always."

"What kind of money are we talking about?"

"He had a car and all the gadgets—y'know, the Xbox and the iPhones and that kind of stuff. It kinda pissed me off that he had money for that shit and never offered to help out with the food and rent until I asked him for it."

Store managers didn't make that kind of expendable money. The kid was probably dealing, and something stronger than weed. Opiates were an issue upstate. He said, "Did he give you money when you asked?"

"Couple of hundred here and there."

"And he lived with you even though he had money?"

"Maybe that's *why* he had money. Anyway, I never bothered him and he never bothered me. He lived in the basement. It's a big basement with two rooms and a bathroom. If he ever got his own place, I was gonna rent it out." She bit her lip and wiped her eyes. "Guess that's not a problem now."

"How did he behave with you?" When Jennifer looked confused, Decker said, "Was he rude or apathetic or physical—"

"No, he never got physical with me even when he was out of control."

"Out of control?"

"Typical teenage stuff—drinking, smoking marijuana, not going to school, not coming home at night. He still goes out at night on occasion, but in the morning, he's sober enough to go to work."

"And you said he's also in school?"

"Night school. That's what he told me. Maybe it's true, maybe it's not. The kid used to lie for the hell of it. Shades of his father."

"Did Brady ever have problems with the law?"

"Not that I know of." She looked at him. "Can't you look that up?"

"I did. No record as an adult, but juvenile records are sealed."

"He used to be truant. Couple of times, cops brought him back home. But then he dropped out of high school so truancy wasn't a problem. He went through some low-paying jobs—fast-food counter, things like that—until he got a job at Bigstore. Like I said, it must pay well, because he has spare money."

Decker thought about Brady, working in the electronics department. He could also have been involved in warehouse theft. Working for a bigger ring and it caught up with him? Both sidelines—dealing and theft—were dangerous enough to explain his corpse.

"And you don't know where he went to college?"

She continued talking. "A year ago, he said he was

taking some classes at community college. Like I said, don't know if that was true or not."

"Do you know if his money may have come from something other than a job?"

"Wouldn't know that, either. You mean like drug dealing?"

"Do you think he was dealing drugs?"

"I don't know, Detective. When are you going to release the body?"

"I'll call you as soon as I know." Decker waited a beat. "Do you know of anyone who'd want to hurt Brady or held a grudge against him?"

"No." A quick response. "Is that all?"

"I'd like to take a look at his basement room, Mrs. Neil. Would that be okay?"

"I don't have the key."

"Can I bust open the lock?"

Her eyes started to water. "Sure."

"Thank you." She was quiet. Decker said, "Mrs. Neil, would you know the names of any of Brady's friends?"

"No. The basement has a private entrance. He came and went as he pleased. I know that occasionally he had people down there. I could hear voices. But that's all I know."

"Male? Female?"

"Mostly male, but a woman now and then."

Decker mentioned the names of the thugs who were probably responsible for the mailbox vandalism. "Any of those names ring a bell?"

Jennifer shook her head no.

"How about friends from when he was a teenager?"

She gave the question some consideration. "You might try Patrick Markham or maybe Brett Baderhoff. Those are the only two I can think of. You also can try his sister. I'm not on speaking terms with her. But that don't mean that the two of them didn't talk."

He needed a pair of bolt cutters to break open the padlock. Once Decker was inside, he wondered why all the secrecy. It was an ordinary living area, only much neater than he had expected from a young adult living at home.

The space was divided into a small living room with a kitchenette. It had a two-burner cooktop and an apartment fridge. No oven. Brady had a sofa, a couple of big chairs, and a big-screen TV. Jennifer was right. He had a massive game console set. No photographs of himself or anyone else. Off the living area was a shower, toilet, and sink.

The bedroom was taken up by a queen bed. It had two doors, one from the living area and the other that emptied into a one-car garage that also held a washer/ dryer. The sole vehicle inside was a maroon Ford Focus that was around five years old. Brady may have owned the car, and that may have put him a step ahead of his mother, but it wasn't exactly a showpiece.

Decker went back inside and began his search in earnest. He checked drawers and cabinets. He looked inside the pillows' cases and pockets. He peered under the mattress and did find a half-dozen photographs of a much younger Brady with a girl. He looked around fifteen, the girl a few years older. The boy had dark brown hair and intense dark brown eyes. The girl was a blonde with blue eyes. The boy's stare pierced through even though the couple was mugging for the camera.

The inspection took about thirty minutes because Brady kept a spare apartment. He wasn't much of a drinker—a couple of six-packs in the fridge. And not much of a doper except for a dime bag of weed. No hidden pills. No hidden powders and no drug paraphernalia. There were no closets brimming with electronics and no stash of phones. If he was involved in illegal activity, he was operating elsewhere.

Jennifer was waiting for him at the top of the stairs. She said, "Find anything?"

"A little marijuana." Decker climbed the steps. "Nothing that makes me think he's dealing."

She nodded. "What does it look like down there?"

"It's pretty tidy. If he was having wild parties, he cleaned up after himself."

"I don't think I can go down there just yet." Her eyes watered up. "I suppose I'll have to do it eventually . . . especially if I'm gonna . . ."

Her words drifted off. Decker filled in the blanks: *if I'm gonna rent it out.* Jennifer was a little short on maternal feelings, but there didn't seem to be open hostility between mother and son as far as he could tell. He took out a photograph. "Mrs. Neil, could you tell me who's in the picture with Brady?"

"That's my daughter."

"Brandy?"

"Yes." A pause. "I remember this picture. It was during the summer, and we were visiting a corn maze. I took the photo on Brandy's phone."

"How old were they?"

"Sixteen and twelve. Shortly after that, Brandy ran away after a blowout fight. I didn't even try to stop her."

"Where'd she go?"

"No idea."

"What about her dad?"

"Not likely. He's been in jail for the last twenty years. He's up for parole soon, but he probably won't get it. The family still lives in town."

"The family of the victim?"

She nodded.

"What's he in for?"

"Murder." A pause. "Double murder. A man and his wife who owned a jewelry store. They weren't supposed to be there when he did the job. I mean, robbery is wrong no matter what, but he didn't go in with the idea of murdering the old folks."

"I understand. Do you know if either Brandy or Brady have visited their dad in jail?"

"No idea."

"Okay." A pause. "And you don't know where Brandy lives?"

"No. Out of the blue, she called me about five years ago just to tell me she was okay. She gave me her phone number. Told me not to call unless it was an emergency. I don't know if this is an emergency, but I think she'd want to know. I'd want to know."

"I'll call Brandy."

"Thank you again."

Decker paused. "Do you remember the names of the victims your ex murdered?"

"Lydia and Glen Levine. Levine's jewelry store. The business was taken over by the son. He was there during the robbery, hiding in the closet, and was the key witness against Brandon and his partner." A pause.

"I know this is going to sound stupid, but I'm going to tell you anyway. My ex and his partner, Kyle, swore up and down that all they did was tie up the couple, that they both were alive when they left. They swore up and down that someone else must have fired the shots after they left. It's probably bullshit, but I don't know . . . Brandon was a lot of things. I never pictured him a killer."

"What did the witness say? The son?"

"That he was there and he saw my ex and Kyle shoot his parents."

"But you don't believe him?"

"He could have shot them after Brandon and Kyle left. And, on the stand, it came out that the son was a party kid, that he spent a lot of money, and there was even talk about his parents cutting him off. But since Brandon and Kyle were caught with the stolen goods, it was pretty much open and shut for conviction."

"What was the son's name?"

"Gregg Levine. Like I said, he still runs the place."

"Okay. Were you married to Brandon Neil at the time of the robbery?"

"My last name is Neil. He's Brandon Gratz. Yes, we were married. That's why I couldn't be made to testify against him."

Decker nodded. "Twenty years is a long time in jail.

But it's a light sentence for a double murder. Was that the recommendation of the jury?"

"Jury recommended life without parole, but the judge gave them twenty each with a possibility of parole. But like I said, they probably won't get out." She caught his eye. "You think there's something to what Brandon was saying, about him being set up?"

"I have no idea." Decker smiled. "I might want to come back and search Brady's room again. Would that be okay?"

"Yeah, but not forever, you know. I got plans." She looked down. "I need the money."

"I understand, Ms. Neil. Thank you for your time and help."

"Detective, I may seem a little hard, but please find out who hurt my boy. We weren't close. Still, no one should get away with murder." She looked down. "I didn't rat out my ex-husband. It was my constitutional right not to say anything against him and I didn't. But once he was convicted, I was secretly glad he didn't get away with it."

Chapter 4

"How are you and Officer Baccus working out?"

McAdams said, "Let me call you right back."

Decker hung up. He bought an espresso at an independent coffeehouse, and as he was walking back to the car from the café, his phone rang. "You okay, Harvard?"

"Just wanted privacy."

"How's the new kid doing?"

"She's quiet. I appreciate that."

"Anything else?"

"The coroner just left."

"Anything else about Baccus?"

"She takes copious notes. She was probably a good student. Have you called your daughter yet to find out who we're working with?"

"Haven't had time. The coroner didn't say anything else other than blunt force trauma?"

"Two blows. Either one would have knocked him cold, so the second one was for good measure. She didn't find any obvious bullet or stab wounds. She'll know more once she gets him on the slab. How'd the death notification go?"

"Jennifer Neil wasn't close to her son even though they lived together. She's also estranged from her daughter, but she told me that Brady and Brandy might be in communication."

"Brandy and Brady?"

"You heard me correctly. I'm going to set up a date to meet with her. See if she might be more useful to rounding out her brother. Their father, Brandon Gratz—Jennifer's ex—is serving a sentence for double homicide."

"Now we have Brandon, Brandy, and Brady."

"Just be sure to write the names properly when we're identifying the cast of characters. Brandon's sentence is twenty years, so he will be up for parole soon. Jury recommended life without parole, but the judge overruled them. It's odd."

"Uh-oh, you've got that tone in your voice."

"What tone?"

"The tone that says, 'Even though this isn't my case, I'm curious about it.'"

"I am."

"It's not only *not* your case, it's not even in your jurisdiction, plus it's been adjudicated."

"I realize that. I'm just wondering if Brady's death might have anything to do with the sins of the father."

"It was twenty years ago."

"Twenty years ago, you were eight. Twenty years ago, I was a very good homicide detective. It was a long time ago for you, but not for me. It's worth checking out."

"But not in the immediate."

"I agree with you there. It sounds like Brady Neil may have done some dealing in the past. Also, he works in the electronics department. Theft and drugs could also be motives for murder. Anyway, I have a phone number for Brandy Neil. I'm going to call her up and break the news—hopefully in person."

"Now?"

"Sometime today. He and his sister were close at one time. I found pictures of them together when they were younger."

"Where'd you find the pictures?"

"In Brady's basement room. There was nothing there to indicate that he was involved in something illegal, but his mom claims that he always had money. She has no idea where he got it from. I'll tell you all the details when I see you." A pause. "When will I see you?"

"Two of the punks you asked me about this morning are coming to the station house—four in the afternoon."

"Which ones?"

"Uh, hold on. Here we go. Dash Harden and Chris Gingold. Riley Summers will come in tomorrow morning at ten. I haven't heard from Noah Grand or Erik Menetti. When I'm done over here at the scene, I can drop by their houses and see if the lads are home—ask for their cooperation." A pause. "Do I have to take the girl?"

"Officer Baccus. Yes, take her with you."

"Decker, I'm an only child. I don't share well."

"Then here's a chance for some on-the-job training. Go find the lads, but be back at the station house when the punks come in. You and Kevin can take one, and Baccus and I will take the other."

"She's not going to be any help to you, boss."

"I don't need help, Harvard. I could use a little luck. And if I don't get luck, I'll just have to rely on my backup plan."

"Which is?"

"Lots and lots of hard work."

On the station house computer, Decker plugged in "Homicide Lydia and Glen Levine." As expected, there were hundreds of references in the general media as well as in-house police information. The original files were probably now archived. Plus, it was going to take time to go through all of it, and since he had a genuine homicide to deal with, Decker knew where his obligations lay.

He picked up the phone and called Brandy Neil. A few rings, and then it went to her message line. He left his name, his rank, and his phone number—cell and station house—and then hung up. He was about to phone his daughter when something on his computer screen caught his eyes.

One of the papers—the *Hamilton Courier*—had offered up a quote from the lead investigator of the Levine double murder case.

Victor Baccus.

Decker stared at the twenty-year-old article. Nabbing two murderers responsible for a double homicide could make a career in a town the size of Hamilton.

It's not only not your case, it's not even in your jurisdiction, plus it's been adjudicated.

He realized he was still holding the phone. He put in a call to Cindy's cell. When she answered, he said, "Do you have a moment?"

"What's wrong?"

"Nothing." Decker waited a beat. "Do I sound worried?"

"You don't usually start out a call with 'Do you have a moment?'"

"You're right. Hi, princess, I love you. Do you have a moment?"

Cindy laughed over the line. "Around five minutes. What's up?"

"We found a body here in Greenbury, but it's possible that the murder took place in Hamilton—"

"You want to know if you should cede jurisdiction?"

"Does that sound like me?"

Another laugh. "Go on."

"Of course, I'd like full access to Hamilton's files. The police chief was willing, but he had an arm-twisting request."

"Which is?"

"Introduce his officer daughter into the wonderful world of Homicide—"

"Oh, wait. I know where this is heading. Hamilton Police. Lenora Baccus."

"Yes. Apparently, she worked with you."

"She did. Did she tell you why she left the department?"

"Sexual harassment. I'm not calling to debate the validity of the charge, but I would like your opinion of her. She told me she was on your team that took down a major GTA ring."

"That is true."

"What did you think of her?"

"Hard worker, very diligent, willing to learn, good firearm skills, good skills with people, and a great team player."

"That's an endorsement. Anything to add?"

"Like is there anything negative?"

"Whatever you want to add."

"As an original thinker? Not so much. And, truthfully, not the most robust personality on the force. No woman should have to take any kind of sexual harassment, including rude comments, but there are realities of life. She's very good-looking. I would have thought she might have been a bit more prepared. The constant comments were obnoxious, but they seemed to blindside her. Like she's never had unwanted male attention."

"Maybe she was sheltered."

"Could be, but c'mon. Like I said, we women shouldn't have to put up with this crap, but it helps if you're the type of person who can ignore the shit and just get on with the job. Life is not one big safe space."

"I'm surprised about that, especially since Baccus came from a police family."

"I don't think her father was Mr. Supportive about her career choice."

"Sounds like someone else we know," Decker said.

WALKING SHADOWS · 43

"Daddy, once you were reconciled to my stubbornness, you were not only supportive, you were a wonderful source of information and knowledge. You were tough on me at times, but I always knew where the criticism came from. Whenever these jerks get to me, I hear your voice in my head. Just do the friggin' job."

"You're still having to deal with jerks?"

"All the time, Dad. But the good news is, I'm starting to outrank all of them."

Decker beamed. "What do you think my approach with Baccus should be?"

"Give her specific assignments—look up this, call that person, check out this alibi."

"Questioning a suspect?"

"Never seen her do it. My intuition is it's not her natural forte. But you're a great teacher. She's lucky to have you as a mentor." A pause. "I've got to go."

"Thank you, princess. I love you to death."

"Right back at you, Daddy."

Decker decided to try Brandy's number again. This time, the line clicked in with a human voice. He said, "Brandy Neil?"

"Who is this?"

"Detective Peter Decker, Greenbury Police. Is it possible that we could meet in person?"

"Why? What's this about? How'd you get my number?"

"From your mother."

"Why?"

"It's about your brother, Brady." A long pause over the line. Then a longer pause. "Ms. Neil?"

"It has to be bad news."

"Could we meet?"

"Is he dead?"

"I'm afraid so, yes."

"Murdered?"

"It looks that way."

"Ah, Jesus!" Swearing over the line. "How?"

"I'll tell you everything I know. But it would be helpful to meet in person."

"Where? Hamilton police station?"

"Uh, if you could, I'd rather meet at the Greenbury station. Your brother died in our jurisdiction, so we're running the investigation. I don't want to intrude on Hamilton's space. If it's too far for you to travel, I'll come to you."

"I almost never go to Greenbury. It would take me like a half hour to get there."

"Like I said, I can come to you."

"No, I'd rather meet at a police station, no offense. I don't know who you are."

"I think that's prudent of you. When can you come down?"

"Not now. It's two o'clock. I'm still at work. I suppose I can make it around seven."

"That would be fine." He gave her the address of the station house and his cell number. "I'll see you around seven. Please call if there's any change of plans. And thank you very much."

She spoke before he could hang up. "Where is my brother now?"

"He's still at the morgue."

"And if you got my number from my mother, she must know, right?"

"She does."

"Ah, Jesus! This is just horrible . . . *just terrible.*"

"It is terrible. I'm very sorry."

"Did he suffer?"

"No," Decker told her.

Not a lie, not the truth. He didn't know one way or the other, and since he didn't know, there was no reason to cause her any further misery.

Chapter 5

Dash Harden sat in the chair. His manner said defiance while his face said fear. He was used to vandalizing—a nonconfrontational crime—and now, he was face-to-face with the enemy. He was eighteen and stood about five eleven, his body slowly turning into a man's, with the wiry arms giving way to actual muscle. Light brown hair and a face spangled with freckles and acne. His hair was cut short, his features more bulldog than eagle. He kept insisting he had been home all night. Since Decker didn't have any proof that Dash had vandalized, he told Lennie Baccus that he'd be stretching the truth a little. Her job was to listen and take notes, especially the nonverbal reactions, because the interview was being recorded. Concentrating on things like the kid's posture, his fidgetiness, what he did with his hands, eye contact with Decker, eyes looking up or looking down or away. While words were easier to understand superficially, gestures almost always told the truth.

"Dash, it's the third time those mailboxes have been overturned," Decker said. "We installed a closed-circuit TV camera after the second time." That part was true. "You and your friends were caught on tape."

Shaking leg. "I wasn't there."

Decker had yet to tell the kid about Brady Neil. He and Dash had been at it for twenty minutes, so it was time to turn up the heat. "Do you really think I'd go through all this trouble to interview you here if it was just about a couple of broken mailboxes? Well, more than a couple of broken mailboxes. Anyway, that's not what I'm after."

Harden continued to squirm. "I wasn't there."

"Yes, you were."

Sweat on his forehead. "I swear I wasn't."

"You were there."

"No, I wasn't."

"I saw you on CCTV."

A long pause. "It wasn't me."

"Okay, it wasn't you."

The kid's face brightened. "I can go?"

"No, you can't go."

"Why not?"

"Because I saw you on tape, and what I saw matters more than what you say."

"It wasn't me."

"Dash, your buddies and you have been vandalizing mailboxes, walls, street signs, and buildings in Greenbury for a long time. Then you run back to Hamilton, where you think you're safe. Not this time. Just tell the truth and you're done here."

"I wasn't there."

"Yes, you were." Decker poured the kid a drink of water. "Son, the first one of your gang to tell the truth gets the most leniency, because you're all going to be charged. I know that you know about the dead body. That means I bump up the charges from destruction of property—federal property—to murder—"

The kid jumped out of his seat. "I didn't *kill* anyone."

"I believe you, Dash." The kid was quiet. "Come on. Sit back down."

The kid cooperated.

"Tell me what you know about it."

More sweat on his pimply forehead. "Sir, I don't know anything about a dead body."

Decker looked at Lennie and gave her a slight eye roll. "Dash, I think you're a good kid. You're the first one who came in to talk to us. And that's why you'll get leniency if you start telling me what really happened. If you don't talk, you'll force my hand. Then I go over to the next interview room, where my colleague is making the same offer to Chris Gingold."

"I don't need an offer." He bounced his leg up and down. "I didn't *do* anything."

"Okay, you didn't do anything. Tell me what you know."

"I know my rights. I can ask for a lawyer."

"I haven't charged you with anything. But if I do charge you and you get a lawyer, he or she is going to tell you the same thing. Start talking. It's your best chance. Otherwise all of you will be charged with murder. You were on the tape; you were all there."

"If there really is a tape, then you'd know that we had nothing to do with it."

Decker's thoughts whirled around for a split second. "How would I know that?"

A long pause. "That's all I got to say."

Decker sighed. "I'm a good guy, Dash, so I'm going to be honest with you. And it's just between you and me."

The kid was silent.

"There are gaps in the tape. We can see you swinging at the mailboxes, but we didn't get a clear picture of what happened to the body."

"Then you have no evidence against me."

"We have circumstantial evidence. We have you boys swinging at anything upright, and with a track record like yours, it'll carry weight. It doesn't take a whole lot of smarts to infer what else you did with those baseball bats."

"I *didn't kill* anyone." His voice cracked.

"I believe you, son. But you're not giving me much to work with."

The wheels were turning in his peabrain. "What happens to me if I tell you that we saw the body and then we all got spooked and took off?"

"Is that the truth?"

Harden nodded.

"You need to answer yes or no for the tape. Did you see the body while you were on Canterbury Lane while you and your friends were vandalizing mailboxes?"

The kid nodded again.

"Dash, you need to answer yes or no."

"Yes. Okay . . . okay." He exhaled, sighed, exhaled again. "We were . . . you know."

"I do know, but you need to tell me for the tape."

"Having a little fun."

"What do you mean by having a little fun, Dash?"

"Okay . . . okay. We were just, you know . . ."

"Dash, let's get this moving. Just say what you were doing, okay?"

"Whopping down mailboxes. I mean, it's no big deal. It's not like we were busting headlights or something."

Decker had had calls about busted head- and taillights. Be easy to goad him into talking about that, but right now, all he cared about was Brady Neil. "Go on."

"Life is so fucking boring! My mom smokes pot all the time, my stepdad drinks, and whenever they get mad or drunk or stoned, which is all the time, I'm the fucking punching bag. And don't tell me to go to Social Services. I've smoked that doobie. It's useless. I got no choice but to live at home. I get a bed, food, and heat in the winter. I'm working toward a car. Once I get a set of wheels, I'm never coming back."

"You won't have a job if the courts find out what you've been doing."

"Meaning I'm fucked no matter what."

"Not necessarily, Dash. If you promise to stop whacking the mailboxes, you can walk out of here. But, first, you have to tell me about the dead body."

Harden looked down. "I saw it first—at the corner house with the woods in back." His eyes got a faraway look. "Scared the shit out of me. I came back and told the bros and we all went over to look. Then we heard something and took off."

"Heard what?"

"I dunno. It sounded like it was coming from the woods. We just took off."

"What time was this?"

"Around three."

"Three in the morning? As in today?"

"Yeah."

"Could you identify the body?" No answer at first. "Dash, do you know who the dead—"

"Yeah, Brady Neil."

"You knew that the body was Brady Neil?"

"Not at first. When I got there, the body was lying facedown. Riley turned him over."

"Why'd he do that?"

"To see who it was. To see if he was alive. He wasn't. That's when I saw it was Brady. His head was . . . caved in." A long pause. "We took off."

"How'd you know Brady?"

"Just from hanging around."

"Did Brady sell you drugs?"

"No."

"His mom says he had cash. What do you know about that?"

The kid averted his eyes. "Nothing."

"What do you know, Dash? It's all going to come out anyway. I might as well hear it from you first."

"I don't know anything!"

Decker didn't speak. He exchanged glances with Lennie. She had been calm throughout the interview and had been taking a lot of notes. If Brady Neil wasn't a dealer or a poker champ or hadn't made a lucky bet on the horses, there was only one other way where a kid could get easy cash.

Decker said, "By any chance, did Brady pay you for stolen property?"

"No. I never stole nothing."

Most probably a lie. Decker said, "Did Brady pay you to fence stolen property?"

"It wasn't stolen." Dash realized his mistake and shut his mouth.

"What kind of stuff did he ask you to fence?"

"It wasn't stolen."

"What was it, first of all?"

"Shitty stuff—mostly old and broken electronics. Told us he got it dumpster diving."

"What kind of electronics?"

"Old phones, laptops, and broken game systems. There's a market for that—recycling old shit. I went where he told me, met a guy on the street, and gave him the crap. A couple of days later, Brady slipped me some cash."

"How much?"

"Around ten to twenty bucks for the load."

"Why didn't Brady fence it himself? Why use you as a middleman?"

Dash said, "I have no idea. But it was easy money for me, so I didn't ask questions." He had averted his eyes. "And really it looked too crappy to be hot stuff."

Again, the kid was probably lying. Decker said, "And that's the *only* thing you did for Brady? Give this man junk?"

"Yep."

"What about your pals?"

"Brady didn't trust them. Said they were too stupid."

Dash was the smart one, then. The world was in serious trouble. Decker said, "Occasionally was there was a new iPhone or a new laptop?"

"I don't remember. Whatever. Brady said he got all the stuff from dumpsters."

"And I bet Brady also told you that you couldn't get into trouble because you're underage. Not true, you know."

"It was only junk," Harden insisted. "If he was jackin' swank, I didn't know about it."

"How long were you selling junk for him?"

"A couple of months . . . maybe six months."

Decker said, "And you never tried to run your own scam?"

"It wasn't a scam. He had the contacts and he found

the stuff in the garbage. Me? I don't dive in shit for twenty dollars. Once he cleans it up, I'll run errands. What the fuck?"

"You stay right here, Dash. I'll be back." Decker got up and Lennie followed.

Once they were out of earshot, Decker said, "What do you think?"

"The scheme sounds plausible."

"Yes, it does, but do you think he's being truthful?"

Lennie paused, then said, "I don't think he killed Brady Neil."

"Why?"

"I believe he may be hiding something—like peddling stolen property. He's nervous—like shaking his leg and looking everywhere but at you. But I don't think he's hiding murder. He isn't acting nervous *enough*."

"Maybe to him, human life is expendable."

She thought a moment. "Would he really stick around if he had just murdered someone twelve hours ago?"

"He might if he was a dumb kid, which he is . . . despite being the smart one."

Lennie smiled. "Smart is a relative term."

"It is indeed." Decker shrugged. "I agree with you. I don't think he murdered Brady Neil, but he's not telling the entire truth. Let's see how his story lines up with what Chris Gingold says. Go into the other interview room and pull out McAdams and Butterfield."

It turned out that Gingold mostly verified what Harden told them. Dash was the first one to find the body, and Dash told them that he knew Brady Neil. As for Chris, he denied knowing Neil. That was probably a lie, but with nothing definitive to keep the boys locked up, they were released after promising to be good citizens and stop whacking mailboxes.

Decker said, "We have Riley Summers coming into the station tomorrow at ten, correct?"

"That's what he told me," McAdams said.

"Let's see what he has to say." Decker turned to Lennie. "You do the interviewing." He turned to Kevin Butterfield, a seasoned former detective who, like Decker, had semiretired. He was tall and bald and had a professorial gaze, as if giving each question its due deliberation. "Do you mind sitting in with Officer Baccus?"

"Not at all." He turned to Lennie. "We should talk before—say nine-thirty tomorrow, after you've thought about what you want to ask?"

She said, "That would be great. Thank you."

McAdams said, "What's the plan now?"

Decker was reading a text on his phone. He looked

at the time: six minutes to six. "Uh, it looks like Brady Neil's sister has decided I'm legit. She wants me to come to her apartment at seven-thirty instead of her coming here." He looked up at Tyler. "As long as you're getting a salary, you might as well come with me."

"Want me to check up on the canvassing?" Butterfield said.

"They didn't hear the mailboxes being whacked right in front of their houses, so I'm not too hopeful on that regard," Decker said. "On the other hand, the elderly have insomnia. Maybe someone peeked through their shades and saw a car drive off."

"I'm gonna grab a sandwich and then I'll go back to Canterbury," Butterfield said.

"Fine." To McAdams, Decker said. "You should grab some dinner also."

"You're not eating?"

"Pick me up a toasted bagel and cream cheese at Bagelmania. And a cup of coffee. The station's stuff is swill."

"I can do that," Lennie said.

"Okay. Thanks."

"Anything else?"

"Have you ever interviewed before?"

"A few times."

"Prepare some questions, then."

"I'll do it as soon as I come back with your bagel."

"Get yourself one on me."

"I brown-bagged it." A half smile. "Working in Homicide for the first time, I guess I figured it would be a long night."

Chapter 6

Before interviewing Brandy Neil, Decker hoped to glean some background, looking over the numerous articles online on the Levine double murder case. Eventually, he was able to flush out a story.

Over two decades ago, at four in the morning, Gregg Levine had made a 911 call from Levine's Luscious Gems. In a panicky and stunned voice, he explained that his parents—Lydia and Glen—had been robbed, tied up, beaten, and shot in the head. Police were immediately dispatched. Arriving at the bloody, gruesome scene, the officers took an initial statement from Gregg. He and his parents had been working through the night, taking annual inventory, when two men with ski masks charged into the store. Gregg had been in the back and peeked out, long enough to see his parents whacked over the head and kicked and beaten by the robbers. Fear-ing for his life, Gregg hid inside a utility closet behind the water heater as he heard the sound of screams and finally two gunshots. Those sounds were followed by the clang of broken glass and muffled voices. He did not open the door until two hours later, after he was fairly positive that the intruders had left the store.

What he saw was pure horror: his parents, bound, gagged, and dead, sitting in their own vomit, blood, and filth. Although Gregg had only a quick look at the killers, he was able to offer a vague description of one of the men. Apparently, one of them got hot and whipped off his mask. Gregg made a guesstimate as to the heights and weights of the men, and he was pretty certain that the man he saw was Caucasian. If asked if he could identify that man if he saw him again, Gregg said probably.

After investigating layers of known criminals, snitches, and fences, the police narrowed down their options. They found as persons of interest Brandon Gratz and Kyle Masterson. The two of them had been long gone from Hamilton since the robbery/murder, and a BOLO was sent out for the men and their missing vehicles. Warnings were issued: the men were "armed and dangerous" and "do not approach" without sufficient backup. After an exhaustive manhunt, the two men were found in Nashville with the stolen items on their persons.

Based on the jewels in their possession and Gregg's eye-witness testimony, they were charged, jailed, extradited, tried, and finally sent to prison. Most of the items were recovered, but a few very valuable stones and statement pieces remained missing at the time of their sentencing.

Victor Baccus had been the lead homicide investigator, but he had a team behind him. When interviewed by newspapers, Baccus was quick to pass around the credit. He was also spent time raising money for the Levines' five orphaned children. At twenty years old, Gregg Levine, a party boy, was forced to leave his cushy college life and take over the business to support his siblings and himself.

There was nothing unusual in the reporting, and in his reading, Decker didn't smell anything other than good, dogged police work. A crime was committed, there was an intensive and time-consuming investigation, and two very bad felons were apprehended. Everything made perfect sense.

Still, Decker wondered about an alarm. There was no mention of anything going off, which usually points to an inside job, and it didn't seem plausible that the Levines would be working late without the alarm being set. He wrote down the word, *ALARM?*, in his notebook and would check on it if he ever looked at the original files.

McAdams walked into the station with Lennie Baccus. He said, "We got your bagel."

Decker looked up from the screen. "Thanks. You guys have dinner?"

"A new café on Princeton Street. Indian-Thai fusion. That means everything they served kills your taste buds while causing excruciating pain in your gut."

Lennie laughed. "I liked it. In Hamilton, we don't have anything like it. It reminded me of Philly. The restaurants there are phenomenal."

"You two went together?"

"By chance," Lennie said. "Tyler was already seated. The place was tiny with a sizable line for tables. He was kind enough to offer me a chair."

"I've done my good deed for the summer." McAdams looked over Decker's shoulder. "What are you reading?"

"Lennie, go call up Detective Butterfield and ask him if he needs help canvassing."

"Of course."

"And thanks for the bagel." Decker unwrapped the sandwich and took a bite. Cream cheese oozed out of the sandwich. His eyes went back to the computer.

McAdams made a face. "Why are you reading articles on a twenty-year-old case? I thought we decided that was a dead end."

"No, you decided it was a dead end." Decker turned

to him. "If I'm going to talk to Brady Neil's sister, it behooves me to find out all I can about the family." He pointed to the computer. "Brandon Gratz is family."

"Brandon Gratz?" Lennie hung up the phone. "Why are you looking up Brandon Gratz?"

"Good question," McAdams said.

"He's Brady Neil's father. His mom changed the surnames of her children after Brandon Gratz was arrested and convicted."

"Oh my God! I'm so stupid!" Lennie hit her head and clicked her long nails. "Wow! Of course!"

"Why of course?" McAdams asked.

"Because Brandon Gratz and Kyle Masterson dominated my childhood."

Decker said, "What do you remember about the case?"

"I was seven when the news broke on the double murder. It scared the crap out of me and all my classmates. That something so terrible could happen. I remember I had this babysitter I adored. After the murders, she wasn't allowed to watch me anymore. Her mom didn't want her out alone at night. I was heartbroken, but I understood. To tell the truth, I wouldn't let my parents go out at night for a long time."

"Did you know the family?"

"No, I didn't. Hamilton's population at that time was

maybe eighty thousand. Now it's over a hundred. The town has three high schools. Brady and I are about the same age, but we didn't live in the same school district so I never really knew him. He grew up in the Bitsby neighborhood—working class and welfare poor. Lots of the parents drank. Some were on drugs. Some were in jail. Lots of lost kids. It's still that way. I grew up about six miles away in the Claremont area. Blue-collar working class but positively Beverly Hills compared to Bitsby."

"Did you happen to know the family of the victims?"

"The Levines? They lived on the border between Claremont and Bellweather. Their house looked like a mansion to me when I was growing up, but in fact it's just a two-story brick house probably not more than twenty-five hundred square feet. Which isn't small, but it's far from Lower Merion."

"That's the posh area in Philadelphia," McAdams said.

"I'm aware," Decker said. "And you didn't know the Levines?"

"Actually, I knew the youngest daughter, Ella. She was a grade older than me, and after it happened, they pulled her out of Hamilton, and she went to live with relatives for about a year."

"How many kids were there?" McAdams asked.

"Five. The oldest was Gregg, who I thought was really old. In fact, he was only twenty or twenty-one when he was a state's witness against the accused. It must have been horrible for him."

"Really horrible," McAdams said. "Not more than a kid himself."

"Yeah, but he pulled it together. He quit school and took over the family business. After a few years, he brought them all back under one roof. There were grandparents in the mix, but Gregg and the next oldest, his sister Yvonne, continued on with the business while looking after the remaining three kids. Ella was the youngest, but the other two were in high school, so they must have been teenagers. The community helped out as well. I remember my dad taking me to a special police dinner to benefit the family."

Decker said, "Hell of a lot of responsibility for a twenty-year-old boy and his teenaged sister."

"The store is still a going concern, twenty years later. The other three kids don't live here anymore. I don't know what happened to them. But Gregg and Yvonne are still in town. They both married locals and have kids of their own. They do lots of charity work with foster care and disaffected youth. Drawing from their own experiences, no doubt."

Lennie sat down and shook her head. "I haven't

thought about Gratz and Masterson in ages. They should be up for parole soon."

"Next year."

"It won't happen. Not if the family has their say-so."

"Any idea why Brandon Gratz and Kyle Masterson didn't get life without parole?"

"You'll have to ask my father about that. He and the entire community thought it was the biggest miscarriage of justice ever to happen around here. The judge retired after the case and moved out of the area. I don't remember her name. It was a she. I remember my father ranting about the bleeding-heart liberal justice system."

"Your father was lead investigator on the case."

"I know he was. He worked it night and day. I don't think he slept a wink until Gratz and Masterson were apprehended, charged, and convicted."

Decker nodded. "I was looking over the articles on him. He and his solid police work were credited for the convictions."

"Like I said, he worked day and night."

To Lennie, McAdams said, "Kinda strange he didn't tell you that Brady Neil was Brandon Gratz's son."

"I'm sure my father just *assumed* that I knew." She looked at Decker. "Did my dad tell you about Brady's father?"

"Not when Radar spoke to him, but at that time, we didn't know who the victim was. If I ask him about it, I'm sure he'll tell me what he knows. Whether the double murder had something to do with Brady Neil's death?" Decker shrugged. "Right now, we're in the beginning stages and everything should be kept under wraps. Like McAdams keeps saying, it's best not to get distracted by twenty-year-old cases that may not be relevant."

The room was quiet. Lennie picked up her backpack. "I'm going to help Butterfield out in the field until it gets dark. Should I come back here?"

"It'll be after nine. Nothing is urgent. Just go home."

"Thanks. I want to prepare my questions for tomorrow morning's interview."

"Absolutely." Decker paused. "Lennie, do you live far from here?"

"No. I'm just across the border. Why?"

"If I need help as the case progresses, I'm more likely to ask you to come in if you're close by."

"Fifteen minutes. I live in a studio apartment where I can touch the walls if I spread my arms wide enough. So anytime you want help, just call."

"Thank you. Go. I'll see you tomorrow."

Decker waited for her to leave, then shut down the computer. "We should leave if we want to get to Brandy Neil's place on time."

"That was an odd question," McAdams said. "How far she lives from the station house. You never asked me that."

"You were in the district."

"No, that's not it." McAdams waited.

Decker said, "Tyler, what's the normal way you ask a question if you want to know where a person lives?"

"Where do you live?"

"And what would she have thought if I asked 'Where do you live?'"

"She would have thought that you were asking where she lives."

"Maybe also with whom she lives."

McAdams thought a moment. "Aha! You want to know if she lives with her parents. You don't want her yakking about the case to her dad around the dinner table."

"Victor Baccus is her father, and he's bound to be interested in anything that has to do with the case that made his career. And until we find Brady Neil's killer, Chief Baccus is going to be curious if there's a link. He may ask his daughter a question or two." Decker stood up and wiped his mouth. "Hopefully she'll be so busy, she won't have time for dinner with the folks and a lot of extraneous yakking. Let's go."

"Why don't you just tell her to keep the case confidential?"

"I already told her to keep the case under wraps. She was a detective. She's a trained police officer. She knows about confidentiality, and so does the chief. If I make a big deal about it, it'll seem like: (a) I don't trust her—which I don't—and (b) I'm suspicious of her dad—which I'm not. If there's tension between father and daughter, it'll make my life harder. Let's go."

They walked out of the station together toward Decker's car. McAdams said, "Do you think Chief Baccus put his daughter on the team to keep an eye on the investigation? It was an odd request."

"Yes, it was. I don't know what his motivations were. So far, I'll just take him at his word and concentrate on the case in front of us."

McAdams climbed into the passenger seat. "I still think it's weird."

"Harvard, you're a cautious guy. I'm a cautious guy. Until we know what's going on, we'll keep the conversation between us. Just think about what I said the next time you go out with Lennie for lunch."

"I didn't go *out* with her," McAdams insisted. "I just offered her a seat at my table." He paused. "Do you think she was trying to pump me for information?"

Decker turned on the ignition. "What'd you talk about?"

"Just shooting the shit. I talked about Harvard Law, she talked about her time with Philadelphia PD. I didn't tell her about Cindy, by the way."

"Of course you didn't." Decker edged out of the police lot and onto the street. "It would have been bonehead stupid if you did, and you're not bonehead stupid. If you talk to her outside of work, keep it neutral. That's all I'm saying."

"You don't trust her?"

"She's new. I don't trust anyone new. In reality, I don't trust anyone unless I've worked with them for a very long time."

"So cynical."

"No, you're cynical. I'm just wary."

"How long before you trusted me?"

"About a year. After you got shot."

McAdams was shocked. "I needed a hit with a lethal weapon before you trusted me?"

"I would have trusted you eventually, Harvard." Decker smiled. "Taking a bullet for me just sped things up."

Chapter 7

The Bitsby area was one step above blighted. It had an oversupply of bail bond houses, twenty-four-hour convenience stores with bars on the windows, seedy motels, OTB outlets, deep discount electronics stores, and pawnbrokers. There were blocks of weed-choked lots and junkyards secured by chain link. The uneven roads were pocked with potholes, and the sidewalks were tattooed in graffiti. Streetlights looked few and far between. Decker had no idea how bright the lamps shone because the sun was still out when he and McAdams arrived at Brandy Neil's apartment.

The woman who answered was thirty with a thin face that bordered on emaciated. She wore no makeup, her filmy blue eyes looking tired and sad. Oddly, her face was framed with luxuriant chestnut-colored hair that had been set in waves and curls. She wore denim jeans and a black T-shirt. Her feet were bare. After Decker made the introductions, Brandy invited them in; her voice was soft and sober.

Stepping over the threshold, Decker thought about Lennie's description of an arm's-span apartment. This one was made even more claustrophobic because the ceiling was low—an acoustical, popcorn top, which meant the place was probably built in the '60s or '70s. It was spare in furniture and spare of personal items. The couch was floral in yellow and blue, the material torn and worn. She invited them to sit on it, and the men complied.

"Coffee?"

"Water, if you wouldn't mind," Decker said.

"And you, Detective?" She was looking at McAdams.

"Water as well. Tap is fine."

"Times two." Decker pulled out his notepad.

She got up and went to a back counter that held a two-burner cooktop and a microwave oven. The fridge was bar sized and sat under the cabinets. She took out glasses and filled three cups from the tap. She handed out the water, and then she sat down. "I don't know what I can tell you that will help. I don't know a lot about Brady's life. I mean, about his life after I left. When we lived as a family under one roof, it was hell."

"How so?" Decker said.

"Well, I'm hoping you know about my dad so I won't have to get into all that shit."

"I do know. You were shunned after he was jailed?"

"We were terrorized. We had to move thirty miles north to Grayborn—a little shit town with a nice name. We lived there for about three years until Mom brought us back to Bitsby and enrolled us in school under her maiden name, Neil. By then I was around fourteen. Of course, my classmates knew who I was, but now we were all teenagers. They fell into two categories about me. In the first group, I was a total pariah. In the second one—the bad kids—having a parent in prison for murder was cool. Guess which group I fell into."

"Not hard to understand."

"I dropped out at sixteen. I was a druggie and a groupie and a horrible influence on Brady. Mom and I fought all the time, but I never expected her to kick me out." She looked down. "But she did, and things worked out well. Being self-reliant made me get my act together very quickly. I got a job with a very kind boss who knows who I am and what I went through."

"What do you do?" McAdams asked.

"I'm a bookkeeper, believe it or not. I was always good with numbers. So was Dad, and that's probably what got him in trouble initially. Dad gambled. Mom used to tell me he had a system. It worked for a while, but then it failed and he got into debt. Real bad debt. Hence the robbery—robberies. The Levines were probably not the first."

McAdams said, "Forgive me for saying this, but you must have a very unusual boss."

"Every week, I go over *everything* with his wife or with him. All invoices, payments out and payments received. I leave nothing up to chance."

"What business is your boss in?" Decker said.

"Paper supplies. He wholesales out everything from typing paper and lined notebooks to high-quality stationery. I've turned my life around. I've got a little money in an IRA and a little money in the bank. I live in this shithole place in this shithole area because it's cheap and all I want is somewhere to rest my head at night. I'm not saying my party days are over. If someone else foots the bill, I'll go out. But I'm not paying for drinks that are pissed out in an hour and leave me with a bad headache. Most of the time, I live like a monk."

"And you're still on nonspeaking terms with your mother?"

"She is positively toxic. So, no, I don't talk to her. I do send her a Christmas card with a hundred-dollar check every year, and she always cashes it. That way, I know she's still alive."

Decker said, "She didn't mention that."

"She wouldn't. To her, I'm just a bad girl who doesn't care." A long sigh. "What the hell happened to my baby brother?"

"We were hoping you could maybe help us out with that. What do you know about Brady?"

"Not a lot. We did talk, but not too often."

"What did you talk about?" McAdams asked.

"Mostly we talked about how we were coping."

"How was he coping?"

"He said he was okay. He had a job, he had a few friends. Mom basically ignored him and he ignored her. Plus, he had the entire basement for his living quarters. About four times the space of this apartment and no rent. Mom always favored Brady. Me? Not so much."

"Did you know any of Brady's friends?"

She paused and shook her head. "I knew a few of his school friends, but that was a long time ago."

Decker paged through his notes. "Patrick Markham and Brett Baderhoff."

"Yeah. Wow, haven't heard those names in a while."

"Anyone of a more recent vintage?"

Brandy smiled. "Yes, come to think of it. He had a pal from work. Boxer. He was a warehouse worker. I never met him, but Brady told me that he and Boxer would go out drinking sometimes. He was an older guy—around thirty-five or so. Sounds like loser company, but I'm not one to judge."

"Is Boxer his first or last name?"

"Don't know. Brady just called him Boxer."

"It sounds like a nickname," McAdams said.

"It might be."

"What about girlfriends?" Decker asked.

She shrugged ignorance. "He never mentioned anyone specific."

"I have to ask you this. Did you know of any activities that might have compromised Brady in some way?"

"If he was dealing, I didn't know about it."

"Your mom said he always had cash."

"Then ask my mom about it."

"I did. She had no idea how he got it."

"Neither do I."

Decker wondered how much he should say to her. Brandy appeared to be truthful. Maybe it was worth the chance. "I pulled in a couple of punks this afternoon. Both of them told me that Brady was selling used and out-of-date electronic equipment to recycling dealers."

She waited. "Okay. Is there something wrong with that?"

"No. The kids said he found the stuff dumpster

diving. Does that sound like the kind of thing your brother might do?"

"Maybe." She shrugged. "Brady could be . . . entrepreneurial. But his business wasn't always legal, to put it mildly."

"He dealt drugs?"

"Nothing big, but yes, he sold pot and pills in high school."

"And that's all?"

"He didn't peddle tar or crack, if that's what you're asking." A pause. "At least, if he did, I didn't know about it."

"So it's possible he could have dealt harder stuff."

"Maybe." She looked at the ceiling. "Something got him murdered."

"True enough," McAdams said. "Was he good at computers?"

"I've never known him to be a whiz or geeky or anything like that. But he did work in the electronics department at Bigstore, and he was promoted to manager. So maybe he was more adroit than I knew."

"Was Brady good at numbers like you and your dad?" Decker asked.

"Yes, he was, come to think of it. He was no abstract math genius, but he could add and subtract in his head. I imagine that a gift like that would come in handy working in retail. Today, with calculators and computers, his skill doesn't bring much to the table. But it's a great party trick."

"How about if you're betting and the odds keep changing?"

"I don't think Brady was a gambler. We both had our fill of that life from Dad." Brandy checked her watch. "I'm sorry to be rude, but I have to meet my mom at the mortuary tomorrow and I'm just dreading it. I need a little time to relax. If you have more questions down the road, I'm fine with it. Just not now."

The men got up and gave Brandy their cards. "Call if you can think of anything else," Decker told her. "You've been very helpful."

"Have I?"

"Very much. Thanks for your time, Ms. Neil."

"Just call me Brandy. It's kind of a stripper name, but I like it. It's about the only thing I've kept from my old life."

After they got into the car, McAdams said, "If Brady was a gambler like his old man, it could explain how he wound up dead. Maybe he borrowed money from the wrong person."

"It's a thought, but a true gambler usually doesn't

have cash lying around. They spend it as soon as they get it."

"A professional poker player?"

"Living in the basement of his mother's home?"

"A mediocre professional poker player?" When Decker didn't answer, McAdams said, "Well, what do you think?"

"I don't have any definite theories right now. But what do you think about a manager of the electronics department of Bigstore keeping company with a warehouse worker?"

"He was stealing from the inventory?" McAdams said. "Don't they keep meticulous records?"

"I'm sure they have records . . . how meticulous?" Decker shrugged. "If he was dealing in broken-down parts, what's to say that a box here and there didn't get accidentally dropped and ruined?"

"Then Bigstore would return it to the manufacturer."

"Yes, if it was a really big, expensive item. But Bigstore sells a lot of glasses, decorative pots and vases, and kitchenware and small appliances and food in jars. Stuff they wouldn't ship back because it's too little. If it was a smaller item—a phone or a cheap game system—maybe the store would elect to lump it all together under its breakage insurance policy."

"Okay. Suppose Neil and Boxer were occasionally lifting broken items. That's a good theory for explaining Neil's extra cash. But it doesn't explain how he got whacked in the head and ended up dead."

"No, it doesn't." Decker's phone rang and Butterfield's voice emerged on Bluetooth.

"Hey, Deck."

"Hey, Kev. How did the canvassing go?"

"Between that and CCTV, I have a few things. I'm at the station house. Where are you?"

"We're just coming back from talking to Brady Neil's sister. We'll be right over."

"Is the kid with you?"

"The kid is right here," said McAdams. "When do I lose the moniker? I mean, is it really proper to call someone a kid if he's been shot two times in the line of duty?"

Over the line, Kevin Butterfield said, "You're right. You are now officially Harvard. The girl can be The Kid. Because I'm sure you can't call any female a girl anymore without getting into trouble by the PC police."

Decker smiled. "Okay, Lennie Baccus is officially the kid."

"Good to have the rules down," Butterfield said. "See you both later."

After he disconnected, McAdams said, "You didn't tell him about Lennie's supposed sexual harassment."

"It's not supposed, it's real. My daughter confirmed it. I didn't tell Butterfield because I don't want to bias his opinion of her. She needs to be judged on her own merit."

"Even though she's a spy for her father."

"I never said that. You did."

"But you did tell me that you don't trust her."

"That has nothing to do with who she is. It has everything to do with who I am. I'm very cautious."

"Indeed," McAdams said. "I started out cynical. You've turned me suspicious. If I keep going at this rate, I'll be downright curmudgeonly before I hit thirty."

Chapter 8

"There was a woman." Butterfield was flipping through his notes. He was wearing a white shirt under a light blue sports coat and tan pants. "She had insomnia. She heard something around three-fifteen in the morning. It might have been a car motor. She peeked through the curtains but couldn't see because it was too dark and she didn't have her glasses."

"Okay. That could mesh with what the punks told me. That they were there around three and the body was already there. Dash Harden also said they heard something a little later and they all took off. Maybe that's what she heard."

"Maybe," Kevin said. "That's convenient. I've been looking at tapes from CCTV close to Canterbury Lane. It took me a while to locate CCTV because not too many businesses have them, and it took me an even longer time to see anything on them, because Greenbury is a ghost town at that time in the morning."

"Got it. What'd you find?"

"See for yourself. This baby had a time of 3:17:34 and was taken from CCTV perched at the intersection of Tollway and Heart. It's heading away from Canterbury Lane."

"Where did you find this camera?"

"It's mounted on the front of Sid's Bar and Grille on Tollway. The place is four blocks from the body dump. Sid's closes at two, and I checked the make and model with the owner. It doesn't belong to him or any of his employees."

"What is the make of the car? I can't tell."

"From this picture, it's hard to see. But at 3:23:17, it shows up again blocks away from Sid's on Tollway in front of the Bank of Northeast. I'd say it's a 2009 or 2010 Toyota Camry—dark gray or black."

"I agree. It might be heading toward the highway. You have any more sightings?"

"No, I'd just started looking in all directions when I found these two tapes. Tomorrow, I'll go pull any CCTV tapes along Tollway and see if I can spot the Camry again. I'll also try to pull current registries for 2009 and 2010 Camrys from the DMV."

"Good work." Decker stared at the screen. "I can't

see the face of the driver." Another pause. "This blob over here. That might be someone in the passenger seat. Can you enlarge it?"

"I tried already. All it did was make the blurry images even blurrier. We don't have the proper resolution equipment. I could try Hamilton. They're a real city."

"Leave Hamilton out of the mix for the time being."

"Why?"

"I don't want to impose any more than necessary on Chief Baccus." The excuse sounded lame to Decker's ears.

"I'd think he'd want to know about this," Butterfield said. "The mailbox felons live in his city."

Decker had to backtrack. "Yeah, you're right. Give Hamilton a call."

"Unless you think there'll be turf issues," Butterfield said.

McAdams came to the rescue. "Baccus wasn't too hot on giving us access to their files. Now that things are heating up, I think he'll want the case back."

"Really?" Butterfield said. "Even with Lennie on our team?"

Decker said, "Give Hamilton a call. Find out what kind of equipment they have to enhance this tape."

Butterfield thought a moment. "I have a few buddies

in NYPD in Queens and in Brooklyn. They're way more likely to have the kind of equipment we need. I can give them a call. If it's there, we can email in the tape."

Decker said. "I'll leave it up to you."

"I'll make some phone calls tomorrow."

McAdams said, "It would be interesting if there were five figures in the car—our mailbox felons?"

"I thought about that," Butterfield said. "I checked out the felons' cars and the cars of their parents. Only one of them—Noah Grand's dad—owns a Camry. It's a 2006 and it's light silver. That car on CCTV is too dark to be light silver."

Decker looked at his watch. It was almost nine-thirty. He'd been working for over twenty hours and decided to call it quits for the day. "Kev, continue this in the morning. Let's go home and get some sleep."

"I've got the Riley Summers interview at ten. Lennie Baccus is doing the questions, remember."

"Right," Decker said. "I forgot about that. How about if I prep Baccus. You make the phone calls to the DMV. Then, you and McAdams check out the businesses on Tollway and see which ones have CCTV. See if you can spot the car and where it's heading."

"Sure, boss." Tyler paused. "You know what goes in, must come out. We have a car driving away from

Canterbury Lane. How about a car driving toward Canterbury Lane?"

"Too true," Butterfield said. "I haven't checked all the tapes. And I've just looked for the cars between the time frame of one a.m. and four a.m. If a car came in earlier, I wouldn't know. Plus, the mailbox felons could be off on their time frame."

"Or lying," McAdams said.

"Always a strong possibility," Decker said. "Get the tapes and we can all watch some TV tomorrow. Right now, let's go home."

They all walked out to the parking lot together. McAdams said, "You're taking me home?"

"Unless you want to walk."

McAdams said, "What are you going to do after Riley Summers?"

"Well, assuming I let him go, I suppose I'll go track down Brady's friend Boxer."

Butterfield smiled. "Boxer?"

"Apparently he works in Bigstore's warehouse department."

"Maybe Brady Neil's friend is a dog. Or maybe Boxer is the name of his profession? Or his favorite hobby?" McAdams started jumping around feigning punches. One came near Decker's face, close enough that Decker jerked his head back.

"What is wrong with you?" He was annoyed. "Did you take your Ritalin this morning?"

McAdams looked chastened. "Sorry."

Butterfield said, "Where'd you learn the moves?"

"I've been taking mixed martial arts classes in Boston."

"Really?"

"No joke. I started with Brazilian jiujitsu. On the first day of class, I grappled with a five-foot, ninety-nine-pound girl and she took me down. After that, I switched to boxing."

Decker smiled. "There's got to be a lesson here somewhere."

"Of course, there is. Don't get hurt. However, if you do get hurt, you can always sue."

At eleven the next morning—after an hour of interviewing Riley Summers—Decker was having a hard time deciding if the kid was a deft psycho or if he was just another confused and/or stoned teen. The few coherent statements he did make seemed to jibe with the statements given by Dash Harden and Chris Gingold. Perhaps they all colluded, but it was hard to believe that these guys could keep a false story straight without tripping up. In the end, Decker released the kid, giving him the same stern warning that he gave Harden and Gingold yesterday: keep your nose clean and don't go anywhere too far away.

"Does that mean I don't have to go to work?" Riley was wearing jeans and a T-shirt and was scratching a pimple on his face.

Lennie looked at Decker for guidance. He said, "You can go to work, Riley. Just don't go anywhere far. Where do you work?"

"Eddie's Gas."

Decker said, "On Milliken, off the highway?"

"Yeah."

"What do you do?"

"Pump gas. Eddie don't use automated machines."

"Why not?" Lennie asked.

"'Cause that way he can charge for full service. That's why I pump gas. I also wash windows and check oil."

Maybe Harden was the smart one. "It's okay for you to work, Riley."

"Fine. Can I go now?"

"Yes." To Lennie, Decker said, "Could you see him to the door, Officer Baccus?"

"Of course."

After they left, Decker picked up his car keys. He met Lennie as she was coming back into the station. "I'm going to Brady Neil's place of work, specifically to interview a guy nicknamed Boxer who works in the warehouse of Bigstore in Hamilton."

"There are two Bigstores in Hamilton. Which one?" Decker showed her the address. "That's near me in Claremont."

"Where's the other Bigstore?"

"Right outside Bitsby."

"The Bitsby one is nearer to Brady Neil. I wonder why he didn't work there?"

"The Bigstore in Claremont is bigger and has higher-end things."

"Ah. Do you shop there?"

"I'll buy food and household stuff. Sometimes I'll get coffee and a muffin in the café. It's cheap."

"Are you there often?"

Lennie thought. "Once a week."

"And you know some of the employees?"

"A few by name. Most by sight. Do you want me to come with you, boss?"

"Yes. While I interview this guy, Boxer, you ask around. I'm sure by now everyone has heard of Brady Neil's murder. It made front-page news. There are bound to be some rumors floating around the place, some sotto voce. It's your area store. It's in your city. People will feel more natural around you. See what you can pick up."

"Of course. What do I tell them if they ask me questions?"

"You tell them nothing, but you make it sound like you're telling them something. You're going back to Hamilton after this investigation is over. You've got to get along with the people you serve. So just dodge their questions. But be really nice about it."

"He's not here."

"Okay." Decker looked around the warehouse. It was enormous, with enough supplies to outfit a third-world nation, and he hadn't even made it to the food storage section. He was talking to a guy in his late twenties—beefy build with muscled arms. He had pierces in his thick lips and a shaved head that was tattooed except for a natural colored red/orange mohawk running down the middle. He was Phil G. Decker knew this because his green Bigstore name tag told him so. The kid was halfway up a ladder stocking some game systems, when Decker asked, "Do you know when he's coming back?"

"No idea." Phil pushed the three boxes he was carrying on an open shelf and climbed down. His forehead was beaded with sweat. No A/C in the place, just a bay with barn doors that were open. He faced Decker. "Boxer didn't show up yesterday and he didn't show up today. Tomorrow's his day off . . . if he still has a job."

"Has anyone tried to call him?"

"Wouldn't know. I didn't call him. He wasn't a pal. Ask the manager."

"And where would I find the manager?"

"In her office."

"And where is her office?"

"All the way in back. When you get to the barn doors, hook a left, then go past the food warehouse, then hook a right and the offices are there. Her name is Barbara Heiger."

"Okay. Thanks, Phil. Do you know Boxer's real name? It's obviously not Boxer."

"Nah, it's not Boxer, but that's what everyone called him."

"Did he box?"

"You've never seen him, huh?"

"No, I've never seen him."

"Scrawny guy. Around five eight with stringy arms."

"You didn't like him."

"Didn't like him, didn't hate him. We didn't hang. He was Brady's friend. They hit it off right away." Phil looked down. "Poor Brady. I talked to him now and then when he came into the warehouse. Once in a while, he'd bring in pretzels and chips for us ghouls to snack on. He said they were leftovers from a party, but the bags were always unopened. What the hell happened to him?"

"That's what we're looking into. You thought Brady was a good guy?"

"Yeah, from the little contact I had with him. He worked resale. He'd come in to talk to Boxer but would always acknowledge me . . . the other guys. It goes a long way, you know."

"What do you mean goes a long way?"

"To most people, we're furniture. Brady made you feel human. But like I said, he mostly talked to Boxer."

"And because Boxer was Brady's friend, we just wanted to ask him a few questions. Any idea where he lives?"

The lightbulb went off in Phil's head. "You think something happened to Boxer?"

"The thought crossed my mind."

"Oh Jesus! That would be . . ." Phil's jaw was working hard. "Is there something going on with this store? I mean, two guys working here. That's a little coincidental, right?"

"If you're just doing your job, I don't think you have anything to worry about."

"Whadaya mean by that?"

"I mean if you keep out of trouble, you should be okay."

"Was Brady in trouble?"

"I'm trying to figure that out. And once I do know what's going on, I'll tell you. Here's my card." Decker handed it to him. "If you think of anything strange or unusual or just something that you think the police should know, call me. I want to find Boxer, if for no other reason just to know that he's safe."

"Yeah, I get it. Boxer did his job but isn't as big as some of us. He's vulnerable."

"Nobody is immune to vulnerability, Phil."

"But some are more vulnerable than others." Phil scratched his head on his tiger tattoo. "I mean no harm when I say this, but Boxer . . . there's something about him. Some people are just born with a Kick Me sign plastered on their asses."

Barbara Heiger was out to lunch. Decker wandered over to the next open office. It belonged to *C. Bonfellow, Bookkeeper.* He appeared to be in his midforties, short and overweight with thinning sandy hair and dark suspicious eyes. He sat behind a scarred desk that was piled with paper in slotted trays. "Can I help you?"

"I hope so." Decker showed C. Bonfellow his badge.

"Police? What's this about?"

"Do you make out the salary checks?"

"Me, personally? No. It's all done by computer. And if you're looking for someone in particular, I'm not the guy. You need to talk to Susan or Harold in HR. I just balance the numbers."

"Where is HR?"

"Three doors down. Who are you looking for, by the way?"

"A guy named Boxer?"

"Don't know him."

"You're not the only one. Thanks."

Decker was about to go, when Bonfellow said, "If you leave your card, I'll call if I hear of anything."

"Sure." Decker handed the bookkeeper his card. "What kind of things do you usually hear about, Mr. Bonfellow?"

The man turned pink. "Not that I gossip. I don't. And most of the time, I'm behind a desk. But people don't notice me a lot. They kind of talk like I'm not there and I pick up things . . . keep things filed in storage." He pointed to his head. "I'll keep my ears open for this Boxer person. I'll call you if I hear anything juicy."

"Thanks. Don't put yourself out. If someone found out you've overheard a private conversation, it might make them mad."

"Oh, I know that, Detective." Bonfellow smiled. "I'm a very careful man."

In HR, there were two people to approach. Decker homed in on Susan Jenkins, who was kind enough to look up the name in the company computer. She was in her midthirties, short but with a very long neck. She reminded Decker of a swan. She wore a black T-shirt and jeans. "There is no Boxer assigned to the warehouse, but . . . there is a Joseph Boch."

"That's probably the guy I'm looking for. Do you have his address and phone number?"

"I do, but I can't give it to you. Company policy." She smiled. "I'm going to the watercooler. I'll be right back."

"Take your time," Decker said. Once she left, he looked on the screen. Joseph Boch was thirty-five, and by the date of his employment records, he'd been working there nine months. Decker quickly copied the address and phone number in his notebook.

She returned a moment later with a conical paper cup and sipped water. "Is there anything else?"

"Thank you very much, Ms. Jenkins. You've been a big help." He paused. "How long does your average employee work here?"

She looked up at him. "I really couldn't tell you. What I can tell you is that we have a lot of turnover, specifically because we have a lot of temp teens working in the summer."

"And you have no idea about the working life span of your permanent employees?"

"If I had to guess, I'd say not more than a few years. It's barely more than minimum wage unless you're in management. And most management isn't from the bottom up."

"Where do they go—the ones who quit after a year?"

Susan was thoughtful. "I couldn't tell you personally, but it's the same old story in Hamilton. I think a lot of them have alcohol or serious drug issues. Or both. When they're sober, they can hold down a job. But it's a really boring job, so they start getting high again. And when they're high, they can't hold down jobs. It's a vicious cycle. Sad, but not unpredictable. What else does Hamilton have to offer?"

"You're here."

"I grew up here, but I never intended to stay. I went to Clarion College on a scholarship; met my husband, who was at Kneed Loft; and we moved to Phoenix. He came down with an illness that does much better in cold climate. So here we are."

She brought out a brown bag and unwrapped a sandwich.

"I have my mother and sister here. It's not so bad now that I'm married with kids. But when I was growing up . . . geez, all I wanted to do was get out of here." Biting into her sandwich, she said, "Probably told you way more than you wanted to know."

"Not at all, Ms. Jenkins, it's always good to get background."

"I can tell you're not from these parts."

"I work with Greenbury PD. Before that, I was with Los Angeles Police for thirty-five years."

"Wow, that's a change of scenery. What drew you to Greenbury?"

"Change of scenery as well as a change of pace. Compared to L.A., even Hamilton seems idyllic."

"I'm probably making Hamilton more horrible than it is. We have our doctors, lawyers, hospitals, libraries, schools, police, churches, yadda, yadda, yadda. It's a decent place, but it's not exceptional. We're what politicians call God and gun people."

"Nothing wrong with that."

"I don't know about that, Detective. With God, it's a round-trip ticket. The Lord destroys, but the Lord also creates. With guns, it's strictly a one-way fare."

Chapter 9

Lennie Baccus was eating a muffin and chatting up one of the women who worked behind the counter. When she saw Decker, she stood up, wiped her mouth, and said her good-byes. She took her coffee in her right hand, another to-go coffee in her left, and met up with the boss. "I thought you could use one of these."

"Thank you."

"Black, right?"

"You're a quick study. Let's go."

"Where are we going?"

"I think I got Boxer's address. We'll talk in the car."

Silently they walked across a big expanse of asphalt. The parking lot was half full, mostly small cars and pickups. Once in the car, Decker put the keys in the ignition. As soon as he pulled onto the street, he said, "You go first."

"Not too much." Lennie pulled out her notepad. "I talked to four people—the two women who work at the café—Marie and Gilliam. Neither of them know Boxer, but they did know Brady Neil. He used to come and buy coffee and a croissant, and he was always friendly. They felt really bad and a little worried, like it has something to do with the store."

"It might," Decker said. "Joseph Boch a.k.a. Boxer hasn't shown up for work in two days."

"Since Neil's death. Wow. That's a little creepy."

"The guy I talked to in the warehouse—his name is Phil—described Boxer as a little guy and kind of a wimp. If he and Neil were stealing electronics, I can bet who ran the show."

"If the company found out," Lennie said, "they'd just fire them. Not kill anyone."

"No, you're right about that. But we have to start somewhere, and since Boxer didn't show up at work, we need to find out why. You said you talked to four people. Who are the other two?"

"Buss Vitali, who worked alongside Brady Neil. Said he had no problems with Brady, that he was a nice guy. Always willing to carry an extra load to help someone out."

"Could be he was a nice guy. Or it could be because he was a nice guy, his coworkers looked the other way."

"You really think he was stealing."

"I think he was pulling off some kind of scam. Especially now that Boxer is AWOL. Who's the last person you talked to?"

"Well, Buss pointed me toward a girl named Olivia Anderson, who works in clothing. She and Brady went out a couple of times. She didn't show up yesterday for work, but she was there today. It looked to me like she'd been crying."

"What'd she say to you?"

Lennie checked her notepad. "They were dating for around two months, but then he broke it off. Neil told her that he had something he needed to work on. But he never told her what."

"When did he break off the relationship?"

"About six months ago."

"When you get back to the station house, call her and say that I'd love to talk to her. She can either come to the station or I'll interview her at her home."

"She seemed like a nice girl."

"And by all accounts, Brady was a nice guy. But something got him killed."

"Can I come with you when you interview her?" Lennie bit her lip. "I think she trusts me. It might make things easier."

"I'm sure you would help, Baccus, but this isn't a

look-see. I need someone experienced to play off of. It's going to be McAdams. Did you give her your phone number?"

"I gave her my card, yes."

"Good. Then she might call you after she's talked to us. If she wants to talk to you, that would be fine. But do it in an open place. Do not go to her house, okay?"

"Got it."

"Did she say anything else other than Brady was a nice guy?"

"Just that he paid for everything. Consistent with the mother saying he always had cash."

"Do you see him earning that much cash from re-cycled parts?"

"Enough for a dinner at Steaks! and a movie. Not enough to take her on a trip to Paris."

"Yeah, having an extra fifty bucks qualifies as having lots of cash around here. And it's certainly possible to make an extra fifty bucks in recycled parts. Especially if you didn't pay for any of it."

"True, but would an extra fifty bucks get you killed?" Lennie asked.

Decker said, "I've seen people killed for less. Especially if you're an addict. But addicts don't usually take a body from the crime scene and dump it in a second spot. They just take the cash and run."

"And it's a definite that Brady Neil wasn't killed on Canterbury Lane?"

"The blood loss at the scene doesn't fit the severity of the wound. Plus, we have a second person of interest who's missing. This *seems* like something more than some random mugging."

"Maybe Joseph Boch a.k.a. Boxer can shed some light on the situation."

"One can always hope." Decker smiled. "And one can always be disappointed."

The address was in an impoverished area on Crane Street. It was a small bungalow with a wraparound porch, the house built around the turn of the twentieth century. The outside lawn was brown even though the weather was no longer cold, but there were a few weeds popping up, giving it spots of green. No planting along the border or the steps, but there was a giant oak tree that shaded a crumbling stone pathway to the front door. Although the place had a dirt driveway, there was no car parked outside. The whitewashed flooring of the porch was missing boards, and what was still there was splintered and looked none too safe to walk on.

When they reached the front door, Decker pulled back a torn screen and knocked on the sash. After announcing himself several times, he closed the screen. He went around to the side yard and peeked over. "Don't see a car."

He eased his shoe into a chain link and hopped over the fence.

Lennie said, "Do you want me to follow you?"

"Nah, just going to have a look around. See if there's any visibility from a back window inside the house."

The backyard was as brown as the front but with no tree to give it any life. The area was fenced off from its neighbors by chain link alternating with rotted two-by-fours. Spare automobile parts were strewn about—a few rusted hubcaps, a piece of a fender, several spare tires, and three or four wheel-less bicycles. The house had two windows that looked out to the backyard, but the curtains had been pulled. He knocked on the back door.

No answer.

"Detective Decker?" Lennie yelled out.

"Over in the back. I'll be with you in a moment."

"You okay?"

"I'm fine." Decker took a last look around, and then he scaled the fence and landed on his feet with a thud. Thank God for rubber-soled shoes. "Quiet as a tomb."

"Just leave our cards?"

"No, I'm going to try his phone. You call up records

and find out who the house belongs to." Decker punched in the numbers, and the line went straight to voice mail. While he was considering his next move, Lennie interrupted his musings.

"The tax bill goes out to Jaylene Boch. She's fifty-nine and bought the house twenty-five years ago."

"Call up the station and ask whoever is there to look her up."

"Greenbury or Hamilton?"

"Greenbury." Decker looked through the front windows, which were obscured by curtains just like the back of the house. "If they don't have anything on her, we'll try Hamilton. And while you're talking to someone at Greenbury, find out what they pulled up on Joseph Boch."

"Right away."

Decker tried the front-door handle. It was locked, but by jiggling it, he could tell that the spring pin wasn't very tight. He picked up his phone and called McAdams, who was still pulling CCTV from Tollway Boulevard. After a brief recap of his morning activities, Decker said, "I have Lennie on several calls. Can you get a cell-phone number for Jaylene Boch?"

"If I were at the station house, I could. But not here in the field."

"Right. Who's there now?"

"Nickweed might be there. Kev is here with me. I bet Radar's there."

"I'll give him a call."

"Can't you jiggle the lock?"

"I could, but that wouldn't be legal."

"The guy's been missing for two days. Can't you justify a forced entry?"

"He's an adult. And you're the law student. What do you think?"

"Your hands are tied, unless you smell something weird."

"The windows are shut, so if something's rotting away, it hasn't leaked out in the open. Lennie just got off the phone. Let me see what she's come up with. Talk to you later." He walked over to Baccus. "What's up?"

"I spoke to the captain. He says he'll call you back with the background information and the phone numbers. What do we do now?"

"We wait around until Radar gives me a call. Want a cup of coffee or something? I think I saw a place a couple blocks away."

"No, thanks, I'm pretty coffee'd out."

Decker said, "I'm going to call my wife."

"Do you want privacy?"

"I'll take a walk down the block." He walked away for a short distance, then phoned Rina. "Hey."

"Hi, I'm in the car. Can I call you back in ten minutes?"

"It might not work. I have a lull right now, but I don't want you talking while you're driving."

"Everything okay?"

"Just a whole lot of nothing . . . well, that's not entirely true." He told her about Boxer and his disappearing act.

Rina said, "That doesn't sound good."

"No, it doesn't. Not with Brady Neil being dead. I'm trying to get information on Jaylene Boch from Radar, who's busy right now. We seem to be a little shorthanded."

"Have you tried looking her up on the internet on your phone?"

"And what's that going to tell me?"

"Maybe nothing, but you never know. Hold on. I'll pull over."

"Nah, don't bother."

"Just hold on. There's a space right here." A moment passed. "Okay. What's the name?"

"Jaylene Boch." Decker spelled it.

"Unusual name. Let's see if she has any hits."

"How are you doing?" Decker asked.

"I'm fine. I just spoke to my mom."

"How is she?"

"Okay. It's been a while since we've visited either

mother. Since they both live in Florida, it should be part of our summer plans."

"Yeah, you're right. We'll go, but not in the summer, please. It's so hot and humid."

"Fair enough, but no more excuses." Rina shook her head. "Okay, here we go with Jaylene Boch. There are six citations, all of them having to do with a car accident eight years ago."

"Car accident?"

"Yes. I'll pull up the article . . ." A pause. "This is sad. She was plowed into by an eighteen-wheeler semi. She got a pretty good settlement. But the poor thing is in a wheelchair."

"Well, that certainly changes things. If Boxer was her son and he disappeared, I'm wondering who is taking care of Jaylene. And that might justify a welfare check. I'll call Radar and see what he thinks. Thank you, honey. As usual, you've been a big help."

He hung up and called Radar, who said, "Jaylene Boch is on disability."

"Yeah, I just found out that a car accident left her a paraplegic eight years ago. If Joseph Boch is Boxer and he's missing, who's taking care of Jaylene?"

"I've got her phone number. Call it and let me know if she answers. If she doesn't, go ahead and make a forced entry, just to make sure she's okay. Knock hard."

"Got it." Decker hung up. He called Jaylene's cell phone. After three rings, there was a beep and Decker left his name and number. But he still didn't feel comfortable about walking away. He went over to Baccus. "We're going to do a forced entry for a welfare check. Turns out Jaylene Boch—"

"Is a paraplegic."

"Looked it up on your phone?"

"Yep."

"Radar gave me her cell phone. No one is answering. I just want to make sure she's not in there, lying on the floor and incapacitated. Agreed?"

"Absolutely."

"All right, let's do this." Decker took out a set of lock picks, and then he backtracked and put them away. Instead, he took out a credit card. After working it back and forth, the bolt retracted and the lock popped. As he opened the door, the stench was overwhelming. Involuntarily, he turned his head. Then he brought out a handkerchief. Lennie was a few steps behind him. She had turned ashen.

Decker took out his revolver. "Watch my back. I don't think this is a fresh kill." He waited for her to respond. "You do have a firearm, don't you?"

"Yes, sorry. Of course." Lennie disengaged her gun from her shoulder holster.

Single file, they walked into a messy living room—paper cups and plates, food wrappers, soiled clothes, dirty towels, all of it scattered on tables, the sofa, and the two chairs opposite the sofa. Off the living room was the kitchen in an equal state of disarray and mess. Dirty dishes and used pots and pans piled in the sink. Ants were crawling in neat little roadways on the counters, down the cabinets, and onto the floor.

Decker said, "These two rooms are clear. I'm going to check out the other rooms. You okay?"

"Fine," she said.

Slowly he walked down the hallway that had three doors. With his back to the wall, he opened the one closest to the living room. As soon as he did, the stink grew stronger.

He pivoted, gun drawn, and went inside.

She was tied to her wheelchair, head lolling to the side, her eyes closed, her lips parched and cracked. A rag was stuck in her mouth.

"Damn it!" Quickly, Decker checked out the room closet. Empty. He felt for a pulse and was shocked to find something thready and weak. He turned to Baccus. "She's alive. Call an ambulance!" Carefully, he removed the rag from her mouth. She had defecated over herself, down the chair, and onto the floor. Decker patted her sweaty forehead with his handkerchief. As he did this, she moaned. "Mrs. Boch, we're the police. We're taking you to the hospital. Just stay with me, okay."

Baccus said, "Ambulance is coming. I also called for additional officers and SID."

"Which police station?"

"Hamilton, sir. It's in their jurisdiction."

"It's related to our case, but you're right. It's their call."

Jaylene moaned again.

Lennie said, "Is she going to be okay?"

Decker put his fingers to his lips. "Just hang in there, Jaylene. Just a few more minutes." To Baccus. "We've got to clear the two other rooms. Otherwise emergency services won't come in. C'mon."

"We just leave her alone?"

"You have to protect my back, Baccus. We have no idea who else is in the house."

"Yes." Lennie wiped sweat off her brow. "Of course."

The door across the hall was a bathroom—broken toilet, cracked tile floors, and a browned acrylic tub/ shower for the handicapped. He took out his hand-kerchief, ran it under the faucet, and wrung out the excess water.

"C'mon," Decker said. "One more to go."

The last room was all the way in the back and looked over the rear yard. He stood with his back against the wall and threw open the door. The stench was horrible. Blood was everywhere—on the walls, on the floor, on the bed linens, and on discarded clothing. Decker quietly walked over to the closet and opened it. It was the only area of the room not smeared with blood.

Definitely a crime scene, but no body.

He rushed out of the room and back to the old lady and wiped her brow with his damp handkerchief. To Baccus, he said, "Stand guard over the back bedroom. No one goes in without my say-so."

"Got it."

The wail of the sirens got louder. Within moments, paramedics were knocking at the door. Decker let them in. "House is clear. Follow me."

Once Jaylene was being ministered to, Decker walked over to the back bedroom and peered inside. He took off his shoes. "See that over there?"

"What am I looking at?"

Decker said, "He tried to make it to the door. He didn't get there. You can see a massive amount of spray on the door and on the walls near the door. He runs to the closet—see the footprints? Doesn't make it to the closet, either. He's mowed down there. See these smear tracks? They're dragging the body out . . ." He looked at the hallway. "Nothing bloody here." He went over to the windows. Blood was dripping onto the floor even before he opened the drapes. Once he did, he opened the window and saw blood on the bottom of the frame. "They pulled him out the window."

He paused, then looked outside.

"No real visible blood outside. They might have washed it down. I'll take a closer look."

"How could they have dragged him away without leaving blood outside?"

"Someone's waiting on the other side with a trash bag." Decker walked back into the first bedroom to check on Jaylene Boch. They had taken off her soiled clothes and were cleaning her body. Decker looked away, but not before noticing an IV was in her arm and an oxygen tube was in her nose. He went back into the hallway as two paramedics were bringing in a gurney. "How is she?"

"Badly dehydrated. She's conscious but barely so. It's hard to tell what damage has been done."

Ten minutes later, they put her on the mobile gurney, leaving the dirtied wheelchair behind, and loaded her into the ambulance.

"Where are you taking her?"

"St. Luke's."

The major hospital in Hamilton. "I'll meet you there," Decker said.

The paramedics nodded.

Baccus was still guarding the back bedroom. Decker said, "I'll wait with you until Hamilton police arrive. They should be here any moment."

"I'm okay by myself."

"This is a crime scene. Who's to say someone's not coming back, or someone could be hiding outside. I'll wait with you."

A few moments passed, and then they heard sirens. "Okay," Decker said. "You wait here and direct Hamilton police to guard the house. No one in or out until you've talked to a detective. Don't tell him or her too much. Just that I'll call later on. Then you all stand guard until Forensics comes out. If you get lip from the detective—someone tries to throw around weight— you stand your position. If someone gets nasty, tell him your last name is Baccus. That should shut the person up. When SID comes, you take them to the crime scene. And then once that's taken care of, you give Hamilton PD the case—temporarily. I'll call later and let them know what's going on and why we were there."

"What are you doing now?"

"I'm going to the hospital. If Jaylene becomes conscious and sentient, I'm going to want to talk to her. Unless you want me to stay and help you out?"

"No, no, I'm fine. Thanks for the trust." She looked at Decker with pleading eyes. Her nails were clicking a mile a minute. "That poor woman. Will she make it?"

"I don't know, Lennie, and that's the truth."

Tears formed in her orbs. She wiped them with her finger. "I'm sorry."

"For what?"

"Just . . ."

"Don't apologize for normal emotions. When it stops getting to you, that's when you need to worry."

Chapter 10

The waiting room in the ER was furnished with orange plastic chairs and a ceiling-mounted TV that had settled on CNN news. Doctors, nurses, orderlies, and volunteers went back and forth between two doors, looking very busy with white coats and clipboards. Triage was located behind glass windows with phones constantly ringing. It took a while before Decker made contact with someone who knew about Jaylene Boch's welfare. ER docs were generally young, and the one who came up to Decker appeared to be in his late thirties, slim build with bags under his brown eyes. His name tag said Dr. John Nesmith.

"You probably found her just in time," he remarked.

"She'll pull through?" Decker asked.

"No guarantees, but I think so. She's sleeping, but even if she were awake, it'd be useless for you to talk to her. She was barely conscious when she was brought in. She didn't even know her name. But that's par for the course with extreme dehydration."

"Could I try to talk to her? Her son's missing, and there was a lot of blood in her house."

"She's sedated, Detective. And if she can't remember her name, she won't be able to tell you anything. Stop by tomorrow. Twenty-four hours could make a big difference."

Decker knew that Nesmith was right, but it didn't make it any easier to accept. "Could someone call me if she's up and alert later in the day?"

"Up, yes. Alert?" Nesmith shrugged. "But sure. Give me a number."

Decker gave the man his card. "We might place someone on her."

"You mean for her protection? She wasn't killed the first time."

"Until we know what's going on, it's better to err on the side of caution. Any objection?"

"Not from me, but you'll probably have to run this by hospital security."

"Thank you. I'll come by tomorrow."

As soon as he left the building, he called up McAdams. "Where are you?"

"At Crane Street, in a pissing contest with Hamilton

Police over jurisdiction. Since it is in their city, we don't have much of a case. On the other hand, if they want our information, it would behoove them to cooperate. I'm trying to impress them with my impeccable logic, but I'm getting mixed results."

"How long have you been there?"

"Maybe an hour. Detectives and techs from Forensics are all over the place."

"Who are the detectives?"

"Randal Smitz and Wendell Tran. Do you know them?"

"No."

"They seem competent. Kevin's here as well. They're less proprietary than the uniforms. Radar has a call into Baccus's office to help smooth the way, but he hasn't called back. Are you still at the hospital?"

"Yes. Jaylene Boch will probably pull through, but I couldn't talk to her because she's heavily sedated. Is SID from Hamilton there?"

"Yep."

"They've got a bigger department and more man-power, so that's okay. Ask them to take numerous blood samples around the room. It could be Neil's crime scene as well as Joseph Boch's. Is anyone canvassing the neighborhood?"

"Hamilton is on it, but Kevin put a couple of our

own officers with them. The police know what they're doing. Judging by the city's crime statistics, it's not their first rodeo."

"What have you told them about Brady Neil?"

"Just that his murder brought you to the house. They pressed for details. I told them I didn't know the full story yet and that you'd fill them in."

"Perfect answer. That means they'll talk to me."

"That's my motto, boss. Always leave them asking for more."

Senior investigator Wendell Tran spoke with a broad southern accent. He was born in Louisiana, the son of a Vietnamese shrimp fisherman, and had come to the Hamilton Police Department about ten years prior. How he got here was anyone's guess. He was thirty-eight and average height with black, straight hair and brown eyes. He and Decker were doing the five-minute small-talk thing on the rotted front porch outside the house, sizing each other up before getting down to the case. Inside, Forensics was collecting and dusting, but the house was so disorderly it was hard to know what was normal and what might have been tossed.

"How do people live like this?" Tran asked.

"She's in a wheelchair."

"Then I reckon her son isn't much of a house-keeper." Tran pronounced *I* as *Ah*. He shook his head and looked Decker in the eye. "You want to tell me your connection?"

"We found a body dumped in our jurisdiction yesterday morning. He was identified as Brady Neil. He lived in Hamilton with his mom, Jennifer Neil. He and Joseph Boch—a.k.a. Boxer—worked together at Bigstore." Decker filled him in on the details. "Neil wasn't murdered where he was dumped. That's why I asked SID for multiple samples. I think this might be his murder scene."

"Which would make Neil's murder in our jurisdiction."

"Yes, that is true. I'd like to see this through, but it's your call."

"I heard you were a Homicide detective from L.A."

"Fifteen years as a lieutenant detective, thirty years in Homicide, thirty-five years in police work."

"I won't lie, I could use the help," Tran said. "We have a significant crime rate, but it's the usual drunks at the bar or gang shooting or drug deals gone sour. I looked up the names. These boys don't fit into any of those categories."

"I agree with you. I don't think Neil was a dealer. For one thing, they didn't kill the old lady. If it were pro dealers, she'd be the first to go." Decker paused. "Brady Neil has a background. His father, Brandon Gratz, is in prison for a double murder."

Tran's eyes widened. "Huh! I didn't see that when I pulled up his name."

"Different last name. I think the family has been trying to expunge the connection for years. His mom told me about the father when I interviewed her yesterday."

"That was the couple who owned the jewelry store— the Levines. Before my time, but it dominated the headlines a long while. Interesting."

"I suppose you know that Chief Baccus was the lead investigator on that."

"I do know. Is that relevant?"

"Not necessarily, no."

"Y'all think that these murders have something to do with those murders? Like a revenge thing?"

"I don't have a clue, Detective. But I'd like to talk to the surviving children, specifically Gregg Levine, who runs the store. He was the only witness against Gratz and his partner, Kyle Masterson."

"Gregg Levine is a big man in the community, Lieutenant. He and his sister, Yvonne, are very generous with the charity."

"That's why it's better if I talk to them. I don't deal with either one on a regular basis like you. And by the way, Pete is fine. Or Deck."

"I sure hate to bring up skeletons in the closet."

"Neil Brady's death has already done that. With this gruesome scene, how long before people make the connection?"

"I reckon so."

"And I'd like to talk to Brandon Gratz."

"Were he and his son in contact?"

"I don't know, but I think we should find out. Because people are going to start asking the same questions you're asking. Can I leave one of Greenbury's detectives with you to search through the house while I go do some interviewing?"

"Sure, if you take one of Hamilton's detectives with you to talk to Levine and Gratz."

"Already done."

"Excuse me?"

"Detective Baccus. She's been here the whole time."

"I know. I spoke to her." A pause. "I thought she was called out by Hamilton."

"No, she's been working with me."

Tran stared at him. "Why?"

"Chief Baccus wanted her on the Brady Neil homicide case. It was a deal we made since jurisdiction for Neil's murder was debatable. If I took her on, he'd give me access to Hamilton's files if I need them."

"What did he get out of it?"

"I guess the chief wanted Lennie to get some on-site experience."

"Well, that's more than a little insulting," Tran said.

"Maybe he wanted someone who wasn't under his authority, someone who felt no compunction about correcting her mistakes."

Tran made a face. "How's she working out for you?"

"Well, so far." And that was the extent of what Decker was going to reveal. "Then you have no problem with my talking to the Levines and to Brandon Gratz?"

"None. You're right about one thing. Gregg needs to be told about this. It is probably better coming from you."

Decker checked his watch. It was almost three in the afternoon. "I'll see if I can talk to Levine today. I probably won't get the paperwork done to talk to Gratz for a while. Is it okay if Tyler McAdams stays with your boys here?"

"The curly-headed kid from Harvard?"

"Yeah, he's a good detective. How'd you find out the Harvard connection?"

"One of your guys called him Harvard."

"He just finished two years of Harvard Law."

"That's aaall riiight," Trans drawled. "I won't hold it against him."

Levine's Luscious Gems of old was now Levine's Jewelry, located in the small but nicely appointed business district of Bellweather. It was located three streets away from the original murder scene, in a spacious building with bulletproof-glass windows that displayed things that sparkled. While the pieces weren't the size and scope of a showcase in Beverly Hills or midtown Manhattan, they stood out in a working-class city like a beacon from a decaying lighthouse. The street had free diagonal parking, and Decker pulled up in front of the store. It was necessary to buzz in. He turned to Lennie.

"Take out your ID now. I don't want to have to reach into my pocket once we're in there. They may be a little gun wary."

She nodded, and Decker rang the bell. They were buzzed in a second later. He gave the room a quick once-over. Dozens of glass cases displaying rings, earrings, necklaces, bracelets, charms, and chains sat on either side of a small hallway that ran down the middle of the room. An armed, muscular security guard stood watch in the back. A teenaged girl was manning the counters. She was thin and gawky with a long face, long curly hair, and round hazel eyes. She wore a miniskirt and a sleeveless white blouse that showed a rose tattoo on her right shoulder.

"May I help you?"

Decker offered up his ID. He spoke while she examined his billfold. "I'm Detective Peter Decker from Greenbury Police Department, and this is Detective Lenora Baccus from Hamilton Police Department. We'd like to speak to Gregg Levine."

Her eyes grew darker in color. "Mr. Levine is out at the moment. Can I ask what this is about?"

"When do you expect him back?" Decker asked.

A door opened from the back wall, and a well-dressed woman stepped out. From old newspaper pictures dated twenty years ago, Decker knew that the woman was Yvonne Levine. She was now in late thirties with strawberry-blond hair and bright blue eyes. Her curvaceous body was shrink-wrapped in a red dress with a hemline that fell slightly below her knee. Spiked heels on her feet. "Dana, why don't you grab some lunch, sweetheart."

The girl looked at her Mickey Mouse watch. "It's almost four."

"Then grab a cup of coffee."

"What about the rule, Mom? Two of us in the shop at all times."

"It's the police, Dana. What could happen? Anyway, Otto is here."

The girl heaved a resigned sigh, picked up an oversize denim bag, and left. The woman went over to the door and switched the Open sign to Closed. "Otto, don't let anyone in." She turned to Decker and Lennie. "Yvonne Apple. Let's talk in the back office."

Leading them through the paneled door in the wall, she walked down a corridor and then opened the second door and invited them inside. The space was small and contained two desks with chairs, two computer monitors, two printers, a landline phone, and a large bank of video camera monitors hanging on the wall. They showed every imaginable angle and space of the store plus the exterior down to the street. Decker supposed she wasn't taking any chances this time.

She said, "Sit anywhere you'd like."

Decker looked around and pulled out a desk chair. "You've been expecting us."

"Wondering what took so long. It happened yesterday." Yvonne found a chair for Lennie Baccus, placed it next to Decker, and then sat on the desk. "He popped up on my newsfeed. His death did. Brady Neil's death."

"You keep track of him?"

"I keep track of all the devils' relatives—Gratz and Masterson. After you've experienced something that horrific, you never trust again." She stared at the security monitors, watching Otto pace. "What did the little shit do to get himself murdered?"

"We don't know." Decker paused. "Since you've been keeping track of all Gratz's relatives, you probably know more about Brady Neil than I do."

"Just where he lives. Up until yesterday, he has seemed to live a quiet life, like his sister and his mother. Kyle Masterson's family is another story. His son, Jason, is a chip off the old block. He's in prison for armed robbery. Nine-year sentence. He'll get out and fuck someone else's life up again. Kyle's ex-wife moved to Georgia after their daughter, Norma, was killed in a motorcycle accident. So that now makes two down, one locked up, and one to go. Maybe I'll get lucky and Brandy will come down with painful cancer or something like that."

Decker said, "Does your brother know about Brady Neil's death?"

"Yes."

"Where is he?"

"Playing golf . . ." She looked at Lennie. "With your father."

"Regularly scheduled game?" Decker asked.

"No, not at all. He called up the chief this morning after I told him about the death, wanting to make sure it was true. I'm sure he wants details."

"Brady Neil is a Greenbury homicide," Decker said.

"Baccus is the chief of police. I'm sure he can get all the details he wants." Yvonne looked at Lennie, whose face was unreadable.

"When do you expect Gregg back?" Decker asked.

"Soon."

"An hour?"

"Perhaps."

"Could you call him for me, please?"

"Sorry, no cells allowed on the golf course. And Gregg just isn't important enough to carry a pager. I will tell him you dropped by."

"Mind if I ask you a few questions?"

"If you must."

"From what you know, Brady Neil has been living a noneventful life for all these years?"

"Obviously not if he was murdered."

"And you don't have any idea about that?"

"What kind of ideas? Do I know who killed him? No, I do not. Do I care that he died? No, I do not."

"Mrs. Apple, where were you Tuesday at around two in the morning?"

"At home, in bed with my husband."

"And last night?"

"Same answer. He can verify that if you want him to."

"I'm sure he can. What does your husband do?"

"He owns a real estate company—does business all over the area. Why?"

"Sake of completeness. With that in mind, where do your other siblings live?"

"Matthew lives in Columbus, Ohio. Martin is in Seattle. Ella's in Brooklyn. She's a tattoo artist. The rose on Dana's shoulder was courtesy of her." Yvonne regarded Baccus. "I believe you knew her."

"She was a grade above me."

"Ah, so you do talk." She made a face. "Then you're twenty-seven."

"I am. I remember when it happened. I'm very sorry."

The sudden sympathy caught Yvonne off guard. Her eyes moistened. "Ella probably suffered the most. She was younger than Martin by eight years. She was shipped out to my aunt, who couldn't deal with all the psychological ramifications of such a massive, horrid event. Later, after Gregg married, he brought her to live with him. It was difficult on Maran, his wife, but she really did try. Then Ella got mad and moved in with me for a while. My husband was fairly tolerant, but Ella grew harder to manage. We tried our best, but we were grieving ourselves, as well as trying to run the business and live life. She fell into the wrong crowd. Now she seems to be doing a little better. At least she has found an outlet for her artistic talents other than graffiti."

Yvonne's face tightened. "Do you have any idea what horrible old wounds this opens up?"

"I'm sorry for your loss and for your pain," Decker said. "I can't even imagine how hard it was for you. And I know you're still suffering. But I'm just doing a job. Brady Neil was murdered, and I realize that this is bound to affect every member of your family—especially once the press gets wind. I'm surprised they haven't been pestering you already."

Yvonne was silent.

"You should be prepared for some phone calls," Decker went on.

"Haunting us even after the little shit died."

"It's terrible. I'm sorry. I need your siblings' phone numbers just to verify where they were when Neil died. Can you get them for me?"

"I suppose."

"Thank you. And when do you think we could talk to your brother?"

"Call him up. I'm not his secretary."

"If you could get me his number, it would help."

She turned to Lennie. "Why don't you just ask your father?"

"I don't talk about my cases, even to my father. But if it's bothersome, I'll find out Mr. Levine's number for Detective Decker."

"Oh fuck! I'll give it to you!" She regarded the monitors. "Dana's back. I need to open up." She stood. "I'm sure this wee conversation has not been very illuminating."

Decker stood and Lennie followed. He said, "Thank you very much for your time, Mrs. Apple. And if you think of anything that might be important, please call."

"Important about what? Helping you find out who killed Brady Neil? If I knew who it did, I'd give that guy a medal."

Chapter 11

When they were in the car, Lennie said, "Do you seriously think that Gratz and Masterson had something to do with Brady Neil's death? They've been incarcerated for almost twenty years."

"We look into everything, Lennie." Decker turned on the motor. "What do you think your dad and Gregg Levine were talking about?" He pulled away from the curb. "Do they often play golf together?"

"I don't know. I don't follow the comings and goings of my dad. But I do know that the Levines—well, Gregg and Yvonne—are important members of the community. They have done a lot of charity work for the police department. I don't see what's odd about Gregg calling up Dad and asking him about Brady Neil's death."

"Nothing odd," Decker said. "Just checking if they've done this before."

"Like Yvonne said, Gregg Levine probably wanted details."

"Sounds reasonable."

"And since the latest incident happened in Hamilton, Gregg probably feels that he's entitled to know the details. It could have something to do with his family."

"Like what?" Decker asked. "Are you suggesting that one of the Levine family members was behind Brady Neil's murder?"

Lennie was quiet. "Do you think that the Levines had something to do with Neil's murder?"

"Nice deflection of my question." Decker smiled. "I'll answer yours. I don't know. I'm still gathering information."

"I probably sound a little defensive about my dad. For the record, I haven't said a word to him about this investigation."

"You don't get a medal for that, Lennie. I wouldn't expect anything less."

"I know." Silence. "He's being stupid."

"Pardon?"

"My dad. He shouldn't be talking to Gregg Levine in an unofficial capacity. The conversation should be at the Hamilton PD station house, not the golf course."

"Have they played golf before?"

"I don't know. Truthfully, I keep my distance from

my father. I want people to judge me by what I do, not who I am."

"That's impossible. If you want that, you can't work for his police department."

"I know. I should have stayed in Philadelphia. Just ignored the jerks and taken the heat. I was really doing well, too. In my mind, I just crashed. What is wrong with me?"

"Lennie, how about you save the self-flagellation for another time and concentrate on the case? Does your father routinely play golf with members of the community?"

"I know he plays a lot of charity games to help raise money for all sorts of good causes. On the weekends mostly."

"Then playing with Gregg Levine would or would not be unusual?"

"The game wouldn't be unusual. But I wouldn't expect him to take three hours off in the middle of the workweek to play golf, especially when there's a blood-bath in his district."

"He probably doesn't know about Jaylene Boch and her missing son, especially if they don't allow cells on the course."

She was quiet. Then her face visibly relaxed. "That's a good point."

A call came through the Bluetooth. When Decker depressed the button, Radar's voice said, "Why are you visiting Yvonne Apple?"

Decker was taken aback. "News travels fast."

"She called her brother, her brother told Baccus, and Baccus called me."

"That's strange. She just told me cells aren't allowed on the golf course."

"Decker—"

"FYI, Captain, Officer Baccus is in the car with me."

"Hello, Officer. I hope Detective Decker is showing you the ins and outs of Homicide."

"Very much so."

Decker said, "Why is Chief Baccus calling you about my homicide investigation?"

"Why are you talking to people who were victims of a double homicide that happened twenty years ago?"

"Because my corpse is the son of the Levines' killer. I have to consider all possibilities, Mike."

"This has nothing to do with the Levines."

"Why do we know that, sir?" Radar was silent. Decker said, "Captain, I'm just trying to get as much background information as possible. And I'm not the only one who's curious. Why else would Gregg Levine call up Victor Baccus for golf?"

"Golf?"

"When I went to their jewelry store, Yvonne Apple, the sister, informed us that her brother had called up Victor Baccus for golf this morning. Hence my statement that phones aren't allowed on the golf course. Yvonne told me that when I asked if I could have his cell number to call him up."

After a moment of silence, Decker continued talking.

"Now maybe it was just a spur-of-the-moment friendly game. But my intuition tells me that Gregg is probably trying to pump Baccus for details of the Neil murder."

Lennie said, "Captain, did Chief Baccus say anything about Joseph Boch's disappearance? It was a nasty scene at the house. A woman was nearly dead. I would think he'd rather be there than the golf course."

Decker glanced at her and nodded.

Radar said, "He didn't know about it until I told him. He's probably on his way there now."

"Then I'll see him there and bring him up to date," Decker said. "I don't know why he would be pissed that I went to see Yvonne Apple. It's relevant."

"You'll find out soon enough, especially if he pulls the case from you."

"Joseph Boch is his case. Brady Neil's death is in *our* jurisdiction. Let's hear it for interdepartmental cooperation."

"If the forensics show that Neil was murdered at Boch's house, then the murder case will go to Hamilton. If they want your input, that's up to them. If they want to do it themselves, that's also up to them."

Decker paused. "That's fine."

Radar also paused. "You're okay with that?"

"What can I do?"

Lennie said, "Why on earth would my father pull the case from Decker when he assigned me to him to work this murder case?"

"I don't know, Officer Baccus," Radar said. "Maybe he'll choose to keep everything in-house. And it's his right."

"But I am in-house," Lennie said. "I work for Hamilton."

Decker held up his hand to her. "This is all supposition. Let me talk to the man first. But I do have one request, Mike."

"Speak."

"I want to interview Brandon Gratz."

A pause. "*Why?*"

"Because if Brady Neil's blood does not show up at the Boch house, his murder is still mine. And I am very thorough. Brandon Gratz is Neil's father. They might have been in contact. He might be able to shed light if

Neil was into something dangerous. Neil could have also been doing something at his father's behest."

"If so, why would Gratz want to talk to you?"

"Because Neil was his son, and his son was murdered. It's an avenue we need to explore. If you could grease the skids with the paperwork, I'd be appreciative."

"What prison is he at?"

"Bergenshaw Maximum. It's near Poughkeepsie."

"I know the prison. I don't know the warden. I'll do what I can."

"Thanks," Decker said.

Doing what you can is sometimes enough.

More often than not, *doing what you can* is a date with failure.

On the front lawn of Jaylene Boch's home, Victor Baccus was surveying the activity, looking straight ahead, while talking to Decker. An hour ago, he was playing golf in appropriate course clothing. Now he was impeccably garbed in a black police uniform, including starched white shirt, tie, and spit-polished black shoes. He was average size but muscular—broad shoulders and a thick neck. He had pink smooth skin and intense dark eyes. He looked at Decker, arms folded across his chest. "It's not that I mind you investigating the Levines. I understand. It's good policing. But if you would have told me first, I could have helped you. Yvonne has always been tougher than Gregg. When it happened, she was the one who held it together. That girl is pure steel. Gregg just fell apart."

"He also was the one who witnessed the shootings. That image isn't burned in her brain. What I'm asking is why'd she feel it necessary to call you, Chief?"

"Yvonne doesn't trust too many people. I'm not sure she trusts me. But she trusts me more than she trusts you. It might have helped to have someone from Hamilton with you."

"Sir, I had Officer Baccus with me. It didn't seem to make a difference."

Baccus made a sour face. "Pete . . . it's all right if I call you Pete? We're about the same age."

"I'm older than you by a decade. But Pete's fine."

"What I meant was I could have sent someone a little more experienced. A real detective."

Decker was taken aback by the insult. "Officer Baccus is doing a fine job, Chief. Couldn't ask for anyone better."

"I'm sure that's a lie." Decker was quiet. Baccus sighed. "I love my daughter, Pete. She's the apple of my eye. She's a good cop—persistent and dogged. But she's better behind the scenes than on center stage."

"That's why it worked well, sir. She did exactly what I told her to do and did it well."

"Whatever you say."

"You sent her to me to learn. She's learning."

"This case isn't for a newbie."

"Dump cases are rarely cut-and-dried." He paused. "Why did you send her to me?"

"Honestly? I didn't see Neil's murder as a whodunit. You asked for the files of some punks in my district. I thought Brady Neil was one of them. Guys get drunk or high, they fool around with guns . . . something goes off accidentally, shit happens."

"He was beaten to death with a bat."

"The point is she's too green for something this messy."

"I think she's doing fine."

Baccus turned to him. "How so?"

"She's a quick learner, Chief. Let her go the distance. You might be surprised."

"Meaning let you go the distance."

"Of course, let me go the distance. I'm a very experienced homicide detective. As such, I like to finish what I start."

Baccus's eyes went back to the house. "If you coordinate with Wen and Randy, I won't pull the rug from under *your* feet."

"What about Lenora?"

"I'm pulling her off the case. This is no time for her to get her feet wet. You normally work with the kid? Harvard, you call him?"

"Yes, but I can use all the help I can get, including Lennie. But it's your call, of course. I'll coordinate with your guys. We all want a quick resolution. And to that end, I'd like to talk to Gregg Levine. Anything that has to do with Brandon Gratz has to do with him."

"But we don't know if it has anything to do with Gratz." When Decker was silent, Baccus said, "How about getting a little further along on this mess and then I'll approach Gregg."

"Sounds reasonable," Decker said. "About Officer Baccus. What's the verdict?"

"She's off." He turned to Decker again. "You tell her that it's my verdict. Put the onus on me."

Chapter 12

"Did he give you a reason?" Smoke from her nostrils. Her nails were clicking faster than a court stenographer's fingers. "Other than I was green and a newbie?"

"Those were the reasons, Len."

"And you agreed with him?" Her face was red.

"Not that it's your business, but no, I didn't agree with him," Decker said. "But it's his call. He put you on the case, he can pull it from you. He could have pulled it from me, but he didn't. Not letting you see this out, in my opinion, is a mistake."

She bit her lip, silently seething.

Decker said, "Listen to me for a sec." No response. "Are you listening?"

"I don't need a pep talk."

"Don't speak to me like that. I'm still your superior."

That got her attention. She sighed. "I apologize, sir."

"Apology accepted. Are you listening?"

"Yes."

"You're no longer on the case. I will not actively discuss what's going on and what progress we're making. But we did work together on it, and I might have to call you from time to time to ask you a couple of questions about the interviews we conducted, okay? And I could see where it might be appropriate for you to ask me some questions as points of clarification, so you know what I'm asking."

Her eyes locked with Decker. "I'll help you any way I can."

"Like with that girl Neil dated."

"Olivia Anderson."

"Yeah, her. I'd still like to talk to her, but maybe she'll want to talk to you also. That would be okay. You want to help me and yourself, go back to your father and ask him what assignments he'd like you to do. Have a good attitude and, above all, be a professional."

"You think he might change his mind?"

"No idea. But it's the right way to behave."

"Okay." She took a breath and let it out. "Call me anytime you have questions for me. And thank you for the privilege of working with you."

"You're welcome."

She paused. "You know, what I do on my own free time is my own business."

Her posture was calm and her red face was gone, but there was something in her eyes. Decker recognized that look because he had seen it so often when he looked in the mirror.

Fuck you, I'll do what I want.

It wasn't his plan to gain her as an ally. But he wasn't displeased with the outcome. Still, he had to act professionally. "Don't go there, Lennie. Nothing good will come from it. Go coordinate with your superior. Good luck."

"Thank you." She smiled. "My last sergeant was smart, perceptive, and very fair. You remind me a lot of her."

Decker smiled and watched her walk away.

Other way around, kiddo. She reminds you of me.

Recapping his conversation with Baccus, but away from prying eyes, Decker and McAdams were a few blocks from the scene, grabbing coffee to go, talking as they walked back to the Boch house.

Tyler was aghast. "He *fired* her?"

"Pulled her off the case."

"Why?"

"Don't know."

"Did she fuck up?"

"Nope. He just didn't want her on a real homicide case. At least, that's what he said."

"You believe him?"

"It's not a matter of do I believe him. There's some dynamic between the two of them that I'm not privy to." Decker smoothed his mustache. "She mentioned something about helping us on her own time—to which I said no. But it's not going to stop her."

"She's going to spy on Hamilton for us?"

"I wouldn't call it spying, Harvard."

"Maybe she's a double agent. She's feeding you some information while telling her dad what you said to her."

"If she is a double agent, she's doing a fine acting job. In my opinion, she's a young woman who doesn't fully have the trust of her dad, and she's working hard to prove herself."

"Don't we all want Daddy's approval?"

"Maybe." Decker's father had been a very nice but remote man. They didn't talk much, but they built a lot of homemade projects together. Wood and tools had been their primary form of communication. He took a sip of coffee and said, "What CCTV tapes did you pull from Tollway?"

"We got about halfway before we were called here. Neither Kevin nor I had any chance to look at them."

"That should be our next step. What about the house? Did you and Kev go through it thoroughly?"

"As much as we could without impeding Forensics. Probably the best thing to do is come back after they finish up."

"I agree. Let's start viewing the tapes. We're dealing with a murder and a missing person and a bloodbath. I want as much information on that car as possible. Go get Kevin and we'll go back to the station. I'm still waiting for a call from the hospital regarding Jaylene Boch. If she regains full consciousness, maybe she can tell us something—if she's all there."

"Why wouldn't she be all there? She's not *that* old."

"No, she's not that old, but she's suffered a trauma and she's had it hard since her accident. If she gives me anything useful at all, I'll be a happy man."

Once at Greenbury station, they divided up the tapes from the CCTV cameras on Tollway Boulevard. The three men sat looking at three monitors for a little under two hours, attempting to discern a license plate or, at least, get a bead on the route the car took.

It took a long time to get enough frames to get enough angles to get an entire license number, and that information turned out to be a bust. The plate was taken from a '78 Caddie Seville—of Linda and Barry

Mark, who lived two blocks down Canterbury Lane, about three blocks from the spot where Brady Neil had been found murdered.

Decker took his car keys and said, "You two keep with the tapes. I'm going to talk to the Marks. Call me if you get anything interesting."

"I'll come with you," McAdams said. "My eyes are getting a little buggy."

"It isn't a two-person job, Harvard."

"I'll wait in the car in case it does become a two-person job."

"Suit yourself."

Ten minutes later, Decker was sitting in the Marks' living room furnished with contemporary pieces—all sleek and monochrome—as well as paintings with abstract blotches done in oils. Weird because the outside of the house was still upstate bungalow. Light was coming in through the windows, hitting the walls and concrete floors at odd angles. The effect, combined with the interview, almost qualified as performance art.

Linda wasn't home, but Barry was game to talk. "Does that mean we have to get a new license plate?" He was over seventy, maybe even closer to eighty, with thin, white hair and a jowly face. He wore dark blue sweats with a sizable gut hanging over the waistband.

"If I were you, I'd do that," Decker said. "It will avoid confusion."

"Damn inconvenience. It's already after five o'clock."

"There's no immediate worry, Mr. Mark. We'll inform other agencies so that anyone who calls it in will know that it's a stolen plate. In the meantime, I'll write you out a report regarding the stolen license plate that you can take to the DMV."

"Damn inconvenience." He paused and then coughed. "I suppose it's better sooner than later. I don't want to get arrested."

"There's lots to worry about in the world. Getting arrested isn't one of them."

"Is that supposed to be funny?"

"No. It's just a statement of fact."

"Okay. I'll do it first thing tomorrow morning. Is the car stolen as well?"

"We're checking that out. It's hard to do without its proper plates."

"Glad they didn't steal my car."

"Yes, that would have been very . . . inconvenient," Decker said.

"It's a classic, the Seville."

"Nice set of wheels."

"Alex Delaware drives a Seville."

"Pardon?"

"You know, the psychologist in the books. He works with that policeman . . . what's his name." A pause. "Milo Sturgis. They work together solving crimes. You don't read mysteries? You should. Damn good novels."

"I'll ask my wife about it. She reads a lot of mysteries."

"You should read it. Maybe it'd give you a tip or two. You know. WWAD."

"Excuse me?"

"What would Alex do." He laughed and wheezed at the same time.

Decker said, "Thank you for talking to me, and I'm sorry for the hassle. You can come into the Greenbury police station anytime and pick up the report for your stolen plate."

"Sure. I'll bring you a couple of novels if you want. They're paperback, might have some coffee stains, but hey, it's for free."

"Your donation to the Police Department is much appreciated. Thank you, sir."

"Might entertain you on all those stakeouts."

"I'm sure they would, but unfortunately when you do a stakeout, you have to pay attention to what you're looking at."

A long pause. "You want audio instead?"

"Mr. Mark, whatever you want to donate to the police is appreciated. Thank you for your time." Decker left before he started laughing to himself. McAdams was waiting in the car.

"What?" he said.

Decker slid into the driver's seat, still chuckling. "I love people."

"Since when?"

"Since always. You're the curmudgeon." He put the key in the ignition. "Okay. We need to pull the rest of the CCTV along Tollway and see where the car was headed, especially since we now know the plates were stolen." Before Decker could turn on the motor, his cell rang with Butterfield on the other end. He put his phone on speaker.

"The hospital called, Deck. Jaylene Boch is conscious and is asking for her son. They don't know if they should say something or . . ."

"They should tell her that he's missing because that's all we know right now."

"They don't want to upset her."

"It's going to upset her. What do they want us to do about that?" Decker paused. "They want *me* to tell her?"

McAdams said, "You wanted to talk to her anyway."

"Jeez, so now I have to be the therapist?"

"I guess they figure you do death calls."

"And hate every one of them." Decker sighed.

"Fine. Tell the hospital I'll be right over, Kev. And can you finish picking up whatever CCTV tapes you can at this late hour? We'll go through those tomorrow."

"Sure. If you don't mind, I'll go home afterward. Unless you want me with you at the hospital."

"Not necessary." Decker looked at McAdams. "You want to come with me?"

"Oh sure, now that your new best bud, Lennie, has been dismissed, you'll take me as your leavings." When Decker laughed, McAdams said, "I'm serious."

"Aw, c'mon, Harvard! You can't be that pissy."

"I can and I am."

"Lennie's gone?" Butterfield asked.

"Her father took her off the case," Decker said.

"Why? I thought Baccus was adamant to have her on the case."

"I know. And she was doing fine. Weird, huh?"

"How'd she take it?" Butterfield asked.

"Not happy."

"Did he give you a reason?"

"He told me he didn't want her on a 'messy' homicide. Maybe he's worried about her safety. Anyway, see what you can do about the CCTV."

"I'm on it." Butterfield cut the line.

McAdams said, "I still think that she's working undercover—like a spy-counterspy thing."

Decker said, "Why would she want to spy on me?"

"You told me to be careful around her, that you didn't trust her."

"I didn't trust her, but that doesn't mean I think she's spying on us. Fact is she's gone now so it doesn't matter what either of us think."

"I'm just saying that maybe, as you're getting close to the truth, her dad wants her for other things."

"What other things?"

"Poking around your office when you're not in."

"McAdams, what tabloids have you been reading? No one is poking around in my office. And what truths are you talking about? Who killed Neil? I hope I'm getting closer, but it sure doesn't feel like it." Decker rolled his eyes. "Are you coming with me to the hospital or not?"

"Can I come to dinner at your house afterward? I'm a little tired of canned chili."

"You're welcome anytime for dinner. Let's go."

"By the way, have you checked this car for bugs? She could have planted something and now knows everything we've just said."

"What is *with* you?" Decker was stunned.

"Her dad just pulling her off like that. Something's wrong."

"Maybe, but I can't worry about that. And I guarantee

you this, Harvard." Decker started the car. "The only bugs in my car are the splotches on my windshield."

Jaylene Boch stirred and moaned as she drifted in and out of sleep. She had a tube in her nose and needles in her veins with IVs dripping from hooked poles. A machine beeped out her heartbeat. Her blood pressure was high, and her oxygen level was low. Perfect conditions to be delivering bad news.

Gently, Decker shook her arm. The woman turned in his direction and managed to open her eyes. The orbs lobbed from one side to the other as they tried to focus. He got close and spoke soothingly. "Jaylene, can you hear me?"

Nothing, then a faint nod.

"I'm Detective Peter Decker from the police. This is Detective McAdams. We're come to see how you're doing."

"Joe . . ." Her eyelids fluttered.

Decker gathered his thoughts. "Do you know where you are, Jaylene?" No answer. "You're in the hospital."

Jaylene was quiet.

"Someone broke into your home. Do you remember anything about that?"

The woman stared at Decker and then pointed her finger at him.

"Yes, I was there. I called the ambulance for you. Do you remember that?"

She was silent. Then she said, "Joe . . ."

"Do you mean Joseph, your son?" No answer. "I don't know where your son is, Jaylene. We've been looking for him. Do you have any idea where he might be?"

No answer.

Decker said, "Do you remember anything from the last few days?"

Again, she pointed her finger at Decker.

"You remember me?"

She looked at Decker, then she looked at McAdams and pointed a finger at him.

"You remember Detective McAdams?"

"I wasn't there," Tyler said.

Decker held up a hand to silence him. "You remember Detective McAdams and you remember me?"

She let her hand drift to the side of the bed. She closed her eyes. "Joe . . ."

"Joe is missing," Decker said. "We're looking for him. Would you know anything about that?"

Tears ran down her face, but she kept her eyes closed. As she lay there and minutes passed, her breathing became more rhythmic.

"We're done here." Decker got up. "Let's go."

Once outside the room and in the corridor, McAdams said, "She's confused."

"She is."

"I mean, I wasn't even there."

"It's still early in her recovery. She obviously needs more time."

"Do you think her memory will come back? Traumatizing events like this are often blocked out of consciousness."

"I know that. She's not that old, but she's not young, either. And she's sick. I don't expect much, but when she gets better I'll ask anyway."

"Do you even think that she understood that her son's missing?"

"Yes, I believe so." Decker sighed. "Even worse, I fear she thinks he's dead."

Chapter 13

"Welcome back to Greenbury, Tyler." Rina set a hot plate of chicken onto a trivet. "This is probably not the start you were looking forward to."

"I'm surprised that our little town has racked up multiple homicides in the last couple of years." McAdams put his napkin on his lap. "We're nothing but a bunch of students, professors, and retirees."

Decker said, "The murders took place in Hamilton."

McAdams said, "Yet here we are on the scene again."

"You'll have to tell me all about it." Rina had tucked her hair into a kerchief. She was wearing a midcalf jersey dress that was a size too big on her. But it was comfortable, and that was all she cared about. She sat down, picked up Decker's plate, and gave him some sliced white meat. Sides were coleslaw and coleslaw.

Decker said, "Do you want some wine, darlin'?"

"No, thanks." She sat down. "Tell me what's going on?" After McAdams filled her in, Rina said, "Poor woman. How awful."

"Yeah, it's probably worse for her son. Something very bad happened in there."

"And you don't know if Joseph Boch was a victim or a perpetrator?"

"Not yet," Decker said. "Scientific Investigative Division is taking multiple samples. We'll see if we have multiple blood types."

"It sounds horrible," Rina said. "Brady Neil was bashed on the head, right?"

"Yes."

"Could his wound produce as much blood as you saw in the back room?"

"Not in my opinion." Decker put down his fork and knife. "Too much blood and way too much splatter. That kind of damage is more consistent with a stab wound that severed a major artery."

"And you have no idea where Joseph Boch is?"

"No. I don't know anything about him, but I'm going to find out."

"You're going back to Bigstore?" McAdams said.

"At some point, yes." Decker paused. "Joe Boch didn't seem to make much of a mark at his workplace, so I don't think that will tell me a lot. I'll have to do a

little research—find out as much as I can about him."
He looked at Rina. "How was your day?"

"Much less eventful than yours."

"What's today? Wednesday?"

"It is," McAdams said. "Can I come for dinner on
Friday?"

"Yes," Rina answered.

"Can I sleep over?"

"No," Decker answered.

Rina laughed. "You have your own apartment,
Tyler."

"I get lonely. You know me, Rina. I hate people, but
I like your company."

"Aww," Rina said.

"The answer is still no," Decker said. "Friday
nights are for my relaxation. I don't want anything that
reminds me of work." Again, he turned to his wife.
"Can you do me a favor, Rina? Whenever you have a
free moment, could you scour the internet and look up
everything out there on the Levine's Luscious Gems
jewelry store robbery and murder case? I found some
old newspaper coverage, but I couldn't go into depth
because I had other work to do."

"I can do that," McAdams said.

"No, you coordinate with the Hamilton detectives
on the Boch case. We can't devote that kind of time

to reading when we have an active homicide to look into," Decker said. "Especially now that Lennie's off the case, we're short a person."

"Lennie's off the case?" Rina asked. "Why?"

"Her dad pulled her off."

"I'm thinking she was a spy for her father," McAdams said. "Victor Baccus was the lead investigator on the double murder. Then Brady Neil was murdered. I think the elder Baccus wanted to know why and see what we were up to."

"Then why pull her off the case?"

"I'm still working that part out."

Rina said, "Is there any indication that the chief didn't handle the double murder well?"

"I haven't read anything that indicates misconduct, but I also haven't seen the original files, either. They're archived, no doubt, but I'd love to look at them at some point." Decker shook his head and hooked a thumb toward McAdams. "First, he tells me that Brady Neil has nothing to do with the double murders, and now he's on to conspiracy theories."

"*He* is here in the room," McAdams said. "So why do *you* think Baccus pulled her off the case?"

"I don't know, Harvard. I can just repeat what Baccus said, that he didn't want her involved in a messy homicide." He turned to Rina. "There's some rationale for that. He wants more experienced people now that the homicide has spilled over to his area."

"And you're okay with that explanation?"

"No, I'm not. Especially since I told him she was doing fine."

"That's why I changed my mind," McAdams said. "Flexibility is a trait of the thinking man."

Decker was deep in thought. "He's an interesting guy, Baccus. He pulls her off the case but more or less gives me free rein to do what I need to do. I hope he's as forthcoming when I ask for the files. Or maybe I'll ask Tran to get them for me. I think I trust him more than Baccus."

"Go with your gut," Rina said. "I'm free tomorrow. I'll go down to the Hamilton library and look up every old newspaper that had articles on the case. Even if the papers haven't been computerized, I can comb through the microfiche."

"Yeah, that's a great idea. Computerization wasn't quite as common twenty years ago, especially in the smaller towns. I bet you will find out a lot more on microfiche."

"And you think the police did a righteous investigation?"

"So far, nothing tells me otherwise."

Rina said, "Then why are you looking into it?"

"I'm looking for a motive for Neil's murder. When I don't have a reason, I look into the victim's background. And that means I look into his father's background. Also, this is really sticking in my craw: when Glen and Lydia were doing inventory the night they were murdered, there was no mention in any of the papers about an alarm going off. That's odd." He paused, then turned to his wife. "While you're at the library—if you have time—could you also look up Glen and Lydia Levine and find out what you can about them? I hope that's not asking too much."

"I don't teach during the summer. As long as I have time to work in the garden and catch up on my reading, I'm happy to be your researcher. I like it, actually."

"Speaking of reading, do you read mystery novels?"

"I mostly read biographies, but I have my favorite crime series novels."

"Do you know an author named Alex Delaware?"

"He's not the author, he's a fictional character. They're terrific books. Why?"

Decker smiled. "Someone mentioned that the guy— Alex—drives a Seville. I'm thinking either that the character is a retro hipster or it's a very long running series."

"It's the latter. And that's a rather esoteric factoid. He must be a devoted fan."

"You read mysteries?" McAdams asked.

"I do. This guy doesn't."

"What do you read?" he asked Decker.

"Travel books. I read about remote areas where you can contract horrible diseases or get eaten by wild animals and bitten by venomous snakes or bugs that cause you protracted, painful deaths. Places I don't know anything about and I'll never visit."

McAdams laughed. "I love this guy."

"I agree with you there," Rina said.

"Can I please sleep over Friday night?" When Decker didn't answer, McAdams said, "I promise I won't say a word about work. And if I stay the night, I don't have to come back for Saturday lunch."

"I don't recall inviting you for Shabbos lunch," Decker said.

"You meant to do it, boss," Tyler said. "But with everything that's going on, it just slipped your mind."

Arriving at the station house at seven in the morning, Decker put in a call to Detective Wendell Tran, asking the secretary to have him call back as soon as he checked in. If Tran and his partner, Smitz, were going to revisit Bigstore, he wanted McAdams with them.

While waiting for a call back, he turned on his computer in hopes of finding out more information about Joseph Boch a.k.a. Boxer. The guy had been arrested a couple of times for DUIs and possession of weed, but nothing violent. He served probation and did community service for all his offenses, the two judges going easy on him because he was solely responsible for his mother's care. Decker did some poking into county records and eventually found his birth certificate. Boxer was born in Hamilton, and the year of his birth put him at thirty-five. His father was listed as Joseph Boch, making Boxer a junior. The old man was thirty when his son was born.

Immediately, Decker switched the search to Senior. Decker found an old tax return filed in Hamilton. The man had worked a variety of low-skill jobs: roofing, construction, and a short-order cook. There was nothing on him more recent than twenty years ago—at least in Hamilton's computers.

Decker needed something a little more recent.

Tapping the keys, going from one agency to another, it took another fifteen minutes, even with department software, for Decker to find a birth certificate: the old man was born in Leavenworth, Kansas, sixty-five years ago. More searching produced a death certificate dated ten years ago from a mortuary in Salina, Kansas. An autopsy was performed and death was determined to be natural—atherosclerotic heart disease. Decker found several tax returns in the state of Kansas, the last one dated twelve years ago, when Joe Sr. had worked as a janitor at the local municipal airport.

Decker couldn't find any divorce papers, so he assumed that Joe had taken his family with him when he left Hamilton and went to Kansas.

He earned money as a janitor, and he did file taxes, but it was barely enough to support a family. How did they live? And what had drawn the Bochs from Hamilton to Joe Sr.'s home state?

And if Jaylene had gone with her husband, what had drawn her back to Hamilton?

And if she didn't go with her husband, why was that?

More questions than answers.

Decker's cell phone rang.

A voice over the line said, "Tran here."

"It's Peter Decker. Thanks for calling me back. Have you gone over the Boch house yet?"

"No, because Scientific Investigative Division didn't finish until late last night. Randy and I did a preliminary yesterday, but with all the forensic personnel, it was hard to move. We were planning to go out first thing, but we just got called out to a slash and grab. The woman's in the hospital."

"When do you think you'll make it over?"

"Couple of hours."

"Do you mind if I get a jump start?"

"Fine with me. Do you have a key?"

"No, actually, I don't."

"You caught me just as I was ready to leave. I'll put it in an envelope and give it to Anna—she's the receptionist. I'll tell her to expect you in, like, fifteen minutes?"

"Half an hour. I appreciate it, Wendell. Thanks."

"Call me Tran. I'm named after some old shrimp fisherman who gave my dad a break. Which was nice in theory except people keep expecting me to be ninety years old."

"Thank you, Tran. Also, are you going over to Big-store in Claremont? Where Neil and Boxer worked?"

"Eventually we'll get there."

"Would you mind taking McAdams with you when you do go?"

"No problem, but it won't happen today. Let me know if you find anything at the Boch house. I'll call SID later and find out what they came up with. There was a lot of evidence to bag and test. Blood was every-where."

"I'll be careful where I step. Talk to you later."

After disconnecting the call, Decker phoned the hospital. After being on hold for ten minutes, he found out that there was no change in Jaylene Boch's status.

They were easing up on her sedation, but the woman was mute and very confused.

Decker realized he was shifting his focus from Neil's murder to the missing Boxer a.k.a. Joseph Boch Jr. investigation, which wasn't officially his case. He shuffled some papers in the Brady Neil file and found what he was looking for.

Brett Baderhoff and Patrick Markham with accompanying phone numbers.

Better to concentrate on what you have control over.

Carrying an armful of CCTV tapes, Kevin Butterfield walked in the room at eight. He laid them on his desk and said, "These are the last of them. I'm gonna grab a cup of coffee and start viewing. Anything new?"

"I was looking up Joseph Boch Senior." Decker gave him a recap.

"Leaving for his home state around the time of the Levine murders," Butterfield said. "That has to be more than a coincidence."

"Probe and ye shall find."

"They're connected then: Joe Senior and the Levine murders?"

"It's certainly a thought worth pursuing. I've put in necessary papers to interview Brandon Gratz at prison. Who knows what he'll tell me. But . . ." He held up a finger, then picked up the phone. "I can call

Jennifer Neil. She might know something about her ex-husband's friends."

Decker looked up her number and punched them into his cell phone. A moment later, he was told that the line was no longer operable. He checked to make sure he had the correct number.

Butterfield noticed a look on his face. "What?"

"Jennifer Neil's line is disconnected." Decker paused. "I'll try the daughter." No one was home, but at least Brandy's line was working. He left a message. "Kev, we need to interview these two young men." He handed Butterfield the slip of paper. "Could you call them and set up a time? If they can't come here, I'll go to their houses."

"Who are these guys?"

"High school friends of Brady Neil's. I got the name from Brady's mother and sister. Maybe they know something. I'm free this afternoon and all day tomorrow."

"I'll call them right now."

"Thanks." When McAdams walked in, Decker said, "Don't bother sitting down. We're going back to the Boch house to do a thorough search."

"Ugh!" McAdams wrinkled his nose. "It's going to stink."

"Death always stinks. Let's go."

Butterfield hung up the phone. "I left messages with the two men. Gave them my phone number and your phone number."

"Perfect, Kev." To McAdams, he said, "Ready?"

"Not really. I'm wearing three-hundred-dollar sneakers."

"Ever heard of shoe protectors?"

Butterfield said, "Why don't you just wear normal, rubber-soled shoes, Harvard?"

"Good question," Decker said.

"I like good shoes. They make me feel good. What's wrong with that?"

"Under ordinary circumstances, nothing." Decker rolled his eyes. "This is your fourth case dealing with homicide, dude. If you don't learn from prior experience, then I have nothing more to say."

McAdams sighed, took off his sneakers, and put on some beaten-up oxford rubber-soled shoes that he kept under his desk. "I got shot in these. I keep them under my desk to remind me that I am not invincible."

"Whatever keeps you humble."

"Let's hope lightning doesn't strike three times." He gave them a sniff. "They stink . . . of death."

"As long as it's not your own," Decker said. "Let's go."

Chapter 14

On the way to Hamilton, Decker filled in McAdams about his research on Joseph Boch Sr. "I don't know if Brady Neil's murder has something to do with the Levine murders, but I'm beginning to think that more people were involved in the robbery than just Brandon Gratz and Kyle Masterson."

"Do you think that Gratz was the one-in-a-million con that actually told the truth?"

"From my experience, probably not. Most convicts are con men. Can't believe a word they say. I'd really like to talk to Gregg Levine since he was an eyewitness. I've called him twice. I've left a card at his house. He's avoiding me."

"Why?"

"Good question." Decker thought a moment. "He's too old to be a chum of Neil—or Boxer, for that matter.

I'm trying to find a link between Brady and Boxer other than Bigstore. They couldn't have been school chums. Boxer is ten years older than Brady. I'm having Kev put in a call to Brady's high school buds. Maybe they can tell me something. Because I have to consider the past bubbling over to the present."

"Okay," McAdams said. "For argument's sake, let's assume that Boch Senior was connected to the Levine murders. And assume that he ran away to the Midwest after everything went down. Then are we assuming that Jaylene went with him?"

"My feeling is that if Joe Senior was in big trouble and went underground, Jaylene would run as well."

"Then why would she come back to Hamilton with Joe Junior after Joe Senior died?"

"I don't know." Decker pulled over to the curb and parked in front of the Hamilton Police Department, intending to pick up the key to the Boch house. Instead, he didn't get out of the car. "Harvard, I'm a little queasy about Jennifer Neil's phone line being disconnected."

"Jennifer Neil knows something and got the hell out of Dodge?"

"Who knows?"

"If you're that worried about Jennifer Neil, let's just go to her house."

Decker checked his watch. It was nearly ten. "How far away is it?"

McAdams pulled up the address and said, "About ten minutes, according to Waze."

"The Hamilton detectives were called out on a case. They aren't going to be ready for another hour. Okay, go get the key to the Boch house, and then I'll feel better if we drive by Jennifer Neil's first."

"Not a problem. But if something happened to her, it's going to be Hamilton's case."

"Hey, they could have done exactly what we're doing. If they're late to the party, well, then it's their faux pas, not mine."

The little bit of lawn fronting the bungalow was turning weed choked. Bunches of dandelions sprouted a carpet of spiky leaves and yellow blooms. An oversize pine tree dominated the front. Not a shrub in sight. Brady's car—which Decker assumed Jennifer was using—wasn't in the driveway or parked at the curb, but it could have been in the garage. There were hardly any vehicles on the street—a stretch of pocked asphalt with tar seeping out. Infrastructure in the neighborhood was minimal. But it was quiet. The birds and bugs didn't seem to mind a bit.

Decker and McAdams walked up the pathway and

stepped onto the porch. They knocked at the door, and when no one answered, Decker tried the doorknob. It held tight. "I could pick it, but there isn't much justification for that." He peeked into the living room windows, partially obscured by sheer drapes, but he could still see inside. Nothing looked out of place. From what he remembered from the last time, the place was spare and pretty neat. "I'm going to take a look around the back."

Just then, the Ford Focus pulled into the driveway. The men waited as Jennifer Neil got out. She stared at them and they stared at her. "Can I help you?"

"Police, Mrs. Neil," Decker said. "Remember we talked?"

"Of course I remember. I'm not senile. Are you releasing my boy for burial?"

"No, ma'am, unfortunately we still need a little more time."

"So why are you here?"

"I wanted to ask you a few questions. Do you mind if we talked inside?"

"No, I don't mind." She went over to the back of the car and popped the trunk. She took out two Walmart bags and headed up to the door. McAdams walked over and tried to relieve her of the bags, but her grip on them was strong. "I'm fine."

When she got to the door, she paused, put the bags down, and fished out her keys from a black leather handbag. Opening the door, she said, "Come in." She set the bags down along with her black handbag. "What questions?"

Decker looked at her purchases and gave a quick glance around. Nothing appeared disturbed. "Your phone is disconnected."

"I know. I disconnected it."

"May I ask the reason for that?"

"I got a few calls asking about Brady."

"From whom?"

"TV stations. Local paper. I don't want to talk to anybody. It's none of their business."

"Do you have a new phone number?"

"Not yet. Just a new phone." She reached down into her Walmart bag and pulled out an iPhone still in the box.

"Can I see that?" She handed it to Decker. It was the latest incarnation from Apple. "Very nice."

"About time I did something nice for myself."

"No time like the present," McAdams said.

"That's for damn sure, young man." Jennifer nodded. "The man at the store told me he'd set it up for me once I get a new phone number. Why are you here?"

"We swung by to make sure you're okay, Mrs. Neil."

Jennifer's eyes narrowed. "Why wouldn't I be okay?"

"For one thing, your phone was disconnected." Decker took out a small notepad. "Also, you must have heard about what happened to Jaylene Boch."

She was quiet, didn't seem overly perturbed. Then she said, "Some people are bad. I've known a couple in my day. I heard her boy was missing."

"Joe Junior," Decker said. "Yes, he is missing. We found out about Joe Junior—he goes by the name of Boxer—because he worked with your son. They were friends."

Jennifer was silent.

"Did you know they were friends?"

"No." Quick answer. Then she thought a moment. "You think he killed my boy?"

"Maybe. Or possibly Joe Junior was murdered as well. Something bad happened in that house." Decker said, "What do you know about the Boch family?"

"I know who they are. It's not that big of a town in our area. I'm not talking about the snooty people in Bellweather or Claremont. Here, we all run into each other now and then."

"Are you friends with Jaylene?"

"I see her around in the grocery store with her son.

We'll chat a minute and that's that. The boy seemed pretty dedicated to her."

McAdams said, "What do you know about the father, Joe Senior?"

"He was no good: a lazy drunk with a big mouth."

Decker said, "Did your husband, Brandon, know him?"

"Probably. Brandon seemed to know every lowlife in town. I'm not saying his company turned him bad. I'm saying Brandon was bad so he kept bad company."

"Were they friends—Joe Senior and your husband?"

"I have no idea. Brandon didn't tell me what he did at night. Most of the time, he'd come home drunk with perfume on his clothes. Then there were those other nights, when he came home sober. Scary sober, if you know what I mean. Never laid a finger on me, but I sure didn't cross him when he had that look in his eye. If I was honest, I preferred him drunk."

"He had money when he came home on those sober nights?"

"He didn't tell me anything about his finances. But there was always enough to keep the kids in milk and cookies and new shoes."

"Do you remember when Joe Senior and Jaylene moved out of Hamilton? It was shortly after your husband was arrested."

"No, I don't remember. I was a little busy with my own problems, Detective. Are we done? All these questions make me depressed. And I don't see what this has to do with Brady."

"Probably nothing, but a few more questions, if you'll indulge me." She didn't answer. Decker said, "I came out because I was concerned about you. I still am concerned. Do you remember when Jaylene Boch moved *back* into Hamilton?"

"Not specifically, no. Just one day I ran into her with the boy." She paused. "What is Joe Junior now? I know he's older than my kids. Must be older than thirty."

"He's thirty-five," McAdams said.

"And you're saying that Brady and Joe were friends?"

"They worked together at Bigstore. It seems they became friends."

Jennifer made a sour face. "Don't know anything about that. Still, it's sad about Jaylene being in the hospital."

Decker said, "Mrs. Neil, would you mind if I searched your entire house?"

"You already did that."

"I searched the basement. It's possible that Brady might have hidden something in your part of the house."

Her eyes narrowed. "Like what?"

"Could be anything . . . papers, electronics . . . possibly drugs."

"Doubt it."

"I'd still like to look."

"Okay, but not today. I'm too tired."

"Tomorrow?"

"Sure." She walked over to the front door and opened it. "Call me before you come."

"You don't have a phone number."

"You're right. I don't." Jennifer smiled. "In that case, just wait until I call you."

Once in the car, McAdams said, "I know what you're going to ask. How can she afford a new iPhone when she's living on assistance? My answer to that is to look at all these scumbag criminals. They may live like shit, but they all have money for phones."

"But hers was new and it was from Walmart. She didn't even go to Bigstore, where no doubt she could get a discount. And did you notice her purse? It's also new—Kathy Spode made especially for Walmart—at least a hundred bucks. Where is she getting all that spending cash?"

"She found a stash of cash that Brady had hidden."

"It's as good an explanation as any." Decker thought a moment. "We should check to see if Brady had a life insurance policy."

"You honestly think?"

"Long shot, but you never know. Rule one is victims are usually murdered by those closest to them. Rule two is follow the money trail. Jennifer seems to be looking good in both those categories."

"She murdered her own son?"

"I don't know, Harvard. They weren't close. I've been focusing on her husband because he's a bad guy. And he's worth looking at. But he's been in prison for a very long time. I'm beginning to think that my time is better spent looking closer to home."

"I haven't been at this as long as you have, but how many cases have you worked where parents have murdered their children?"

"With children over five, maybe two or three times. One of the messiest was a divorce case. The dad was getting even with the mom and murdered the entire family. Murdering your child for insurance money does happen. But it's rare."

"There you go."

"There I go nothing," Decker retorted. "Rare doesn't mean never."

———

The library catalog was computerized, but old copies of the *Hamiltonian* were still on microfiche. The machines sat in a remote corner and looked like they hadn't been used in ages. Rina took out a pair of strong reading glasses and decided to start with the year of the Levine murders. She'd work forward, and then she'd go backward.

The murders had dominated the front pages for six months. The information was pretty much what she had read on the internet, but seeing the amount of space given over to the double homicides brought home how shocking it had been to the community.

It was clear from the get-go that the motive was robbery—the whydunit—but the whodunit was not as immediate. It took a month before Brandon Gratz and Kyle Masterson were arrested for the robbery/murders. Gratz was identified from a lineup by Gregg Levine, then twenty. He swore that Gratz was the man he had seen removing his mask. A search of their hidey-hole in Nashville produced jewelry taken from the robbery. Not all the pieces, but enough to tie the noose around Gratz's and Masterson's necks.

At the trial and faced with the evidence against them, Gratz and Masterson admitted to the robbery. But both adamantly refused to confess to the murders and continued to profess their innocence. And there were inconsistencies that backed up the claim. Though both owned guns, the firearms that were legally registered did not match the firearm that was used in the murder. But that meant nothing according to the D.A. Robbers used unregistered or stolen guns. Between possessing stolen gems and the eyewitness testimony, the case was a slam dunk, yielding convictions for both robbery and the double murders.

After the sentencing of the two men to twenty years to life—looked on by the community as a travesty for such a heinous crime—the murders slowly faded from print. What took its place were human interest stories regarding the Levine family. Since the children weren't talking to the papers, it fell to the reporters to sidestep direct quotes and infer stories about a family struggling to come to terms with such horror.

As if it were ever possible.

Those columns lasted a few months. Eventually the Levine family was only mentioned as participating in charity functions and at the anniversaries of the deaths of Glen and Lydia Levine.

It was eleven in the morning by the time Rina finished reading about the murders. Her eyes were tired, and her shoulders and neck ached from hunching. What she had learned wasn't new. She broke for a quick lunch, eating a sandwich in the car. Then she took a walk around the block to buy a cup of coffee and tried to clear her head.

Forty-five minutes later, she was refreshed enough to squint and strain her eyes for round two of reading. This time, she'd work from the murders and go back in time, trying to flesh out Glen and Lydia Levine.

It was harder to find out information about them while they were living. The one thing that stood out was their copious amount of charity—always giving to the community: the police, the firemen, the schools, the homeless, the halfway houses. Two years before he was murdered, Glen was elected president of his temple. Two years before she was murdered, Lydia ran for city council but lost to the incumbent.

Rina kept searching and searching and searching until her eyes got buggy and blurry. But she soldiered on, going back a year before the murders.

Ten minutes later, she hit a front-page article that caused her heartbeat to quicken and her head to swim. The article headline was about a couple who skipped town the previous week, a few days before they were to be sentenced for fraud and embezzlement. She had to read it twice to make sure she wasn't making a mistake.

Time seemed to pass quickly. Going back in the records: two years before the murders when the first charges were made.

And then she read—and she read—and she read.

Chapter 15

The two men got out and walked to the front entrance of the Boch house, blocked by a banner of yellow crime scene tape. Decker ducked under the ribbon and inserted the key in the lock. As soon as he opened the door, a whiff of warm fetid air rushed out. Having been sealed for twelve hours, the interior smelled ripe. He and McAdams gloved up and went inside. Fingerprint dust was everywhere, revealing numerous hand and shoe prints. Decker said, "Watch where you step."

"It stinks of excrement. That's shit in layman's terms."

"Probably from where the old lady was tied up. She was here for a few days. Unable to move. She soiled herself."

"Poor woman. How is she doing?"

"Better than when I found her, but basically no

change from yesterday." He gave McAdams a face mask and then put one over his mouth and nose. "It doesn't do too much with the smell, but we shouldn't be breathing in human biological matter. I'll take the two bedrooms where it smells really bad. You go through the living room, kitchen, and bathroom."

"Thank you. Am I looking for anything specific?"

"Just the usual: stashes of money or drugs, old documents, papers. Anything hidden will be significant." A pause. "Something that could explain the slaughterhouse in the back bedroom."

"Didn't Hamilton PD already comb the place?"

"SID was doing their thing, and the detectives didn't have a lot of room to conduct their search. Tran and Smitz are planning to meet us here. They want to inspect things more carefully."

"When?"

"Maybe thirty minutes. Let's get a head start."

Decker focused his search in the back. That room had been gone over with someone opening the interior of the mattress and rummaging through the closets. There wasn't much left to do except reexamine what had been examined, and that took all of fifteen minutes.

Jaylene's bedroom was the most odiferous. And while the mattress hadn't been ripped apart, it had been stripped and moved, exposing the box spring. Decker took a quick peek under the mattress and examined the box spring for alteration—nothing to the naked eye. He felt the top; he ran his hand over the bottom. Nothing out of the ordinary. He studied the underside of the bed. Lots of dust bunnies on the floor but nothing suspicious. He searched the closet: the clothes, the pockets in the clothes, the lining in the pockets. There was a cabinet inside the closet that had canes and braces and several walkers. At one time, Jaylene might have been more mobile. Or perhaps she couldn't walk too well before the accident. Along with the medical equipment, there was a shoebox on the top shelf.

He took it down and looked inside—old photographs. Lots of them. Some of them were in the era of one-hour-development photo shops; some were old colored Polaroids that were brown and faded. There were even some scalloped-edged black and whites. Decker decided to bag the box and the contents as evidence. He'd sift through them later.

Perhaps if there was a box with old photographs, there was also one with old letters and mementos that might be significant. He searched the closet but didn't find any more shoeboxes—or any other boxes, for that matter.

On a top shelf in the closet was a set of luggage— two suitcases and a carry-on. The insides were empty.

Decker studied the lining to make sure it hadn't been tampered with. Everything seemed intact. Then he patted down the lining around the bags to make sure they didn't feel thick. He hoisted them up to see if he could see something in the light.

Nothing.

Once he was done with the closet, he went through the nightstand, opening the top drawer. Inside was a collection of nothing: a comb, a brush, a nail file, a nail scissors, three pairs of glasses, a box of bandages, and random hardware. On the open bottom shelf was a pile of three paperbacks. Jaylene's dresser held mostly clothes. Other items included old buttons, rubber bands, desiccated sachet packets, and odd bits of junk.

The bathroom cabinet held lots of OTC medication as well as prescription drugs including Vicodin and OxyContin. No surprise there. The woman must be in constant pain. Decker looked inside vials and pill bottles and smelled the contents. Without analyzing the substances, he couldn't swear that the pills were what the label claimed they were, but there was nothing telltale in sight or in odor. He closed the medicine cabinet door. The tiled counter was lower than normal to accommodate her handicap. It held another brush, several tubes of lipstick, some makeup powders, and an eyeliner. The old woman still cared, and that was nice.

Decker checked around the toilet. It had a cracked seat, but the commode was intact. He gave the handle a flush. Nothing was backed up, but it did leak water onto the floor. He checked the tank for drugs—nothing. She had a wheelchair shower. Decker looked for hidden cubbies inside the tiled walls, but he didn't find anything. He left Jaylene's bedroom and joined McAdams in the kitchen. Together they went through cans and boxes and bags of food, scouring through the contents and finding nothing untoward—no unwanted pills, crystals, or powders.

An hour later, Decker's cell rang. It was Wendell Tran.

"We just got called out on another assault. This is unusual. Something must be in the air."

Decker pulled down his face mask until it dangled around his neck. "Yeah, it does go in waves."

"Are you out at the house?"

"We are. We're just about done."

"Did you find anything?"

"Just a box of old photographs. I'd like to take it back and sift through the contents, if that's okay."

"It's fine with me. We're pretty tied up at the moment. Give the box back when you're done. Also, drop off the key. At some point, Randy and I need to go back to the house."

"Not a problem. Thank you." Tran cut the line, and Decker stowed his phone in his pocket.

"Are we just about done, or were you just cutting him off?" McAdams asked. "With you, I never can tell."

"Did you check all the sofa and chair cushions?"

"Yes, I did. Nothing, to my eye, has been tampered with."

"All the seams looked untouched?"

"Yes, everything looked intact."

"How about trapdoors?"

"I didn't find anything. Did you?"

"No. If there's something valuable hidden in here, I can't find it." Decker shrugged. "I found a shoebox filled with photographs. I didn't find anything with mementos and/or old letters."

"You find that suspicious?"

"Not really. Jaylene doesn't impress me as a letter writer. I'll go through these snapshots eventually . . . see if anything stimulates my brain cells. Which might be a bit difficult because I'll have no idea who I'm looking at."

"At whom I'm looking," McAdams said.

Decker gave him a sour expression. "What would you have done if I would had said the sentence grammatically correct?"

"I would have made fun of your proper English."

"In other words, I can't win."

"Precisely. Can we get out of here? I think my nose has become desensitized, but I find it all very depressing."

"Sure. Let's go." Decker locked up. He took off his gloves and mask and almost made it to the car. But then he stopped cold.

McAdams sighed. "What is it now?"

"I just thought of something. You can wait in the car. It won't take me long."

"No, boss, someone has to watch your back." McAdams did an about-face and started walking in the other direction. "Are you coming?"

Decker smiled. The once spoiled and petulant kid was becoming a seasoned detective. He jogged to catch up and then unlocked the front door. Both of them went inside. He slipped on another pair of gloves but didn't bother with the mask. His nose, like McAdams's, had become inured to the smell. He went into Jaylene's bedroom and Tyler followed.

"You had to pick the stinkiest room in the house."

"I did it on purpose." He went over to her soiled wheelchair and felt the back strap—a thin piece of black leather stretched between the steel framework of the chair. When that seemed normal, he examined the stitching on the strap. Everything seemed okay.

Next came the seat pad, black leather still flecked with fecal material.

Whoever said life was easy.

Decker tried to take the pad off the chair, but it had been sewn on. He felt the top of the seat and ran his gloved hand over the arc of the seat cushion. It felt smooth from every direction. His next step was examining the stitching.

"You're dedicated," McAdams said. "I'll give you that. Sticking your nose that close."

"Not pleasant, but I've smelled worse."

"You also don't bitch a lot. Why is that?"

"Waste of energy." Decker continued to inspect the stitching. "Aha! Look and learn, Harvard. Examine the sewing on the left side."

"It's irregular. She could have had the seat restuffed and repaired."

"True enough." Decker took out his phone and snapped several pictures. Then he pulled out a Swiss army knife and cut the stitching until he was able to lift up the yellow foam seat cushion inside the leather. He was silent. Then he said, "And we've got something." Again, he took pictures on his phone. Then he wiggled his fingers between the cushion and the wooden bottom that supported the seat. Carefully, he pulled out a sealed manila envelope. The flap was glued down, and additionally, there was string latching the flap to the body of the envelope. Decker felt the contents.

"Nothing too lumpy." He pressed down on it again. "Feels like papers, but it could be drugs. Powder wrapped up in another envelope. I'll take a picture of it unopened, and then drop it in an evidence bag. We'll examine it at the station house—put it through the scanner before we crack open the seal."

"Good find, boss. I'm impressed."

"It was the only thing that I didn't check out." Decker smiled. "Process of elimination."

McAdams paused, then doubled over in laughter. "Who knew you were a natural punster?"

Decker started laughing. It felt good to release the tension.

The kid said, "Any idea what's in there?"

"Like I said, I didn't find any old letters."

"But why would Jaylene hide them?"

"No sense guessing. Let's go back and find out."

"You are going to phone Tran and Smitz about this, right?"

"Eventually. They just got called out on an assault.

I don't want to bother them with anything until I know what I found."

McAdams gave Decker a skeptical look. "No turf battles, then, huh? You're just being considerate."

"Harvard, I'm a very nice guy."

The scanner didn't reveal anything that looked like organic matter. Decker took the package into Radar's office. The captain and McAdams served as witnesses when Decker undid the string, then slit open the flap.

Inside were black-and-white grainy photographs—five of them. The long shots were clearer than the close-ups, but nothing was sharp and in focus. They all had one thing in common—the same woman in all the frames. Sometimes it was the woman with a man, but sometimes it was just the woman. She looked to be in her late forties or early fifties, but that was just a guess. Caucasian, medium build, probably brunette, although it was hard to discern with black and whites. The close-up blurred the features. The woman had a long face. There were two different men in the pictures. One had a round face, and the other one had a longer, older face. Two long shots showed the woman walking on a sidewalk among buildings—probably a city, because nothing looked very quaint—and drinking out of an espresso cup at a small, round café table.

As the three of them sifted through the snapshots, McAdams said, "And the million-dollar question is . . ."

Radar was staring at the photos. "I've been here a while. No idea who they are."

"The quality is so poor," Decker bemoaned. "I'm trying to see if I can find a landmark or the name of a store . . . something to home in on."

McAdams said, "The coffee cup . . . there's a logo on it . . . maybe it's writing."

Decker said, "Maybe we can get it enhanced?"

"It's so blurry, I don't think it'll work," Radar said. "Let's see if we can find something better."

"Let me take it to my desk and work at it," Decker said.

Kevin Butterfield knocked on the door's sash, then walked into the office. "Patrick Markham is here." When Decker looked confused, he said, "You did tell me you were free the entire afternoon."

"Yes, of course." Decker's watch read a little past three in the afternoon. "Thanks, Kev. Put him in an interview room. I'll be right there. Did you find out anything new with the CCTV?"

"It looks like our car was indeed headed for the highway. I'm going through the tapes again, starting much earlier in the evening. Maybe I can pick up the car going the opposite direction to the murder scene."

"Good idea. Are you able to get a face view of the driver or any passenger?"

"Shadows only. The quality is really poor. But the one thing I will say is it is probably two people. What are you looking at?"

"Also poor-quality images. Photographs. They were hidden in Jaylene Boch's wheelchair."

Butterfield scanned through several of them. "I take it no one knows who these people are?"

"Nope," McAdams said. "We're trying to see if we can find a name or landmark that'll at least let us know where these were taken."

Butterfield said. "From the dress and hairstyle and cars, these are maybe fifteen years old."

"I agree," Radar said. "I should call up Baccus. You found these hidden at a house in his jurisdiction."

"Let's leave him out of this for the moment." To Butterfield, Decker said, "I'll be with Markham in a minute. Thanks for setting it up."

"Sure. No problem."

After Butterfield left, Radar said, "No Baccus?"

"Not quite yet, if you don't mind."

Radar was silent. Then he said, "Who's Patrick Markham?"

"A high school friend of Brady Neil's. I'll tell you more after I'm done. Anything else?"

"No, you can go," Radar said.

Decker walked out of the office, pulling McAdams along with him. "Since Kevin is still going through CCTV, could you go through these snapshots to see what you can nail as far as ID?"

"No prob." McAdams paused. "Maybe there's a watermark on the film with a date. Sometimes that happens." He stared at a picture of the woman and older man drinking coffee or tea in a café. "Who are you?"

Decker stared at the pictures. "These do look to be about fifteen years old."

"Is that significant?"

"Yeah, I think so. First of all, really good cameras were available fifteen years ago. My first thoughts are that these were taken by an amateur with either a cheap phone or a bad camera."

"Ah, good thinking. Why black and white?"

"Don't know. Maybe these were taken at night, so they just look like black and white. Actually, the shots do look like night. These were taken in a clandestine manner."

"So, boss . . ." McAdams smiled. "What was going on fifteen years ago in Hamilton that you don't want Chief Baccus to know about?"

"Nothing significant for him. But maybe something significant for Jaylene Boch." Decker looked up from the photos and at McAdams. "Jaylene's husband, Joe Senior, was still alive fifteen years ago."

"You think the old man in the pictures might be Joe Senior?"

"I don't know, but why else would she hide pictures of strangers in her wheelchair. They must have significance to her."

"Or maybe Joe Junior hid them without his mom knowing. Fifteen years ago, Junior was twenty. It could have more to do with him than with her."

Decker conceded the point. "You're right. Jaylene was left to die. But Joe Junior's room was the crime scene."

"Yeah," McAdams said. "His room was . . . not hers."

Chapter 16

Patrick Markham was wearing a jacket and a red-on-red striped tie. Unusual for anyone his age, very unusual for anyone in Hamilton. The caramel-colored corduroy jacket had leather elbow patches and sat over a red-tan-and-white-plaid shirt. He wore denim pants and sneakers with no socks. He told Decker he had been coming home from work when he got the message that the police wanted to talk to him. He decided it was easier to drop by.

"What do you do?" Decker asked.

"Today I was teaching at one of the community colleges—practical electrical science. That's a fancy title for being an electrician."

"You must be good at what you do to teach."

"I have a BA in electrical engineering, but I mostly work as an electrician. I have my own company. But I teach because it's a little different even though it pays close to nothing. These days, with so many courses being offered online, I admire anyone who shows up for face-to-face instruction."

Decker regarded Markham. He looked to be around six feet, solidly built with dark eyes and auburn hair. On his left fourth finger was a gold band.

Decker took out his notepad. "You're married."

"My high school sweetheart. She was a cheerleader, I was the running back. Everyone was shocked when we married and she *wasn't* pregnant. Most guys are afraid to take the plunge. I'm afraid of dying alone. Particular neurosis of mine that's not shared with most of my peers. Anyway, that's more than you probably wanted to know. I realize this is about Brady. God, it's been a tough couple of days."

"You two were close?"

"During high school, yes."

"But not afterward?"

Markham paused. "What do you know about Hamilton?"

"I've been here for over three years. But I live in Greenbury. I know it's a different demographic than Hamilton."

"One hundred eighty degrees. Greenbury is an upscale college town. Hamilton is larger than a town, not quite a city, and not at all on the economic upswing. The local high schools are not great, and that's the best you can say about them. I kept my sanity by playing football, dating Mel, and actually studying for exams. Most of my teammates partied on the weekends with crystal meth and mollies. Lots of them had parents who had scripts for Vicodin or OxyContin. Whatever they could find that was easy."

"What about Brady Neil?" Decker asked.

"Brady straddled all the different social options. He was popular despite his old man. Or maybe it was because of his old man. He was smart, but he could play the bad-boy image when it suited him."

"He was a small guy to play football."

"He didn't." Markham looked upward. "But he was a smart guy. He made a name doing other things."

"Like?"

"He did a lot of chemicals in his senior year. Whatever he could find was up for grabs—for recreation and for money."

"Ah," Decker said. "Dealing."

"Unfortunately, yes. Enough to keep some bills in his pocket. Certainly, his mother didn't help him out. She could barely cope herself. Or maybe she did help him out, but inadvertently. I know he stole stuff out of her medicine cabinet."

"Did his dealing continue after he graduated?"

"I don't know. We didn't talk as much after high school. I was busy with college, and Brady . . ." Markham's voice trailed off. "It was really too bad. Brady could have gone to a four-year college, but he wasn't interested. I won't say he was lazy, but he certainly wasn't ambitious. He used to hang around in his mom's basement, get high, and screw girls. My wife hated him. Brady and I drifted apart."

"Understandable."

Markham nodded. "It's hard carrying that monkey on your back. He never could quite shake it. I don't judge him, but there it was, and no matter what he did, it would always come back to his dad."

"And you haven't had recent contact with him?"

"Actually, it's weird, because he called me up out of the blue about six months ago. I mean, you call somebody up after years of no contact? I thought he was in deep trouble or had something important to tell me. But no. We just shot the shit for about twenty minutes and that was it."

"What did you talk about?"

"Life." Markham thought a moment. "I've been going over that conversation in my head since he was found dead—murdered. Did I miss something that he was trying to tell me? Was he giving me a warning? I don't think so, but I wasn't paying attention to every word."

Decker said, "Did he do most of the talking?"

"Yeah, come to think of it. He talked about how he was going back to school in coding and computers and how well he was doing. He talked to me about his job at Bigstore. Offered me discounts if I wanted any upgrades in my phone or computer or TV. He said something about doing a little business in recycled electronics. There was a lightness to his voice. I was happy for him. It seemed like old times. I did call him several times after that initial phone call. Left messages on his voice mail, but he never called me back. Frankly, with a business, a wife, and two kids, I was involved with my own life. I forgot about him until a few days ago. It felt like a punch in the stomach."

"Any idea why he was murdered?"

"Lord, no. When we spoke, it didn't sound like he was leading a fringe life. He sounded like he was getting it together. I'm totally baffled."

"You said Brady had money from dealing?"

It took a while for Markham to answer. "Yeah. Why?"

"His mom reported him as always having cash. I'm wondering if Brady was dealing."

Markham said, "I can't tell you yes or no."

"If Brady was dealing back then, who would he sell to?"

"This is taking me back." A long pause. Markham said, "I don't know, Detective. I tried hard to keep my nose clean. While Brady was my friend, I kept away from his darker life."

"Fair enough," Decker said. "Do you know if Brady kept in touch with his father?"

"Not when we were in high school. If he resumed contact with the old man, he didn't tell me in the one conversation we had."

"I heard Brady was close to Brett Baderhoff as well."

"Yeah, we were a trio. Brett did okay for himself. He moved to Florida and became a nuisance hunter. He traps alligators and lizards and boas and other types of snakes. He always liked deer hunting, so it's not too weird. We talk like once a year. When the news hit, I spoke to him soon after. He was as bummed as I was."

Decker looked at the number he had stored in his phone for Brett Baderhoff. He showed it to Markham. "Is this current?"

"No, it's old. I have to look up his current number. If you hold on a sec . . ."

"Not a problem."

"I gotta tell you. He doesn't have any idea about

what happened, either. I know because I asked. Besides, he hasn't lived in Hamilton for over four years."

"I understand, but I'd like to call him anyway."

"Right." Patrick read off the number. "You can tell him I gave you his number. I'm sure Brett wouldn't care."

"Thanks. Patrick, when you were close to Brady, was he friends with Joseph Boch?"

"Who?"

"Joseph Boch."

Markham opened and closed his mouth. "The guy in yesterday's paper who's missing?"

"Yes, him. He and Brady were friends. They both worked at Bigstore. Do you know if they had a previous relationship before this one?"

"No idea." A pause. "I thought I read that Boch was in his midthirties."

"He is."

"That's around ten years older than us. Why would he know him from before?"

"If Brady was dealing, unless he had a lab, he had to get his meth from someone."

"And you suspect that this Boch guy was supplying him with drugs?"

"I don't know. I do think Boch going AWOL and Brady's murder are connected."

Markham made a face. "I don't know who supplied Brady in high school. I never asked."

"Why were you and Brady friends?" Decker asked. "You don't seem to have much in common."

Markham sighed. "We just clicked. I think . . . it was easier to be friends because we weren't in the same social groups. Even though my wife hated him—for obvious reasons—I always found it easy to talk to the guy."

He checked his watch.

"Speaking of my wife, I should get home, help Mel out with the kids."

"One more thing, please." Decker took out one of the black and whites hidden in Jaylene Boch's wheelchair. "Would you happen to know who these people are?"

Markham studied the photo. "No . . . sorry." He handed the snapshot back. "Is that all?"

"Yes, it is." Decker stood up. "How many kids do you have?"

"Two."

"Boys, girls?"

"Boys. One and three. Live wires, both of them. They simple exhaust my wife. I keep telling her to go back to teaching. Working is easier than caring for those two wild animals." Markham smiled. "They are cute. I do look forward to the days when my business card reads Markham and Sons." He stood up. "Yes, I know. I'm an old soul in a twenty-six-year-old body. My teachers used to tell me: 'Pat, you're so serious. Lighten up.' But I never did."

"Being studious and dedicated never hurt anyone," Decker said.

"That could be my epithet: Studious and Dedicated." His eyes twinkled. "Still, I look forward to my twenty-fifth high school reunion. We'll see who has the last laugh."

In the station house, McAdams was poring over a photograph with a magnifying glass. Decker said, "How's it going, Sherlock?"

"Come here for a sec." McAdams focused in on the espresso coffee cup. "What do you see?"

"May I?" After McAdams gave him the magnifying glass, Decker peered at the cup. "It looks like an insect. Maybe a butterfly?"

"More like a dragonfly to my eye. Look at how skinny the wings are."

Decker looked again, then handed him back the lens. "I do believe you're right."

"How many cafés would have a dragonfly as a logo?"

"Look it up."

McAdams typed in "café, dragonfly" as keywords into Google. A surprising number of cafés showed up—from Portland, Oregon, to Massachusetts. "So much for a slam dunk." He looked away from the screen and sat back in his chair. "I'm achy and tired, and I'm starved."

"Did we eat lunch?"

"I sure as hell didn't."

It was a little past five. "Let me call up Rina and see if she made dinner. If not, I'll pick up sandwiches at Kosher Mart."

"Anything sounds good at this point. My shoulders are killing me."

"Kvetch, kvetch." Decker punched in Rina on his phone. She answered two rings later.

Her voice was a whisper. "Hold on." A minute later, she spoke in her normal voice. "I've been in the library more or less since ten. It's good to see sunlight." A pause. "Is it really five o'clock?"

"It is," Decker said. "What's been so engrossing?"

"A lot of stuff. How about you?"

"Things are getting interesting."

"We'll catch up at home. It's too much to tell you over the phone."

"Okay. Should I pick up dinner at Kosher Mart?"

"That would be lovely. Smoked turkey on rye with mayo, mustard, lettuce, tomato and onions on the side. Pick up a pint of coleslaw and a pint of potato salad. Is Tyler coming over? It'd be easier to talk to both of you at the same time."

"Yes, he's coming. Can I have a hint?"

"You asked me to dig into the Levines before the murders, and that's what I did. And that's all I'm going to say. Otherwise we'll be on the phone for a while, and like I said, it's too much to deal with if we're not face-to-face."

"Fair enough. We'll be home in about a half hour."

"Good. I believe I'm starved, but I haven't had enough time to think about it."

"Well, I know I'm starved." He checked his watch again. "Although eating at five-thirty is a little early, don't you think?"

"Eating early is good for the digestion."

"Now we're really sounding like old people."

"We are old people. Or at least, one of us is."

"Did I ever tell you that you're a mean woman?"

"Did I ever tell you how handsome you are?"

Decker smiled. "Especially for an old guy?"

"Especially for *any* guy, gorgeous. You know I'm a sucker for a guy in uniform."

"Rina, I haven't worn a uniform in over thirty-five years."

"I know. But I have all those old photos of you in your salad days. It's enough to make any girl dream."

Chapter 17

Decker dropped a forkful of potato salad on the printout he was reading. They were given to him by Rina, and every time he finished a sheet, he passed it on to McAdams. "I'm such a slob."

"You're tired," Rina said. "We're all tired."

Decker smiled. She was giving him an out. At his behest, she had been studying the blurred photographs, as well as the photographs in the shoebox found in Jaylene Boch's closet, at the dinner table. "I am tired, but I'm also a slob."

For the last half hour he had been reading about Margot and Mitchell Flint—a case of embezzlement, grand larceny, and money laundering that went back twenty-five years. At that point, Mitchell Flint had been partners with Glen Levine for a decade. The two men had grown up together. Mitchell was a lawyer by trade, and Glen was a certified gemologist and jeweler. Flint, who had a thriving practice, had bankrolled the store for his friend, who had an unerring eye for jewels but not much of a head for business. Lydia— Glen's wife—had grown up in the area. Margot came on the scene later. The Flints were part of the small Hamilton Country Club set. Margot became a society woman, her name often mentioned in charity functions and politics. The Flints were a handsome couple: he was tall and dark, she was tall and blond. Her picture, even more than his, was everywhere.

Lydia and Glen, on the other hand, were average in looks and stature. He had a round face with a bulbous nose; she had an attractive face—large eyes and a sweet smile—but carried a little extra weight. They had worked hard in their business, and although the two couples were friends, they traveled in different economic circles. The Flints did well, lived in a big house, and had the cars and the trappings. The Levines scraped by, wondering why all their hard work was not paying off.

It took Glen Levine almost six years to realize that someone was stealing from the till. It took him another two years to come to conclude that it had been his partner and best friend, Mitch. But once he was sure that the proof was irrefutable, Glen enacted justice as swift as the wheels would grind. It took almost two years for Mitchell—along with his wife, Margot, thought to be the ringleader—to be tried and found guilty of embezzlement, grand larceny, and the biggest insult of them all, money laundering. Two days before they were due to be sentenced, the Flints went out for dinner and never came back. They left behind two teenaged boys and a massive amount of debt. The house and everything in it was sold off to pay the lawyers and for the judgment given to the Levines. Nothing was left for the children. An aunt and uncle took the homeless boys in.

No one seemed to know where the Flints went or what happened to them. While on bail, they had surrendered their passports, so rumor had it that they were still in the United States, but where was anyone's guess. A follow-up paper article with the children, ten years later, illuminated nothing. As far as the boys—now young men—were concerned, their parents were as good as dead to them. They had deserted them and cast them off like garbage to save their own skin. The rage in the interview jumped off the print.

Wiping a cube of potato up with a napkin, Decker stared at the pictures in the paper. Mitchell had milky blue eyes, high cheekbones, and a wide smile. Margot's blond hair was flipped back at the sides with feathery bangs in front. Her eyes were lake blue deep, and they stared from any photograph she was in. She had pouty lips that showed a hint of two big front incisors. "Do you think it's them in those black-and-white photos?"

"I can't tell." McAdams took another bite of his sandwich. "The black and whites are terrible quality, and the newspaper pictures of the Flints are over twenty years old. Maybe someone could match the faces, but I sure as hell can't."

"They could have also undergone plastic surgery," Rina said.

"Right." Decker put the papers down. "I know that there are two bad guys in jail for the Levine murders. It would take a lot to convince me that Gratz and Masterson didn't do it. But just as a matter of procedure, I wonder if the police ever considered the Flints as suspects."

"The dates are a little funky," McAdams said. "Why wait almost two years to kill the people who put you in jail?"

"It takes time to plan murders of this magnitude," Rina said.

"What good would it do them to kill the Levines after the convictions?"

"Revenge," Rina said. "And it was a robbery also. The Flints were fugitives. They were in debt from legal fees and needed the money."

Decker said, "I'll agree with you there. Also, I remember reading in the papers that some of the bigger jewelry pieces had never been found."

Rina said, "And who would know the layout of the store better than a partner?"

"I'm sure they changed the safe combinations and the alarm code after the Levines found out they were stealing," McAdams said.

Rina said. "The alarm wasn't on." She turned to Decker. "You thought that was odd. Maybe someone had turned it off."

"Maybe." He waited a beat. "You know, alarms can be set and disarmed with more than one code. If the Levines just put in a new code and didn't actively delete the old code, the old code might still work."

"You should ask Gregg Levine about that," Rina said.

"I would, except he doesn't answer my calls."

"So why don't you pop in on him at the jewelry store?"

"If Yvonne's there, I'm not going to get past the front door. She doesn't like me."

"That's impossible," Rina said. "Everyone likes you."

Decker smiled. "I do have my detractors, believe it or not."

"You think they'd be that careless?" McAdams said. "Not to get rid of their old alarm code?"

"I don't know, Harvard. But regardless of whether the Flints were in on it or not, they had to be considered suspects at the time of the murders. I'm going to need to see the original files. I just have to figure out how to access them since Brady Neil's death is just a thread of a connection to the Levine murders."

"When are you giving these photos back to Tran and Smitz?" McAdams said. "You know you have to do that."

Decker took out his cell. "I'll call them right now. They've been cooperative, and for selfish reasons, I need their help. You find anything of interest in the shoebox, Rina? Anything that looks like Margot and Mitchell Flint?"

"Most of these pictures are more like forty years old. Pictures of a young girl—probably Jaylene. Some are Polaroids. But a lot of them look like they were taken with a Brownie camera."

"Mitchell and Glen grew up together. Maybe they were friendly with Jaylene Boch. Joe grew up in Kansas, but she grew up here." Decker thought a minute. "Any pictures of her with a kid?"

Rina stared at him. "No, come to think of it."

"How about Joe Boch?"

"I'm not sure what he looked like."

"He was older that Jaylene by about ten years."

"These pictures were mostly teenagers. I have no idea what Mitchell and Glen looked like as boys, but I suppose I could go down to the local high schools and check out yearbooks."

"If you have time tomorrow, it might help. Although even if we found pictures of them with Jaylene, I don't know what that would tell us." Decker played with his cell. "Maybe I should wait until tomorrow to give back the photos."

"Not cool, boss."

"I agree," Rina said.

"All right, all right." He dialed Tran's number and explained the situation. Then he said, "I didn't want to bother you today because you seemed pretty busy. But going forward, I wanted you to know."

"Liar," Rina whispered.

Decker smiled, listened, and then said, "As long as you have a busy tomorrow morning, can I keep the photographs? I'll drop them off in the afternoon and bring you up to speed on what I know." Another pause. "Sure, I'll be happy to check with Forensics tomorrow. Not a problem. Oh, one thing. Is there any way I could get access to the original Levine murder files?" Decker listened. "Could I get access to the archives?" Another pause. "Sure, I'll talk to Chief Baccus. No problem. Thanks, Tran. I'll see you and Randy tomorrow afternoon."

He hung up.

"Just what I didn't want. Getting Baccus involved."

"Why are you so opposed to dealing with him?" Rina asked.

"Because he was the lead in the murders. I don't want him thinking that I'm checking out his breakout case for improprieties."

"Which is what you're doing," McAdams said.

"No, I'm not," Decker defended himself. "As far as I know, he did nothing wrong. I'm just trying to be as complete as possible."

"Complete how?" Rina asked. "What do the murders have to do with Brady Neil?"

"I don't know." Decker was pensive. "According to his friend, Patrick Markham, Brady called him up to tell him that he's doing well. Plus, his mother, Jennifer, told us that he always had money. Now we find out that Levine's old business partner and his wife are fugitives. We've got old pictures sewn into Jaylene Boch's wheelchair. Then we've got Joe Junior and Brady—who are ten years apart—working together. And one is dead and one is missing. You tell me what picture I'm seeing."

McAdams said, "They found out where the Flints are hiding, and Joe and Brady were blackmailing them. The Flints got tired of paying them off and had the boys murdered."

Decker shrugged.

Rina said, "Why now?"

"Maybe the Flints were running out of money," McAdams said. "They couldn't pay the kids off anymore."

"We have the photos until tomorrow afternoon," Decker said. "Let's enter them into the Greenbury system before we hand them over."

"I can do that," McAdams said.

Rina said, "I'll check out the local high schools for yearbooks of Glen and Mitchell."

"Thanks." Decker rubbed his eyes, then looked up. "Anything for dessert? I need a sugar fix."

"Biscotti in the freezer. Lemon and almond."

"I'll get them."

"I'll get them," Rina said. "I know exactly where they are. You can clear while I make coffee."

"Sounds like a plan." Decker stood up and looked at McAdams. "You can help, you know."

"Do I get a tip?"

"Yeah, buy high and sell low."

"Actually, boss, I think you've got it backward."

"Aha!" Decker smiled. "No wonder I can't scratch a dime in the stock market."

At eleven on Friday morning, after scanning the photographs into the Greenbury computer, Decker drove down to Hamilton PD, returning the originals to the detectives assigned to the missing persons case of Joseph Boch. In the detectives' squad room, as Wendell Tran shuffled through the blurry black and whites, he said, "You think these people are Mitchell and Margot Flint? The woman is with more than one man."

"I don't know who they are," Decker answered. "Show them to Chief Baccus. He was around when the Flints went underground. Maybe he'll recognize them. Or maybe Gregg Levine will know who they are. The Flints were family friends. He was in his teens when the couple disappeared."

"I'll try Baccus first before I disturb a civilian. He's out until the afternoon. Did you find anything else sewn into Jaylene Boch's wheelchair seat?"

"No." Decker paused. "Have you gone over Jaylene Boch's house yet?"

"Today." Tran looked up. "I suppose that looks negligent, but we're a small outfit. Yesterday was un-usually busy, and we had real victims to talk to."

"I get it."

"We did put out an APB on Joseph Boch. But we can't find a car registered in his name. It's going to be hard to find him, if he's still alive. There hasn't been any activity on his credit cards."

"How many does he have?"

"Two—one is a Bigstore credit card, the other is a Mastercard, and neither one has had any charges since your guy, Brady, was murdered four days ago. Boch has a checking account with about fifty bucks in it. No activity there, either. Have you made any headway with Brady Neil's murder?"

"One detective is checking cars in and out of the area on CCTV. We've hooked on to one that looks promising. Stolen plate from an old Cadillac was put on a Camry. Looks like there are two people inside the car. We're following that up. I also talked to Patrick Markham, his best friend from high school. Back then, Neil dealt mollies and weed and would steal his mother's prescription drugs."

"Well, that could explain a lot about what happened to him, especially if he advanced to opiates."

"Of course. He could have been dealing. He always seemed to have pocket change. But drug dealers usually don't bother with full-time jobs, especially things like being a manager of an electronics department at

Bigstore. I thought at first he was stealing merchandise and that's how he got spare cash, but now I'm not so sure."

"Why's that?"

"What got him killed should be bigger than a few stolen items, although I've seen people murdered for all sorts of reasons."

"Maybe it was a ring."

"Sure, that could explain it, especially if the ring spanned several states." Decker paused. "I'm very curious about those black and whites in Jaylene Boch's wheelchair. Someone took great care to hide them."

"Yeah, good job on finding them," Tran said. "We need to identify the people, obviously. What about the shoebox you found in the closet. Was it hidden as well?"

"It was on a shelf. Pretty much out in the open."

"Then what significance could the shoebox pictures have?"

"I don't know if they have any significance," Decker said. "I scanned everything into Greenbury's computer system. There's several forensic programs that takes faces and progressively ages them. There are also programs that age-regress photographs as well."

"You know they have apps like that on your phone."

"The resolution on the old photos stinks. Once I downloaded them, the resolution would be even worse.

Even if they were great, those apps aren't reliable. The good ones take money, and I can't justify spending cash for that."

"It might be worth a shot."

"If all else fails, sure."

"Let me know what you come up with. I'll see what I come up with on my end. We'll compare notes."

"Thanks." Decker winced. "Also, I'd really like to take a look at the original Levine murder files."

"I told you to talk to Baccus about that." When Decker didn't answer, Tran said, "Why don't you want him to know about it?"

"Chief Baccus was the lead investigator."

"Do you think he did something wrong?"

"Not in the least. But no one wants their old adjudicated cases being looked over."

"Then why do it?"

There was big-time hesitancy in Tran's voice. Who could blame him. Decker was asking him to sneak around his superior. He said, "It would help me understand Brady Neil."

"Brady was a kid when the old man went to jail. How would it help?"

"Put it this way: I want to see the file for the sake of completeness. I hate to put you out, but . . ."

"The files have been archived, and that's in a different building. It's already Friday, and I'm swamped. I'll see what I can do next week." Tran looked him in the eye. "I don't know if I can keep it from the chief. I don't know if I want to keep it from the chief."

"I don't want to upset him, but that's got to be your decision."

"Right." Tran shook his head. "Are you always this meticulous about your murder cases, looking into every detail of a background like this, or are you just bored?"

"Maybe a little of both."

"I'll get back to you next week. By the way, I got the forensics report on my desk. Several DNA profiles. More than two. First thing we need is a sample from Jaylene Boch and a sample from Jennifer Neil. Jaylene's not hard because she's hospitalized and they've drawn multiple tubes of blood from her. You should contact Jennifer Neil because Brady is your case."

"No problem," Decker said. "Thanks for your cooperation. I really appreciate it. Not all departments are so helpful."

"Yeah, we're all small departments around here."

"Sometimes the small ones are the most territorial," Decker said.

"Nah, that never works," Tran said. "Your department is small, our department is small. Working together, maybe we can create something bigger."

Chapter 18

At Urgent Care, the fingerstick took all of twenty seconds, although the wait time was considerably longer. Jennifer Neil sat in stony silence until it was her turn. Afterward, Decker walked Jennifer back to the Ford Focus. She unlocked the driver's door, and Decker helped her in.

Before he closed the door, she said, "I don't know why I had to go through with that. Doesn't bring him back to life to know *where* he was murdered."

"No, it doesn't," Decker said. "But as I explained over the phone, every detail that I find out will help me solve this."

"Don't see how," Jennifer said. "You haven't made much progress."

"No, but it's early days."

"I heard if you don't solve the crime right away, your chances of solving it are real low."

"Sooner is always better than later. Most murders are obvious. This one isn't. From what I've discovered, Brady wasn't doing anything high risk, although he did deal drugs in high school. Whether that continued on, I don't know."

She was silent.

Decker said, "He seemed to be making something of his life. He had a job and he was going to school."

Jennifer's eyes watered up. "He was a good boy."

"I can see that." Decker took out a copy of the blurred black-and-white photographs found under Jaylene Boch's wheelchair seat. "These are old snapshots. Do you happen to know who these people are?"

She sifted through them. "Where'd you get these?"

"I found them when I was searching the Boch house. Do you know who they are?"

"No idea."

"Take another look."

Instead, she handed them back to him without a further glance. "No idea. If you found them at Jaylene's house, ask her." A pause. "How's she doing?"

"Better."

"Good for her. I can go now?"

"Of course. Call me if you have any other questions." When she didn't respond, Decker closed the driver's door. Within moments, she was gone physically. Emotionally, with her vacant eyes and her flat voice, she had checked out years ago.

Since the hospital was just five minutes away, Decker decided to pay an unannounced visit to Jaylene Boch. He parked and stopped by the Critical Care Unit. Jaylene Boch's condition had improved, but she was still being closely monitored. Her lunch tray had been pushed aside, and she was staring into space. There was a butterfly needle on the back of her hand, although she wasn't hooked up to an IV. There was also an oxygen tube in her nose. Her hospital gown had remnants of her meal: looked like applesauce and pudding. That she was eating was a healthy sign.

"Mrs. Boch?" No response. Decker pulled up a chair and sat down next to the hospital bed. "I'm Detective Peter Decker. Do you remember me?"

Nothing.

"How are you feeling?"

She nodded her head. At least she could hear him.

"That's good. You seem to be on the mend. That's great."

Silence.

"Well, I'm glad you're feeling a little better. When you're all better, I'd like to ask you some questions."

Slowly, she turned her head to Decker. "What . . ."

Her voice faded out. He tried to fill in the blank. "What questions?" When she nodded, he said, "I have some photographs of some people. I found them in your house. I was wondering if you could tell me who they are?"

A nod.

Going better than expected. He pulled out the black and whites and held them up to her eyes. "Do you know the names of these people?"

He showed her the first picture. When he didn't get a reaction, he showed her the second and then the third and then the fourth. "Do you know any of them?"

She didn't answer.

Decker stowed them back in his briefcase. "Thank you, anyway."

Frail fingers grabbed his forearm. "Joe?"

"Ah, your son. Unfortunately, we haven't found him yet. We're looking very hard. Not just us, other police departments. We're putting in an all-out effort." Silence. "I'm sorry the news couldn't be better."

She seemed to take it all in. "You were . . ."

"Yes?"

"My house?" she whispered.

"Yes, I was at your house. I called the ambulance. Do you remember me?" When there was no answer, he said, "I was there along with Detective Baccus. The woman. Do you remember her?"

"Baccus." She pulled her fingers away. "Baccus."

Decker waited for more, but instead she closed her eyes. Within minutes, she had fallen asleep, sitting upright with her head tilted back and her mouth open, snoring loudly and seemingly without a care.

Sabbath started on Friday night: Decker's comma, a pause in the week to take a breath before rushing off to finish the sentence of one's life. Sometimes, it came at inconvenient times, and then there were other times, like today, where nothing was going wrong exactly, but nothing was going right, either. In the summer, the time of rest started later, which allowed for a relaxed shower before sundown. Rina, as usual, was busy in the kitchen. He had just finished dealing with the lights and time clocks—they didn't use electricity once the sun set—when the doorbell rang. Tyler was in jeans and a polo shirt with sandals on his feet, carrying two bottles of kosher wine.

"Shabbat Shalom. Late, yes or no?"

"I think you're early, but no matter. Come in. Can I take the bottles from you?"

"Be my guest. I got these after reading an article in *Wine Spectator*. They're supposed to be great Israeli wines. They should be at what they cost."

"Thank you. Never had either one. Since they're both reds, which one should I open?"

"Both. After this week, I could go through a bottle myself. I have never scoured that much CCTV in my life."

"Find anything?"

"Nothing other than the Toyota Camry, going outbound from Canterbury Lane to the main highway. Definitely two blobs in the front seat, but we can't discern anything more than that. But we've got other tricks up our sleeves. Kevin suggested that we pull CCTV from the main roads from Jaylene Boch's house to Canterbury Lane where we found Brady Neil."

"That's a good idea."

"In theory, yes. In practical terms, you stare at blurry black-and-white tape for five hours and then you offer your opinion."

"You're still standing at the doorway, Tyler. You can come in."

Rina had appeared in the living room. She was wearing a yellow paisley caftan with three-quarter sleeves and a yellow scarf on her head.

McAdams said, "Are you going to read my palm?"

Rina laughed. "I haven't dressed yet. You're early. I told you seven, not six-thirty. The days are longer now, and it doesn't make sense to start Shabbos too early."

"My bad, then. Anyway, you can remain in your Madame Zola clothing. You should be comfortable."

"Thank you very much, but I've already picked out a dress." She took the bottles from Decker. "Nice wine. I'll open it and then get dressed. I'm starved."

Twenty minutes later, McAdams was serving mushroom soup while Decker and Rina sat. Waitering and wine were his contribution to the free meals that he often mooched off them. Decker was wearing a short-sleeved shirt and jeans like Tyler was. Rina was in a white dress, cinched at the waist with a gold belt. Tyler sat down. "Smells great. The roast looks amazing. I almost cut myself off an end."

"Don't do that," Rina said. "It needs to rest."

"Not as much as I do," Decker said. "Although I didn't do much today. And as a result, I didn't get anywhere. Wendell Tran said he'll try to pull the Levine murder files out of archives for me next week. Let's see if he follows through."

"Why wouldn't he?" McAdams asked.

"Because his attitude at best could be described as reluctant."

"Because Victor Baccus was the lead on the case," Rina asked.

"Exactly. And I kind of hinted that I didn't want Baccus to know what I was doing. Tran wasn't happy about that."

McAdams refilled everyone's wineglass. "You think he'll say something to the chief?"

"I don't know. I left it up to him." He turned to Rina. "Soup is outstanding, darlin'."

"Thank you." Rina took another spoonful. "I did get a chance to rummage through some of the Hamilton high schools' yearbooks."

"You did?" Decker was happy. At least someone was accomplishing something. "And?"

"Well, Jaylene Boch and Brandon Gratz went to the same high school. But different years. Jaylene was four years ahead of Brandon. She graduated, but I didn't see a graduation picture for him. Jennifer Neil went to a different school. She's four years younger than Brandon, which puts her eight years younger than Jaylene. She didn't graduate, either. I did got copies of their yearbook pictures, but I didn't have time to see if they matched any faces from the shoebox."

"Good job. What about Mitchell Flint and Glen and Lydia Levine?"

"Lydia was Lydia Frost back then. All three of them went to a third high school in Bellweather—the posh area of Hamilton. Mitchell and Glen were in the same year. Lydia was three years behind. I do have graduation pictures of them, but if you're looking to match faces to the black-and-white pictures you found under the wheelchair, I couldn't tell you yes or no. Some people carry the same face from toddler to oldster. Others change drastically as they age. I'd try looking at the newspaper photos. They're more recent."

"I've been looking at that," Decker said. "Comparing newspaper photos with the black and whites. I can't make out features well enough. What I can do—if Radar gets me the money—is send them to a forensic reconstructionist to take measurements. Even if the couple did things to their faces, there are basic bone measurements that stay the same."

McAdams said, "Plastic surgery is expensive."

Rina said, "Maybe not as much in Mexico. I had a friend in L.A. She did everything in the world to her body—face lift, nose reduction, tummy tuck, eyelids lifted, ribs taken out to make her waist smaller. She had this doctor in Mexico who catered to Americans. The clinic, according to her, was a resort on the Sea of Cortez. Like a five-star hotel except that everyone was walking around with bandages. And she claimed because it wasn't as regulated, it was almost half the price of the States."

McAdams said, "Maybe we're looking in the wrong country."

"Or maybe they did the surgery abroad and came back with new names, new passports, and totally new faces." Decker was twirling his spoon. "I honestly don't know too much about capturing fugitives. It was never something I did in all my years of police work."

"Who captures fugitives?" Rina asked.

"Depends. If you're on the FBI's Most Wanted list, they take the lead. If it's a dangerous criminal, it could be the US Marshals in the individual areas where the fugitives were spotted. It could also be bounty hunters. It's just something I've never done."

"You probably know as much as anyone around here does," Rina said.

He thought a moment. "I'll call Cindy and see if she can help me out."

"I thought you said she was in GTA," McAdams said.

"Yeah, she is, but she has resources that we don't have. Anyway, I do have a bit of good news. Jaylene Boch seems to be improving."

"That's great," Rina said.

"Was she able to answer questions?" McAdams said.

"No, but she did talk—more like say a few words. Specifically, she asked about her son."

"Poor woman," Rina said.

"Yeah, it's really sad. I wish I could tell her something."

"Did you show her the black-and-white pictures?"

"Actually, I did," Decker said. "She didn't verbalize a yes or a no, and nothing in her face has me leaning in one or the other direction. So maybe later on, once she's more coherent." He paused. "I'm just frustrated. Four days and I still don't have anything that points to why Brady Neil was murdered beyond his dealing in high school."

Rina said, "It could be that Joseph Junior was the target and Brady was in the wrong place at the wrong time."

"Maybe," Decker said. "Anything's possible, sure."

McAdams said, "Do we even know if Brady's blood was in Boch's house?"

"I just got blood from Jennifer Neil. We'll send it to Forensics and find out soon enough."

Rina said, "If he was dealing, Peter—even a little— that would put Brady with the wrong people."

"Yep." Decker took a deep breath and let it out. "Well, I can't do anything at the moment. And, frankly, I don't want to think about work for the next twenty-four hours. Can I serve the next course?"

"Sure. It's salad," Rina said. "Bowl is in the fridge, along with the salad plates. The greens are already dressed. Remember to bring in the tongs."

"I'll do it, boss," McAdams said.

"No, I'll do it," Decker said. "That way I know you won't steal the end of the roast."

"Which means that now you have means, motive, and opportunity yourself to steal the end of the roast," McAdams retorted.

"Why don't you both go in?" Rina suggested. "Keep an eye on each other." Slowly, they both rose from the table. When they came back, they both smelled like gravy. She shook her head. "How did it taste?"

Decker said, "Delicious. After the salad, I'll carve and bring it in."

"If you carve, there won't be anything left," McAdams said.

"Will you two stop squabbling? There is plenty of meat for everyone, Mr. and Mr. Caveman."

The table went silent. Then McAdams said, "We'll both carve."

"Sounds like a plan."

The men got up and headed toward the kitchen.

"Wait!" Rina said. "You didn't finish your salads."

But it was too late. She had lost them both to a standing rib roast.

The greens never stood a chance.

Chapter 19

At eleven in the evening on Saturday, Decker's mobile lit up with Cindy's cell number. It was a little late to be saying hello, but his daughter knew that he and Rina observed the sabbath. It probably wasn't an emergency. Otherwise she'd have called at any hour.

"Hey, princess."

"How was your Shabbos?"

"Restful. I only thought about work a hundred times instead of a thousand."

"That sounds like you, Daddy. And now I'm going to contribute to your workaholism."

"Why? What's going on?"

"I got a call from Lennie Baccus this afternoon—"

"Don't tell me," Decker interrupted. "She's pissed because I didn't defend her to her father and she wanted to vent."

Cindy paused. "Maybe, but that's not what she called about."

"Oh. Sorry. What's the story?"

"Dad, maybe you could give me a little background? I know she was working on your team regarding Brady Neil's murder. She told me her father—not you— pulled her off the case when a friend of his went missing. What's going on?"

Decker filled her in as best as he could. "It was a very bloody scene in the back bedroom, but what was worse was Jaylene Boch being tied up and nearly starving to death. Chief Baccus said he was pulling Lennie off because he was worried about her safety. Which didn't make sense. There wasn't anything vaguely threatening. She was doing fine. Murder scenes are ugly. That's what you see when you're a homicide detective. I didn't understand it then, and I still don't."

"Okay, that helps explain a few things. Who are the Levines?"

"A couple that was murdered in Hamilton twenty years ago. Two men are in prison for the homicides, and one of the guys is Brady Neil's father. I've been trying to see if there's a link between Brady's death and his father's crime, but so far I haven't found anything."

"And why would you think that there's a link twenty years later?"

"I'm not saying there is. Still, Brandon Gratz is . . . was Brady's father. I'd like to look at the original murder files for the Levines."

"So why is that a problem?"

"It shouldn't be except Victor Baccus was the lead detective on the investigation. I asked another Hamilton detective who was assigned to the Boch disappearance to get the files out of archives for me. I also asked him not to say anything to Chief Baccus. Naturally, he's reluctant, though. I haven't found a whiff of wrongdoing, by the way."

"But you haven't seen the original files?"

"No. Why?"

"O-kay. Here's the deal. It seems that Lennie has been doing a little research of her own about the Levine case—"

"Oh fuck!" Decker's face was sour. "Sorry."

"It is 'oh fuck!'" Cindy said. "Your friends aren't going to find the files because Lennie has already checked them out of archives."

"That's not good, Cindy. If anyone else in the squad goes to check them out, they're going to see Lennie's name in the book. What's that going to look like?"

"That she was either hotdogging it on her own or you were conspiring with her. But let me get to the punch line, Dad. Lennie is fairly certain that there are pages missing. Plus, what she has looked through has been heavily redacted."

"What kind of pages?"

"She didn't specify. She wants to talk to you, but she's afraid of dragging you into a mess."

"What's been redacted?"

"I don't know, Dad. She didn't say."

"Sometimes departments redact names of suspects who had ironclad alibis. They don't want cops thinking ill of their good citizens."

"Well, then, that makes sense. She told me that there were hardly any other suspects interviewed other than the culprits."

"That's odd. It took them a month to catch Brandon Gratz and Kyle Masterson."

"Brandon Gratz is Brady Neil's father?"

"Yes. There should be other interviews—with workers and friends and relatives before Gratz and Masterson were apprehended. They should have an interview with the Levines' son Gregg. It was his ID of Gratz that got Kyle Masterson and Brandon Gratz arrested."

"Maybe it's there. She was fuzzy on the details. Lennie thought about asking her father, but then he'd know that she was investigating this on her own. And now you tell me her father was the lead? How dicey is that?"

"Why is she dragging you into this?"

"Because she feels comfortable with me, and I'm objective and far away. She doesn't know we're related, Dad. Anyway, she feels her two options are to work on this by herself or go to you since you're actively working on the case. But then she said that you specifically told her not to do anything on her own. Which of course is good advice. From what I gathered, after her father pulled her off the case so suddenly, she just got curious."

"Or pissed at him."

"Yeah, that could be. I immediately told her to stop. You don't want to find out bad things about your colleagues without going through proper channels. Lennie said almost all the detectives involved have retired because it was twenty years ago. Then I reminded her the people who were young patrol officers back then are probably now officers in senior positions. I told her that she can't cowboy it on her own."

"Great advice."

"Except now the only person she trusts is you. To buy you time, I told her that I'd call you up and let you know what's going on. I told her when I talked to you about her time in Philly that you seemed like a reasonable person."

"There's your first lie, princess. Me being reasonable."

Cindy laughed. "I know I'm putting you in a very bad position—well, I'm not, but she is. Anyway, I wanted to give you a heads-up."

"And she doesn't know we're related."

"I haven't said anything. She's a decent detective, but up until now, I never saw her acting with initiative. You should talk to her, Daddy. I know you don't want her doing this, but if she has sensitive information, it's good to let someone else know about it."

"And you're sure that she didn't access the information illegally?"

"No, she signed out the boxes, which makes it worse. Anyone can trace her. Plus . . . this is really bad. She took the file home."

"Good heavens, what is wrong with her? Is she trying to get herself fired?"

"At least you can see what she's talking about."

"Cold comfort. I have to think about this. But one way or the other, I want to see those files. I've already asked Wendell Tran to get them out of archives, and now if he does it, he'll see that they were already checked out by Lennie. God, what a mess!"

"Who's Wendell Tran?"

"The missing persons detective assigned to the Joe Boch Junior case. Jaylene Boch lived in Hamilton."

"Okay. Can I ask you a question?"

"Sure."

"Why do you want to see the files if the murderers are in prison?"

"I wanted to find out if anything in those files might be related to Brady Neil's homicide."

"And?"

"What makes you think there's an 'and'?" Cindy waited. Then Decker said, "Okay, here goes nothing. Glen Levine had a partner—Mitchell Flint. He and his wife, Margot, were convicted of embezzlement, fraud, and money laundering. A few days before they were to be sentenced, they skipped town."

"How did they manage to do that?"

"They were out on bail. They had surrendered their passports and weren't considered a flight risk because they had teenaged children."

"Interesting." She paused. "I take it this was before the murders?"

"About two years before the murders."

"If they were involved in the homicides, they waited awhile."

"Yes, they did. But like Rina said, it takes time to plan something like this, especially if you're a fugitive. I'm not saying they had anything to do with it. But their names should be in the files as suspects in the murders. I want to see if anyone mentioned them."

"I agree. Do you know where they are?"

"No. I don't even know if they're in the country."

"Can I help? Our databases are more complete than yours."

"I don't want to get you involved, but if you happen to be curious . . ." Decker spelled the names for her.

"Not a problem." A pause. "What are you going to do about Lennie?"

"I have to tell Mike Radar about this. We'll come up with something."

"Good." A pause. "Sorry about this."

"Why? What did you do?"

"I suppose if I'm letting you handle this, it takes me off the hook."

"Hey, I called you about her in the first place. If anyone started this chain of events, it's me. And call me if you need anything, Cyn. Help is a two-way street."

"True. But help from parent to child is always more trafficky than child to parent."

Decker smiled and hung up. His grin was short-lived. It was now his firm duty to call up Mike Radar and let him know what was going on. The captain's reply was predictable.

"We need to call Victor Baccus."

"With all due respect, Mike, I'd prefer to leave him

out of it until I've seen the file. There's something screwy going on."

"Yeah, and screwy is named Lennie Baccus. She not only disobeyed direct orders from her captain, she's flouting protocol. She took the file home, for Chrissake. She's rogue."

"She's trying to prove herself."

"By going rogue."

"Let me see the files, Mike. I can tell right away whether they've been messed with."

"How do you know she isn't presenting you with false files or that she hasn't messed with them herself?"

"I wouldn't know that. But I won't know anything until I've seen the pages."

"I don't deal with rogue cops. Especially ones who seem to be setting you up. It's going to look like you were colluding with her."

"I know, but Baccus isn't going to fire his own daughter."

"Why not? He didn't have any qualms about yanking her off Homicide."

"Mike, I'm not letting her hang out to dry. What's the worst you can do? Fire me? I've had a long career. I have a pension that's untouchable. Certainly, looking at a file that may be related to my case is not a criminal offense. And what the hell is wrong with an officer of Hamilton PD looking over an old case?"

"And taking it home?" When Decker didn't answer, Radar said, "Why is she sticking her neck out?"

"Like you said, to prove herself to her dad. Or maybe it's to spite him. It's irrelevant. I'm not deserting her just because she's showing a little spine. Look, Mike, I'm just telling you because if something blows up, I want you to know what I'm doing."

"What could blow up?"

"I don't know. A couple of years before the murders, Glen's shady business partner and his wife went underground. Then the Levines were murdered. Although some of the gems were recovered, bigger pieces are still missing. Neither Gratz nor Masterson got life without parole—which would have been the natural sentence. Corruption comes to mind." A pause. "Maybe there was a payoff in jewels for a lighter sentence."

"That would mean not only corrupt officers but bribing a judge. Do you have any evidence?"

"If I did, I wouldn't be holding back. I know I'm getting ahead of myself. Let me see what the files look like and I'll tell you everything I know. But please. For the time being, let's leave Victor Baccus out of it."

"I'm coming with you."

"Don't involve yourself, Mike."

"You've already involved me. I'm coming, and so is McAdams. This way, we all know what's going on and there's no collusion. I'm trying to help you out, Decker."

"I realize that. You're putting your own integrity on the line. I really appreciate it."

"Stop with the flattery. I'm pissed. Now I've got to deal with a neighboring captain who's going to find out about this and be pissed that I didn't call him."

"Call him after we look at the file."

"Doh, why didn't I think of that?"

Decker laughed. "Sorry."

Radar laughed as well. "Give Officer Sticky Fingers a call tonight and set something up. Hopefully, the homicide file looks like a homicide file and we all go back to work on Monday. But either way, I'm going to have to make that phone call and I'm pissed about it. And no, I don't want you to make the call to Baccus. Let me know when you've got a time and a place. And try to make it before dinnertime. Sunday may not be your sabbath, but it is mine."

"I'm sorry about this."

"No, you're not. You're excited and you're trying to hide it. You've got a bug up your butt, Pete. Let's hope when it bites you, it's not carrying anything lethal."

Chapter 20

At nine in the morning, Decker, McAdams, and Radar met outside Lennie's apartment building. The street was tree-lined with big leafy oaks. Because it was Sunday, the neighborhood was quiet except for some excitable birds being chased by ravens. A bright sun, sitting in deep blue sky, was already warming the day. McAdams had on a white shirt and blue linen pants, ringlets cascading down his neck. Radar was wearing an open-neck white shirt and tan slacks. Decker was the only one dressed in a suit. But he went Friday casual in a white short-sleeved polo shirt. He said, "She's on the third floor. I'll call her and let her know we're here."

He punched in the numbers and, unexpectedly, got voice mail. She knew they were coming. He had confirmed it an hour ago. Where the hell was she?

Decker looked at the others. "She's not answering."

Radar narrowed his eyes. McAdams walked up to the glass door that led to a small lobby. It was locked. "We have to be buzzed in."

Decker said, "Is there a house manager?"

"Yeah." McAdams pushed the button. When a voice came over the intercom, he announced himself as the police. The door buzzed, and they all walked inside. They took the elevator to Lennie's floor and walked over to her unit. When McAdams knocked, the door fell open. He started to go in, but Radar stopped him.

"Take a picture on your phone, then announce yourself."

Decker looked at the doorjamb. "It's been jimmied." He took out his own phone for evidence pictures.

Finally, the men stepped inside. The apartment looked neat, and there was the distinct smell of coffee brewing. A quick look around revealed an apartment with few adornments—a living room with basic furniture that opened into a kitchenette with a breakfast bar. On the fake granite countertop were mugs, spoons, sugar, and Splenda. Moments later, Decker heard footsteps. He stepped back into the hallway and saw Lennie carrying a carton of milk. She wore a cotton jersey red T-shirt over jeans with moccasins on her feet.

"So sorry I'm late. I made coffee, but I ran out

of milk. I know you take yours black, but I wasn't sure—"

"Lennie, someone broke into your apartment," Decker informed her. "When we got here, your door was open and the doorjamb looked pried open. How long were you gone?"

She stopped walking and stood slack-jawed. "About forty-five minutes."

"It takes you that long to get milk?" Lennie was silent. Decker said, "I think someone was watching you. Let's go inside. You tell me if anything's missing."

The two of them went back inside the apartment. Lennie put the milk on the counter. Her face still registered shock. "My laptop is missing." She looked at the men. "I don't keep anything important on it. I keep private stuff on my iPad mini—which is in my purse."

McAdams said, "We tried calling you. You didn't answer."

She checked inside her handbag and pulled out her phone. "Sorry. It was off."

"Where is the Levine file?" Radar asked.

"Oh shit!" She ran to the bedroom and the others followed, watching her as she pulled out a dresser drawer and rooted through a pile of sweaters. "Gone."

She clamped her long fingers over her mouth. "How did this happen!"

Decker blew out air. "Now what!" He turned to an ashen Lennie. "What was in those files that warrants a break-in?"

"I have no idea. You can see for yourself." Lennie took out a USB flash drive. "Last night, after I talked to my old sergeant, I had a bad feeling. This morning, I scanned the contents onto a computer at a twenty-four-hour place in Jackson, emailed a copy to my old sergeant, and downloaded the contents onto a USB stick."

Radar said, "Officer Baccus, you can't willy-nilly send police files over the internet even if you sent it to another officer at a legitimate police organization. What is wrong with you?"

Lennie looked down. "I erased everything on the computer."

"It's still on the hard drive, Lennie. You know that. Why do you think we confiscate computers from our suspects?" Decker turned to Radar. "We'll get hold of the machine and destroy it."

"The file is twenty years old. I figured who'd care?" When no one answered, Lennie said, "I know, it was really dumb."

"It was dumb of you to take home the file in the first

place," Radar said. "For precisely this reason. This could be your career."

"I have no career as long as I'm under my father's command." She was suddenly frustrated. "He has no faith in me. I suppose I emailed a copy to my sergeant because I really trust her—more than my father. It's the weekend. She probably doesn't even know she has it on her email."

"I'll call her." Decker stared at Lennie. "We've been talking a lot about you."

Lennie winced. "She probably thinks I'm a doofus."

"A little bit. She also thinks that you might be out of your league." A pause. "Or maybe she identifies with you because her dad is also a cop."

McAdams cleared his throat. Lennie started clicking her nails. Decker put his hand over hers. "Why do you do that? Play with your nails. It's annoying."

She clasped her hands together. "I used to bite them to the quick. So now I put gels on. I don't bite them anymore, but I guess it's one bad habit replacing another." She made a face. "Sorry."

"I'm edgy right now. I'm sure you are as well." Decker backed off. "Let's see what you have on your USB stick. I think we'll need a computer for that."

"We're not using the station house computer," Radar

said. "I don't want a Hamilton file in our files without permission."

"I have a laptop that I use exclusively for school," McAdams said. "How about we go over to my apartment and I'll make coffee?"

"I think you left your laptop at my place," Decker said.

"Uh, yes, that is true," McAdams said. "How about we go over to Decker's house and I'll make coffee?"

Radar said to McAdams, "There's closed-circuit TV when you enter the lobby. You come with me and we'll get the manager to pull the tape. If it's pros, they've probably put something over the lens. But sometimes when you're in a hurry, you slip up." To Decker, he said. "Take Officer Baccus and we'll meet you at your house."

"Let's go," Decker said to Lennie.

Her smile was sad. "I'm going to get fired."

"I'd certainly fire you," Radar said.

Lennie winced again. "Then I might as well see this through. I have nothing left to lose."

"Not true," Radar said. "You've got your safety to think about, Officer Baccus. You've made someone angry. You've also made someone desperate. Angry and desperate is not a good combination."

After securing the CCTV tape from Lennie Baccus's apartment lobby, Radar and McAdams joined Lennie and Decker, who had already downloaded the files from the USB stick. Rina came out with a coffee set and put it down on the dining room table. She stared over her husband's shoulder as McAdams slowly scrolled down the pages. It started with the crime report, then moved into the crime scene photos and evidence lists, followed by autopsy reports. It ended with pages centered around the investigations into the homicides.

Decker said, "It's on the thin side."

Radar asked, "How many crime scene photos do we have?"

"Too few for a double homicide."

"I'm counting twelve evidence cones in these photos alone," the captain remarked. "What was listed in evidence?"

McAdams said, "Fifteen items, but not the murder weapon."

"What about evidence found when they searched the suspects' home?"

Lennie said, "A gun was taken, but it wasn't the one that killed the Levines."

Radar asked, "What weapon killed them?"

"No weapon was recovered. They found .38-caliber ammo, probably from a .38 Special Smith and Wesson."

"Standard police weapon back then," Decker noted.

"I realize that," Radar said.

Decker said, "At the murder scene, is there anything on the evidence list about recovering .357 cartridges?"

McAdams said, "Three-fifty-seven cartridges?"

"I know what you're thinking," Rina said.

"What's he thinking?" McAdams asked.

"You can fire .38 Special S and W ammo from a .357 Magnum. Down at the range, I saw this guy do it and asked him about it. He said .38 ammo is much cheaper that .357, but you have to be careful. But if you're a criminal, I suppose it's also a good dodge. The police would be looking for a .38 Special Smith and Wesson and not a Magnum. By the way, you can't use Magnum ammo in a .38 Special. Too powerful."

"Gold star for you," Radar said. "I'm impressed."

"You're absolutely right, Rina," Decker said. "It is a good dodge because it's something that not everyone knows about. If there were any .357s . . . even one . . . we could consider a Magnum as the murder weapon."

Rina shrugged. "Who wants coffee?"

Hands all around. Radar said, "Did they ever find the weapon that killed the Levines?"

"If they did, it wasn't in the file," Lennie said.

Radar shook his head. "I don't know if something stinks or not, but you're right about one thing, Baccus. The file is thin and heavily redacted, and that's not normal."

Decker said, "Maybe these murders were part of a bigger investigation with another agency. When that happens, there's a lot of redacting to hide the identity of undercover officers."

"Want me to ask around about that?" Lennie said.

"You don't say a word to anyone until we find out what happened at your apartment this morning." Radar looked up. "You've made your safety my concern. Now I'm in charge and this is what we're going to do. Baccus, you and I are going down to the station to look at the CCTV tape. You tell me who belongs at your complex and who doesn't."

"I'm going to print out the pages," Decker said. "McAdams and I will go through them word by word. We'll meet up with you in a couple of hours."

"Sounds good. Keep an eye out. I don't like this at all."

After Radar left with Baccus, Rina said, "What can I do?"

"We're fine," Decker said.

McAdams said, "Actually, it'd be great if you can start looking up dragonfly cafés and see if you can find one that matches the logo on the coffee cup in those black and whites. I was going to do that today, but now it looks like I have other things to do."

"Happy to do it, but you know those photos are old. That café might not even exist anymore. But I suppose it's worth a try."

"Thanks, Rina," McAdams said. "Can I print these pages off your laptop? I don't want to transfer them to my home computer."

"Sure, send them to me and I'll print everything for you," Rina said. "Does anyone want breakfast? I can get some fresh bagels."

"Don't put yourself out," McAdams said.

"I want to get out anyway," Rina said. "I need to clear my head."

"Why?" Decker asked. "What's on your mind?"

"Nothing, really," Rina said. "Just a lot of buzzing and static. Nothing that a good walk won't take care of."

Decker looked up. "If you're going out, take the car. After the break-in at Lennie's apartment, I don't want you alone and vulnerable."

"Nothing's going to happen to me."

"Says the woman who was nearly attacked a year ago. After what happened at Lennie's apartment, it's possible that we're all being watched. If you need to walk, go to the gym and hop on a treadmill. If you're going to get bagels, please take the car."

"Fine." Rina picked up her purse and a recycled paper bag.

"Check your mirrors." As she left, Decker shouted, "And keep your phone handy."

Without answering, she closed the front door and tried not to get too annoyed. That was Peter: worried about everyone's safety.

Except, of course, his own.

Gregg Levine's statement to the police was complete and unredacted. Decker read it several times, poring over the jumbled words, hearing a young, disoriented man of twenty trying to make sense of the horror he had just witnessed. Haltingly, Levine portrayed a story. The shock of seeing his parents shot—blood and brains spattered across the walls—must have etched a gruesome image in his brain for life. Who knew what kind of nightmares Gregg Levine had suffered throughout the years. There had been rumors that his father had been angry at the young man's party lifestyle and had threatened to cut him off. But since Decker couldn't find anything in the files to substantiate the rumor, he put it down to empty chatter.

No other witnesses were found. The shops in the

surrounding area were all closed as everything took place in the wee hours of the morning. No one was found wandering the neighborhood, and no one heard shots fired. The files did contain statements about the Levines from friends, neighbors, and people who knew them from business or their local synagogue. No one had a bad word to say about the couple. Several people did mention Mitch and Margot Flint as people to look into. But by the time the murders had occurred, the Flints were long gone—deep underground.

Brandon Gratz and Kyle Masterson were arrested about a month after the crime. Neither one had been interviewed before, and how the police got that information was up for grabs. There was a reward of ten thousand dollars for information leading to the arrest. If it was claimed, there was no mention of it in the files.

The confession statements came seventeen hours after the arrests. Decker rarely got confessions from professional robbers. Almost everybody—from the most sophisticated criminals to the lowliest punks— knew to lawyer up as soon as the police brought them into the interview room. After finding purloined jewelry in their possession, the men admitted the robbery, but they never copped to the murders.

It was generally a bad strategy to admit to anything. Decker had to wonder if there was some kind of off-the-record deal, because the perps got twenty years to life with a chance of parole for a double murder instead of life without parole, which would have been more appropriate. If there was more to the story, the two convicted killers weren't talking.

Rina had returned from her bagel foray. "Safe and sound." She kissed her husband's head. "All that worrying for nothing."

"It must serve a purpose for me. Otherwise I wouldn't bother."

"Yes, the purpose being to drive me crazy," Rina said.

"Harsh."

"What have you learned about the Levine murders?"

"Nothing that I didn't already know."

"Are you hungry?"

"As long as you bought fresh bagels, I might as well be a gentleman and eat. Toasted everything bagel with cream cheese, please."

"Just because you said please." She looked at McAdams. "Tyler?"

"Same, thanks."

Decker went back to reading. Victor Baccus was the lead investigator. Other detectives involved were George Tor, Jack Newsome, Harvey Jacques, and Ben Pearson. He turned to McAdams and scratched his head. "Newsome seems to work directly under Baccus. The other detectives more or less float in and out."

"Yeah, I'll go along with that."

Entering Jack Newsome on the Hamilton PD website, Decker learned that the man had retired over a decade ago. "Tyler, find out all you can about Newsome, including where he is now."

"Is he still alive?"

"No idea, but that should be easy enough to find out. If he is still with us, I'd like to talk to him." Decker's cell rang. It was Radar. After listening, Decker hung up and said, "The captain wants us down at the station house. They found some things on the tape. Nothing definitive, but enough to warrant a second pair of eyes. Also, the lab got a kinship DNA match between Jennifer Neil and one of the blood samples taken at the Boch house. It looks like Brady Neil was killed at the Boch house, although most of the blood wasn't his. The vast majority belonged to a kinship match with Jaylene Boch."

McAdams clucked his tongue. "Boch being the intended target and Brady was collateral damage."

"Maybe, but he's just as dead."

"But it shifts the focus of the investigation onto Boch rather than Brady Neil. And Joseph Boch is not our murder case."

"But we need to find answers for Joseph Boch's

murder to solve Brady Neil's homicide. The cases are still linked even if Neil was just in the wrong place at the wrong time." Decker started stacking the file papers. "Help me clean up. I'll store everything in my gun safe."

Rina brought them wrapped bagel sandwiches. "I'll look up Jack Newsome if you want. Spell it for me."

Decker complied. "Thanks, that will help."

"Did Radar say what he spotted on the CCTV?" Rina wanted to know.

"No, he was cagey. Oh. Important. I got permission to visit Brandon Gratz in prison tomorrow."

"And you still think that's necessary even if Brady was an innocent victim?" McAdams said.

Rina said, "Why do you think he's an innocent victim?"

Decker said, "I'll explain later. Yes, I still want to talk to Brandon Gratz. I've got a lot of questions." He looked at Rina. "Want to keep me company? It's a three-hour ride one-way."

"Of course I'll come. I just got *Friends Divided* on audiobooks. It's about Adams and Jefferson, and the reviews I've read make it sound a lot more political than dense, dull history."

"Do I really want to hear something political?"

"Yes, you do. There's comfort in knowing that human nature never changes."

Chapter 21

"They enter the lobby . . . you can see them walking up the steps, heads down wearing hoodies," Radar said. "They step out of the range of the camera, but we see the door to the building opening and a set of shoes walking inside."

"How'd they get the door open?" McAdams said.

"No idea. It's out of the camera's range."

"Can you go back a few frames?" When Radar complied, McAdams said, "What's this guy carrying up the steps? It looks larger than a briefcase."

Decker said, "Some kind of man purse. Big enough for a laptop."

The two figures disappeared out of range. Radar ejected the security disc. "Now this one is from the camera inside the lobby." He put on another disc. "As soon as they walk through the door, one of them heads toward the back where the elevator is. He's the bigger of the two guys."

"He's also the one with the man purse," McAdams said.

"He is," Radar said. "The thinner guy puts his hand over the lobby camera lens for around twenty minutes. The film goes dark. I'll fast-forward through that." A pause. "Okay. Here we go. They're now leaving, walking with their backs to the camera."

"And fatter guy is carrying the man purse, where the Levine files were stashed."

"Probably." Radar paused the machine. "Baccus said she hasn't seen anyone stalking her house before."

"I wasn't looking," she said. "I should have been more vigilant, but I think I would have noticed two guys loitering around."

"Any strange cars?" Decker asked.

Lennie shrugged then shook her head. "There are always cars parked outside the building. I honestly didn't notice. Stupid."

"Don't beat yourself up over it," Decker said. "I'm sure you'll see things now that you've never seen before."

"That's for sure."

Decker turned to Radar. "Could you play the second disc again, but on slo-mo?"

"What are you looking for?"

"I'll let you know if I see it."

The group once again witnessed the disc frame by frame. Decker said, "Stop. Right there. Okay. The guys obviously didn't want to be recognized: hoods over their heads, long sleeves, long pants. But look here at the heavier-set dude. When he raises his hand to adjust carrying the man purse, his sleeve rides up. Could you advance it a frame?"

Radar complied.

"Another one. Another. Another. Okay. Stop." Decker pointed to the monitor. "His wrist and a third of his forearm is showing. That blotch on his skin. I think it's a tattoo."

"You're right," Lennie said.

"Every single criminal between the ages of three and three hundred has a tattoo," McAdams said.

"And each one is a little different," Decker said. "You work with what you have. We should get it enhanced to get some detail out of it."

"I'll get it to a lab," Radar said.

Lennie was squinting at the screen. McAdams said, "What are you staring at?"

"You can see the back of the thin guy's hand in this frame . . . before he raises his hand and covers the lens . . ."

"And?"

"For some reason, to me it doesn't look like the hand of a young person."

"No, it doesn't," Decker concurred. "It looks mottled."

"Liver spots," she said. "Hamilton has an aging population. Anyone with a brain leaves." She sighed. "My dad always assigns me cases dealing with the elderly—aging people who are confused and angry. Someone calls the police to get them to calm down. I think this guy is older. Not old, but in his sixties, maybe?"

"Good observation," Decker said. "So it looks like we're working with two older men who stole a twenty-year-old police file."

McAdams said, "Maybe they were cops on the case who want to find out if the files have something incriminating in them."

"But it's been redacted."

"Maybe they don't know that."

"Then following the logic, we should be looking for old detectives who were involved with the Levine murder cases."

"And one of them might have an arm tattoo," McAdams said.

Decker said. "That should narrow down our list of suspects."

"It could have been a patrolman," Radar pointed out. "Doesn't have to be a detective."

"Absolutely," Decker said.

McAdams said, "It could be that these two guys aren't cops, you know. Maybe a crooked cop hired someone to steal the files."

"No, I disagree," Decker said. "You don't hire a criminal to get something for you if it contains potentially damaging information about you. He'll read it and then he has something over you. I'll bet you that these guys were involved in the Levine case."

Radar nodded. "Look through the files, as thin as they are, and make a list of everyone who worked the case."

"We can do that. But if the guy's name is redacted, I'm not going to find it. But"—Decker smiled—"I can interview the cops we do have names for and ask them about it." A pause. "If I go that route, it's going to get back to Victor Baccus. How do you want to handle it?"

"I've got to think about that," Radar said. "Let's enhance the image first and make sure it is a tattoo."

Decker nodded, then turned to Lennie. "And you positively don't remember seeing strange men hanging around your house?"

"Unfortunately, no." She looked up from the screen. "But I'll certainly remember them now."

Radar said, "Let's get some names from the file, and we'll start checking off people tomorrow."

Decker said, "I won't be at work tomorrow morning. I've got a date with Bergenshaw."

"Who's Bergenshaw?" Lennie asked.

"It's not a who, it's a what," Radar said. "It's a maximum-security prison."

"Brandon Gratz?"

"Brandon Gratz," Decker echoed.

It was a perfect day for a trip to the penitentiary. They started early Monday morning, when the air was still cool, but within an hour, the day had turned warm and the bugs and birds were fully awake in a silky blue sky. As the sun rose, its light and heat were filtered through the leafy boughs of the forest trees. Since the highways were jammed with weekday traffic, Decker elected to drive the back roads even though it added time to the trip. They passed miles of untamed foliage and rode over several one-lane bridges that spanned creeks and rias. Eventually he merged onto the tollway where the idyllic surroundings turned into a blurred background of industrial gray.

Rina wore a purple sundress that fell below her knees and a light white shirt to cover her arms. Decker was dressed in a suit and tie befitting his role as a law enforcement agent. All the while, they listened to the audio CD of their chosen book while drinking coffee and eating breakfast sandwiches that Rina had prepared from scratch. The time passed quickly, and they made it to the gate around ten in the morning. The prison was newer and medium-sized, with two guard towers and thick, high cement walls covered with barbed wire.

Decker had added Rina's name to the roster. A while back, at his behest, the department had given her a civilian badge that gave her some kind of police standing. Still, the guard was unsure about letting her through the gate. But Decker remained calm, and eventually they were both cleared and he inched the old Volvo into the parking lot.

Rina said, "I suppose I should have worn something dull and official."

"He was just being a jerk." Decker pulled into a visitor's parking space. "Petty bureaucrat."

"In all fairness to him, I could be hiding something under my petticoat."

"Petticoat? How quaint." Decker turned off the ignition. "That's why there are metal detectors. Do you want to come in, or would you rather wait in the car?"

"How grubby is it?"

"Never been inside here, but it's a prison. You can't

come in the interview room, but there is a waiting room."

She took out her phone. "Take your time. I wanted to look up some stuff anyway. And I have a book. As long as I have something to read and coffee to drink, I'm fine."

"They're giving me a half hour with Gratz. Before we meet, I'm going to check the visitors' log to see who he's been talking to. I'll probably be an hour or so, unless he shuts me down."

"Why would he do that?"

"Criminals are not cooperative people." He gave her the keys to the car. Then he leaned over and kissed her. "Lock the doors."

"Good luck."

"Thanks." Decker walked toward the entrance to the cement fortress, which held not one but two sally ports. Then he was checked by guards. Since he wasn't carrying his service gun, he proceeded to a metal detector. On the other side was the front desk to the prison. After presenting the paperwork, he was given the current month's visitor log to look over. There were a lot of inmates who had entertained company over the past thirty days. Decker started by checking the names one by one.

Three weeks before the murder, Brady Neil had

signed in to visit his father. It had been on a Tuesday. Decker looked at the previous Tuesday, but he didn't find Brady's name. He went back and began to reread the names in the log, making sure he didn't miss anything. As far as Decker could tell, Brady had visited his father just one time in the previous month.

The next step was to check last month's log. But since time was growing short, it seemed more economical to just ask Brandon about it. If he was uncooperative, Decker could always come back and scour through the previous logs, looking for Brady's name.

He handed the book back to the desk clerk. She was tall and rangy with short gray hair. Maybe in her early sixties and probably once in law enforcement. She looked at Decker's signature and checked it against his driver's license. "It'll take a few minutes."

"That's fine," he said. "I'm ready whenever they are."

"Just finalizing your paperwork. Take a seat."

Decker sat.

A few minutes turned into a quarter hour. Eventually, a tan-uniformed guard picked him up and led him through a labyrinth of hallway and into an interview room. It had a steel table and four chairs, all the furniture bolted to a cement floor. It took another ten minutes before the prisoner was led in. He was handcuffed in back but wasn't wearing leg irons.

In his fifties, Brandon Gratz had a broad chest and big, long arms. His hair, silver in color, was clipped short. His salt-and-pepper beard was thick over his chin but well trimmed on his cheeks, exposing a faint scar running down the left side of his face. His eyes were a skeptical, milky blue; his nose was crooked; and his lips were thin. He was wearing orange prison scrubs and step-in orange shoes. He nodded to Decker, and Decker nodded back.

Gratz said, "Can I take the cuffs off?"

"Fine with me, but I don't make the rules," Decker said.

The guard pulled out a key. He uncuffed him from the back, cuffing his left arm to a metal ring on the desk while leaving the right arm free. Then he pocketed the key and stood by the door, hand on his holster.

"Thanks." Gratz sat very still in his chair and waited.

Decker broke the ice. "I'm sorry about your son."

Gratz's eyes scanned Decker's face. He pursed his lips. "Are you in charge?"

"Of your son's murder investigation? Yes, I am."

"Then you're with Hamilton PD?"

"Greenbury PD."

"Greenbury?"

"Your son was found in Greenbury's jurisdiction, near the border of Hamilton. It's officially my case."

"You worked a lot of murder cases?"

"I have." Decker waited for another question. When it didn't come, he said, "I noticed Brady visited you a couple weeks before it happened."

"Yeah? Maybe."

"It's a fact. I saw his name in the visitors' log. How often did he visit you?"

The man scratched his head. "Were you looking for his name?"

"Yes."

"Why?"

"Because I want to know if you two had a relationship."

"Is that relevant?"

"It might be."

"You think I had something to do with the murder of my own son?"

"Nothing I've heard would lead me in that direction. But in a murder investigation, you leave no stone unturned. How often did he visit you?"

"What have you heard?"

Decker sat back. "Brandon, I only have"—he looked at his watch—"another twenty-plus minutes with you. If you don't mind, let me ask my questions and if there is leftover time, I'll answer yours. How often did Brady visit you?"

Gratz shrugged. "I don't get many visitors."

"All the more reason why you should remember how often your only son visited you."

A smile perched on his lips. It quickly disappeared.

Odd, Decker thought.

Finally, Brandon said, "Maybe three or four times. It started about six months ago."

"Was it out of the blue?"

"Yeah."

"What did you two talk about?"

"Catching up."

"Why do you think he suddenly contacted you?"

"He said that he wanted to get to know me."

"Did he talk about himself, or did he want to hear about your life?"

Another scratch, this time to his face. Gratz said, "Little bit of both."

Like smart inmates, the man didn't volunteer any information. Decker said, "People I've talked to said that Brady was doing okay."

Gratz nodded.

"How about you, Brandon? Are you doing okay?"

He folded his arms across his chest. "I don't back down, but I don't cause trouble." A pause. "I'm up for parole. I probably won't get it, but even in the worst case, I should be out in ten years. Less than ten for good behavior. If people leave me alone, I play nice."

"Smart." Decker leaned forward. "Why do you think you'll be out automatically in ten years?"

"Lawyer told me they usually are more lenient with people over sixty."

"Good luck then." Gratz was silent. Decker said, "Okay, sir, this is the deal. I'm going to just lay it open for you and you decide whether or not to talk to me." Again, Gratz was quiet. "Brady seemed to have kept his nose relatively clean. He had a job, he had a car, and he was going to school part-time. I understand he dealt drugs in high school, but if he was still doing it, it wasn't obvious to me or anyone who knew him. I'd say he had turned into a good citizen except he seemed to have expendable money and no one knew where that came from.

"I don't know who murdered your son. But once I find out the why, the who may be easier to find. I'm going to ask you this, and I hope you'll be honest with me. Do you think his murder has anything to do with you and your past? Because if you do think your past is a factor, I'd really like to know about it."

Gratz didn't talk for a moment. Then he said, "What do you know about my past?"

"I know you never admitted to the Levine homicides. And I have a feeling that there's a lot more to it than Hamilton PD is telling me."

"What's Hamilton telling you?"

"What I've been reading in the papers."

"Why do you think there's more to it?"

"Call it detective's intuition."

Again, Gratz didn't say anything. Then he said, "Time's almost up."

"Yes, it is."

"I'll say this: you shouldn't believe anything, whether it's in the papers or what people could have told you. People lie, you know."

"I know. What should I believe?"

Gratz shrugged.

"Okay," Decker said. "Maybe you want to think about that one. What did you and Brady talk about? Specifically."

"Lots of things. I don't have time to get into it. Specifically."

"I can come back."

"We'll see about that."

"One thing before you go. It's important." When Gratz looked upward and remained silent, Decker pulled out the black-and-white photocopies and said,

"Do you know who these people are?" He put the snapshot copies on the table.

Gratz's eyes moved downward. Slowly, his finger touched the corners of the copies until they were lined up in a row. "Where'd you get these?"

"You answer my question, I'll answer yours. Do you know these people?"

A pause. "Do you know about Mitchell and Margot Flint?"

"I do. They were scheduled to be sentenced for embezzlement and grand theft, but they fled underground. This happened about eighteen months before the Levine murders. When I read the murder files, I wondered if they were considered suspects before you were arrested."

Gratz was on the edge of his chair. "And?"

"I didn't see their names in print because the file has been heavily redacted—blacked out." Decker pointed to the photocopies. "Is it them?"

"Can't say. It was a long time ago."

"Give it your best shot."

"Why should I help you?"

"Because right now, we have a common goal: finding out who murdered your son."

"It might be if I ever gave a shit about my kids."

Cold, Decker thought. "It's a simple yes or no. Do you know who these people are?"

A few moments passed. Then Gratz said, "I knew Mitch better than Margot. The guy doesn't look anything like Mitch."

"And the woman?"

Gratz smiled. "Who knows? Women can change their appearances—dye their hair, get a nose job, fiddle with their boobs. Margot was a hot number—a blonde with big boobs. This woman is a brunette with normal knockers. You decide. Where'd you get these?"

"At another murder scene."

His face registered surprise. "Who got murdered?"

"Joseph Boch Junior, known as Boxer. Does the name sound familiar?"

For just a moment, Gratz seemed at a loss for words. He stammered, "I knew the old man—Joe Boch Senior."

"Then you must know that he was a wife beater, a petty thief, and a real lowlife. About the time of your arrest, he moved to Kansas. He was from the Midwest, but his wife, Jaylene, was a local Hamiltonian. You know Jaylene. You went to high school with her."

Gratz shrugged. "She's older than I am, but yeah, I knew her."

"She's in a wheelchair from a car accident. The people who broke into her house and murdered her son left her tied to her chair to die a slow death."

"Sorry to hear that." Said without emotion.

"She'll probably make it. What do you know about Joe Senior?"

"You already asked me that." Gratz stared at Decker. His lips formed a slow, joyless smile. "You know, not all criminals hang, especially if they're stupid idiots who beat their wives." He looked at the guard. "Take me back."

The guard cuffed Gratz behind his back and said to Decker, "Someone will be here in a moment to escort you out."

Decker said, "Solving your son's murder may be beneficial to both of us, Brandon."

Gratz turned his head. "It would help you, not me."

"What if I were to say that I believe that you may be innocent of the Levine murders."

"I'd say you were shitting me in hopes of getting something from me."

"Like what?"

"You tell me, because I got nothing to say right now."

"Brady was your son," Decker said. "Keep an open mind about the future. I'll come back whenever you feel like talking."

"Don't count on it." Gratz sneered. "You're a cop. You're the enemy. End of story."

Chapter 22

Decker knocked on the passenger window, startling his wife. When she unlocked the doors, he said, "Sorry I scared you."

"It's fine. How'd it go?"

"As expected—frustrating." He recapped the conversation. "Gratz insists that he and Brady were just playing catch-up, but there was something deeper going on. Maybe whatever they discussed got Brady murdered."

"No wonder he wasn't talkative," Rina said. "He doesn't want his son's death on his conscience."

"I don't think he has a conscience."

"Brady is still his son."

"He told me he didn't give a shit about his kids. Could be bravado, but it could be he's truly apathetic."

"Do you think he'll see you again?"

"Maybe, but I'm not positive what good it'll do me unless *he* wants to talk. And he'll only want to talk to me if I can do something for him—which I can't."

"You never know, Peter. He might think about it afterward and give you a call."

"Sure. But it's too far to be making trips out here for a fishing expedition." He started the ignition and pulled out of the parking space. "Unless he has something genuine to offer, there's no purpose for a second round. Thanks for coming with me. What have you been doing?"

"Trying to locate Jack Newsome—the Hamilton detective on the Levine murder case."

"Yes. And?"

"He lives in Florida. Looks about sixty-five or so."

"So that means he retired around fifty-five. Pretty typical for the force."

"Unlike someone else we know."

Decker smiled. "You'd hate it if I retired."

"No, I wouldn't."

"Rina, you don't want me around all the time."

"Not *all* the time, but most of the time."

Decker laughed. He left the prison lot and headed toward the highway on his way back home. "If Newsome is in his midsixties, he would have been around forty-five when the Levines were murdered."

"You can do math."

"Very funny. Where does he live in Florida?"

"Not far from your mother. Hint, hint."

"Ah, I see where this is going." They rode a few minutes in silence until Decker said, "It might be easier to just call him up, Rina."

"Don't you always say it's better to talk to someone face-to-face?" A pause. "Peter, she's in her nineties. She's still healthy, but you never know. Even if it's hot and humid, we should see her before it's too late. Then how would you feel?"

"You're right—as always."

"Don't be too sentimental."

"The trouble with Ida Decker is she's too sharp. She loves to needle me."

"So do I."

"Yeah, but you don't really mean it." Decker blew out air. "Okay, we'll go—combine business with business. Did you get a phone number for Newsome?"

"I did not. But I'm sure as an officer of the law, you'd have no trouble doing that. And I'll be happy to entertain your mom while you interview Newsome."

"If he'll talk to me."

"Why wouldn't he talk to you?"

"Some detectives might consider it disloyal to talk against their former colleagues."

"You're not accusing anyone of wrongdoing. You're just asking for information from someone who was there."

"He'll be suspicious and rightly so. I don't know if he'll talk to me."

"Maybe that's the reason he moved out of Hamilton—to get away from his former colleagues."

"Or maybe he's tired of freezing cold winters."

"You won't know until you call him up and sound him out. If he refuses an interview, well, that says something, doesn't it?"

"How about this?" Decker said. "If we're going to take the trip to visit Mom, maybe I shouldn't call him. It might be better just to show up at his doorstep. That way I could say I was in the area and I had a couple of questions. He might think it's a little strange, but I doubt that he'll slam the door in my face."

"Most likely he won't. But you still might want to call him. People often don't like surprises. Are we taking Tyler with us?"

"I hadn't thought about it." He paused. "It might be better for him to stay . . . keep an eye on Lennie Baccus."

"You're worried about her safety, or you don't trust her?"

"A little of both." He thought a moment. "I'll leave

him here. Besides, I don't think prime time's ready for Tyler McAdams versus Ida Decker."

"You know, it just might be Ida Decker *and* Tyler McAdams versus you."

"Come to think of it, that probably is what will happen. Lucky for me that you're on tag team, right?"

"Of course, darling." She patted his knee. "I always have your back." A pause. "You know my mother is only a short plane ride away from your mother."

Decker exhaled. "Yes, I know, and yes, we'll visit your mother as well. At least she doesn't needle me."

She leaned over and kissed him. "Thank you. You know what they say, Peter. One mitzvah leads to another."

"Do they say anything about one headache leading to another?"

"No, there is no commentary on headaches." Rina made a face. "It's probably because the sages never met either one of our mothers."

They were almost at Greenbury when the Bluetooth kicked in. Wendell Tran's voice cut through the line. "I went to check on the Levine murder files. It seems they've been checked out by Lennie Baccus. You wouldn't happen to know anything about that?"

Tran sounded pissed. How to handle this delicate

situation? Decker looked at Rina and made a face. He said, "Can we meet somewhere, Tran?"

"You don't want to talk over the phone."

"Never said that," Decker answered. "But I do like talking in person."

"I'm not calling from the station house. The conversation isn't being recorded."

"Great. Where would you like to meet? I can come to you in about twenty minutes. The timing is perfect because I want to fill you in on the conversation I had with Brandon Gratz."

A long moment passed in silence. "You spoke to Gratz?"

"Just getting back from visiting him in prison. I was wondering if Gratz was doing something that ultimately led to his son's death."

"And?"

Decker cleared his throat. "Where would you like to meet?"

"Name a place."

"How about Jaylene Boch's house? It's still taped up. And we should go over it together . . . see if we can find something that might lead us to Boxer."

"You read the forensic report, Decker. You know that no human being could sustain that much blood loss and still be alive. We should be looking for a body.

The area around the house is very wooded. We're talking acres, if not miles."

"Has anyone searched beyond the immediate vicinity?"

"Smitz and I poked around over the weekend. We didn't get too far because we've both been tied up on this robbery case."

"I'd be happy to help you search . . . if you want help."

There was a long pause. "We've got about three hours of daylight left," Tran said. "I'll meet you at the house."

Rina gave him the thumbs-up.

Decker said, "See you then." He hung up the phone and pulled into the driveway. Then he shut the motor. "I should change into hiking boots."

"Be careful, Peter. You don't know if he's a good guy or a bad guy."

"Tran? He's fine."

"Take your gun."

"Rina—"

"I'm serious. You said yourself that the room was a slaughterhouse."

"I'll take my gun, but nothing's going to happen unless I get eaten by a bear."

"All the more reason to take a gun."

Decker opened the car door. "Thanks for coming with me."

Rina got out of the car. "You're shining me on. Do you want me to fix you something to eat?"

"No, I'm fine. Want me to pick up some takeout for dinner?"

She opened the front door. "No, I'll make something."

"You sure? It's been a long day."

She turned to him. "If you find a body, your day will be even longer. This way, at least I'll have something to eat."

The inside of Jaylene's house was hot and sticky and smelled like spoiled meat. Wendell Tran was dressed in a short-sleeved blue shirt and blue cotton pants. Decker had changed from a suit and tie to a long-sleeved cotton shirt and jeans. Both of them were wearing boots. Tran said, "Want to tell me why Lennie Baccus checked the Levine murder files out of archives?"

"I don't know why, but I'm guessing that my probing made her curious." Decker looked around the living room. The walls were dirty with fingerprint dust, and there were boards over the floor so footprints wouldn't contaminate whatever was left on the wood laminate. "I didn't ask her to do it. I asked you." When Tran didn't answer, Decker said, "For the record, it's hard to tell what the original murder investigation team did because the papers were heavily redacted."

"You've seen the files, then."

"Not the originals, just a copy."

"She made a copy of the original files?"

"That's what she's telling us."

"And someone broke into her apartment and *stole* the original files. But she just happened to make a copy of them?"

"You think it's bullshit."

"It sounds like bullshit to me."

Decker looked at Tran's face. His expression was incredulous. "Let's start looking in the woods. It's past seven. Not a lot of daylight left, and it stinks in here."

They walked through the back door and into the woods, going up through a well-worn pathway. Tran said, "Baccus took the files home against protocol. Then she called you, and you went over to look at them."

"Basically, yes, but not exactly in that order. Let me start at the beginning."

As Decker explained the situation, they scoped out the hills, dodging rocks, loose dirt, and tree roots. The afternoon was warm. In Los Angeles, temperatures dipped as the day headed to twilight. In the East, warm afternoons often meant balmy nights.

"I have two theories on why Lennie Baccus took the files. The first is like I said: she got curious and decided to branch out on her own. She took the files home. Someone found out about it, wanted to see what the original files contained, and stole them. We know that two men in hoodies went into her apartment building while she was out running errands yesterday morning. We saw the CCTV. One of the men had a tattoo. We're trying to get an ID."

"Since you've seen the files, what's in there that's worth stealing?"

"Nothing from my standpoint, because everything is blacked out. But I think the guys who pinched them didn't know that." The trail was getting smaller, and Decker began bushwhacking his way through the brush. "My second theory is Baccus took the original files on the order of someone higher up and she's playing me. She might have even been instructed to show me something bogus. Like I said, the files I saw were heavily redacted."

"Then you think it's bullshit, too."

"Maybe."

Tran switched topics. "What'd Gratz and you talk about today?"

"According to Gratz, his son, Brady, had been visiting him for six months. Gratz told me that their conversation was strictly catch-up. I don't believe him, but he's not ready to talk. He may never talk. He may not even have anything of value to say."

"And that's all he told you?"

"No." Decker tripped and caught himself before he landed on his face. "I showed Gratz the black-and-white snapshots that we found in Jaylene Boch's wheelchair. He implied that maybe the woman was Margot Flint, but he also told me that the man wasn't Mitchell."

"Do you think he's playing you?"

"No idea." Decker exhaled. "Boxer is missing—probably dead—and since the pictures were well hidden, I have to think that whoever made the mess was looking for them. If it is Margot Flint in the snapshots, then the case has something to do with them."

"About the Flints and not the Levine murders?"

"They went underground because of the Levines. I have to think there's some kind of connection, especially since the murder file is all blacked out. My question is, who knew that Lennie Baccus took the files?"

"You did. She told you Saturday night."

"I did know, but I didn't steal them from her apartment. It's more likely that—" Decker didn't finish his sentence.

Tran said, "That it's someone from our department who was on the original Levine case."

"The thought crossed my mind."

"The only one that I know who worked the Levine case and is still on the force is the chief," Tran said. "If you have suspicions, you should take it directly to him."

"Right." They walked in silence, looking for signs of animal activity that might indicate a dead body. Decker said, "There's nothing in the files that makes me suspicious of Victor Baccus. But there are lots of other people who worked the case."

"They're probably retired."

"That doesn't mean I can't call them up and ask them questions."

"You can do what you want, Decker." Trans stopped walking and looked around. He was breathing hard and sweating. "But I'm not probing anyone in my department without a reason."

"I get it," Decker said. "Since Gratz identified the woman in the black-and-white photo as possibly Margot Flint, we should probably have a look at the Flint files."

"Who's we, Lone Ranger?"

"Wendell, I don't know who in your department worked the Flint case, but the files are relevant to me because Brady Neil's blood was in the slaughterhouse. We're on the same side. I'd really like to see the files."

Tran looked up at the sky. The sun was sinking quickly, and puffy white clouds were edged in bright pink. "I'll see if I can pull the original files out of archives. Unless Lennie Baccus took those home as well."

"If she did, I don't know anything about it."

"Why didn't you tell the chief about Lennie after you found out she took the files home?"

"I told my captain. It was his decision. Can we move on, please?"

Tran shook his head. "Let me figure this out. I'll give you a call once I have the Flint files."

"Thank you."

"This is not going to endear me to my buds in the department." He waved his hand in the air. "What the hell." He checked his watch. "It's getting late. If Joe Boch Junior is buried out here, he'll keep for the night. Let's get out of here."

They reversed directions and headed toward the house. It took them around forty minutes to get back, and by that time, the crickets were in full chorus.

"I appreciate your help," Decker said.

"Your appreciation doesn't do me a whit of good. You've got your pension. I don't." Tran stopped in front of his car and disarmed the alarm. "If Baccus did something sketchy, he's going to know that I'm poking around."

"If your inquiries make you suspicious of him, don't go it alone."

"Shit. I hate anything that smacks of corruption."

"I understand." Decker exhaled. "I'd like to interview Gregg Levine about the night of the murders. His statement was one of the few things that wasn't blacked out. But there's a problem with that. The guy is avoiding me, and I don't know why."

"Maybe it's painful for him to resurrect all this."

"Probably. But I still need to talk to him."

"I'll see what I can do. As long as I'm there when you talk to him. Someone needs to keep an eye on you. I'll let you know if I get hold of him. Don't call me, I'll call you."

"Got it." Decker went back to his car, turned on the ignition, and sat while the motor ran. Wendell was a good one, sticking his neck out for someone he didn't know. He hoped it wouldn't come back to bite him.

Decker's watch said eight-thirty. He made a quick call to Rina and told her he'd be home for dinner if she hadn't already eaten. She hadn't. The lasagna was just coming out of the oven.

His timing, in the case, was perfect.

Chapter 23

McAdams was at the dining room table, sorting through papers. He was dressed in shorts and sandals and grunted something when Decker crossed the threshold.

"Excuse me?" Decker closed the front door. "I didn't catch that."

McAdams grunted again.

Decker took off his boots and left them in the hallway closet. He went into the bedroom and came out wearing a clean T-shirt and slippers. "Do you ever eat at home?"

"Not really." McAdams kept his eyes on his papers. "I did bring dessert."

"No doubt something fattening that I can't eat."

"Can we talk business for a moment?" Tyler looked up. "Rina brought me up to date at the prison. She said you're going down to Florida to speak to Jack New-some but that you want me to stay here to keep an eye on Lennie Baccus."

"Yep." Decker picked up the morning paper and perused the headlines.

"Did you know that her dad put her on suspended leave until he can figure out what happened to the Levine files?"

Down went the paper. "Who told you this?"

"She did. She was upset but not surprised. I told her to watch her back. She claims she's being very vig-ilant. From personal experience—being on the wrong end of a bullet twice—I'm a little concerned about her safety."

"I am as well, unless she's working for the other side."

"Yeah, Lennie the spy. I thought you didn't buy into that."

"Now I'm considering everything."

"Ah. Open mind. I like that. Yes, she could be play-ing us. If that's the case, I'll save my nervous energy until there is a reason to expend it." A pause. Then McAdams said, "Do you really think she's spying on us?"

"Don't know." Decker went into the kitchen. "Can I help?"

Rina was cutting up a vegetable-and-cheese lasagna. "You can take out the salad and the garlic bread." Her squares were perfect. "How did it go this afternoon? Is Wendell Tran friend or foe?"

"He's not happy because I'm still asking him favors."

"You want to see the Mitchell and Margot Flint files."

"Yes, I do."

"And is he going to get them for you?"

"I got a resounding *maybe*." A beat. "I think he's honest, but he's upset because I'm putting pressure on him to do things he doesn't want to do. Like spy on his colleagues."

"Anyone would be peeved about that. Has he seen the Levine file?"

"He says no. I'll send him my copy. He said he'll call me when he has the Flint files. I guess I'll just wait."

"And while you wait, we might as well think about going to Florida. I can get a good deal if we go this weekend. I'm thinking Thursday through Sunday."

"Rina, why don't you go visit your mother on Thursday. I'll come down Friday afternoon and we'll spend Shabbos with her. I mean not at the retirement home, but at the hotel around the corner. We can get takeout. We'll go visit my mom on Sunday and, hopefully, I'll squeeze in an interview with Jack Newsome."

"Both moms will be thrilled. It's been a while. Then I should book the tickets?"

"Go for it."

Rina took out a serving fork. "Peter, do you think it's possible that Tran might call up Newsome and give him a heads-up about your visit?"

"He can't tell Newsome about a visit that he doesn't know about." Decker went to the refrigerator and took out the salad with one hand. In the other, he held a platter of garlic bread. "I'm starving. Let's eat."

When they placed the food on the table, McAdams cleared the papers and put them in his backpack next to his chair. "Radar is working on enhancing the CCTV mystery man's tattoo. He found someone in Boston who specializes in that kind of thing. He's FedExing the original image up to him and keeping a copy. Compared to LAPD, it must be hard for you to work for a department still stuck in the Stone Age."

"Technical things are never at your fingertips," Decker said. "Greenbury doesn't have much, but it moves much faster than the dinosaur I used to work for." He picked up the plate. "Can I serve you, Rina?"

"Sure."

McAdams said, "Have you talked to Butterfield today?"

"Yes, we finally connected," Decker said. "He's compiled a list of thirty-four Toyota Camrys in the vicinity. He's checking them out one by one . . . gone through about a third."

"I can help."

"Good," Decker said. "What'd you do today other than worry about Lennie Baccus's safety?"

"While you were talking to Gratz and trying to get on Wendell Tran's good side, I was looking into the employment record of Joseph Boch Senior."

"Okay." Decker gave himself two pieces of lasagna and passed the platter to McAdams. "And?"

"He had filed taxes for the following occupations." McAdams took a piece, set the platter down, and then poked around in his backpack. "I haven't had a chance to look at his employment record once he moved to Kansas, but in Hamilton, he worked two primary fields—in the building trades as a roofer and as a line cook in local diners. Never held a job longer than nine months and never filed for more than twenty grand a year."

"Not very exciting," Rina said. "I hope there's more."

"There is," McAdams said. "One stint of employment stuck out: Joe Senior worked for six months doing night security at City Hall."

Decker stopped eating. "He did security?"

"For six months."

"Huh." A beat. "Why didn't I pick that up when I searched?"

"It took me a while to find it. I don't even think it was listed on his tax forms."

"It had to be if it was the government."

"In a small town, sometimes people cut corners. As I said, it didn't pop out immediately."

"Good work," Decker said. "You know, to get that job, at one point, he had to have been vetted."

"Or maybe he just knew someone who put in a good word," Rina said. "Like Tyler said, small towns."

"If he worked security, he had to be familiar with alarms," McAdams said.

"Maybe," Decker said. "When was this?"

"He quit working at City Hall six months before the Levine murders."

"Convenient," Rina said.

"Exactly," McAdams answered. "I know it was a long time ago, but I could go down to City Hall in Hamilton and see if anyone remembers him."

Decker nodded. "Give it your best shot." A beat. "Do we have anything that links Joe Senior with the Levines?"

"Like did he work security for them?" McAdams

said. "I couldn't find anything, and I looked. But the Levines could have hired him anyway and been paying him under the table in cash. That way, they wouldn't have to pay employee tax and Social Security, and he wouldn't have to declare income for tax purposes. Plus, the Levines might have hired him without references since he had worked for City Hall."

Decker said, "Right. Any link between Senior and the Flints?"

"Still looking," McAdams said. "Maybe the link is between Jaylene and the Flints. The pictures were hidden in *her* wheelchair."

"Right. I should probably go see Jaylene tomorrow. See if there's improvement."

"She's still in the hospital?" Rina said. "It's almost been a week. Is she not over the hump?"

"I don't know. I'll talk to her doctors."

McAdams said, "Maybe she can finally tell you what happened."

"That would be ideal," Decker said. "First, let's see if she can talk."

It was past eleven by the time Rina came to bed. She expected to find Peter out for the evening. Instead, his nightstand light was on and he was reading out of his little black notebook, flipping through the pages. She pulled the covers over her chest and faced him. "You're still at it?"

"Sometimes it helps to review."

"I'm sure it does, but not right before you're ready to call it a night. I mean, you do want to sleep, right?"

"Something was bugging me, and I found out what it was." Decker hit the notebook with the back of his hand. "This guy . . . C. Bonfellow. He works at the Bigstore where Brady Neil and Joseph Boch were employed."

"That's his name? C?"

"No, that's what his name tag said. It's probably Chris or Carl or something like that. Anyway, the guy made a point of telling me that he knows secrets, that people talk around him because they ignore him." He looked up. "He's got a chip on his shoulder, that's for sure."

"You think he might have had something to do with the murders?"

"I don't know, but he was a weird guy. He claimed he didn't even know who Boxer was. But that was before I knew that Boxer was Joseph Boch. And a lot has happened since the first time I talked to him. It might be worth paying him another visit."

"Okay. Sounds good. Can we go to sleep?"

"Sure." Decker put his notes down and turned off his light. "And while I'm there, I can talk to the co-workers again. They're usually a gossipy lot."

"Gossip isn't all bad, you know." She leaned over and gave Peter a kiss. "I mean, where would detective work be without gossip?"

"That is very true. It's a misconception that science solves most crimes. It doesn't. What science does is convict criminals. It's plain old gossip that solves most of the cases, because people *love* to talk."

The room was a semiprivate, but Jaylene's bed had the outside window. It let in light and a little blue sky, but it was still a hospital room with its hospital smells and a foreboding of a bad outcome. It was Tuesday, seven in the morning, and Jaylene was up and eating break-fast when Decker arrived. Her eyes landed on his face, her expression a mixture of confusion and apathy. She was still being fed supplemental oxygen, but her color was better. He drew a curtain for privacy and pulled up a chair bedside.

"Hello, Jaylene. How are you feeling?"

She didn't answer, bringing a shaky spoon of corn-flakes to her mouth. Milk dripped down her chin and onto a bib that covered her blue-and-white hospital gown. Emaciated arms poked free from oversize sleeves. He waited until their eyes met before he spoke.

Then he said, "Do you remember me?"

She put the spoon down. "The boy?"

"By the boy, do you mean your son, Joseph?"

She didn't answer. Then her eyes watered. "He left me."

Decker said, "I don't know if he did or didn't, Jaylene, but I can't find him. Any idea where you think he might be?"

"Kansas."

Decker tried not to react. "Kansas?"

"Yeah, Joe's from Kansas."

"Okay." She was mixing up the two Joes in her life. "Do you know anything about Joe's friends?"

Another spoonful of cornflakes. "All gone or in prison."

"Yes, Joe Senior's friends are all gone or in prison. What about Joe Junior's friends?"

A blank look. "The boy?"

"Yes, the boy. What about his friends?"

She gave him another blank stare. Then she said, "Who are you?"

"I'm Detective Peter Decker from Greenbury Police. I called an ambulance for you to go to the hospital last week. Do you remember that?"

She didn't answer; then she gave a small shake of the head, indicating no.

"Do you remember how you got here? In the hospital?"

Her eyes moistened. "A car accident."

Again, she was mixing up two traumatic incidents. It wasn't the time to correct her. And now that she was talking, there was the possibility that her thoughts would become more coherent as time passed. "You look better," Decker said.

Another stare. "Who are you?"

"I'm a policeman. My name is Peter Decker. I came to visit you in the hospital after you were admitted."

She stared at him with intense eyes. "A policeman."

"Yes." Decker paused. "Someone broke into your house, Jaylene. Do you remember that?"

"Ask the boy."

"I'm trying to find Joseph, but I can't seem to locate him."

"He was there."

Decker bit his lip, trying not to rush things. "Joseph was there when someone broke into your house?"

"Someone broke into my house?"

"Yes. What do you remember about that?"

"Ask the boy."

They were going in circles. Decker said, "What

would the boy say if I asked him about people breaking into your house?"

"I don't know." Jaylene pushed aside her cornflakes. She picked up a coffee cup, but then put it down. "It's cold."

"I'll get you some fresh hot coffee."

"Thank you."

Decker walked over to the nurses' station and snagged a busty, short woman who looked to be in her sixties. She had gray, curly hair and light brown eyes. Her tag told Decker that she was Aileen Jackson, RN. "Excuse me, could someone get Jaylene Boch a fresh cup of hot coffee?"

Her eyes narrowed. "This is a restricted area, sir."

A smoker's voice. "I'm Detective Peter Decker from Greenbury Police." He showed her his badge. "I needed to talk to Mrs. Boch regarding her missing son, but her memory isn't sharp. I'll come back tomorrow and see if she's a little less confused. In the meantime, can I get her a fresh cup of coffee?"

"You shouldn't be here talking to her, especially after yesterday." A hard stare. "You guys don't give up, do you?"

"You guys?"

"You and the two who were here yesterday."

Decker took a deep breath. "Who was here yesterday?"

Aileen sneered. "Don't you people talk to each other?"

"Ma'am, what are you talking about?"

"The two policemen who came here yesterday, right after we moved Jaylene into her hospital room. They said they needed to talk to her about something important, but as soon as they entered the room, her blood pressure and heart rate shot straight up. I ordered them to leave, had to shout at them, actually. It took us a while to stabilize her." When Decker didn't answer, Aileen suddenly because cautious. "Fellow cops, right?"

"Not my colleagues."

"They were policemen. I saw their badges. They were legitimate."

"If you saw their badges, did you get their names?"

"Well, no." Aileen swallowed hard.

"They didn't say their names when they identified themselves?"

"No, but they showed me their badges."

"Which should have had their names and ID numbers." When Aileen went silent, Decker said, "Which police department were they from?"

"I think it was Hamilton PD."

"They were from Hamilton PD?"

"I think."

"Were they in uniform?"

"No." She glared at Decker. "You're not in uniform."

"No, I'm not. I haven't worn a uniform in thirty years." A beat. "Was one of the detective Vietnamese, by any chance?"

"No. Two white men."

"Okay. Young? Old?"

"I don't know if I should be talking to you."

"Actually, I'm the one you should be talking to, because I went through the security desk as witnessed by my fancy stick-on visitor's name tag. Plus, you know my name and where I'm from and I didn't cause Jaylene Boch to have a panic attack. What did the two men look like?"

"They were older white men. Nothing remarkable about the way they looked. I didn't give them much thought until they came into the hospital room and Mrs. Boch's vitals went through the roof. We had an emergency situation."

Decker's jaw began working overtime. "I'm going to call someone from my department to send a police guard to watch her room. No one who isn't on staff goes in or out without my permission."

"Why should I take orders from you? I don't even know who you are."

"Yes, you do," Decker said. "I'm Detective Peter Decker of Greenbury police, and right now, I'm the one in charge. But just so everyone feels okay with this, I will clear this through the hospital administration. I have to go back to the room to keep an eye on her. I don't think it was an accident that her vitals went nuts after she saw those two men. They might have had something to do with the attack."

"What attack?"

"Jaylene Boch was attacked." Decker headed back until he was in front of the doorway to Jaylene's semi-private room. Nurse Jackson had followed him. He said, "You didn't know?"

"I knew she was brought in here severely dehydrated."

"Because she had been tied to her wheelchair and left to die. Her son is missing. She needs to be protected. No one in or out without my permission no matter how many badges they flash."

"They looked legitimate—their badges."

"The men may have been legitimate, ma'am, but without names, I can't verify anything." He looked at the forlorn lady. "It's not anyone's fault, Ms. Jackson.

They might be detectives. I just have to find out who they were." He took out a cell phone. "I need to make a couple of calls. Could we get her a fresh cup of coffee, please?"

"I'm not leaving you alone. I don't know if you're spinning me a yarn or what."

"Then could you call someone to get her a cup of coffee?"

"I'm not budging from this spot, and you really shouldn't be using the cell phone out here. There's an area right down the hall."

"I'm not budging, either, Nurse Jackson. It looks like we're at a Mexican stand-off."

"I could call security."

"You're not going to do that." Decker brought up his Favorites list on his cell phone and punched in Tyler's name. "Then you'll have to admit you were snowed by two men posing as cops."

"They might have been cops," she said. "You said that yourself."

Tyler's voice mail kicked in. Decker left a message and hung up. "Yes, I did say that." He thought a moment. "I know you said that you don't remember what they looked like. But maybe if you sat with a police artist."

Her face softened. "Maybe."

"Could I arrange something? It would really help us out."

"If it would help, I suppose I could."

"Could you get Mrs. Boch a fresh cup of coffee?"

"She shouldn't be drinking anything too hot. In case you hadn't noticed, she has limited control over her right arm."

"Can you still get her a fresh cup of *warm* coffee?"

"I'll see what I can do." She stared at him. "You want a cup?"

"That would be grand. Just black—no cream or sugar." Decker smiled. "See, it's better to be friends than enemies, right?"

"I wouldn't say that," Aileen countered. "With my enemies, I know where I'm at. With friends, you never, ever know."

Chapter 24

With a Greenbury uniform outside Jaylene Boch's room, Decker spent over an hour coordinating with the hospital. Although there were forms to fill out and hurdles to jump, he found the administration to be cooperative. It took over an hour for the paperwork, and once that was out of the way, Decker left St. Luke's for work. Once in his car, he excoriated himself for being so slow to find the two men in the Toyota Camry. Greenbury was leisurely, downright soporific, compared to the pace of Los Angeles, but a homicide is a homicide, and he should have gone at it with full force. After beating his chest in the Latin *mea culpa*s and the Hebrew *al chait*s, he stopped the rumination and was back in business mode. From his car, he called up Wendell Tran and gave him a brief update.

Over the line, he said, "I'm going back to Greenbury to pull out a police Identikit. Aileen Jackson, the nurse who actually saw faces, agreed to meet us there in the afternoon. Would four o'clock work for you?"

"Randy's got a court case, but I'll be there." A pause over the phone. "Who are these guys, and why do you think they're from our police department?"

"I'll answer your second question first. The nurse believes that the badges she saw were from Hamilton, but she isn't sure. I don't know if they're actually from your department or just pretending to be."

"Well, nobody I know in Hamilton was assigned to go to visit Jaylene, but I'll check just to make sure I didn't miss anything. My opinion is they're frauds."

"I agree," Decker said. "These two guys may be the same ones we found on CCTV leaving Canterbury Lane the night Brady Neil was murdered. They may also be the same ones who broke into Lennie Baccus's apartment and stole the original Levine murder files. What those two things have in common is anyone's guess. But we do know is that Jaylene Boch panicked when she saw them. I've got a uniform watching over her room."

"From Greenbury?"

"Until we know that they're not associated with Hamilton—present or past—I think that's wise."

Tran reluctantly agreed. "I'll update Baccus. Have you gotten anything out of Jaylene?"

"No, she's still confused. I'm hoping that her brain will clear with time. Her panic at seeing those two men is the most revealing thing we have so far."

Tran said, "You know what bothers me?"

"Yeah, why Jaylene wasn't murdered along with the boys. I can't answer that. Maybe she had a heart attack or a stroke with all the stress. I'm sure whoever did it thought she'd die."

"Why not just kill her? Why leave it up to chance?"

"I don't know. That is the most surefire way to make sure she wouldn't talk again. Just whack her head." A thought. "Getting rid of Boch Junior was the main goal. She may have been an afterthought."

"Still, if he—or they—killed two people, why not three?"

"Sparing her life does seem weird." Decker paused. "Maybe he knew her, had a soft spot for her."

"If she knew him, all the more reason to kill her, not just tie her up and hope she dies."

"Yeah, you're right about that." Another pause. "Maybe he didn't notice her at first. She heard what was going on and played dead. I've seen things like this before where families have been murdered, but one person is spared. The killer doesn't perceive that remaining person as a threat—a child or a baby or an elderly person. The maniacal frenzy has subsided, the adrenaline rush is gone, he doesn't have it in him anymore. All he wants to do is escape."

There was a pause over the line. "Then why tie her up?"

"I don't know, Tran. Could be he was intending to finish the job after he killed Boxer, but after the frenzy, he forgot about her. Maybe he was tying her up when Boxer came in and the murderer shifted his attention. Maybe he didn't want to kill her, but he didn't want her calling for help."

"Did she have a phone nearby when you found her?"

"No, she didn't. Maybe the killer took it, because Jaylene does have a cell phone number."

"Makes sense." Tran was quiet for a moment. "I'll relay what you told me to the chief. I'll see you at four."

Decker hung up. When he returned to the station, it was a quarter to three and he was wiped out. Talk about adrenaline depletion. He was so tired that he poured himself a cup of rotten stale coffee. After taking a couple of sips, he spit it out.

McAdams and Butterfield emerged from an interview room, both of them wide-eyed at the bright artificial light. Tyler said, "Don't drink that swill. Use the new pod machine I bought."

"Not strong enough, kiddo. I need a *caffeine* fix." Decker shook his head. "Not a lot of sleep last night, and age creeps up on you."

Butterfield nodded. "Ain't that the truth. Anyway, I was about to get Harvard and me some fresh cups from the new café across the street. I'll pick you up something full strength while Tyler fills you in on our CCTV tapes."

"Yeah, what's going on?"

"Nothing so revealing as seeing their faces clearly, but we have a couple of side views. It's definitely two people in the car, Pete, but we can't even see if it's male or female. They're going by fast, and the quality is really poor."

"We'll work with what we have. How are we doing with our Camry list?"

"Nothing in the area looked promising, so I've expanded the search. I've also asked for any recently stolen Camrys. No luck on either front. Our next step is rented cars."

"I'm working on a list of places within fifty miles," McAdams said. "I'll start making calls after we're done looking at all the CCTV tapes. But if the car was stolen, we're sunk." He gave a small shrug. "Every-thing squared away at the hospital?"

"Jaylene's got a guard on her." Decker recapped

what happened to Butterfield. "I have to organize my thoughts before Aileen Jackson comes in at four. Do we have anything in the way of a police artist?"

Butterfield smiled. "No. It hasn't come up all that often."

"Do we have anyone on the force who can draw?"

"Melanie Sarzo," McAdams said. "She's uniform. When I first came on, she drew me in a caricature."

Butterfield grinned. "I remember that. It was really funny."

"Funny is in the eye of the beholder," McAdams grumped. "I've held a grudge against her ever since. But this'll give her a chance to redeem herself."

"I'll contact her," Butterfield said. "Four o'clock, right?"

"Yes. And while you're making phone calls, ring up Lennie Baccus. She's entitled to see who probably broke into her apartment. And there's always an off chance that she'll recognize them from somewhere else."

"No prob." Butterfield rubbed his eyes. "But first I'll get us all some coffee. After the last two hours, I need to see daylight."

It was a large interview room, but it held a crowd. Besides Decker, there was Melanie Sarzo, the artist cop; McAdams; Butterfield; and Radar from Greenbury. Representing Hamilton was Wendell Tran. Chief Baccus was due to arrive any moment. Lennie Baccus had the unique status of straddling between police stations. It was warm outside, and she was dressed in black cotton pants and a crisp white shirt. Aileen Jackson, the star of the show, had just come from work, so she was still in uniform.

"He had a round face . . ." Aileen was rifling through the police Identikit. "Kinda like this one." She pointed to a figure. "Not as round. It was longer. A long, round face. Like a guy who might have had a long face when he was younger, but he gained weight and now it's round." A glance at Decker. "I really don't know exactly. I just saw them for a few seconds. My focus was on the patient."

"Aileen, you are all we have," Decker said. "Do the best you can."

She nodded with grave solemnity. Whatever job she was assigned to was serious business. Twenty minutes later, they got their first peek at one of the two men who almost gave Jaylene Boch a heart attack.

Melanie Sarzo said, "Is there anything you'd like to add or subtract?"

Aileen stared at the rendition of Person of Interest #1. It took her several moments before she spoke. "Something's off."

"Take your time," Decker said. "We're here for you."

Aileen said, "It's the eyes." Silence. "He gave me a death stare, I remember that. Not that I cared a whit. Glare all you want, just get the heck out the room." A pause. "It was like looking into a vacuum. There was no there there."

"Maybe his eyes were lighter?" Melanie began to erase the shading.

"No, it wasn't just the color; it was something in the eyes themselves. There was no life in them."

"When people are angry, their eyes dilate," Decker said. "If his eyes were dark and dilated, it looks like you're peering into a black hole."

"Maybe."

Melanie went from erasing the shading to darkening it. "Like this?"

"Kinda yeah. Except . . ." She paused. "Maybe the eyes were closer set? Like when you focus on a face that's too close to you. The eyes go together. Am I making any sense?"

"Perfect," Mike Radar said.

When Melanie made the changes, Aileen nodded. "Yeah." Another positive nod. "Yeah, that's it."

Melanie handed it to Decker, who handed it to Tran. "Look like anyone you know?"

The man studied the likeness for a long time. "There are three station houses in Hamilton, and while I don't know everyone, I know most people by sight. He doesn't look familiar. He also looks way older than most of the guys I know."

"Yeah, he looks around my age," Decker said. "If he had been an officer or detective in Hamilton, he would have been active maybe ten to fifteen years ago. Most normal people retire from a real police force in their fifties."

"I think I'm supposed to take umbrage to that," Mike Radar said. "We've been pretty damn busy since you got here, Decker."

"Yeah, I'm just bad news."

"We'll show it to the chief when he gets here," Tran said. "He's been around for a long time."

Lennie Baccus broke in. "Can I see it?"

Tran handed it to her.

As she studied it, the team waited for her to speak. She closed her eyes, then opened them and looked at the face again. Finally, she said, "There's something familiar, but I can't place it."

"Those two guys who came into your apartment complex," Radar said. "Could it be you're remembering one of them as loitering around your building?"

"It would have to be at a subconscious level, sir."

She shrugged. "I don't remember anyone just hanging around the apartment."

Decker said, "Maybe if he was once a Hamilton officer, you're remembering a younger version from your childhood."

"Again, I can't answer that because I don't know why he looks familiar."

"Forensic artists are able to age people; maybe we can go in the other direction," Decker said. "Melanie, is there a way for you to draw this face as a younger man?"

A hesitation. "Not my forte, honestly."

Aileen said, "Can I describe the other face, so I can get home?"

"Of course, Mrs. Jackson," Radar said. "You've been an enormous help. Let's move this along, please."

Within an hour, Aileen Jackson had given them a pretty decent sketch of the two men she saw in the hospital room. After she was excused, Decker said, "Do these men look familiar to anyone?"

Head shakes all around. A moment later, Victor Baccus blew through the door. His dress was immaculate, but his face was flushed. He seemed winded. Lennie regarded her father. "Are you all right?"

"I'm fine. Why shouldn't I be fine?" Baccus was annoyed. "Just in a hurry. What's going on?"

"We have a composite of the two men who represented themselves as Hamilton police officers." Decker handed him the sketches. "Do they look familiar?"

A quick glance. "No one working for the department now, that's for certain."

"I figured that," Decker said. "They're older men, sir. Maybe they were on the force when you were younger? Take another look."

"I don't need another look, Detective. I don't recognize them."

"Thank you, sir," Decker said. "We should circulate the sketches. Put up posters in the community, because these two represented themselves as cops. That's a crime."

Baccus said, "We're showing them our hand if we do that."

"The community should know, don't you think?"

"I suppose you're right. But give me a day or two. I'd like to post the sketches to other agencies online and through police bulletin boards. Ask them to contact me if they have any idea who these two clowns are. Then we talk to the community. Can I keep these, Mike?"

"Let me make copies and I'll give you the originals." Radar left with the sketches and came back a minute later. "Here you go."

Baccus stowed them in a briefcase. "We'll get to the

WALKING SHADOWS · 321

bottom of this. I'll have one of my tech guys post it first thing tomorrow."

"Thank you, Victor. And thank you for your cooperation."

"More than I can say for your people . . . dragging my daughter into your problems." The room went silent. "I'm not being fair. She dragged herself in all by her lonesome. I didn't want her involved in a messy homicide. Maybe if I hadn't pulled her off, she wouldn't be in this fiasco. My bad. But now she's on suspension. She's no good to either of us."

"Sir, I'm in the room," Lennie said. "I'll participate in whatever you need."

"I need you to be safe so I don't have to waste my time babysitting you," Baccus said.

Lennie turned red. Decker stepped up. "I'll take her back. That way I can watch her."

"She's still part of Hamilton PD. You'll do no such thing. Anything else? I need to get home to my wife. She hasn't been doing well lately."

"I'm sorry to hear that," Radar said.

"That's MS," Lennie said. "Like hope, it waxes and wanes."

"For the last six months it's been doing way more waxing than waning." Baccus stood up. "We'll talk tomorrow, Mike."

"Sounds good." After he left, Radar said to the gang, "Let's break it up and get back to work." He turned to Tran. "Thanks for coming down. Can you act as a liaison between us and Hamilton? It would be easier than contacting the chief every time I have a question."

"No problem."

"Thanks." To Decker, Radar said, "A word in my office, Pete?"

Decker raised a brow. That didn't sound good.

As soon as they were alone the captain barked. "Why are you baiting him? *'I'll take Lennie back.'* It makes my life harder, and in return, I make your life harder."

"For the record, none of us *dragged* Lennie into her current situation. Even if she messed up a little, someone should stick up for her."

"Be a knight in shining armor to someone else, okay? Stop making my life so difficult."

"Why did he put her on my team in the first place?"

"Fuck if I know. Maybe she was bugging him to do real homicide and he wanted her out of his hair. Maybe if she was going to make mistakes, he wanted her to do it in someone else's department."

"Then why yank her? I wasn't complaining. And don't tell me it was because he was worried about her safety. As it happens, she's in more danger now."

Radar stared at him. "What exactly are you saying?"

"I'm saying that maybe—just maybe—Baccus wanted to know what was going on with Brady Neil and put her with us to get information on our investigation. When she wasn't forthcoming, he pulled her."

"He didn't need her for information; he could have asked me."

"C'mon. There's always chatter between detectives that you might not be aware of."

"Just back off Hamilton, okay? Stop asking the detectives for favors."

"I want to see the Flint files. If Tran can't get hold of them, can you ask Baccus for them for me? Aren't we supposedly all friends."

"No dice unless you can show me a connection from the Flints to Brady Neil's murder."

"The woman in the hidden photos at the Boch house is probably Margo Flint, and Brady Neil was probably murdered in the Boch house. There's your connection."

"Too tenuous."

"Ah, c'mon!"

"Get me a positive ID that the woman in the photos is Margot Flint and I'll go back to Baccus."

"Okay. Then I'll show the black and whites to Yvonne Apple and Gregg Levine. They were family friends. They could tell me yes or no."

"Let Tran show the sketches to Yvonne and Gregg.

He's in Hamilton, and Gregg and Yvonne live in Hamilton. And before you accuse me of stonewalling, you said yourself that Gregg isn't answering your calls. And we know Yvonne is pissed at you. Am I right?" When Decker didn't answer, Radar said, "There is no conspiracy, Pete."

"I'm not saying there is."

"From everything I know about the Levine murders, it appears that the right people are in prison. I don't know if those black and whites are significant, but until we definitely know who the people in the pictures are, they are insignificant to you. Just concentrate on Brady Neil."

"How about this, Mike? The two guys who were in the hospital are probably the same ones who dumped Brady's body and who broke into Lennie's apartment. I can't separate one from the other. How can I solve a case if I keep hitting roadblocks?"

This time it was Radar who didn't answer.

Decker threw up his hands. "Okay, Captain. What do *you* want me to do?"

Radar blew out air. "I'll see what I can do about getting you the Flint files. But you let Hamilton handle Yvonne and Gregg. In the meantime, don't you have people you need to talk to regarding Brady Neil?"

"Yes, I do have some names."

"Follow them up, and let Hamilton handle its own people."

"Mike, do you believe that Baccus doesn't know who the guys are?"

"Why should I not believe him? Answer that question and I'll answer yours."

Decker didn't push it. He had plans to visit Jack Newsome that weekend. Maybe he'd get some help there. "What about Lennie Baccus? I'm concerned for her safety."

"Her father is as well. Let him handle it. Or don't you trust him with his own daughter?"

"I'm not sure if I do or don't."

"Well, Decker, you're entitled to your thoughts, but stay out of it. If you don't like it, too damn bad. Starting now, you work *with* Tran instead of cajoling him to do your bidding." Radar turned and went back into the bowels of the station house.

Decker had no choice but to follow. Chin up, chest out, grin and bear it. *If you don't like taking orders, you shouldn't have joined the club.*

Chapter 25

He slept in fits and starts—a restless night— waking up before dawn. Tiptoeing out, he went into the kitchen and started the coffee. As quiet as he was, it didn't help. Rina, even on good nights, slept like a shark with one eye always open, and within minutes, she was padding around in the kitchen. Decker attempted a weak smile.

"As long as you're up, I might as well shower and get dressed."

She pointed to a breakfast room chair. "Sit."

He sat.

Then she sat. "I didn't probe last night because it wasn't the time. I decided to wait you out. But that strategy doesn't seem to be helping. I know it takes something big to ruin your sleep."

"I'm fine."

"No, you're not." Rina took in a deep breath and let it out. "Look, if Baccus isn't hiding anything, it makes sense that he doesn't want you running the show. If he is hiding something, he doesn't want you nosing around. Guilty or innocent, it's his territory. And you'd be exactly the same way."

"Yeah, I know."

"Forget about Hamilton. Forget about the Levines and the Flints. Forget about interviewing Gregg Levine. That's probably not going to happen anytime soon. You know that, right?"

"Right."

Rina got up to get the coffee. "With those limitations in mind, what's your approach going to be?"

"I have a few options."

"Talk to me." She thumped a coffee mug in front of him.

"Today I thought I'd check out the guy at Bigstore—Carter Bonfellow."

"Ah, C is for Carter."

"C is also for correct." When Rina smiled, so did he. "I was planning on going yesterday, but then all this business with Jaylene and her cop visitors came up." Decker made quotation marks.

"It's better that it all happened yesterday. If these two guys in the sketches were after Boch and Neil, they might have shown up at Bigstore looking for them. Now you can show the drawings to Carter Bonfellow. See what he has to say."

"Yeah." Decker took a sip of coffee. "Yeah, you're right. I never thought about it that way. Thanks."

"You're welcome. And while you're at it, you'll show the sketches around the entire store. You'll want as much input as possible."

"Of course. I'll be there anyway."

"Ergo, you're in better shape today to interview people than you were yesterday."

"Absolutely."

"You have every right to investigate Bigstore because Brady Neil worked there."

"So did Joseph Boch. Hamilton also has a right to be there."

"Yes, but the place opens at seven. Do you think that Wendell Tran or Randy Smitz will be at Bigstore when someone in a blue, orange, and white apron unlocks the doors?"

Decker chuckled. "No."

"Exactly." Rina took a swig of coffee. "Right now, those two are busy trying to find out the identities of those fake-o cops. And if they aren't fake-o cops, they'll be busy trying to figure out who they actually are and what they're up to. In the meantime, you get yourself a jump start with the sketches."

"Baccus didn't want the faces shown around the community. Not that it'll stop me, but it might piss Radar off."

"Oh please. Bigstore is not the community. It is the workplace of your murder victim." She shrugged. "Call Radar after you're done with your business there if you're concerned."

"You're absolutely right."

Rina looked at her watch. "You have an hour— enough time to get ready and finish your coffee. Would you like a refill?"

"Sure."

Rina filled up his cup. "Are you going to call up McAdams to come with you?"

"No need to wake him up this early. This is a one-man job." A pause. "Thank you. Within five minutes, you've clarified everything. If I need any kind of a partner, it should be you."

"I'll come."

"No, no, no. That was meant as a compliment, not a serious offer. I still have safety concerns."

"I understand. And when you don't sleep well, neither do I. I'm actually a little tired."

"Go back to bed. I'm sorry I was so restless. I should have just woken you up and we could have had this conversation, and then we both could have gotten some sleep last night."

"You weren't ready to have this conversation then. Talking is like comedy. It's all about timing. In the morning everything seems so much more . . . hopeful. There's something new and fresh about the day."

"And a good cup of coffee doesn't hurt, either." Decker got up. "Thank you, Rina. I'm feeling much better. I owe you one. Just add this to the other things that I owe you for."

"You're in deep hock, you know that."

"Yeah, but that'll equalize soon."

"How do you figure that?"

"We're going to Florida, where I've agreed to visit with our mothers."

"You have to go there anyway to meet with Newsome. Is that so terrible, to be a good son and son-in-law?"

"Not at all, but you have to admit that I went along with your idea with a smile on my face."

"When do I beatify you, Saint Peter?"

"Don't bother." Decker stuck out his arms from his shoulders. "It's not worth the holes in my palms, and I don't like hanging upside down."

The sketches sat under plastic sleeves to prevent them from being smudged. The surface was also good for fingerprints if he wanted to go in that direction. Feeling revitalized—showered, shaved, and clad in his usual suit and tie—Decker pulled up into the near-empty lot of Bigstore. The store was located in a gigantic outdoor shopping arena that held the big-box chains as well as a couple of grocery stores, restaurants, small cafés, specialty stores, and two gas stations. It was built at a time when optimism was a bottomless pit. As he parked, he noticed that several of the huge retail spaces had been shuttered, with For Rent signs hanging in the windows. The internet had changed habits, and cruising the aisles with a basket had turned into surfing the web with an icon cart.

In the summertime, the parking lot was often occupied by RVs and campers, people visiting the lushness of New England. A yearly membership fee to the Bigstore chain provided travelers with electrical hook-ups in the lot as well as free showers and discounts at the store. Decker noticed people, waiting with their towels, for the doors to open. He parked and finished the rest of his coffee. He had two minutes to go until opening time when he stepped out of the car. As he walked up to the entrance, he stopped cold.

It seemed that others had the same idea as Rina. "What are you doing here?"

Lennie Baccus was dressed in a long-sleeved white cotton shirt and jeans with espadrilles on her feet. She was holding the sketches in her hand. Her face was as deep red as her fingernails. She looked like an American flag. "I'm on my own time. I can do what I want."

"Not if you're representing yourself as a police officer."

"I am a police officer," she snapped back. "But even if I wasn't, I can show drawings to whoever I want."

"First of all, those sketches are police business. Second, you heard your father. He didn't want this out in the community just yet."

"And here you are doing the same thing."

"I'm a police officer, and this is relevant to my murder case. Furthermore, I'm not under his command." When Lennie didn't answer, he said, "You should go home. You're on suspension."

"I know. I'm totally hamstrung, but it's not going to stop me. Let him fire me."

"If this gets out, he's likely to do just that."

"How will this get out? You're not going to say anything to him. You're already suspicious of him."

Decker said, "That's ridiculous."

"No, it's not. I would be suspicious, if I were you," Lennie said. "I'm suspicious, and I'm his daughter. I love my dad, but he never had much use for me, and he never had any faith in me."

"That's too bad, because you have potential," Decker said.

"Thanks."

Silence settled between them as a young person in an orange, white, and blue apron unlocked the door. Moments later, people started filing in.

Lennie said, "Look, Detective Decker. These two guys showed up at my apartment building and broke into my space. They violated my privacy and scared the crap out of me. I have every right to find out who they are. And if I help the police—Greenbury or Hamilton—I'm also fine with that. But it's secondary. I'm looking after my own safety."

"I don't know if showing the sketches around will help your well-being."

"Maybe not. But a gal's gotta do what a gal's gotta do."

"You've certainly grown a set in the last week."

"I'll take that as a compliment. Time's a-wasting, Detective. I still have to show up at a desk by nine. If I'm a minute late, people will notice."

Decker shook his head. If she was going to tread

his territory, he might as well make the rules. "Okay, Officer Baccus. If we're mining the same ground, we should at least have a plan."

She tried to stifle the smile on her lips. "I want to tell you that if I do find something . . . dicey with my dad, I'm not going to whitewash anything."

"I believe you." Decker raised his eyebrows. "Last week, when we came here together, you talked to people at the café. Start there. Maybe if these two jokers came here, sniffing around for Boch and Neil, they bought a cup of coffee."

"Okay."

"I still haven't talked to Olivia Anderson—the girl who dated Brady Neil—because other stuff kept getting in the way. I need to do that. If she's in today, you can set that up for me."

"She is in. I already checked. And I will set it up for you. What time?"

"I want to talk to a few people before then. How about eight? After I talk to her, we'll compare notes and then you can get back to your desk job."

"Perfect. Anything else?"

"No."

"Can I get you a cup of coffee, sir? Double espresso black?"

"Stop trying to impress me. You've already done

that by showing up. And I'm fine right now. Maybe later." A pause. "Thanks."

She smiled. "I don't know why, but you remind me of my former sergeant."

"We're both redheads. Or at least I was in my salad days."

Lennie looked at him quizzically. "You've never seen her. How do you know she's a redhead?"

Decker paused, surprised she caught his slipup.

Lots of potential.

He said, "X-ray vision, Officer. Don't overstep your authority. I'll talk to you later."

Seven-fifteen in the morning and Carter Bonfellow was at his desk, his focus on his paperwork. When his brown eyes lifted, they widened. He lowered the pen in his hand onto his desk. "I was wondering when you were coming back."

"You've been expecting me."

"I've been expecting someone since Joseph Boch disappeared."

"No one's talked to you?"

"Not yet."

Decker nodded. "When we last spoke, you said you didn't know him."

The eyes narrowed. "I said I didn't know a guy

named Boxer. I do know who Joseph Boch is . . . was."
A pause. "Is it present or past tense?"

"Your guess is as good as mine." Decker flashed him
a smile. "Do you have a minute?"

Bonfellow straightened up in his chair. "Yeah, sure."

Decker pulled up a chair and sat on the opposite side
of the desk. Bonfellow was wearing a red polo shirt.
His build was square and his head was on the smallish
side. With his sandy-colored hair—thin and parted to
one side—he looked like a Bloody Mary with a lemon
slice on top.

Decker said, "You told me the last time we talked
that you were the eyes and ears of the place. I was
wondering if you've heard anything that might help
the investigation."

Droplets of sweat materialized on Bonfellow's forehead. He didn't look nervous, just excited to be included
in the intrigue. "Well . . ." Hands clasped together. "I
never saw anything, but there are rumors circulating
that Neil and Boch were dealing."

"Okay. Want to tell me about it?"

"You want my opinion?"

"I do." A thin smile appeared on Bonfellow's lips. It
was probably the first time that someone ever took him
seriously. Decker was happy to contribute to his ego.
"Tell me what you think."

"Well . . ." A brief smile. "I think people are nervous. If they were involved in something bad—like dealing—it gives a reason to the insanity."

"Good insight," Decker said. "Were they involved in something bad?"

"I don't know. As I said, I never saw anything. But they spent a *lot* of time in private conversation," Bonfellow said. "I remember seeing them talking in the commissary, looking around like someone was watching them. Very hush-hush."

"Any idea what they were saying?"

"No, but it had to be something intense. They sat in a corner, and every time someone walked by and said hello, they stopped talking."

"Let me ask you this," Decker said. "Were there any rumors about them stealing merchandise? I know that Brady used to deal in used electronics."

"There's always a junk pile. People break things. Sometimes the store just takes it off as a loss and doesn't return it. But stealing new stuff?" He shrugged. "I kind of doubt that. They've got hidden cameras all over the place."

"They do?"

"Yeah. Everywhere. And since they were never fired, I have to assume that they weren't stealing new material."

"By hidden cameras everywhere, you mean . . ."

"I mean everywhere. And they change locations so the employees never know," Bonfellow said. "The cameras are meant to catch shoplifters. But I imagine they catch a crooked employee now and then. Lots of cameras in the warehouse and in electronics. But people will steal anything and I mean anything. Security once caught a guy trying to steal a barbell in his rain jacket."

"How do you know about this?"

Again, he straightened his spine. "I listen to people talk. Plus, I've been down in Security when I had to take care of some paperwork for them. It's on the lower level, but you can only get down there with a badge. They've got banks of monitors shooting from every angle possible."

"Who's the head of Security?"

"Benton Horsch."

"Do you have his number?"

"I have Security's extension. Would you like me to call it for you?"

In the last couple of minutes, the little man seemed to have grown in stature. Decker said, "Yes, I would like to speak with them, but not just yet." He took out the two sketches and placed them on the desk. "Do either of these men look familiar to you?"

Bonfellow regarded the drawings. "Are these the killers?"

"Just people of interest. Have you seen them before?"

A long hard stare. "If I've seen them, I don't remember where or when. If I could keep these, I'll look for them."

"No, I don't want you to do that. If the answer is no, then it's no."

"Sorry." A shake of the head. He seemed truly disappointed that he didn't know the men.

Decker said, "Could you call Security for me?"

"Sure." A pause. "Anything else?"

"Just need to talk to Security." A smile. "You've been a big help, Mr. Bonfellow."

A grin. "Thank you."

The compliment seemed to lighten his weighted face.

Decker's good deed for the day.

Security was a cavern that took up the entire footprint of the store above. It was windowless, overly brightened by artificial light in some places and barely lit in others. Dozens of monitors showed dozens of angles, including the warehouse and the parking lot. Horsch was leading Decker into his office, navigating dozens of twists and turns. Judging from Decker's height, Horsch was about six two and broad across the chest: a weight lifter's torso on a basketball player's legs. He appeared to be in his forties. He had dark eyes, dark bushy hair, and a dark, thick mustache. He wore a black uniform with HEAD OF SECURITY emblazoned in gold across his front pocket.

Horsch's office had walls filled with TV monitors that were constantly changing angles. Anyone sensitive to strobe lights would have gone crazy. "Have a seat." His voice was low and raspy. After Decker pulled up a chair, he said, "What can I do for you?"

"Probably a lot. I have to think this through." After a moment, he said, "I'm looking for these two men." He placed the sketches on Horsch's desk. "These two people are persons of interest in several ongoing investigations concerning your former employees—Brady Neil and Joseph Boch."

"Got it." He looked at the sketches and shrugged. "I'm here in the bat cave. I don't do a lot of hunting in the flesh."

"But you have tapes. Lots and lots of tapes."

"For our use only. And they're not typical CCTV tapes. Everything is computerized by dates. It'll take you hours to sort through one day with all those monitors."

"We'd start by looking at the parking lot, the electronics department, and the warehouse. I know it's a lot of viewing, but if these two guys showed up at the store, they wouldn't know they're on camera and we could get their faces. That's much better than a sketch done from the memory of a woman who wasn't really paying attention."

"You're not even from Hamilton."

"True. We're from Greenbury. Brady Neil is my homicide case. But I can get someone from Hamilton PD, if you want."

A pause. "Why do you need the parking lot?"

"I have an idea what they may have been driving."

Horsch bit his mustache with the tips of his lower incisors. "I have to pull off someone to supervise you. That means I'll be one man short, and someone already called in sick. I'm down to seven people watching the monitors and four others monitoring the customers in the stores. How long will you be at it?"

"Depends how many cameras you have on the spots I mentioned."

"Around three dozen cameras, maybe more. Electronics department is noted for pilfering, and we always have cameras in the warehouse and on the parking lots."

"What can I say, Mr. Horsch. We need to do what we need to do."

"Call me Ben." Again he bit his mustache. "When do you want to start?"

"Today. This is a murder investigation."

"I don't know if I can swing it today. I have to talk to my secretary about scheduling. I'll give you a call, and even that won't be until the afternoon."

"I'll take whatever you give me. Thank you very much, Ben."

"You're welcome, Detective."

"Pete."

"You're welcome, Pete."

Joining Lennie Baccus and Olivia Anderson, Decker drank coffee with the women at an orange table, sitting on orange plastic chairs. The girl who once dated Brady Neil was nineteen with poker-straight dishwater-colored hair and hazel eyes. Her complexion was more olive than rose, and she gave the overall impression of beige. She was around five five and stick thin, and it didn't take long for the tears to come. She dried her face on a paper napkin.

"He made me laugh."

Decker nodded, giving her a small smile. "Good sense of humor?"

"I guess." A sniffle. "He just did kinda goofy things." She stared at her coffee cup. "He took me to nice places. He always paid."

"What kind of nice places?" Lennie asked,

"Pastamania, Steaks!" A pause. "He once even took me to brunch at the Marriott. We didn't date very long. He said it wasn't me . . . that he just had important things to take care of." Tears again. "Of course, I thought it was me. That's just what guys say to be nice. But I never did see him with another girl. And Carmen and Rhonda were always flirting with him. If he wanted another girlfriend, he could have had one. But I never saw him with either of them, so maybe it was the truth."

"I think it was the truth," Decker said.

Her head came up. "Really?"

"Yes, really," Decker answered. "When did he break up with you?"

"About six months ago. He was still friendly. I kept hoping that his business thing would clear up and we could date again. But he . . ." Head down, back staring at her coffee.

"Did Brady ever mention his father to you?"

She raised her eyes, a look of confusion in them. "He told me his father was dead."

"Okay."

"He's not dead?"

"No, his father is in prison."

"Oh." A pause. "Well, maybe it was embarrassing for him."

"I'm sure it was," Decker said. "Brady seemed to have zero ties to his dad. Then he started visiting him about six months ago. Any idea why?"

"No. Like I said, Brady told me his dad was dead." A pause. "Wow. In prison. I did not know that."

"What else did he tell you about himself or his family?"

The girl thought hard. "Actually, he didn't talk much about himself. I mean, we talked about work. We had that in common. But we didn't have these long, meaningful conversations. It was mostly a movie, then a dinner, and during dinner we'd talk about the movie. He liked video games. Does that help?"

Decker smiled. "Everything you tell me helps. I don't want to get too personal, but were you two ever intimate?"

Olivia pinkened, the first bit of color she displayed. "I live with my parents. He had his own place in the basement of his mother's house. We'd go there whenever we wanted privacy. Afterward we'd play video games on his iPad or watch Netflix."

"Did you two ever do drugs together?"

She blushed, the pink deepening. "Maybe we'd smoke weed, but it's legal now, kinda. He liked beer, but always had white wine for me. He was a real goofaloof, but he could also be a real classy guy."

"I can see that," Decker said. "Did he ever take strange phone calls in front of you? Things where he talked in privacy?"

Slowly, she shook her head no.

"How about at Bigstore? Did you two hang out on your breaks together? Eat lunch together?"

"No." She took in a breath and let it out. "He didn't want it getting out that we were seeing each other. I don't know why. Tons of employees hang out. I mean, in this town, where else are you going to meet people except church and work?"

"Did Brady hang out with anyone else?" Lennie asked.

"No, I told you I never saw him with another girl."

"How about guys?" Decker said.

"Oh, I get it. You mean Boxer. Yeah, they were friends. They used to eat lunch together almost every day. I never understood why Brady liked him. He's kind of a loser. I mean, thirty-five and still working in the stockroom? Brady was already manager of electronics, and he was ten years younger."

"He had ambition, then."

"Yes, he sure did." Her eyes moistened a third time. "But the two of them seemed to be real tight. Always talking and when I came over, they'd get real quiet. It was weird, but sometimes opposites attract. Like me and my friend Grayson. I'm fun loving, and she's, like, really studious. She wants to be a medical receptionist. We're totally different, but we get along really well."

"All sorts of things go into making a friendship," Lennie said.

"Right." Olivia nodded. "Exactly." A pause. "I really need to get back to work."

Decker gave her his card. "I know you have Officer Baccus's number, but here's mine. If you can think of anything else . . . even the smallest thing, let me know."

"Brady liked M&M candy. Does that count?"

"Sure." Decker showed her his notepad. "See? I wrote it down."

Olivia got up and attempted a smile. It came out as a sour aftertaste. "Thanks for the coffee."

"Sure. And feel free to call me any time."

"Find the guy who did this."

"That's my goal, Olivia, that's my goal."

Walking out to the parking lot, Lennie said, "She didn't tell us much."

"Nothing important," Decker said. "But she did reinforce the timeline. Six months ago, Brady Neil dropped her and started visiting his father. She said he was busy with something. It all fits. He was on a mission."

"What do you think it was? Clearing his dad?"

"Maybe. But that wasn't going to happen. It doesn't matter if Gratz or Masterson pulled the trigger or not. The Levines died as a result of the robbery. Brandon and Kyle are responsible for the deaths."

"But if they didn't shoot them, it means the actual shooters got away." She laughed. "How profound, Officer Obvious."

Decker smiled. "Obvious, but correct."

"What did you find out from Bonfeller?"

"Bonfellow. I found out that the store has hidden security cameras all over the place. And that's all I'm going to say since you're not officially part of the investigation." When she rolled her eyes, Decker said, "Stop that. You're lucky I'm not reporting you to your dad."

"As if." She stopped in front of her car. "This is me." She punched in her code on the driver's door. But instead of disarming the car, she turned on the alarm. "WTF? That's so weird."

"What is?"

She punched in the code again. "I know I put the alarm on. I'm supercareful, especially after what happened at my apartment." She reached for the door handle, but Decker stopped her. He gave her his handkerchief.

"Just in case there are prints."

"Right." She opened the door. The glove compartment was wide open. Her owner's manual, maps, flashlight, and sunglasses were spilled onto the floor. "God, they weren't even trying to be subtle."

"They must have been following you." He was irritated. "Didn't you notice anything?"

"No, I didn't notice anything. And I looked, I swear it. I really, really look around."

"Sorry." Decker took a deep breath and let it out. "I didn't mean to accuse you of being sloppy. They must be real pros."

"This is awful." She started to bite her thumbnail but then stopped. "They have the Levine files. What could they possibly be looking for now?"

Decker just shook his head. He had some ideas, but he was confused as well.

She clicked her nails. "I suppose you're going to call the police."

"We are the police. But if you're asking if I'm calling up Tran and Smitz, the answer is yes. They have to be notified because I want Hamilton's Scientific Investigative Division to go over the car. Let me think for a moment. I've got to figure this out."

"Sure." A pause. "You want that coffee now?"

Decker smiled, but he shook her off. "Okay. This is the plan. You wait here for Tran and Smitz and let them know what happened."

"They're going to wonder what I was doing here with you when I'm supposed to be on suspension."

"You weren't with me, Lennie. I had no idea that you were coming. And if you don't want to tell them that you came to Bigstore to play rogue detective, tell them you get your morning coffee here and shoot the shit with the girls who run the café. You ran into me when the doors opened. You went one way, I went the other way. You can also tell them that I insisted on walking you back to your car. Then you noticed it had been tampered with and we called the police. Shouldn't be hard to remember because it's all true."

"What about Olivia Anderson?"

"Don't worry about that. If it comes up, I'll take care of it, okay?"

"Okay. Where will you be?"

"In Security. Like I said, the place has hidden cameras everywhere, including this behemoth of a parking lot. We know when you came, but I don't know where the cameras are. Maybe—just maybe—we'll get lucky."

Chapter 26

Most of the outside cameras monitored people going in and out of the enormous sets of glass front doors. This was the way that security caught 90 percent of the shoplifters. Those with sticky fingers claimed that they were distracted and just forgot to pay. This worked with little items such as makeup—the number one filched item—but it was a little harder to claim memory loss when trying to stuff a Game Boy under a trench coat. Regardless of the item, Bigstore's policy was always the benefit of the doubt. If the person went back inside and paid for the item, there was no need to involve the police.

Sometimes the items were so well hidden a person could leave the store without triggering the alarms. There were alarms in the parking lot, however, and when the thief attempted to stuff the item into their trunk, a silent alarm went off. The cameras in the parking lot provided backup evidence. Monitors also picked up a fair share of car break-ins.

Supervisor Benton Horsch—miffed, at first, by the interference of police—soon warmed up to the idea of being a linchpin in a real police investigation. He was in his office, at his computer, which was hooked up to dozens of mounted TV monitors. He was checking out squares of black-and-white images. He asked Lennie Baccus, "Where were you parked again?"

"Orange between 2B and 2C."

He moved the mouse over a list of images. "Possibly we can pick you up on this camera . . . hold on." A click of the mouse. "No, that won't work, either. Let's try a different angle. Hold on while I download the videos." The camera was picking up multiple angles, flashing between the images. He pressed pause. "This looks like a Kia Optima."

The image showed the windshield and part of the grille, including the top half of a license plate. Also discernible in the frozen frame was the top half of the passenger's front door.

Lennie shouted, "That's my car!" She announced her license plate ID, which corresponded with the truncated letters and numbers. "Oh my God, I can't believe we actually found something on the cameras."

"It's not that unusual. We do put them at strategic spots." Horsch seemed irritated. "When did you show up at Bigstore?"

"I was here before they opened the doors."

"Okay. Then we'll backtrack the monitor to before seven in the morning." He placed the camera in fast reverse. The video contents flew by fast and blurry. It was impossible to make out images.

"How about"—Horsch pressed the stop button—"we start at six-forty-five since you don't know exactly when you arrived."

"Sure," Lennie said.

Horsch pressed start. At twelve minutes to seven in the morning, the monitor showed Lennie's Kia pulling into the parking spot. She got out a minute later and turned right and soon was out of the range of the camera.

"Great definition of the features on the face," Decker noted.

"We have two-year-old equipment. Not the latest incarnation, but it's pretty new," Horsch said. "It's an all-digital setup, not that grotty CCTV film, and the resolution is decent."

"Best clarity I've seen," Decker said.

The three of them sat in silence, watching people stroll by. There were young women holding babies and toddlers to their chest or wheeling them in a Big-store shopping cart. Others walked quickly, grasping the hands of school-age children. Older couples were pushing empty leg-high shopping carts that they had brought with them. Families were going in with towels and exiting with wet heads, holding bloated Bigstore bags—supplies for the next leg of their journey.

After some time had passed, Decker said, "We were in Bigstore for around an hour and a half. I know you're a busy man. If you want to do other things, we're fine."

"No one touches my equipment except my people," Horsch said. "It's also better if I'm here. I can swear that you didn't monkey with anything."

"I understand. I just didn't want to waste your time."

"Not a waste of time to catch a break-in," Horsch said. "It looks good on everyone's record." To Lennie, "Is anyone processing your car?"

"Two detectives from Hamilton arrived twenty minutes ago. They're waiting for a forensic team to get here."

"Tran and Smitz?" After Lennie nodded yes, Decker asked, "Chief Baccus show up?"

Lennie made a sour face. "He wasn't there when I left to come here, but I'm sure he'll hear about it." Her nails clicked. "No one's going to believe that we came separately."

"Not my problem."

"Tran and Smitz seemed annoyed with me. They can't understand why I didn't pick up a tail. I was looking out of my mirrors all the time."

"It's hard to pay attention to someone following you and drive at the same time."

"I swear I was looking around—"

"Freeze the frame," Decker interrupted. Horsch stopped the digital tape. The image centered on a man who was approaching Lennie's car. His face was turned with three-quarters visible to the camera. To Lennie. "One of our guys?"

"The heavier one?"

"Yeah. Him."

Lennie looked at the composite police drawing and then at the image. "Could be."

Decker said, "Could you slow it down from this point forward, Mr. Horsch?"

"Ben," Horsch replied. "Sure."

Unknown Man stopped at the Kia and looked around. Decker sat up. "Just how much no good are you up to?" Unknown Man checked over his shoulder and bounced on his feet. Miraculously, he turned, and just for a moment, he was facing the lens. He was a stocky fellow. In the black-and-white video, he appeared to have a full face with white hair and dark eyes. He was wearing a bomber jacket—overly heavy in such warm weather. It also didn't go with the board shorts that showed muscular legs and flip-flops on his feet. The big bulky jacket meant he was carrying tools.

Horsch paused the frame and wrote down the time to the exact hundredth of a second. "That's a good image."

"That's a great image!" Decker said.

Lennie looked at the police rendering. "Not a *bad* likeness."

"I wonder if any frames show his wrists."

"For the tattoo."

"Exactly."

"I'll keep going then." Horsch pressed the play button. The camera was advancing at half-speed. Unknown Man kept going in and out of the camera lens as it flashed to other angles of the parking lot, and then back again to the Kia. Unknown Man appeared to be walking around the car, hands in his pocket. Slowly the images advanced. Four minutes, twenty-three seconds later, another unknown man, designated by Decker as UM#2, arrived at the Kia. He was also wearing a jacket. The two men conversed. Then UM#2 went to the driver's side of the car and ducked down—out of range of the camera—for at least five minutes. UM#1 stood at the front of the car, clearly acting as a lookout. After UM#2 popped back up, he fiddled with the front passenger door until it swung open. UM#1 went around so that the door hid most of his body. Then he ducked, probably sifting through the car's contents from the passenger side. Both men were lost to the camera's lens.

They were out of range for over five minutes. When they popped up again, they conferred for a moment, then appeared to go their separate ways. The men were on-screen for twelve minutes, forty-two seconds. Although the camera captured a good image of UM#1, his accomplice male, UM#2, never appeared full-faced in the lens's eye. Horsch stopped the progress of the digital tape.

"I'll splice out this clip and give it to you."

"That's great for evidence if we get them. What I really need are their vehicles. I'm assuming it's two vehicles since they arrived at different times. But it could have been they staged it that way. Or possibly one of them took an Uber." A pause. "Do you have Uber in Hamilton?"

"Uber and Lyft."

"That would be the best of both worlds because then the company would have a record. Anyway, is there a way you can pick them up as they walk to their cars?"

"It would involve using other cameras," Horsch said. "It will take a while."

"It's important."

Horsch said, "I have to fiddle around with other cameras, but I'll do my best."

"Thank you. It's a major case." Decker turned to Lennie. "Why don't you wait here while Mr. Horsch is setting things up? I'll go talk to Tran and Smitz. Possibly those two jokers left behind usable shoe prints."

"I can do it for you—" She stopped, remembering she was suspended, then said, "Uh, good plan. Sure."

Within an hour, Decker got the make and model of UM#2's vehicle. No plates visible. When he checked with the local DMV, he discovered that the same make and model had been reported stolen three hours ago. He recongregated with Lennie, Tran, and Smitz, watching SID work. Tran wore black slacks and a yellow shirt, sleeves rolled up at the elbow. Smitz was dressed in a blue suit and a white shirt but no tie. He was fair to the point of being bleached. He'd burn quickly in the morning sun. Perhaps that's why he was wearing a cowboy hat.

By the time Chief Baccus arrived—clad in uniform—Decker had a good face shot of UM#1 pulled from the digital disc. He presented Baccus with the image; the chief studied it for a long time. "I wish I knew who he was, but I don't."

Decker regarded his face. No deception that he could see. "You can keep that, show it around."

"This guy is around my age, maybe older. People in the department aren't going to know him if I don't."

"Right."

"But I'll post it anyway. Whoever he is, he's not a cop in my department. Maybe you should show it to your captain."

"Absolutely."

"It could be someone from Greenbury's past."

"Absolutely."

Baccus turned to his daughter. "Are you okay?"

"I'm fine. I wish that I knew what they were looking for. Whatever it is, I don't have it."

"What were you doing here at Bigstore in the first place? You know you're on desk duty."

"Of course, sir. I was just getting my morning coffee before work. I come here once or twice a week."

"And you just happened to run into him?" Meaning Decker.

"Yes, sir."

Baccus looked at Decker, who waited for a question. One thing he learned: never volunteer anything. "What about you?" the chief finally said.

"Working on the Brady Neil case. Showing the sketches around."

"I wanted you to wait until I posted the images on police bulletin boards."

"Sir, with all due respect, Neil was an employee here. I was showing them to people he worked with, not a community."

Baccus made a sour face. "Any luck?"

Decker pointed to the clear image of UM#1. "This is luck." A pause. "We've just got to get someone to identify him. I'll post it on our websites and put it in our local paper. If you could do the same for the *Hamiltonian*?"

"I suppose that would be a good game plan," Baccus admitted.

"Thank you, sir."

A woman from Forensics, dressed in blue scrubs and shoe covers, ripped off her gloves. "We're done here. We have a lot of prints." She turned to Lennie. "I know you have a card on file, but it's always better to get fresh prints. We'll need them for elimination."

"Of course."

Baccus said, "I'm going back to work." He turned to Lennie. "My office. Three o'clock."

"Yes, sir." After Baccus walked away, she sighed. "Not going to be good."

"Maybe not for you, but this is a great outcome for the case," Decker said.

"Spoken like a true homicide detective." Tran shook his head. "The only thing that was hidden in Boch's house were those old black-and-white pictures. If that's what they were looking for, why would they assume that Lennie has them?"

"She stole the file, so maybe she also has the pictures," Smitz said.

"I didn't *steal* anything!" Lennie said.

Decker said, "Who, besides a police officer, would know that she had taken the files home?"

No one spoke. Then Tran said, "You think it's someone from our department. I'm telling you that this joker isn't one of us."

"I'm not saying he is. But there is a possibility of a leak."

"Maybe from your department, not from us," Smitz said.

"Maybe." Decker didn't argue. He knew everyone in Greenbury. No one was a candidate for a mole. But Baccus had a point. Decker couldn't rule out that the unknown men were people from Greenbury's past. "If no one needs me, I'm going back to work." He hit the photograph. "I need to let my people know about this." He looked up. "By the way, I'm going to be out of town this weekend. I'm leaving on Friday, but I'll be reachable on my cell. If something comes up, please call me."

"Where to?" Tran asked.

"Visiting my ninety-four-year-old mother."

"Is she ill?" Smitz said.

"No, not ill, just ninety-four. She lives in Florida, and I haven't seen her in over a year. It's time."

"Have a good one," Smitz said.

"A good one?" Decker laughed. "It's clear you've never met my mother."

Chapter 27

After posting the CCTV camera shot and the two sketches on the Greenbury Police Department bulletin board, Decker began looking up the current roster of Hamilton PD. Within a few minutes, Radar was at his desk, peering over his shoulder.

"What the hell are you doing, Decker?"

"No need for profanities, Captain. I'm just thinking that someone had to know that Lennie took the Levine files home."

"Shut that down," Radar snapped. "My office. Now."

Decker was irritated but kept it to himself. He slowly made his way to Radar's office. The captain had a distasteful look on his face, as if he had just bitten into a mealy apple.

"I am not looking for a conspiracy, okay?" Decker closed the door. "I'm attempting to find out how anyone other than a cop could have known about the file being checked out."

"If they posed as cops before, they could have posed as cops to the person who was in charge of Hamilton's archives. A secretary wouldn't know every cop on the force. Between uniforms and detectives, Hamilton must have close to one hundred police officers."

"Well, then let me take the sketches over to Hamilton archives and see if I can't get an ID from the receptionist." When Radar didn't respond, Decker said, "If it is one of them, they're not going to police themselves."

"That's not necessarily true. Anyway, this isn't what I wanted to talk about. What were you thinking . . . working with Lennie Baccus?"

"I wasn't working with her. She showed up—"

"Yeah, to get morning coffee. You really think I'm buying what you're selling?"

"You should, because it's the truth . . . mainly."

"Mainly?"

"She went to Bigstore for the same reason I went to Bigstore. To get an ID on the men in the police sketches. I didn't go with her. We met by chance at the front doors before the store opened."

"You should have just sent her home."

"I suggested it. She didn't take my suggestion. I

don't have control over a grown woman. What did you expect me to do? Call her dad?"

"I didn't expect you to work with her."

"I didn't. We went our separate ways."

"Meaning you two didn't coordinate efforts or anything like that?"

"She was going to ask around at the café. I was fine with that. She knows people there. I went straight to Carter Bonfellow to ask him a few questions."

"Who's he?"

After Decker explained, he said, "Carter was the one who told me about Security's cameras. My thoughts were to see if these guys had ever been in Bigstore. And if they had been caught on camera, maybe I could catch them talking to Brady Neil and/or Boxer. After the head of Security told me it would be at least a day to pull up all those cameras, I decided to interview Olivia Anderson—a girl who worked at Bigstore, and, more importantly, she had gone out with Brady. Lennie set up the interview for me because she was the one who had originally talked to Olivia—when she was still with me on the homicide. After the interview, I walked Lennie to her car. And that's when she discovered it had been broken into. We went back to Security. Luckily a camera was pointed on part of her car, and we saw the guys who did it on the monitor. We got a couple of great frames that showed a full-face shot. It wasn't what I had planned when I went to Bigstore this morning, but it all worked out."

Decker took a breath.

"Now you're up to speed."

Radar was silent. Then he said, "Baccus wants you off the case. He says you're not only butting into his homicides but you're undermining his orders to those under him."

"Ah, c'mon!" Decker stared at Radar, who said nothing. "You can't be serious!"

"I'm not taking you off the case." Silence. "You're welcome."

"Thank you. But we both know it's not Baccus's call."

"No, it's not, but—"

"There's a but?"

"There's a but." Radar rolled his tongue in his cheek. "You wanted Friday off to see your aged mother. You told me Rina's leaving tomorrow." He took in a breath and let it out. "Go with her. Let Victor cool down."

"Right when the case is breaking and we might actually ID these guys, he wants me off."

"If something definite breaks, I'll let you know."

"Nothing's going to break because Baccus isn't going to do a thing to help me ID these clowns."

"Pete, I'm not going to stonewall a murder. Just . . . let Victor settle down so we can work with him, okay? We need his help because the Boch house is in his jurisdiction. Let Forensics go over Lennie's car completely. I'll check up on it myself. You've done a great job. I swear if something major breaks, no one will freeze you out."

"We have to keep a guard on Jaylene Boch at all times. Even if Hamilton doesn't want to give the manpower—"

"Kevin's already got a schedule worked out. Go home and change your airline tickets. Spend a little time with family. I'll see you Monday morning."

"Fine." Decker stood. "Fine."

Radar seemed stunned that he agreed so easily. "Thank you for being reasonable. I have your cell. I'll call you if I need or hear something."

"No problem."

Decker meant it.

The new and unexpected plan would give him more flexibility with Jack Newsome.

There was a God in heaven.

The original plan was to surprise Newsome with a drop-in visit on Sunday. But after reworking the airline tickets, it turned out to be cheaper to see his mother on

Thursday and then go visit Rina's mother for Shabbat. With that in mind, Decker took his chances and called the man up. As it happened, Newsome was planning a fishing weekend, leaving Thursday and coming back late Sunday night. He was willing to talk—he had no idea how he could help—but he could only find the time on Thursday afternoon, and then, only for an hour or so.

Okay, Decker said to himself. He'd take whatever he could get.

At four in the morning, as Decker fit the final piece of luggage in the Volvo, hoping to make a 9:00 a.m. flight from JFK to Gainesville, Rina came out carrying a small cooler of food. She wore a floral tunic/dress over a pair of white leggings and espadrilles. Her hair was brushing her shoulders, and atop her head was a white knitted tam.

She spoke before he did. "I know that we can't take the drinks on the plane, but we can take the sandwiches. We'll leave the drinks in the trunk and can use them on our car ride home. Any other questions?"

"You notice I haven't said a word."

"But you gave me that look."

"What look?"

"The husband look that says, 'Why are you bringing so much stuff.'"

He smiled. "The look actually says, 'Why are you bringing enough food to feed the Turkish army.'"

"It's just four sandwiches, for your information."

"Okay. That's not bad."

"Actually, four kinds of sandwiches, so it's eight altogether."

"You made them, I'll eat them. That's the problem. Let's go before we hit traffic. In New York, it starts early."

Rina slipped into the passenger side, setting the cooler behind her seat and a paper bag at her feet. She had taken out a thermos. "Coffee?"

"Yeah, as soon as I back out of here." He threw the car in reverse and went down their driveway. Ten minutes later, they were on the highway to New York. "I'll take the coffee now. Make sure it's not too hot and just fill it up halfway. I don't want to burn myself."

"Sure. Bagel?"

"In a bit." He paused. "How many bagels did you bring?"

"Two cheese jalapeños, two everything."

"In addition to the sandwiches?"

"One is breakfast and one is lunch," Rina said. "What time are you meeting Newsome?"

"Three in the afternoon. If Radar hadn't told me to

get lost, I wouldn't have been able to talk to Newsome this weekend. Everything worked out."

"Sometimes it happens that way. Do you want me to come with you?"

"To the interview?" When she nodded, he said, "Just handle Ida Decker. That's enough of an assignment."

"That's better for me anyway. I'm cooking dinner. I shipped a five-pound roast to your mom. Randy and his new lady are coming down for dinner."

Wife number four for his brother. His mother kept a special set of kosher dishes and pots and pans for them. It was a very nice concession considering that she was a practicing Baptist. Rina's job was to clean the stove and oven when she went down.

"Chabad is coming at two to blowtorch the oven. It would really make much more sense for me to cook everything in my kitchen, but it seems so important to your mom that I use her kitchen. Besides, she loves to bake, and it's amazing that at her age, she still can do it."

"If you call ordering you around baking."

"She still rolls out her own piecrusts."

"Bless her little heart."

She hit him. "Any idea why Baccus is being such a jerk?"

"I hate to think bad about anyone in the league, but that guy is hiding something."

"About the Levine murders?"

"That I couldn't tell you."

"Do you think he knows who the guys in the sketches are?"

Decker exhaled. "I was watching him. I didn't see any recognition on his face, but he could be good at lying."

"If Baccus is involved, why would he go after his own daughter?"

"If Baccus is involved, why did he ask me to take her on in the first place?"

"Like you said, maybe he thought she'd be a good source of information. And when she wasn't, he pulled her off the case."

"Well, someone thinks she knows more than she does. And probably someone in Hamilton PD."

"Are you concerned for her safety?"

"Yes. McAdams is with her this weekend. I'm also a little concerned about Tyler. He's a cop, but he's not really a cop cop. He's never been on the mean streets."

"I'm sure he's watching his back, Peter. He's been shot twice."

"I know. He saved my life. He has good judgment. But he's still a little green, and I'm not around." He paused. "That's why I've asked Kevin to keep an eye on both of them."

"That's a little insulting to Tyler, don't you think?"

"It is. He'd kill me if he knew. This is the way I look at it, Rina. If McAdams doesn't pick up Kevin's tail, then I did the right thing. If he does pick up the tail, I'll know for the future that he doesn't need me mothering him. Either way, I feel good about my decision."

Florida—a state with year-round warm weather and no income tax—attracted many East Coast retirees eager to exchange freezing temperatures for a beachfront condo. The downsides were hurricanes and months on end of unrelenting heat and stifling humidity.

Gainesville, the city of Decker's birth, was ever changing, consistently rated a top-ten place to live. Housing was reasonable, employment was good, and it was a university town with an undergraduate population of over fifty thousand people from the University of Florida alone. The students basked in the temperate months and cleared out during the summer monsoons, although it could rain at any point in the year and often did. June, heading into July, was typically hot and damp and slapped like a wet towel on bare skin. The rental car had good air-conditioning and a good set of wipers, both amenities needed as Decker drove westward from the airport. His mother's house was outside the city.

It was a modest structure that hadn't been touched in several decades, sitting on a large parcel of land. Once it had been a bog, but his father, long ago, had diverted the waters and turned it into a manicured wetland. Although his mother let the dwelling go to seed, her gardens were still lush and green.

At noon, Decker pulled up in front of a one-story sprawling ranch house with a wraparound porch and white-painted wood siding. The front lawn was emerald green, and the beds surrounding the grass were planted with flowers in every hue of the rainbow. As soon as he stepped out of the car, he whacked the back of his neck. The mosquitoes were out in full force. "I forgot the bug repellent."

Rina stepped out of the car. Beads of sweat congregated on her forehead. "I have it packed in the suitcase."

"Someone's thinking."

"Thinking but not too clearly. I should have put it in my carry-on." She walked quickly to the front door and knocked.

It took several minutes for Ida to make it to the door. It swung open, and Rina was looking down at a diminutive, wizened figure with dark blue eyes and thinning pearly-white hair, dressed in light blue stretch pants and a short-sleeved floral blouse. Both of them smiled. Then came the quick hug.

Ida said, "Come in before you let all the cold air out. You need help, Peter?"

"Sure, you can bring in the suitcases." When Ida started toward the car, Decker held a bony arm. "Ma, I'm kidding."

"Why? You don't think I can do it?"

"I know you can do it, but so can I." He bent down to kiss her proffered cheek. "How are you?"

"We'll chat once you've got the suitcases." She turned and headed into the house.

Rina followed past a neat living room that was in perfect style sixty years ago. The furniture was clean but very, very tired. It didn't reflect the near boundless energy of the ninety-four-year-old woman. The kitchen was the heart of the house: big and cool thanks to a room AC unit pouring out refrigerated air. The appliances were old, colored with enameled avocado, but they still worked well. The countertops were covered in hard plastic sheets in deference to Rina's rules of kashruth.

"I haven't pulled out the pots and pans yet." Ida sat down in the middle of the space at a large round table, covered in a new tablecloth. "I wanted to make sure you approve before I take anything from the cupboards. I changed the sponges and got new kitchen towels. Two sets for meat and milk. I needed to change my old ones, anyway, and they had towels on sale at Walmart."

"It looks perfect. Thank you for doing this."

Ida sighed. "What choice do I have? You won't eat here otherwise."

"Mom, be nice," Decker said.

"I am nice," Ida said. "I did it, didn't I?"

Rina laughed. "Yes, you did. I know you got the rib roast I sent you, Ida. Do you want me to cook it, or do you want to do it?"

"You do it. I'll bake. I got fresh apricots from the farmers' market. I'll make some pies."

"Sounds great," Rina said.

"I could make more if you'd stay longer."

"Mom—" Decker wagged a finger.

"Who comes all the way out here for one day?"

"I'm in the middle of a case."

"You're always in the middle of something."

Decker nodded. "Yes, you're right about that." He checked his watch. "As a matter of fact, I'm going to shower and change. I have to interview someone, and it'll take me at least an hour to get there. What time's dinner?"

"What time do you want it to be?"

"Well, what time is Randy and whatshername coming in?"

"Her name is Blossom."

"Blossom?" Decker held back a smile. "Is she nice?"

"She's forty-two with a tattoo on her neck."

"Randy has tattoos."

"Trash begets trash. And don't tell me to behave myself. I am what I am and at ninety years old, I'm not going to change."

"Um, I think you're ninety-four."

"Nonsense. I'll be ninety-one in September." Ida stuck her chin out in defiance. "Don't you even know how old your own mother is?"

"I thought I knew," Decker said. "I guess not."

She grunted. Rina cleared her throat. "Why don't you go shower now?"

"Good idea. But I still don't know when's dinner."

"I'll call you and let you know." Ida paused. "Blossom's okay. But she's no Rina."

"Thank you, Ida," Rina said. "That's a terrific compliment."

"The woman can't even boil water."

"Maybe she has other talents," Rina said.

"Probably the kind we can't talk about in public," Ida groused.

"I'll see you later, Ma," Decker said.

"Seven," Ida told him. "Dinner's at seven."

"Does Randy know the time he's expected?"

"No."

"Are you going to tell him?"

"You tell him."

"Not a problem."

Ida said, "You will make it back on time, right?"

"I'm planning on it."

"Good. I'd like to see you even if it's only for a day."

"We'll make it longer next time."

"You always say that."

Decker kissed her head again. "I do always say that, don't I. I'm sorry about that, Mom. I promise to do better."

"Ach." She waved him away. "Go do your business. I got cooking to do." With that, she got up and went to fetch the kosher cookware.

But not before Decker saw the tears in her eyes.

Chapter 28

The drive was over an hour from Gainesville going northwest but more west than north. Outside was hot and humid, and the roads hadn't been looked at for a while. The two-lane highway took Decker through lush acreage of dogwoods, live oak, magnolia, and leafy cabbage palms. Newsome's place was in the middle of nowhere—a one-story ranch home on a sizable spread of cleared ground. Greenery was all around—dense and deep—but there were power lines, which meant a decent chance that the man had AC.

The area in front of the house was all gravel, the space taken up by a camper/trailer, an SUV, and a pickup. Decker parked on the pitted asphalt road, not wanting to ruin the undercarriage of the rental. The walk from the road to the house was around one hundred feet. By the time he rang the bell, his back was drenched in sweat.

The door opened and a blessed waft of cool air hit his face.

The man on the other side appeared to be in his seventies. He sported white hair, grizzled white stubble, and wrinkles all over his face—above his lips, on his forehead, creasing his cheeks, and surrounding his dark, perceptive eyes. Wearing a short-sleeved shirt and tan khakis, he was long and lean with big hands, extending one of them for Decker to shake. "Jack Newsome. Welcome." His voice was deep and raspy. "Come in. It's hot out there."

"That it is." Decker walked inside, carrying a briefcase filled with information about his case as well as the sketches. "Thanks for seeing me."

"You want something to drink? Water? Lemonade?"

"Whatever you're drinking, I'll have."

"I have vodka and lemonade. You want that?"

Decker laughed. "I'm driving. Plain lemonade is fine."

Newsome led him into a small living room—more like a parlor with a leather couch, a big chair with a footrest, and a bay window holding a reading nook. One wall was filled with bookshelves that held actual books. "Ever been to Florida?"

"I grew up in Gainesville. My first job was with their PD."

Newsome smiled. "Not foreign territory, then."

"It's my ancestral home."

"How long were you with Gainesville PD?"

"Four years. I signed with the academy right after I came out of the army. I met my ex-wife at the university, and she wanted to go back to Los Angeles after we married. I have to say, I didn't object. I liked L.A."

"You were with LAPD?"

"I was. I ended my career as a lieutenant detective. Lots of pencil pushing, but I didn't mind. Whenever there was a difficult homicide case, I got to work it."

"How long were you in Homicide?"

"Many years."

"What brought you to Hamilton PD?"

"Greenbury, actually. A good pension in my pocket and a slower pace of life."

"Understood. Have a seat." Newsome left and came back with a pitcher of lemonade, a glass filled with ice, and a bottle of Stoli. "Just in case you change your mind."

"Thanks."

Newsome sat down. "I was born in New Hampshire, worked in Boston PD for thirty years. After I got my pension, I thought like you, only I wound up in Hamilton."

"How long were you there?"

"Five years." He shook his head. "I didn't like it. I don't mind small towns, obviously, but I didn't like the small-town mind-set. After my wife died of cancer, I came down here and retired for good. Maybe that's why I don't like Hamilton. I associate it with a really rough patch in my life."

Decker nodded. "What brought you to Florida?"

"It's cheap, for one thing. It's quiet. I don't mind the heat, and I like the great outdoors. I fish in the Gulf, and I hunt whenever I get a chance."

"Sounds nice."

"Do you hunt?"

"No, I don't."

"Too much death after homicide?"

"Could be. But I'm Jewish, and we keep kosher. Which means that meat has to be ritually slaughtered. I couldn't eat what I hunt, so there's no sense shedding blood for sport."

"Oh . . . can you drink?"

"Alcohol?" Decker smiled. "I can and I do, just not now."

"What about fish? Do you fish?"

"I do fish, but I haven't done it for a while."

"Can you eat the fish?"

"Yes."

"I have some catfish frozen. I'll give you a few steaks."

Catfish wasn't kosher. He'd give them to his brother. "Thanks very much."

"Okay, then." Newsome sat back in his chair. "What can I do for you?"

"First . . ." Decker reached in his briefcase and pulled out a still of Unknown Man #1 taken from the digital video. He handed him to Newsome. "Do you know who this man might be?"

Newsome studied the image for a moment. "Where was this taken?"

"At a camera in a parking lot."

"Good resolution for CCTV."

"Everything's digital now."

"What's this guy doing that you caught him on camera?"

"He broke into someone's car."

"Why?"

"I believe he's looking for something."

"What?"

"Don't know."

Newsome regarded Decker's face, then his watch. "I suppose you should start at the beginning."

"How much time do you have?"

"Enough for a quick recap."

"Great, but first: yes or no on the ID?"

"Not positive. But . . . if I had to ID someone, I'd say it's Yves Guerlin."

"Yves Guerlin?" The man had never popped up on Decker's radar. "Who is he?"

"He was with Hamilton uniform when I was there. We didn't like each other."

"Okay." Decker took out a notebook and started writing things down. "Why was that?"

"I thought he was a bully, and he thought I was a snob." Pause. "A little background. I came in as a detective. I think it chafed his hide because he'd been there a lot longer and was still doing patrol. He could have taken the sergeant's exam, but either he was too dumb or too lazy. Didn't stop him from being a know-it-all."

"I know the type." Decker's brain was firing in too many directions. "Would Victor Baccus have known him—Guerlin?"

"There are three station houses at Hamilton. Yves worked Bitsby, which is high crime and high action. Victor was at Claremont/Bellweather, which had far less crime and far less serious crime until the Levine murders. I was only transferred there because brass wanted someone with big-city experience. Between the murders and my wife's death, I decided I'd had enough. I retired for good."

"I can understand that." Decker waited a moment. "Then they *didn't* know each other—Yves and Victor?"

Newsome shrugged. "They ran in different circles. I certainly didn't know everyone in all three station houses. Is there a reason you don't want to ask Vic about him?"

"I did yesterday. He said he has no idea who it is." Decker pulled out the sketches. "A witness helped us with these police composites. I think this one looks like the guy you identified as Yves Guerlin."

Newsome took the sketch. "Fair enough."

"What happened to Guerlin?"

A troubled look on Newsome's face. "No idea. After I was transferred to Claremont/Bellweather, I happily lost track of him. Like I said, we didn't like each other."

"About how old would he be?"

"He was younger than me. He'd be around sixty."

That fit the age of the guy in the image. "Would you know if Guerlin had any tattoos?"

"I couldn't tell you." He looked up and then back at Decker. "He was a redhead when I knew him. But that was a long time ago."

"Twenty years ago, I was a redhead myself."

"I can still see it."

"You're too kind." Decker pointed to the second sketch. "How about this guy?"

A long, hard look. "He looks slightly familiar, but I can't put a name on him."

"Someone that Yves knew maybe?"

"Maybe. He looks younger than Guerlin."

"I agree," Decker said. "Could he have been a cop?"

"Sure. I didn't know everyone. Probably the same with Victor." Newsome checked his watch again. "Now it's your turn. What's going on?"

Decker gave him a ten-minute summation that included Neil's murder, Boxer's disappearance, the crime scene at the Boch house, the black and whites hidden in Jaylene Boch's wheelchair, and the ID of Margot Flint from Brandon Gratz. He talked about Victor Baccus assigning his daughter to the case and then pulling her off the case. He concluded with the break-in at Lennie's apartment after she had taken home the Levine murder files. The amount of sheer information seemed to stun Newsome into silence.

Decker said, "Sometimes crimes have too few pieces to solve. I have too many."

"Man, I'll say. Do you have those hidden black-and-white pictures with you?"

"Copies." Decker retrieved them from his briefcase.

Newsome looked at them. "Don't know the guy. But this does look like an older Margot Flint with dark hair. Gorgeous gal. I remember very clearly when she and her husband went underground. It was a major screwup and a big scandal. Prosecutor got hell for giving them bail, and the Flints' lawyer was accused of abetting their flight."

"Was it true?"

"I think they just wanted a scapegoat. The Hamilton police chief was forced to resign. His name was Rodney Bellingham, if you're interested."

"I'm interested in everything. Why'd they come after him? All the police do is gather evidence."

"The Flints gave a lot of money to community causes, including Hamilton police." A pause. "I kept to myself in the department—busy with my wife. I didn't hear every bit of gossip around. But there was lots of speculation about the Flints: that they were serial criminals, that they had inside help in their escape, that they were involved in the Levine murders. It seemed like everywhere we turned, someone had something to say about the Flints."

"What about the Levine kids? Did they think the Flints had a hand in their parents' murders?"

"I don't know. The Levine son . . . what was his name? Senior moment."

"Gregg."

"Sure. Gregg. The sister was Yvonne?"

"Yes."

"I never heard the kids accuse the Flints of murder, although I'm sure there was talk. I do remember that after Gratz and Kyle Masterson were arrested, all the rumors kind of disappeared. And then my wife died about three months after the arrest of Gratz and Masterson, and I left the area about a month later."

Decker was writing as fast as he could. "You said there were rumors that the Flints had inside help in their escape. Anyone else besides their lawyer come to mind?"

"Nobody specific, but Margot was a gorgeous blonde with a shapely figure. How do I know that? Every time I saw her, she was wearing something tight." He paused. "I didn't know her at all. But the vibe I got from her was . . . calculated. She'd look at you, and you could sense that she was sizing you up—what could you do for her, you know what I'm saying?"

"I do. From the old papers I read, she was always doing something charitable. Sometimes it was an event with Mitchell, but in some of the events, she was the only one involved."

"She had lots of friends in high places. And I think

she preferred to be with her high-placed friends when Mitch wasn't around."

"Friends with benefits?"

"Like I told you, people accused her lawyer of helping them flee. And the chief resigned, so his name was bandied about. I even heard that Glen helped them out because Margot and he had something on the side. Nothing concrete to back up those claims. Glen's statements in court were primarily against Mitchell, his partner, but he certainly seemed angry enough at both of them when he testified." A pause. "It's getting a little late."

Decker put down his pad and took a sip of lemonade. "How much time do I have left?"

"I should leave in thirty minutes. What else is on your mind?"

"Did you know Joseph and Jaylene Boch?"

Newsome nodded as he thought about the question. "Not personally. But I do remember uniforms getting domestic calls. He was a first-class jackass." Another pause. "He . . ." A raised finger wagged in the air. "He also worked for the Levines in security. We considered him a good suspect for a while. But he had an alibi where lots of people vouched for him that night, but that doesn't mean he didn't set something up."

"Right."

"But then Vic arrested Gratz and Masterson and Boch became a footnote in the investigation. Gratz and Masterson never pinned anything on him, so he went way down the list."

He checked his watch a third time. "I need to get my stuff together. But you can call me anytime."

"Thank you." Decker took a final sip of lemonade and closed his notebook. "I'd really appreciate if you kept our conversation quiet."

"No problem. I'm still in contact with my Boston buddies, but I don't talk to anyone in Hamilton. That place was nothing but bad memories."

"Thanks for your cooperation. As an afterthought, what did you think of Victor Baccus and how he handled the Levine murders?"

"I thought he was competent, especially considering he never worked a big-city department. He seemed professional and hardworking."

"No evidence of corruption?"

"None that I saw. Actually, I think the Levine murders were handled well."

"That's good to hear." Decker put away the photographs, the still digital of Yves Guerlin, and the sketches. "One last question and it's a biggie. Who gave up Gratz and Masterson?"

"Anonymous tip. It was a woman. Some say it was Margot, others say it was the wife."

"Jennifer Neil?"

"She was Jennifer Gratz back then. Cold woman as I recall, but then again, Gratz was beating on her. Maybe it was her who made the call."

"What do you think?"

"Didn't know, didn't care. She gave us good information. It was a big case. We were just happy to catch a break."

Chapter 29

Over the phone, McAdams spelled the name Yves Guerlin back to Decker. Then he asked, "Who is he?"

"He was a cop with the Hamilton Police Department when the Levines were murdered." Decker was driving back to Gainesville. There was still daylight, and if he kept up the pace, he'd make it back for dinner with time to spare.

"About twenty years ago."

"Newsome remembered him being there from even longer—to the time when the Flints skipped bail and fled underground. Could you look him up for me?"

"Absolutely. Just give me a second . . ." Clicking of the keyboard in the background. "Okay, this Yves Guerlin appears to be about thirty. He's posing with friends in front of a giant plate of nachos."

"What *network* are you on?"

"Instagram."

"That's probably a son. The Yves Guerlin we're hunting would probably not be on Instagram."

"Some old guys are a lot hipper than you."

"Unless you have a page for the elder Yves Guerlin, look somewhere else."

"Okay, okay." More tapping. "Okay. Google gives me a group picture of men around sixty golfing at a charity event for underprivileged children."

"Now we're getting somewhere. Do you see Yves Guerlin in the photo?"

"The event lists the names in an article, but there's no caption under the picture. It's a very small snapshot, and when I make it larger, I lose definition."

"How old is the picture?"

"Dated two years ago . . . oh wait, this is interesting. It was sponsored by the Levine Foundation."

"Is Gregg Levine in any of the pictures?"

"I don't know what Gregg Levine looks like, and like I said, the resolution is bad at best. Let me look up the actual event."

"Do that eventually, but first I need an address of Yves Guerlin the elder."

"Right. Hold on and let me pull up his driver's license. How are you doing otherwise?"

"Fine. How's Lennie?"

"Back at Hamilton."

Decker was surprised. "I thought she was suspended."

"Desk duty. Maybe her father wants to keep an eye on her."

"If he's any kind of normal father, that would be a priority." Decker waited a beat. "How safe is she there?"

"With her father around, I'd say she is okay. We're keeping in contact via texts, but if something happens, I can't do anything."

"What would happen?"

"It's theoretical. You know I'm totally pissed about you leaving for the weekend. It's a big responsibility to watch Baccus and watch my back at the same time. And to make matters worse, where am I going to eat?"

"You won't starve. Where is Lennie staying over the weekend? I don't want her alone."

"I've offered up my apartment. If someone does break in, there's absolutely nothing to steal. It's really bare bones because I spend so much time with Rina and you . . . Okay, here is Guerlin's address according to his New York driver's license." McAdams gave him the numbers and the name of the street. "I suppose you'll want a tail on this guy?"

"I do once you find him. Be careful. At this point, he has to be expecting it."

"Who do you want on Guerlin's tail while Guerlin's tailing Lennie and me?"

"That would be Butterfield. Where is Kevin?"

"Going through CCTV at Bigstore with Benton Horsch." There was a pause. "Did you put him on my tail, by the way?"

"Kevin?" Decker waited an appropriate moment. "Why would he do that? Why would you ask that, Harvard?" Another pause. "Is he following you now?"

"Never mind. I must be tired."

"I'm sure that's true. Anyway, I'll call Kevin, pull him off CCTV, and put him on Guerlin. Since you'll be watching Lennie over the weekend, you two can go to Bigstore and check the CCTV. Keep you both safe and occupied."

"Neither Baccus nor Radar is going to like Lennie being involved."

"She's entitled to know who's stalking her. Especially now that we have a name. How old is Guerlin?"

"Sixty-two, according to the DMV. If you wait a sec, I'll see if there's an announcement of his retiring."

"Yeah, it wouldn't be good if he was still with Hamilton."

"Hold on . . . ah, he retired eight years ago."

"Good. What else can you tell me about him?"

"Let me see if he has a Facebook profile . . . uh, no, he doesn't."

Decker thought a moment. "What about Yves the younger? Does he have a Facebook profile?"

"Let me check." Clicking. "Yes, he does have a Facebook. He's an electrician . . . went to Andrew Jackson High School in Bitsby . . . thirty-one, unattached . . . he takes a lot of pictures of food."

"Any pictures of his father?"

"Let me see . . ."

It was quiet over the line. Decker asked, "Tyler?"

"I'm going through his photos. He's into snacking in a really big way. I don't see any pictures with any older folks, but this guy has to be the son. How many Yves Guerlins could there possibly be?"

"Is he a redhead? Newsome said Yves the elder was a redhead."

"He is, as a matter of fact. Dark reddish. Like brick color." A pause. "There are a lot of pictures of him with a guy named Phil. Captions like: 'Here's Phil and me getting hammered at Madness.' That's a bar near Claremont, FYI. Phil may be a brother. He's also a redhead."

Something was whirling around in Decker's brain as it flipped through a Rolodex of names and images.

Bald except for an orange mohawk.

His name tag said Phil G.

Right before his eyes, damn it.

Decker said, "Harvard, I need you to listen carefully."

"Okay . . . what's going on?"

"There's a guy who works at Bigstore named Phil G with an orange mohawk. He was one of the first people I talked to after Brady Neil died. I was working on the theory that maybe Neil stole electronics from the warehouse and Phil worked in the warehouse. I talked to him about Neil and about Boxer. This was even before I went to Jaylene Boch's house."

Silence over the phone.

"Tyler?"

"I'm here."

"Find out Phil G's last name for starts. Then find out if he's working today."

"Right. Then what?"

"Good question. I've got to think about how to handle this. If his last name is Guerlin, someone needs to keep an eye on him."

"Him meaning Phil G with the orange mohawk."

"Yes."

"Do you think he murdered Neil and Boxer?"

"No idea, but he knew both of them. He could have easily overheard them talking about a case that might have a big effect on his father."

"The Levine murders?"

"That or possibly Mitchell and Margot Flint going underground. Or maybe something totally unrelated. Whatever it was, it's possible that he passed the information to his father."

"Wow. That's a pretty weird coincidence: Phil, Boxer, and Brady all working together."

"Not so weird," Decker said. "We're not talking about Manhattan. We're talking about three local boys— or men—living in a smallish town, all of them without skills, working nonskilled labor jobs in a big store that hires a lot of nonskilled labor."

"Right. But it's still weird. Second generation involved with first generation."

"Past coming back to bite you in the ass. I know Radar wanted me to take the weekend off, but that's not going to happen. I can't direct from down here. It's too late to catch a plane tonight, but I'll come back tomorrow."

"Want me to let him know?"

"I'll call him, but thanks."

"Is Rina coming back with you?"

"Probably not. She'll still want to visit her mom for the weekend. It's been too long since she's seen her."

"Okay. Then what will you do about Shabbos?"

"We've got a freezer in the garage filled with food. It won't be a problem, but thanks for asking."

"You want company?"

Always an ulterior motive. Decker said, "Sure. Come over. Stop by the house in the morning, pick out what you want to eat, and leave it on the kitchen counter to defrost. Everything's in there from soup to dessert."

"Bring Lennie with me?"

"Absolutely. Just find out Phil's full name and get a watch on him."

"You want me to do it?"

"No, you watch Lennie. Here's what we'll do. Since Kevin's already at Bigstore, instead of me calling him to tell him to tail Yves Guerlin, I'll call Kev and explain the situation about Phil."

"Let me get this straight, boss. You're going to pull Kevin off CCTV to watch Phil G if he's at Bigstore, correct?"

"Yes, exactly. And if Phil G isn't there, you find out where he is, if you can. I'll tell Kevin to tail Yves Guerlin Senior. We were looking for a link between Brady, Boxer, and Unknown Man #1, who turned out to be Yves Guerlin. We've not only found our link, we've also found our leak."

There were two guestrooms in Ida Decker's house. One had a queen bed with an unattached bathroom, and one had a double bed with the en suite bathroom. Rina chose the queen bed because they both spent more time sleeping than the occasional trip in the middle of the night. She was fluffing up pillows when Decker came in the room, towel and toothbrush in hand. She said, "Did you confirm your flight?"

"Yes, I'll be in Greenbury by two in the afternoon. I changed your ticket so you'll be coming into Albany on Sunday instead of JFK. I should be able to pick you up."

"Just send a car, Peter." She climbed into bed. "I'll be fine."

"I'm really sorry about this."

"Honey, my mother loves you. But honestly, without you there, I can direct all my attention to her. And you'd be so antsy, wondering what's going on with the case. You did the right thing. I know this isn't a priority, but be sure to take the food out of the freezer, so it'll have time to defrost before Shabbos starts."

"Tyler will be there first thing in the morning. He's already planned the meals, and I believe he made dessert. I'll be fine." He slid under the sheets. "Thanks for being understanding."

"I'm fine. Are you going to get any sleep?"

"Probably not. I'm still trying to organize everything in my head."

"What have you found out so far?"

"Phil G is Philip Guerlin, and he hasn't shown up for work for the last two days. Yves Guerlin, meanwhile, has gone AWOL since breaking into Lennie's car. I'm concerned about her, I'm concerned about Jaylene Boch—"

"You've got protection on her."

"I do, but Guerlin was a seasoned cop. And if his accomplice was also a former cop, they both know the ins and outs of security. Not to mention all the VIPs in Hamilton."

"Speaking of VIPs, if Guerlin retired only eight years ago, Baccus must have known him."

"Radar called him up. Baccus said of course he knows who Yves Guerlin is. He just didn't recognize the sketch. Seems Yves Senior has gained a lot of weight in the last few years."

"Even so. He's lying, don't you think?"

"Absolutely. It's only been eight years. People's faces don't change that much." Decker exhaled. "This is what puzzles me. Whenever I ask about how Baccus handled the Levine murders, they all said he did a good job."

"He has to be hiding something. Otherwise why lie?"

"But what? Maybe he did do a good job on the Levine murders."

"That may be," Rina said. "But now he's chief of police. He'd not only want to protect his men, he'd also want to protect his reputation."

"Yeah, you're right." Decker sat up. "I don't want to sound like one of those people, but it does sound like some kind of conspiracy of silence. Radar needs to talk to him. It's a terrible thing to accuse a chief of wrongdoing. And we don't know he did anything wrong. But something's not kosher."

Rina smiled.

Decker smiled back. "My mom looked happy at dinner, didn't she?"

"Very happy. It was a lovely evening all around."

"Thanks for cooking and cleaning everything up."

"You helped clean."

"Randy and I brought in a couple of plates. I know who really did all the work."

"Blossom pitched in. I like her, Peter. She's very nice."

"She is, actually." Decker chuckled. "Think my brother finally got it right?"

"We'll see. There's no test like the test of time." She

kissed Decker's lips. "You have to be up very early. Try to get a little sleep."

"At most, I'll get four hours. It isn't even worth it to go to bed."

"You want to get up and work this out on paper?"

"I'd like to at least have a strategy." A shrug. "I'll sleep on the plane."

"Go get dressed and get out of here," Rina said. "Just kiss me before you leave for the airport."

"Darlin', I'll kiss you any time you want."

Chapter 30

At 2:26 p.m., as soon as Decker walked into the Greenbury station house, McAdams handed him a printout. "This guy is Denny Mayhew. He was with Hamilton Police for ten years but abruptly quit right after Gratz and Masterson were arrested. Mayhew was a semilocal boy, attending high school in the nearby town of Sawtooth."

Decker's eyes were sweeping over the printout as McAdams was talking. "How'd you get a name?"

"From Mike Radar, who got it from Victor Baccus. Once Newsome identified Guerlin, Radar went over to Hamilton and pressed Baccus on the other one. He said it was probably Mayhew because he and Guerlin had partnered together for a while. But he didn't really know Denny because he wasn't at his station. He also said Guerlin was unrecognizable from the officer he vaguely remembered. He said that Yves must have gained about a hundred pounds."

"Yeah, I heard that. It's ridiculous. Was Mayhew partnered with Guerlin when the Levine murders took place?"

"Baccus wasn't sure—he was out of uniform by then and wasn't working at Bitsby—but he said it was possible. He'll go through the records and check it out. How much do we trust the chief?"

"We don't."

"My question to you is this: What do Guerlin and Mayhew have to do with the Levine murders? They certainly weren't the first responders when Gregg Levine called 911. I know because I checked."

Decker looked up from the pages. "I don't remember seeing their names anywhere in connection with the Levine murder files."

"Spot on, boss," McAdams said. "I just reread the files that Lennie gave us. There's not even an honorable mention. Then again, the files are heavily redacted."

Decker looked at the printout. "Cowards. Making us do all the work while they hang back in the shadows, watching our every move. At least they should have the balls to show their faces."

"Well, we got their names despite their best efforts to hide."

Decker exhaled. "Do we have any idea where Mayhew might be?"

"He lives outside of Tucson, Arizona. According to his wife, he's been on a camping trip for the last week."

"More like a hunting trip." Decker stared at Mc-Adams. "And Lennie Baccus is still on desk duty?"

"About fifty feet from her father's office."

"If Baccus suspected that the incident at Jaylene Boch's house might bring out two ex-cops hunting for something, it could be why he pulled her off the case."

"Then why put her on in the first place?"

"Yeah, that was strange. Maybe he was telling the truth. Maybe he did want her to have some experience in Homicide. At that time, when we went to him to look at Hamilton police files, I was only interested in the punks that Neil might have associated with. We really didn't suspect that Brady Neil's death had anything to do with the Levine murders."

"You did. You started looking up the murders almost immediately."

"But not until after Jennifer Neil told me about Brady's dad—after Baccus asked me to take Lennie on. Then the Boch slaughterhouse happened and he pulled her off. Baccus probably knew the case was bigger than some juvenile punks gone awry. He was worried for her safety." Decker thought a moment. "I asked Mike to set up an 'informal' talk with Baccus later today."

"When?"

"Around five. You can come if Radar follows through."

"Why wouldn't he?"

"It's a bit sticky, but it has to be done."

Kevin Butterfield walked into the room. The back of his shirt was wet, and he had beads of sweat on his forehead as well as his bald head. "It is hot out there." Frustration was visible on his face. "I knocked on Phil Guerlin's door at least six separate times and left multiple cards. I have canvassed every one of his neighbors. I have tried to talk to every known friend or acquaintance. I have visited every bar or restaurant that Phil is known to frequent. The man is officially a mole and he has gone deep."

Decker said, "Maybe our best bet is to wait for Mayhew to come back from his 'camping trip.' If he has a wife, he has to return home."

"I'll contact the local police in Arizona," McAdams said.

"Before you do, Harvard, you might want in on this." Butterfield turned to Decker. "You've got a visitor, Deck. Gregg Levine. Asked specifically for you."

"You're kidding!" Decker was taken aback. "That

guy has been actively avoiding me since Neil's murder."
A pause. "Any idea what he wants?"

"Nope, and he's not volunteering any information.
But like me, he's visibly sweating. It could be the heat.
But I suspect it's because he has a story to tell."

*It is important to keep in mind that twenty years ago,
this man, now forty, lost his parents in the most brutal
and violent of ways.*

Decker stored that thought in the back of his brain.
Go slowly, go easy.

Butterfield had seated Levine in one of the two
interview rooms. He stood up when Decker and Mc-
Adams came in. He was thin and appeared small in
stature although he was average height. He had a long
face with a long nose and eyes that slanted downward
at the corners, giving him a hound-dog look. His head
was crowned with a receding hairline of curly locks.
He wore a white-and-blue-checked shirt, dark blue
linen pants, and loafers with no socks. He dabbed his
forehead with a tissue.

"Sit down, please," Decker told him. "Would you
like a drink of water? It's hot outside."

"That would be nice." A deep voice, courtesy of the
pronounced Adam's apple in his throat.

"I'll get it," McAdams said. "Would you like some coffee, boss?"

"Yes, thanks," Decker answered.

Levine said, "Could I have some coffee as well?"

"Of course," McAdams said. "How do you take it?"

"Cream and sugar, if you have."

"We do have." McAdams got up. "Be right back."

After he left, Levine managed a weak smile. "Sorry I didn't call you sooner."

"I'm sure you had your reasons."

"And now I'm barging in on you."

"We're the police," Decker said. "We get people coming in at all hours."

"Yeah, but you're not *my* police."

"Meaning Hamilton." When Levine nodded, Decker said, "There's a reason why you're here and not there, then." No response. "Why don't you start at the beginning, Mr. Levine."

"I'm . . . not sure how much I should say because . . ." He looked down. "I don't want to get myself in trouble."

Decker held out his hands. "You're here because something's on your mind. Something must be bothering you—"

"Y'think?" A mirthless chuckle. "I've been living

with this for twenty years. Not that I feel guilty, because . . . well . . . I don't. And I wouldn't be here
except for what's happening lately. Things are making
me nervous."

McAdams came back with the coffees. He distrib-
uted the paper cups and sat down.

Decker thanked him. "What's making you nervous?"

A small sip of coffee. "This is good." Levine took
another sip. "I was expecting swill."

"We have a pod coffeemaker mostly used by me,"
McAdams said. "My financial contribution to our great
team of law enforcement personnel."

Decker gave him a "cool it" glance. It was hard
enough getting people to talk, let alone sidetracking a
train of thought. On the other hand, maybe it calmed
Levine down.

"Yeah, it's good coffee." Silence.

Decker pressed the restart button. "What's making
you jittery, Gregg? I can call you Gregg?"

"Sure, whatever."

"Tell me why you're here. What's making you un-
comfortable?"

Levine let it out in a whoosh. "What happened at
Jaylene Boch's house."

"Okay." Big admission. Give him time to catch his
breath. "Why is that making you nervous?"

"I'm not positive, but . . . I think she was there."

Decker tried to keep his expression bland. He glanced at a wide-eyed McAdams. "By *there*, Gregg, do you mean that Jaylene Boch was present when your parents were murdered?"

Levine looked down. "It's really stupid of me to talk without a lawyer. But I think my family and I need protection more than legal advice."

"Who's threatening you, Gregg?"

"They're not exactly threats. More like reminders." A pause. "You've got to realize that I was a twenty-year-old kid who had just walked into this nightmare." Tears formed in his eyes. "I was shocked; I was beyond scared shitless. I just did what they told me to do."

"Who is they?"

"As if you didn't *know.*"

"I don't know, Gregg. Honestly. When your parents were cruelly cut down, I was with the Los Angeles Police Department working Homicide. I just found out about your parents when Brady Neil was murdered a couple of weeks ago. I'm hungry for information, which is why I was trying to get hold of you. Tell me who you're talking about. Who told you what to do?"

"I was trying to do the right thing."

"Of course you were. Who told you—"

"The *police*." Levine's voice was barely above a whisper.

"Ah." Silence. Decker then said, "And what did the police tell you to do—specifically?"

"They told me unless I said certain things about what happened, the killers would just walk away. I needed to say certain things to make sure they were caught!"

Slow it down. Decker said, "Okay. I'm starting to understand." A pause. "Do you remember the names of the officers you talked to?"

"How could I forget if they keep reminding me that I perjured myself!" He wiped his eyes. "Yves Guerlin and Denny Mayhew. It was Guerlin who did most of the talking."

"Okay." *Keep it clear and understandable.* "These two officers, Yves Guerlin and Denny Mayhew, they told you to perjure yourself on the witness stand?"

"Worse, than . . ." He froze up. "Forget it."

"I'm here to help and protect you—"

"Sure you are." Levine rolled his eyes. "You're one of them. I don't even know why I'm here."

"You're here because you're scared. And that's where I can help. Gregg, I had a sterling career for over thirty-five years. I'm not about to jeopardize my reputation for anyone, including the entire Hamilton Police

Department." A pause. "If you want help, I'll certainly help you. But please help me. Start at the beginning. What happened, Gregg? Talk to me about that horrible night."

Levine didn't talk for a few moments. Then he whispered, "I was supposed to come in to help my parents with inventory." His voice grew stronger. "It's a lousy job. I didn't want to do it. I didn't want anything to do with the shop back then. But after what happened with Mitch Flint—do you know about Mitch and Margot Flint?"

"We do," McAdams said.

Levine turned to him as if he were just aware of his presence. His eyes went back to Decker's face. "Anyway, Dad didn't trust anyone but family members after that. There were times that Dad was so stingy, *I* felt like ripping him off. I didn't, in case you're wondering."

"Running a high-end jewelry store is a big responsibility for anyone, let alone a college-aged young man," Decker said. "I'm sure you had other things you wanted to do rather than help out your parents."

"Ain't that the truth!" Levine looked into his coffee cup as if reading tea leaves. "At the time, Dad and I weren't getting along. At all." He looked up. "You know that the police were suspicious of me because I had said some things in the past and Dad had said some things and none of it amounted to shit. Just two angry people venting steam."

"I hear you."

"On top of everything else I was going through, they questioned me like I was a suspect, the bastards."

"Who questioned you?"

"Victor Baccus. I *hated* that motherfucker back then."

"Back then?" Decker paused. "You don't hate him anymore?"

"No." A small laugh. "Not at all. He's like a father figure to me now."

"We know that you two play golf together," McAdams said.

"It's more than that." Levine was still holding the coffee cup. He put it down. "I couldn't have survived without Victor. He stepped up to the plate, got the entire community behind us. I mean, we were five lost kids and I was the oldest."

"I get it." *Then why are you talking to me instead of Victor?* Decker said, "Tell me about Guerlin and Mayhew. What kind of trouble are they causing you?"

"Oh God," Levine said. "I've got a wife. I have children. I don't know if I can do this."

Decker said, "Gregg, I know you lied about something, otherwise why mention perjury? We're halfway to the finish line. You can do this. Your father had asked you to come to the store to do inventory. Then what happened?"

A big sigh. "Like I was saying, I didn't want to be there. But Dad was furious with me for not helping out. I finally relented and told him I'd come in. But then a friend called me up and we wound up going to a party together. There was lots of alcohol—and other stuff. I knew that inventory taking usually lasted all night anyway. They wouldn't miss me for a few hours." A pause. "I got stoned, I got drunk."

"It happens to the best of us," McAdams said.

"Well, it happened to me a lot back then. I knew I couldn't go in smelling like a weed field or a distillery. Take your pick. I waited until it mostly wore off. By that time, it was real late or very early—like two in the morning. I knew they'd still be working. And I knew my dad would yell at me. But he'd still be grateful for the help. I walked over to the store. I took my sweet time about it."

The tears reappeared.

"Right before I got there, I froze. A police cruiser was parked in front of the store, the strobe going blue to red, blue to red, blue to red. I knew that wasn't good. Dad would never randomly call the police."

"What did you do?"

"I was petrified. I took a step back and hid in the shadows. I was thinking about my next move." Head down and then back up. "About a minute or two later, I saw two guys leave the shop. They were lugging, like, totes: carry-ons that you use for airplane travel. I thought, 'Oh shit. Mom and Dad.' They've been robbed. But then I thought, 'But the police are here!' I was utterly confused."

Decker nodded. "Understandable. I'm confused as well."

"The two men who left the shop walked opposite from where I was hiding. Walking, not running."

"No big hurry," McAdams said.

"No big hurry," Levine repeated. "A car pulled up, they got in, and it took off."

"Okay," Decker said. "Then what did you do?"

"Just stood there trying to figure this out. I couldn't make out any faces—it was way too dark—but I recognized the car. It was a real beat-up clunker. Easily recognizable."

A long pause.

"It belonged to Joe and Jaylene Boch. That's why I told you I think she was there."

Decker waited a few moments to give him time to collect his memories. "Why her and not him?"

"Because I had just seen Joe Boch at this party. He was so wasted, he couldn't even steer a shopping cart."

McAdams said, "This might be beside the point, but what was Joe Boch doing getting wasted with a bunch of kids?"

"He was a motherfucker and an asshole and was constantly coming on to young girls who hated his guts. But"—Levine held up a finger—"he bought the beer and the booze for all us underaged kids. When I left the party, Joe was passed out."

"Ah," Decker said.

"And besides, we all heard that his old lady was fooling around."

"Who with?"

"Some of my friends bragged that they nailed her. In her house with Joe Junior in the other room. God only knows why they'd want to fuck a skank like her. Harsh, I know, considering what happened to her." He looked down. "But it totally wouldn't surprise me that she was doing losers like Brandon Gratz and Kyle Masterson. God, everybody in town knew to stay away from those two. They were all just bad news."

"What about Yves Guerlin? What did you hear about him?"

"I didn't know who Yves Guerlin was until that horrible night," Levine said. "All I know is when I finally made it inside the door, Guerlin and Mayhew were standing there, looking somber. They told me my parents were dead—shot and killed."

Tears ran down his cheeks.

"Things got dizzy for me. I . . . passed out, just hit the floor. When I woke back up, I was still dizzy. Then I got sick to my stomach. I threw up. I think I might have fainted again. I don't remember all of it. I was in total shock."

"What were Guerlin and Mayhew doing all this time?"

"Actually, they were taking care of me. They wouldn't let me go into the room where my parents were—at first. They asked me if I needed a doctor. They asked me if they should call an ambulance. One of them gave me a glass of water. They were . . . nice, I guess. They got me a chair and sat me down . . . let me catch my breath."

He waited a few moments before he continued.

"Like I said, it was Guerlin who did most of the talking. He told me—as much as I remember—that he knew who did this to my parents. Because he saw them running out of the shop when they pulled up the cruiser. I knew that didn't make sense. No one was running anywhere, but I was too stunned to say anything. Then Guerlin said . . . he repeated that he knew who the killers were, but he couldn't prove anything without my help. I was wondering exactly how I could help except by cleaning up my puke." A pause. "Do you see where this is leading?"

"I have an idea," Decker said. "Tell me."

"Guerlin said . . ." A deep breath in and out. "He said that he needed an eyewitness to the shooting. He said he needed me to tell the police that I saw what happened. He said that if I didn't give testimony in court that I saw what happened to my parents, the guys who murdered them would walk."

A long pause.

"Guerlin developed this plan. It sounded like he was making it up as he went along. He told me that they were going to leave—him and Mayhew—and that I should call 911 after they left. That I should be a witness to the crime to avenge my parents. They told me what to say to the dispatch operator; they told me what to say when the cops arrived. I was completely confused. They were the cops! Why did they want me to call 911 if the cops already arrived? I mean, what were they doing there in the first place?"

"Did you ask them about it?"

"I might have . . . I think I did. They said they responded, but it was too late. I was the only one who could get justice for my father and mother. I was so horrified and shocked and I didn't question it. I just did what they told me to do."

"Which was?"

"Guerlin's plan. After they left, I called 911 like it was a new incident. I told them I saw what had happened. I didn't do it exactly like they said because, frankly, I didn't remember exactly what they told me to do. I told them I was hiding in the closet and saw one of the guys when he took his mask off. And after Gratz and Masterson were arrested, I felt I was already in it too deep to admit the truth."

"The truth that you really didn't see what happened."

"Yes. I did not see what happened, but Gratz and Masterson had the jewelry, so it really didn't feel like I was lying."

"But you didn't identify Gratz to the detectives at the time."

"No, I just said I saw one of them and briefly. It was a lie but a small one. Later, they asked me to come in for a lineup. Guerlin paid me a visit. He told me to identify Gratz because my description matched him more than Masterson. And since I knew who Gratz was, I was able to identify him. And I felt okay about it. Guerlin and Mayhew were legit Hamilton cops and those two monsters had my parents' jewelry in their possession. I didn't feel I was doing anything wrong. I see how naive I was, but back then I didn't even fathom a thought that the cops were in on the crime. My mind didn't work that way."

"But now you think they could have been part of it?" When Levine didn't answer, Decker said, "How is Guerlin threatening you?"

"He isn't *threatening* me."

"Okay, Gregg. Then what is he saying to you to make you nervous?"

"Just saying that with everything that's been happening with Jaylene, Joe Junior, and Brady Neil's murder, that I should get my story straight because they—meaning the police—may start asking me questions about my parents' murders."

"And how did you respond to that?"

"I said, 'What about you, Yves? You were there way before I arrived.'"

"And?"

"And he told me that he and Mayhew couldn't have been there. They were called out on another dispatch. If anyone looked at the police log, there wouldn't be a record of Mayhew or him being at my parents' store. Of course, then it hit me . . . it only took me twenty years. They *had* to have been in on it." He shook his head as if to erase the memory. "I don't know if they were in on it from the beginning—or they just happened to take the call and got greedy . . . struck a deal with Gratz and Masterson to keep silent in exchange for loot. Whatever the deal was, it didn't help, because Gratz and Masterson were arrested a month later with jewelry from the store."

"Not all of it," Decker said. "I heard some big pieces were missing."

Levine took in a deep breath and let it out. "Baccus said that the big pieces were probably fenced. They were filled with gems—easy to take apart and sell separately."

"Of course," Decker said.

"Or . . ." Levine sighed. "Yeah, the cops could have taken them in exchange for keeping their silence. I didn't think about it at the time. Guerlin and Mayhew were never in the picture—at all. Not during the investigation, not during the arrest, not during the trial. It puzzled me, but I kept my mouth shut. You've got to remember how frightened I was. I wanted Gratz and Masterson to go away for life. I was shocked when they got off with such a light sentence. Maybe Guerlin got them some kind of deal in exchange for silence. I'm sure judges can be bribed."

"Some can be bought," Decker concurred.

"The thing is . . ." Levine swallowed coffee. "If Guerlin and Mayhew were actually the ones who murdered my parents, you can see why I'm nervous. And since they were actually legitimate cops, you can understand why I don't want to talk about this with Hamilton police."

"I thought Baccus was your friend," McAdams said.

"He is. But he's also chief of police and was the lead investigator in my parents' murders and I don't know what he knows or doesn't know. I just don't want to involve him right now."

"You think he might have been in on it?" McAdams asked.

"No." Levine was adamant. "I can't believe that. But he could have found out something after the fact. I'm not saying he did, but I know if my testimony is thrown out, it screws up the entire case. And this was Victor's breakout case."

"Your testimony will be thrown out," Decker said. "You know I'm going to have to report this, right?"

"Yeah, I guess I was hoping . . . of course. As long as you go after Guerlin and Mayhew."

"That's for damn sure." Decker pulled out a yellow legal pad and a pen. "Write down everything you remember about that night. Every detail, no matter how small and insignificant."

Levine took the pad and pen. "To this day, even now, I never felt guilty about lying about Gratz and

Masterson. I know they robbed my parents. They had jewels in their possession. And deep in my heart of hearts, I know they killed my parents."

"That could be, but the case is going to be overturned. The D.A. won't retry unless there's evidence against them for murder. The case hinged on your eyewitness testimony. And now that's gone."

"My parents had been brutally slaughtered and I did what the cops told me to do. I don't apologize for that."

"But maybe it was those cops who did the murders," McAdams suggested.

"Then shame on them for taking advantage of a horrified kid who was in emotional and physical shock." Levine grew red. "Shame on them, and shame on all of you."

It was almost dark when Decker and McAdams walked Levine out of the Greenbury station. Decker was famished and exhausted, and all he wanted to do was go home to a hot sabbath meal and a warm bed. What awaited him instead were piles of paperwork and endless phone calls in wake of what Levine had just admitted. Everyone had to be contacted—Radar, Baccus, district attorneys, judges. But most of all they needed to find Guerlin and Mayhew and get their side of the story.

Levine had parked across the street. As the trio waited for the light to change, he took out his phone and unlocked the car doors with a smart app. "I can't say this has been fun." He looked up at the sky. "It's been a long time coming. Those bastards served twenty years. I won't say it's enough, but it's something." His eyes went to Decker's face. "Am I going to be prosecuted?"

"That's not for me to decide, Gregg. I will have to present everything you told me to the people in charge and let them decide. For what it's worth, I wouldn't bring charges against you. Even if Gratz and Masterson didn't pull the trigger, it was the robbery that set the whole thing in motion. I don't feel sorry for them."

"Thank you for saying that even if you don't mean it."

"The boss always means what he says," McAdams told him.

Levine managed a smile. The light changed. As they stepped off the sidewalk to cross the street, Levine aimed his phone at his car to start the motor.

The explosion was immediate.

Without conscious thought, Decker hit the ground, taking Levine and McAdams down with him as an earsplitting boom reverberated in his ears. A ball of blinding light and heat with glass and metal flew over his body, some of the shards piercing his clothing. A wave of hot air reeking with gasoline scorched his back.

Then came the stench of burning rubber and melting metal. As Levine started to lift his head, Decker shoved it back down. "Don't move. There could be more than one bomb." He realized he was on top of McAdams and slithered off.

"You okay, Harvard?"

"Peter, your back is pocked with glass and metal."

"Yeah, it feels like it's been hit with a bunch of needles." Slowly, he got up, shards of glass and metal slipping down his back and onto the sidewalk. People were rushing out of the police station. Several moments later, fire trucks were racing down the street, diving into pure chaos.

McAdams stood, bringing Levine up with him. Decker said, "Get him back in the station house."

"You need a doctor," McAdams said.

Decker could hardly hear him above all the noise. That and his ears were still ringing hot from the explosion. Kevin Butterfield suddenly materialized. "What the *fuck*!" He looked at Decker's back. "Oh shit!"

"I'm fine, Kev. Get some officers out here, do crowd control, and secure the crime scene. Do we have a bomb squad?"

"No. I'll handle this, Deck. You take care of yourself."

"Thanks." Decker rolled his shoulder. The heat had

burned through his clothing. He knew his back, on top of being a pincushion, was also sporting a bad sunburn. "We need to get Gregg to safety." Levine had several jagged pieces of metal in his back. "Wait. Don't move. You've got debris in your back, Gregg. I don't want you walking until you've been looked at."

McAdams took out his phone. "I'll call for an ambulance."

"Somebody beat you to it. Go inside and get some face masks. These fumes are toxic." He whispered, "And get a cruiser out to Levine's house ASAP."

McAdams left as an ambulance was careening down the road. Decker waved it forward. Two paramedics—a woman and a man—jumped out.

"He needs attention." Decker was referring to Levine. "I don't know if anyone else was hurt more seriously."

Just then a firefighter from across the street shouted to them. "I've got a woman down!"

Immediately, the paramedics raced across the street. Someone had turned on an arc lamp from one of the fire trucks. The water from the fire hoses let loose, and billows of rancid, oily smoke filled the air. Another ambulance pulled up. Decker said, "There's a woman down across the street. When you're done with that, can I have someone look at his back? I don't want him walking if the pieces are deeply embedded."

Amid the fire, the heat, the smoke, and the stink, two other paramedics dashed onto the scene. One of them was a stout woman named Candy. She tore off Levine's shredded shirt and took a look at his back. It was scratched and burned and had small pieces of metal stuck into the skin.

"Can he walk inside? The fumes are toxic out here."

"Just wait a sec. I'll be right back."

McAdams returned with a box of face masks. Officers started reining in the gathering crowds. Kevin had returned with crime scene tape and was barking orders. Tyler said, "Cruisers are on the way to the Levine house." When Decker told him to go inside and wait in better air, he said, "I'm not going anywhere."

The paramedic returned with a black bag. As she swabbed the area, Levine winced. Slowly, she took out the biggest metal shard. It bled profusely. She applied pressure to the spot. "You're not going to die, but you need to go to the hospital. This should be done by a doctor."

From across the street, paramedics were wheeling a gurney to an ambulance. The woman had an oxygen mask over her nose and face.

"She okay?" Decker shouted.

A paramedic gave him a thumbs-up, meaning she'd live. How seriously she was hurt . . . The paramedic continued to work on Levine's back, slowly pulling out bits and pieces. Five minutes later, another ambulance pulled up.

"Go to the hospital, Gregg." He looked at McAdams. "You go with him."

Levine had yet to speak. He paled and his knees buckled. He whispered, "My wife and kids!"

McAdams checked his phone. "I just got a text. Someone's out there. They're fine."

"*Who?*" Levine panicked. "Not from Hamilton!"

"No, it's our officers," McAdams said. "Your family is fine."

Radar had pulled up and jumped out of his car. "I was on my way home when I heard." His face was horror-stricken—wide eyes and a pasty complexion that Decker could see even in the poor street lighting. "God Almighty! What the hell happened?"

"Mr. Levine's car was bombed—"

"Christ!"

McAdams said, "We have two men from our department out at Mr. Levine's house. His family is fine, but Mr. Levine needs to go to the hospital." He cocked his head toward Decker. "So does the boss, but he's not budging."

"Go with him to the hospital, Decker." Radar's phone rang. "That's an order."

"Not going to happen until I figure out what's going—"

"No, you need to go to the hospital—"

"Can you answer your phone, Mike? The ringing is hurting my ears."

Depressing the green button, he said, "Radar." As the captain listened to the other end of the conversation, Decker saw whatever color Mike had in his face drain away. He had turned a pallid gray. "Gregg Levine is here. Someone just tried to blow up his car but he's okay—"

"What is it?" Decker asked.

Radar shooed him off. "I'll be right there."

"What is it, Mike!" Decker insisted.

Radar pulled him aside, away from Levine's anxious ears. "That was Victor Baccus. He's got a hostage situation. Levine's Jewelry—"

"Shit! Yvonne Apple?"

"Worse. It's her daughter, Dana."

Chapter 31

"They don't really want me down there, let alone you," Radar told Decker. "Baccus called in a SWAT team, a hostage negotiation team, and a bomb squad. The place is completely surrounded."

"Then why are you going there?" Decker asked.

"Baccus wants to be updated on what Levine told you and this—what happened here."

"I interviewed Levine. I was here when the bomb went off. I can fill him in. I'll recap for you on the ride over."

"McAdams will come and tell me," Radar said. "He's in one piece."

"Only because I had the courtesy to land on top of him. If you don't take me, I'll drive myself. And I'm in no condition to drive."

"If you're in no condition to drive, you're in no condition to work."

"Time's a-wasting," McAdams pointed out. "Decker, why don't you take Levine to the hospital and I'll go with the capt—"

"Out of the question!" To Radar: "I'll wait for you in the car." Decker stomped off.

Radar sighed. "Go with Gregg Levine, Tyler. Call up his family and get them a police escort to the hospital." A moment passed. The captain shook his head. "God, he's a stubborn prick."

"He needs medical attention," McAdams said. "I'll call an ambulance to meet you in front of the store."

"Hamilton's already called out an entire medical team." He faced McAdams. "I'll just have him treated there, I suppose. Go." Radar jogged over to his car, opened the driver's door, and sat down. Decker closed the passenger door with a thud. "Look at you!"

"What?"

"You can't hear and you can't even sit back in the seat without wincing."

"I'm fine."

"No, you're not." Radar started the engine and put the siren on the roof of the car. "You look like you have a stick wedged up your butt."

"No comments necessary. Please drive."

With the siren going full force, Radar took off. "The car just happened to blow up just as you were about to cross the street?"

"Mike, you're going to have to talk a little louder with the siren going."

"Never mind."

"No. No never mind. Just speak up."

Radar repeated his comment.

Decker said, "The bomb was set off when the ignition turned over. Levine has an app on his phone and he turned the engine on remotely. He is one lucky son of a bitch."

"He turned it on *remotely*? Who *does* that?"

"What can I say, Mike? Sometimes your time just ain't up."

"Anyone else hurt?" A pause. Radar repeated the question.

"A woman was down. The paramedic indicated that she'd live, although I don't know how seriously she was harmed. Now it's your turn. Who is in the jewelry store holding the girl hostage? Guerlin and Mayhew?"

"I don't know anything other than it's a hostage situation. Dana Apple is the victim."

"There's a guard in the store."

"Then apparently he didn't do his job."

"You know I've been inside the store. I know the layout."

"Great, then you can help the SWAT team."

"I can do this—"

"Decker, I took you with me against my better judgment. But I do admit that you may have something of value to contribute to this situation. There's a medical team in front of the store. While we wait, you get treated. After that . . . we'll see what they need from us. Baccus is in charge. We're just there to help. Got it?"

"How do you know Baccus isn't part of it?"

"Why on earth would Baccus want to kill Gregg Levine?"

"Because he found out that Gregg Levine was coming to Greenbury station to tell us what really happened the night of the murders." Decker gave him a quick recap of the conversation. "Baccus knows that Levine's admission will overturn his big breakout case. Two men incarcerated for over twenty years and a lying witness urged on by the police? That would be the end of the chief's career."

"Levine's lying is unfortunate, but it doesn't mean that Baccus knew about it. There has never, ever been any implication that Baccus improperly handled the case.

You told me that yourself." Decker was silent. "Look, we don't even know who's in that jewelry store. Until yesterday, you didn't even know who Yves Guerlin was."

As much as Decker hated to admit it, Radar was right. "I could be getting ahead of myself."

"Damn right. Let's get you some medical help. And squelch the thought of you going in. I'm shouting and you can barely hear me."

He was right again. "I suppose it might put me at a disadvantage."

"Exactly. You go get some help while I talk to Baccus."

"Sure you want to confer with the chief? We don't know if Baccus is crooked or not."

Radar made a face. "Do you have a shred of proof that he is?"

"If I did, we wouldn't be having this conversation." A pause. "We don't know who is holding Dana Apple hostage. But *if* it's Guerlin and Mayhew, and *if* they killed Joe Junior and Brady Neil, they wouldn't think twice about murdering again."

"That's for damn sure. Let's just hope whoever it is, he isn't building another bomb."

The street was cordoned off with rows of police officers guarding the perimeter. They stood two abreast, arms folded across their chests or with their hands resting on their gun belts. From afar, the scene reminded Decker of the endless TV shoots he had witnessed on the streets of Los Angeles. The only things missing were the catering trucks. Radar showed one of the officers his badge and was grudgingly allowed to park a few blocks away. To get to the heart of the action required walking, and with the passage of time, Decker could feel the fatigue of adrenaline depletion. His ears were still ringing and he was aware of every cut, scrape, scratch, and burn as he walked with Radar. There were still bits of glass and metal embedded in his back and legs, and he winced with each step. He needed to rest, but a desire to see justice compelled him forward.

Radar noticed his limping and slowed down. "I don't know who's crazier. You for being here or me for letting you come with me."

Decker said, "The girl was there when I went to the store."

"Which girl? Dana Apple?"

"Yes."

"Why did you go to the store in the first place?"

"To interview Gregg Levine about Brandon Gratz. I thought it might have something to do with Brady Neil's murder. He wasn't there, so I wound up talking to Yvonne Apple. Don't you remember? Chief Baccus called you up to complain. He read you the riot act and, in turn, you read it back to me."

"I don't recall it being exactly like that, but I do remember you talking to the sister." There were about fifty feet from a group of cop cars that had formed a semicircular wall around the shop. Artificial lights had been set up. On the civilian side of the taped-off perimeter were news and radio vans with reporters setting up mikes and cameras. People from the printed press were there as well. No one seemed to notice Decker and Radar walking through the crowd and stepping over the police tape. "You didn't tell me the girl was there."

"For just a few minutes. She was just an ordinary teenager helping in the family business." Decker paused. "I do remember something about the inside layout, though. I could go in just to direct—"

"You're not in a position to go anywhere except a hospital."

It was dark outside, but where the cops had set up was well lit. There were arc lamps and spotlights, and strobes atop police cars were blinking in random rhythms. Several ambulances were sitting behind the police cars, with paramedics standing by just in case. Decker could hear Yvonne screaming but couldn't make out any words. She was gesticulating wildly to Victor Baccus. A man stood by her side—probably her husband. He placed a hand on her shoulder, but she flung it off. When she noticed Decker, she marched up to him and slapped him in the face. "You shit! You brought this all on."

She was about to whack him again, but Radar caught her arm. "Take a deep breath—"

"Let go of me, you fucking Nazi!" Her eyes were wet, and makeup was running down her face. Her hair looked like a fright wig. There were red scratches on her cheeks, as if they had been raked by combs. Her once perfectly polished nails were ragged and broken. She was wearing white slacks and a red shirt that had come untucked as she struggled under Radar's grip. "Let GO of me."

Baccus had materialized. He took Yvonne's arm. "Stop." He looked at the man by her side. "Take her home, Paul."

"I'm not going anywhere." Yvonne suddenly broke down and covered her face. "You don't *understand!*"

"Of course, I understand, Yvonne. And we're doing all we can. But you can't do that."

Radar said, "This man saved your brother's life."

"I don't give two fucks about Gregg." Fierce Yvonne had come back to life. "This was all his fault! If he hadn't lied—" To Decker, she said, "You started it. Do something!"

Paul put his hand on her shoulder a second time, and once again, she swatted it away. He was taller than she by an inch and broad across the chest. He had a round face, round eyes, and the start of a double chin along with a noticeable sag above the belt line. His hair was thin and his eyes were red and unfocused. He was floating without an anchor.

Decker looked at Baccus. "A moment, sir?"

Baccus said, "Paul, take her home—"

"I'm not going anywhere!" Yvonne shouted to him.

"Then wait here for a moment."

Yvonne took umbrage. She grabbed his arm. "Where are you going, Victor?"

"I'm just filling them in—"

"Don't leave me in the fucking dark." Her eyes shot arrows. "I am part of this!"

"I can't deal with your questions right now, Yvonne."

"I've got every right to ask questions! It's my daughter's life, damn it!"

"Sir?"

Baccus looked left. An officer informed him that SWAT needed his attention.

"Just answer me this, Chief," Decker said. "Is it Mayhew and Guerlin?"

"We think it's Guerlin and we think he's alone."

Decker was surprised but attempted to hide it. "Where's Mayhew?"

"Anyone's guess. His wife has been alerted—"

"Sir? SWAT is waiting."

"Yvonne, I have to deal with the team going into the store. You have to get out of harm's way. Now! Go wait by the ambulances."

"Victor—"

"I can't talk now, Yvonne. If you don't go voluntarily, I'll have to forcibly drag you away."

She stalked off while muttering obscenities directed to the world. Paul paused, then ran after her. Baccus took off toward the SWAT team. Decker had to move quickly to keep up. Every step was sharp and painful. "Does SWAT know the layout of the store?"

"How do I know if I haven't talked to them?" Baccus said.

"I've been inside."

Radar said, "You can't go with them, Pete. You're wounded and can't hear. You're a hindrance."

"I can draw a map."

"Shit," Baccus said. "I should have asked Yvonne to do that for me. Although I don't think her memory is too sharp at the moment. And the last time I was inside was years ago."

Radar said, "Decker's been inside recently. He can help."

"Yes, do that while I talk to SWAT and the hostage negotiator. I'm still hoping there's a way to end this without anyone else being murdered."

"You may be late for that party," Decker said. "They have a hired guard."

Baccus stopped. "Armed guard?"

"Yes. His name is Otto. Either he's being held or he's dead."

"Shit!" Baccus stalked off. As they approached SWAT, Decker saw a very familiar face talking to one of the team members outside the van.

Baccus turned red. He was livid. "Lenora, get the hell out of here!"

She looked at Decker. "How are you feeling, sir? Detective McAdams told me you were pretty banged up."

"Good news travels fast."

Baccus said, "If you don't get out of here right now, I will have you dragged away in handcuffs."

Her voice was steady. "I was just telling Officer Nelson about the layout of the store to the best of my recollection, Chief. If I could consult with Detective Decker, I think my memory would be even better. Furthermore, I think I would be a valuable asset to the team—"

"Get out!"

"Sir, I've taken part in two GTA raids in Philadelphia. In both cases, the team was successful." Determined. "I can do this, Chief."

"Go away, Lennie, before I arrest you."

Lennie's face darkened. She whispered, "If I were anyone else, you wouldn't hesitate."

"You're inexperienced."

"Not as inexperienced as you'd like me to be."

"I'm not sending you in, Lenora. There's probably a dead guard in the store already and I'm not going to be responsible for the look on your mother's face if something happens."

"Dana Apple is Yvonne's daughter. How are you going to face Yvonne if you didn't do everything you could have done?"

Decker nodded to Radar, who held up a palm. Baccus looked more weary than angry. "Go with Detective Decker. He's consulting with Yvonne Apple to get a detailed layout of the store. Maybe you can be some help there."

"I'll stay here," Radar said. "Help the chief in whatever way I can. Go."

To Lennie, Decker said, "C'mon." He turned and walked toward where Yvonne and Paul were standing.

Lennie looked at her father, but then followed on Decker's heels. "You know I'm right!"

"How much experience do you really have in take-downs?"

"I told you I was on two GTA raids. Vests and all."

Decker said, "This guy is extremely dangerous. He's probably killed the guard—"

"Otto. I remember him. If he's still alive, he'd could help—"

"He's probably incapacitated or dead." Decker looked at her. "You know that my daughter is a cop, and I wouldn't send her into this situation even though she's qualified."

"Then you're thinking of yourself more than the public you swore to serve."

"That may be, but an oath doesn't mean a damn thing when you're standing in front of your child's casket. Slow down!"

She slackened her pace. "Sorry."

"It has to be his decision."

"Just put in a good word for me."

"I won't do that, Lennie. I don't want to be responsible for sending you to a grave. You're on your own."

"Will you at least say I'm competent?"

"You are competent. That was never in doubt. But

first, SWAT needs a plan. And to get a good plan, you need a good map."

Yvonne refused to be sidelined. She was uncooperative and wanted to speak to Baccus directly before offering any help. Returning with Decker and Lennie, she marched straight up to Baccus. "One minute you're threatening to arrest me, then the next minute you're asking for my help. If you want my help, I have to know what's going on."

"Not now, Yvonne." Baccus looked defeated.

Decker said, "What's the matter?"

Baccus lowered his eyes. Tears began streaming down Yvonne's cheeks. She rocked back and forth on her feet. "She's dead."

"No, no, not as far as I know." He regarded her and swallowed. "Do you have a room with multiple security cameras on a wall?" Yvonne closed her eyes and nodded. "Is there any part of the store that's not visible to the monitors?"

When she didn't answer, Mike Radar said, "SWAT is trying to figure out how to get inside without being picked off by Guerlin."

Decker said, "How did you find out about the room?"

"Guerlin," Baccus said. "It is Guerlin. He told the

hostage negotiator about the room. He's holding Dana there, just watching all the activity."

"What about the guard?"

"I didn't ask him and he didn't say."

Decker swore to himself. "Does he have any demands?"

Radar said, "A helicopter and money—twenty million dollars or some ridiculous sum."

"He's going to take Dana with him." Baccus swallowed hard. "If he gets what he wants, he'll release her at some point where he feels safe."

Yvonne swooned on her feet. Lennie caught her before she passed out. "Can we get her something to sit on, please?"

Baccus barked, "Take her to a police car, Lennie. Settle her in. I'll be there in a few minutes."

After they had left, Decker said, "Is Dana really still alive?"

"Who the fuck knows?" Baccus spit on the ground. "I just talked to her about a minute ago. So, yes, she's still alive. But that's not going to last. The longer he has her, the more likely that she'll wind up dead."

"Has he given you a time limit for his demands?"

"Three hours."

Thinking to himself, *Well, that's not going to happen,* Decker said, "How about a person exchange?"

"Who? You? Me?" Baccus smiled. "No one on the force is as valuable to him as Dana Apple."

"Except me!" Lennie clicked her nails. Baccus looked at her, but she spoke before he could. "I'm your daughter. You'll move heaven and earth to save me. At least, that's what you've got to say to him."

"You're not going in."

"I am a police officer, Dad, and as a police officer, it is my job is to put my life second to the people I serve—"

"Cut the shit, Lenny. You're not going anywhere. If you go in, all that will mean is we'll have two dead people on our hands. Three with the guard."

"Guerlin can't control Dana and me at the same time. Every time he takes his eyes off me to look at Dana, I'm a threat—"

"Not if she's tied up. Not if he decides to kill you."

"Then convince him that it's in his best interest *not* to kill me." Lennie blew out air. "Look, I'm betting I can get Dana out alive. What happens after that . . ." She threw her hands up in the air and let them fall by her side.

Baccus laughed mirthlessly. "What happens after that . . ." Another laugh. "Get the hell out of here. You're an unwanted distraction right now."

Her eyes pleaded with Decker's. He finally said, "I

have a daughter who's a detective. I wouldn't send her in, either. As a father, I couldn't. But . . . she has a point."

"Get out of here, Lenora!" Baccus repeated.

"Dad, every time I have tried to stretch, you have stood firmly in my way!" She raised herself to her maximum height of five ten and stuck out her chin. "Not this time! You can't afford to show favoritism. No one in the department will ever trust you or me again if you do. You have to let me try!" Silence except for the clicking of her long, red nails. "At least ask him if he's willing to exchange Dana for me."

"Guerlin knows his demands won't be met," Decker said. "They can't be met. But even a psycho like him would probably rather shoot a cop than a kid. Ask him if he's willing for an exchange—any exchange. Use Lennie as a last resort. And even then, he probably won't go for it. Talking to him is a good stall until you can figure out your next move. And it'll not only give him a sense of power, it'll keep the communication open."

"And how many hostage situations have you done successfully, hotshot?"

"Los Angeles is a big city, sir. I've done enough to feel it's worth a try."

Baccus waited before he spoke. Then he said, "I'll tell the negotiator to bring up an exchange."

"You want me to do it?" Decker asked. "Negotiate with him?"

"You're that experienced, Decker?"

"No, but this is my thinking: a guy like Guerlin would rather talk to a working police officer than a civilian hostage negotiator. Cop to cop. Man to man. But it's up to you."

Baccus looked around—at the blinking police cars, at the arc lamps, the news media, the cameras, the ambulances, the SWAT van, the negotiator's van. His eyes took in Yvonne sobbing in the backseat of a police car, shoulders heaving, hands over her face. He regarded Paul standing nearby, leaning against the black-and-white, motionless and pale.

His eyes went to Decker's face. "The negotiator is in the SWAT van. C'mon, hotshot. Let's see what they teach you in the big city."

Chapter 32

It took a little more convincing, but Victor Baccus caved. There was wisdom in Lennie's ideas, and no one else came forward with a better position than hers. If only they had enough time to plan. Instead, decisions had to be made fast and furious.

She was going in weaponless and defenseless except for the vest, police combat training, and her own wits. When she was being outfitted in the uniform, she was shaking. Afterward came the preternatural calm. This is what she had been schooled for. This was her job. She turned to Decker. "You really need some medical attention."

"When this is all over." His heart was going a mile a minute. "He's a mean guy, Lennie. He's a murderer with no remorse. And he probably won't take you seriously because you're a woman—"

"No prob—"

"Don't interrupt. So he may look at you as a pushover—which might work to your advantage. Whatever you do, remain steady. Don't beg, don't buckle, but don't antagonize. To build a rapport, you have to do a lot of listening. Don't offer any advice or any interpretation to what he might tell you. You're a mirror. Reflect back, but change the wording slightly. Otherwise he may think you're mocking him."

"Got it."

"Remember you're going in there as *his* representative. You're there to facilitate his demands."

"Understood." She started to click her nails, but then clasped her hands. "Where's my dad?"

"He's in the van with SWAT, buttoning up the details."

They had told her the strategy in broad terms. They were planning to cut the power to the monitors so SWAT could go in without being picked off. At the moment, they were trying to figure out how the men could sidestep the monitors, so they wouldn't be seen while working on the electricity shutoff.

Decker said, "As soon as the place goes dark, they'll do an immediate takedown. That'll be your chance to get the girl out."

"And that will be in about an hour?"

"We're hoping an hour." Decker checked his watch. "Start checking the clock after forty-five minutes. And I shouldn't have to tell you this. Stall him as long as you can."

"And if they can't shut off the power to the monitors without being seen?"

"They're working on plan B, plan C, right through plan Z. We're all behind you."

"I'd like to see my dad before I go in." When Decker sighed, she said, "Or is he absenting himself on purpose?"

"You know this is killing him." Silence. "I'll get him—"

Lennie held on to Decker's arm. "No, it's fine. Let him do what he's good at. It's certainly not emotion. But if something happens to me, tell him I love him and Mom very much."

"Nothing will happen to you."

"You don't know that."

Of course he didn't. He was lying. "I'll relay the message."

"Thanks." Taking the megaphone from Decker's hand, she announced to Guerlin that she was coming in. Her back was covered by numerous guns pointed at the shop as she walked to the door. It took a minute for Guerlin to open it, and when he did, he had his arm around Dana's neck and a gun to her head. He shouted, "In, in, in, in!"

As soon as Lennie stepped across the threshold, the door closed and everything was shrouded in darkness. She had to squint, but she did see a form lying at the back of the store, motionless. No time to dwell on that. She had to move quickly as he raced through the secret paneled door and down the small hallway: a walking shadow of death and misery. Guerlin settled in Yvonne's office, where the security camera monitors were giving him a bird's-eye view of the activity outside. He motioned Lennie in, closed the door, and took the gun away from Dana's head. He kept his forearm around Dana's neck. He aimed the barrel at a chair. "You sit. Don't move."

Lennie complied. Guerlin pointed the gun at her face as he took his arm away from Dana's neck. "You know the drill, girlie. Sit in the corner. You move, you're dead." He gave her a small push. "Go."

Dana reeled over to the spot. Even in the shadows, Lennie could tell she was beyond petrified. She sat small and huddled, a stick figure of pain and anguish. Burying her head in her arms, her knees to her chest, a nest of long curls looping over her face. It was hard to tell, but Lennie guessed she was silently crying.

Guerlin barked to the air. "You." Meaning Lennie. "Stand up."

Lennie stood.

He said, "Are you wearing a wire?"

"No," she lied. "Just a Kevlar vest."

"If you're lying, I'll kill you. Are you wearing a wire?"

"No."

He did a superficial pat-down. Then he said, "Take off your clothes."

She hesitated a fraction. "You want me buck naked?" He smiled. For some reason, it didn't bother her. His face looked wild but not lecherous.

She stripped nude.

Still waving the gun, he checked her mouth, her ears, her vagina, and her anus. He looked at her skin and felt her scalp. "Take off your earrings."

She did as told. "I'd like them back. They were a gift from my dad."

"Your dad . . ." A snort. "In that case . . ." He threw them across the room.

They tumbled and landed in a corner. And so that's where the microphone sat. Hopefully it would be sensitive enough to record what they were saying. She said, "Can I put my clothes on now?"

He looked her up and down. "Everything but the vest." He opened the door to the office and threw it out. "You might have stuffed a wire in there."

She dressed quickly. "No wire. You can check."

"Sit down and shut up."

"Okay." She sat up, taking in his size and girth. He was a stocky guy, but muscular. Big arms. Even in the dark she could make out a smudge on his wrist that was probably the tattoo: definitely the man who had covered the security camera lens to her apartment. He wore a short-sleeved black T-shirt and black pants. Her eyes tried to engage his, but he was pacing. His eyes were glazed and unfocused. His entire demeanor suggested disorganization. Whatever his plan was, it wasn't well thought out. "What are they doing out there?" He turned the gun to her. "Don't fucking lie."

"They are trying to figure out how to end this without anyone getting hurt."

"What did Mayhew tell you?"

"Mayhew?"

"Yeah, Mayhew. What's he blabbing to you?"

"Mr. Guerlin, we have no idea where Denny Mayhew is."

Guerlin looked confused. "You're lying."

"No, sir, I am not." A pause. "Would you know where he is?"

"Just shut up. I don't want to talk about Mayhew. Lying scum. It's all his fault."

"Okay . . . how's that?"

"Shut up." Lennie was quiet. "Why'd they send you in?"

"I'm Chief Baccus's daughter, Lenora. It's meant to show you that he's serious about negotiations."

"What does he want?"

"To end this peaceably. What do *you* want?"

"I told them what I wanted." He looked at his watch. "Your daddy has a little over two hours. Then I start shooting."

Her emotions wanted to plead with him, but her instructions were to listen. "Okay."

He became agitated. "C'mon, c'mon, what's the plan? SWAT's working on something." He was waving the gun at her face. "Maybe I should tell your dad I just shortened his time."

"You can have as much time as you want," Lennie said. "No one is going to do anything while we're here. And they know you can see everything." She pointed to the mounted monitors.

That seemed to calm him down. "Why'd they send you in? To talk me down?" He snorted. "I am not going to prison, and if I go down, you go down with me." She nodded. "You both go down with me." When she didn't answer, he said, "Why the fuck are you really here? I'm not doing a swap. You had to know that. You have a death wish?"

"No, sir, I do not."

"Then why *the FUCK* are you here?"

She saw his neck artery throb. She took a moment to organize her thoughts. "I won't insult your obvious intelligence. Two people are harder to watch than one. I think we're all hoping that you let Dana go. As long as you have me as a hostage, my father won't do any-thing."

He inhaled and let it out slowly. He said nothing.

The clock ticked.

One minute.

Two minutes.

Five minutes.

He looked at his watch. "They're running out of time."

Lennie looked at him. "Can you give them a little more time?"

"So SWAT can organize better?"

"Up to you, sir."

"Yeah, you'd better fucking believe that it's up to me." He started pacing again. "Why the fuck did you open up the case anyway? It's been settled for over twenty years. Why didn't you just leave it alone?"

"Superior orders."

"Whose? That idiot Dexter? Who the fuck is he?"

"Detective Decker is from Greenbury. He's investigating Brady Neil's death. Neil is Brandon Gratz's son. He thought that maybe Neil's death had something to do with the father, and one thing led to another."

A long pause. "I did that."

Lennie didn't react right away. "Did what, sir?"

"Brady Neil and Joe Boch. I killed them both."

"Okay." Lennie swallowed hard. "Can I ask why?"

"No, I don't want to talk about it."

"Okay," Lennie said. "You're calling the shots."

Silence.

Then Lennie asked, "What about the bombing?"

Guerlin was quiet. "I did that, too. Gregg Levine was a little weasel. As soon as I saw him walking into the police station, I knew it was over. He deserved to die."

"How did you plant a bomb that fast?"

"I planted it three days ago. All I had to do was tie it in to the ignition switch, which took about thirty seconds." He looked at Lennie. "If you get out in one piece, I'd check the undercarriage of your car."

So that's what Denny Mayhew had been doing when he ducked down in the parking lot of Bigstore. He was planting a bomb. How did SID miss it? It must have been tiny.

Lennie said, "Gregg Levine didn't die."

"Huh?" Guerlin looked at her. "What are you talking about?"

"The car exploded, but Gregg wasn't killed."

Guerlin closed his eyes. "Shit!" He gave out a miserable chuckle. "The best-laid plans, huh? Doesn't matter now! It'll all be over soon."

Lennie shuddered, but she didn't say anything. The minutes ticked on. She finally found her voice. "If you killed Brady and Joe, can I ask why you left Jaylene Boch alive?"

He whipped around, aiming the gun at her face. "I told you, I'm not talking about that!"

"Understood."

It *was* a curious thing why he didn't kill her. Maybe she had been in on the original heist and Guerlin didn't perceive her as a threat. Gregg Levine did identify the car as belonging to Joseph Boch Senior. Maybe Guerlin thought she was as good as dead when he left her tied to her wheelchair. Whatever the reason, Lennie knew Jaylene was afraid of him. Why else would she have had a panic attack when they visited her in the hospital? She took a chance and spoke. "I think you left her alive because maybe you were friends with her a long time ago?"

Guerlin sat in Yvonne's chair, his eyes darting

between the monitors and Lennie's face. He said, "I should tie you up."

She paused. "Go ahead, but I'm not going anywhere."

"When this is over, you tell them I treated you good."

Thumbs up. "I will do that."

Another minute passed.

Guerlin said, "I knew Jaylene, yeah." A pause. "I also had dealings with her moronic husband. He was an asshole."

"That seems to be the consensus."

The minutes passed.

"He knew the code—or how to bypass the code. He wouldn't give us the number, the prick. All that asshole had to do was switch off the alarm. He couldn't even do that right."

"What happened, if I may ask?"

"He never showed up." He faced her, gun in hand. "It tripped when Gratz and Masterson went in. I ran over there as fast as I could, but Mayhew was already there, wondering what the hell was going on."

Silence.

Guerlin looked up. "I had to give him a cut. Lucky he was the one who caught the call, because I knew he was bent. I should have just plugged him when I had a chance."

Lennie said, "If Mayhew was murdered, it might have thrown attention on you."

He stared at her. "Maybe." A minute slipped by. "It wasn't my idea . . . the robbery." When she nodded, he said, "Jaylene brought me in. She and Gratz were having a thing." He let out a laugh. "She was having a thing with everybody back then. You wouldn't know it to look at her now, but once she was more than a pathetic old bitch."

"Yeah, she's pretty pathetic," Lennie said. "Why were you brought into the robbery?"

He didn't answer, continued to watch the monitors.

Lennie switched the subject. "Any idea why Jaylene Boch had old pictures of Margot Flint hidden in her wheelchair?"

"Margot Flint?" Guerlin didn't talk. Then he said, "I haven't heard that name in a while."

"Some people say she was behind the robbery."

"Wouldn't be surprised. She was fucking Levine and went apeshit when he pressed charges against her and Mitch. She was another one who got around."

"Do you have any idea why Jaylene hid pictures of Margot in her wheelchair?"

"How the fuck would I know?" A minute passed. "Jaylene hated her—Margot."

"Why?"

"Like I said, Margot got around. You do the math."

Lennie nodded. "Margot was doing Joe Boch. Did he organize the robbery for her?"

"He couldn't organize a trip to the john without stepping on his dick. If anyone organized something, it was Margot. People say she wanted revenge. Maybe she got it."

"Did Joe drag Jaylene into the robbery?"

"Stop asking me questions."

"Sorry."

Five minutes of silence passed.

"I don't know whose idea it was," Guerlin said. "I was paid to keep the patrol cars clear of the area when the robbery took place. They weren't supposed to get shot—the Levines. That wasn't part of the plan." He was silent. "All of them were fucking assholes. I'm an asshole. I got greedy." He checked his watch. "It's under two hours. Call them up and ask where they are with the demands . . . no, fuck that. They'll just say they're working on it."

"Can you give them more time?"

"No."

"Okay."

Another few minutes passed. He said, "They needed someone from the department to act as a lookout."

"Who did? Gratz and Masterson?"

"Yeah. Jaylene knew I was on the take. A lot of people were. A lot of people still are. I could name names but I'm a gentleman." He looked at Lennie. "Jaylene was good at getting shit out of people. She filed the information away for favors. She cozied up to a lot of people. I was dumb—let the wrong head do the thinking. But I wasn't the only one."

Lennie swallowed hard. She had to know. "My dad?"

He looked at her and grinned. A minute later, he said, "Nah, not your dad. She was way too low class."

For some reason, relief flooded her.

Guerlin said, "She made it sound like a no-brainer. Jaylene did. In and out. Gratz and Masterson were good at jobs. I knew that from growing up here, from previous jobs they pulled. I was on watch assignments that night. All I had to do was keep the area clean of cop cars."

"You were at a desk?"

"Until the fucking silent rang, yes."

"What a mess."

"You can say that again." Guerlin had lowered the gun to his lap. He looked at her. "You say you're here for me. What can you do for me?"

"What do you want me to do?"

"Get me a car, Baccus. Get me out of here."

"I'll be happy to make a call for you. That's what I'm here for."

"Nah, don't bother. I know how it works. They'll say let the girl go, then we'll see. The girl isn't going anywhere."

"Why not? You still have me."

"You're trained. She's not."

"That's true. But do I look like a threat to you?"

"I don't fucking know what you look like to me."

"I'm not a threat. Let Dana go and then I can help you."

He didn't answer.

Lennie changed the subject. "Why did you kill Brady Neil? What did he do to you?"

"Shut up! I don't want to talk about it."

"I was just thinking that maybe it was Mayhew's idea."

"I said I don't want to talk about it." Guerlin paused. "Fucking psycho. Mayhew. He's in it as deep as I am. He took payoffs same as me."

"No one is figuring him for a good guy. We do think that you're the brains behind everything because you're smarter."

"Fuck the flattery. It isn't working."

462 • FAYE KELLERMAN

"Just saying."

"Well, don't. I wasn't the brains behind anything. I was just the lookout."

No doubt a lie, but Lennie nodded.

He regarded her. "Your dad has balls—sending you in here."

"You know he's not going to do anything stupid while I'm here." Lennie laughed. "My mom would kill him."

"How is your mom?"

Lennie hid surprise: first, that he knew her mother; second, by the genuine interest in his voice. "Not so hot."

"She's been not so hot for a long time."

"She's getting worse."

"That's the way it is with those diseases. What does she have again?"

"Multiple sclerosis."

"Muscle thing, right?"

"Right."

"You have any brothers or sisters?"

"I don't. Giving birth to me almost killed her."

He was quiet for a very long time. He checked his watch again. By now, even in the gray darkness, she could make out the clock.

A half hour to go before the raid. Mentally she began to prepare herself.

Guerlin said, "This is what I want you to tell them." A pause. "Are you listening?"

"Every word. Please tell me what you want."

"I want you to go out there and tell them to fuck the money and the helicopter. Just get me a car with bullet-proof windows. And no tracking devices. If I find out I'm being tracked, I'll kill the girl." He was breathing hard. "I'm taking the girl with me. As long as no one follows me, no one will get hurt. I don't want anyone to die, but I'm not dying alone. You got that?"

"No one has to die at all."

"Not sure about that. Go on. Get out of here."

"How about letting the girl go—"

"No. Get out of here before I change my mind and shoot you both." As if to emphasize the point, he aimed his gun at her. "Go."

She uncrossed her legs. "Tell me again exactly what you want and I'll call them up."

"No, you tell them face-to-face. When the time comes, I don't want to have to deal with you and her."

"Let her go—"

"Shut up with that, okay?"

"Mr. Guerlin, all I'm saying is it's probably easier for you to deal with me. You're a former cop, for goodness' sake. You've got the gun; you've got more experience than I have. And while I'm here, Dad isn't going to do anything."

"Okay, you blew it." He pointed the gun at her face. His hand was steady and his eyes were focused. But he hesitated. Barrel still aimed at her head, he said, "You have balls."

Lennie felt her eyes start to tear. Quickly she looked down. "I believe everything you're telling me, sir. *Everything.* I don't want to die. But I *really* don't want the girl to die. It was my idea to come in here."

"Proving something to your dad?"

"Yes, probably."

"That I understand." He shook his head. "I'm not a monster, you know."

"I know that. Let the girl go."

He checked his watch again. "I really don't want to shoot anyone."

"Let me use the phone. I'll tell them everything you want me to say."

"It's not a hard demand: just get a fucking bullet-proof car."

"It's easier than a helicopter."

"They got plenty of time to arrange it. Call them up."

"I will. Would you like to talk to them directly?"

"No. You do it." He waved the gun at her face. "Go on."

Lennie picked up the phone on Yvonne's desk. The call was quick and precise. If the hidden mic was working, they already knew what the call was about anyway. She hung up. "They're working on the car. Like you said, it's not as hard a demand."

"They'd better get it right, because time is running out. And I can't take both of you. If you don't leave here soon, you won't leave here alive."

"How long do I have?"

"Why? What's the point in hanging around? You did what you could. It didn't work. Deal with it. Better than being six feet under. And I will shoot you. Get the hell out of here."

Before she stood up, Lennie said, "Can I ask you something? Nothing to do with what's going on right now." When he didn't answer, she said, "Did Gratz and Masterson murder the Levines?"

Guerlin laughed. "Of course they murdered the Levines. They're a couple of psychos. They didn't have to kill them. They probably did it for fun. That's what tipped me over . . . why I told the kid to lie about seeing them. They did it and I didn't want those two assholes running around loose."

"They were convicted of a double murder. Why didn't they get life without parole?"

"Why?" Guerlin rubbed his fingers together.

"There're a few local assholes in this town who call themselves judges. Gratz and Masterson had lots of valuable shit from the robbery. When Jaylene contacted Mayhew and me for the payoff, we knew we were stuck. But it turned out okay. Gratz and Masterson were put away for a while, and they'll get their chance for parole down the line."

"Makes sense." Lennie paused. "But why did Brady Neil and Joe Boch have to die?"

"Shut up about that. Now get out of here before my finger gets itchy. *Now!*"

As soon as she stood up, the monitors went blank, plunging the room into darkness.

Immediately, Guerlin lunged at Lennie just because she was closer.

A tactical mistake.

He should have gone for the girl. Easier to handle, easier to control.

As he caught her, Lennie flailed her arms in a wild circular pattern, knocking the gun from Guerlin's hand.

Score one. To Dana, Lennie shouted, "*Go, go, go, go!*"

The teen bolted as fast as she could to unlock the door. It swung open all the way, hit the wall, then closed back on itself, automatically relocking.

Even without the weapon, Lennie knew that she was at a disadvantage. She had known what was going to happen, and he still somehow got the jump on her. She was struggling against him, as he tried to pin her with a chokehold. She tried to stomp on his instep, but his feet were planted too far back. She tried to kick him, but she couldn't find her balance as he choked her. He was stronger and more experienced. He also outweighed her and could use all of those pounds for extra leverage.

Seconds passed and Lennie heard nothing.

Where the hell was SWAT?

This was not a battle that she was going to win going one-on-one. Conventional strategy and police tactics had just flown out the window. Somehow, she managed to take in a breath before he started squeezing out her air and her life. She clawed at his arm with her sharp red nails. Pain barely registered on his face, he was so pumped up.

Digging deep into his flesh, raking his skin, blood flowing down his arm.

Red on red.

Vaguely aware of distant noises.

Human voices.

She couldn't hold her breath any longer, exhaling

with a whoosh. She tried to hold off inhaling, but the need for oxygen was overpowering her brain. Her eyes began to see sparkles as she started going under. The noises were getting louder, but she wasn't sure how much longer she could hold on. She was still clawing at his arm when the idea hit her.

Going about this all wrong.

She retracted her hand and tried to go under his forearm instead of pulling it off her neck. All she needed was a tiny bit of room to get her hands in between his arm and her neck. Prying up his forearm just enough to take in a half breath of oxygen.

Which was all she needed.

She placed her hands under the back of her head right next to the soft spot in his throat, and with as much force and momentum as she could marshal, she plowed her sharp red nails into the depression under his Adam's apple. Stunned, Guerlin loosened his grip as blood squirted out. He was trying to pull away, but her fingers were still deep in his gullet, keeping him attached to her.

She inhaled deeply, enjoying the rush of oxygen as she pivoted around and bore her nails deeper into his wounded throat. Intent on saving her own life, she barely registered that SWAT had burst through the door.

She knew she could let go now, but her brain was looping as she kept reaming and rotating her nails and fingers into his neck until she had carved a deep, wide ruby hole . . . until her fingers touched the cervical bones of his spine.

Chapter 33

B y the time Decker had his back and legs debrided and treated for minor burns at St. Luke's, it was after midnight. Because his torso and legs had been bandaged, he was walking slowly down the hospital corridors. McAdams was on his right, watching him struggle. He stood close by in case Decker faltered. When they hit the entry lobby, Tyler looked through the glass windows and said, "Ordinarily I'd bring the car around. But I don't want to leave you alone with the press."

Outside the main entrance of the hospital, the pack of media personnel had thinned to several stringers who specialized in nighttime videos and a couple of intrepid reporters, including one from the *Hamiltonian*. At the scene, Chief Baccus had fielded most of the on-the-spot questions. He'd do a formal announcement in the morning.

"I can walk to the garage." Decker tried to roll his shoulders, but he was bandaged too tightly. "Is Radar still at the station?"

"Don't even *think* about going back to work, boss. I promised Rina I'd take you home and watch over you personally."

Decker stopped walking. "You called *Rina*? On *Shabbos*?"

"And you think it would be better for her to hear about it over the news?"

"Tyler, she doesn't watch TV on Shabbos."

"She's visiting her mother in a retirement home, Peter. The news is going twenty-four seven. For your information, she was very grateful to hear about what happened from me and not from some anonymous source. Besides, if she did hear about it on Shabbos, she'd call you immediately. I saved her making a phone call."

That was probably true. Decker continued walking but was silent.

McAdams said, "It was a short conversation. I told her that no matter what she heard, you were fine. I didn't say anything about your being mummified."

"Smart." He shook his head. "Harvard, I really need to talk to Radar."

"Give me a message."

"No, I have to do it in person."

"Why?"

"Because something's bothering me."

"C'mon!" McAdams stopped walking. It wasn't hard, since Decker was shuffling like an old man. "What!"

"The entire time we were out there, waiting for some kind of conclusion to that horrible drama, I did not see Yves Guerlin's sons. Did you?"

"Not that I recall. But I wasn't looking for them."

"You'd think that with their father in a life-threatening situation, someone would have called them down."

"Maybe someone did. Maybe we just didn't notice them."

"No, they weren't there. I'd like to know why."

"You can find out tomorrow, Peter. With Guerlin's death, I'm sure next of kin will be notified."

"Guerlin is divorced. His sons are next of kin. Where the hell were they?"

"It doesn't matter, Peter. Guerlin confessed to killing Brady Neil. Your case is closed."

"I just think it's weird that they never showed up."

"You're not hearing me. Guerlin confessed. Case closed."

"Baccus said he was going to call them—the sons."

"Maybe with everything that was happening, he forgot."

"You don't forget to call next of kin in a hostage situation. You use them to try to talk sense into the kidnapper. It rarely works, but you try every option possible."

"There was a time exigency. Maybe the sons didn't have enough time to get there. I'm sure Baccus will call them now that Guerlin's dead."

"Then it'll be no problem for me to talk to them."

"I'm sure you can do that at some point, but not at twelve-thirty in the morning. No one is going to talk to you right now."

"I just want to look up a few things on the computer. You go home and catch some sleep. I'll catch a cab."

McAdams made a big point of sighing. "I'll take you. And I'll stay with you. I promised Rina I wouldn't let you out of my sight."

"You must be exhausted, kiddo. Go home."

"What about you? Or doesn't Bionic Cop need to rest."

"I'm too wired," Decker said. "There's no way I can sleep until (a) we know where the sons are, (b) we know where Denny Mayhew is, and (c) until I talk to Lennie."

"None of the three is going to happen tonight." They reached the elevator. McAdams pushed the button. "Certainly not Lennie. She's being debriefed. I don't think Lennie will be talkative for a very *long* time."

"She may have more resilience than you're giving her credit for."

They both stepped into the elevator car and rode it to the underground lot. As they walked to the automobile, McAdams said, "You saw her. She's totally traumatized. This wasn't a shooting, Peter; it was hand-to-hand combat. I can't even imagine . . . maybe you can imagine . . ." When Decker didn't answer, he said. "Or maybe I should shut up."

Decker said, "In Nam, combat wasn't my role. I was a medic, not a point man. But I've done one-on-one as a cop a few times. That's how I got shot. And, yes, it did stick with me for a long, long time."

"Then you know what she's going through."

"I do. Somebody needs to tell her that she executed her job perfectly. She needs to understand that."

"Boss, you'll have an opportunity to tell her that. Just not at . . ." McAdams looked at his watch. "Almost one in the morning."

"I want to find out if Radar or Baccus has contacted the sons."

"We're back to that? Why are Guerlin's sons so important to you?"

"After hearing the conversation between Guerlin and Lennie on the wire, I think we do have a better idea of what happened with the Levine murders. But I still don't know why Guerlin would want to kill Brady Neil or Joe Boch."

"And we'll probably never know unless Jaylene starts remembering things."

They found the car. Decker moved slowly but refused help. He slid into the passenger's seat. "Brady Neil is my case, and I want to know why he was killed."

"Well, good luck with that." When Decker didn't answer, McAdams said, "What do you think happened, hotshot?"

"You go first," Decker said.

McAdams sat down and turned on the engine. "I think Jaylene told Joe Junior that Guerlin and Denny Mayhew took payoffs from the Levine murders: money or possibly the spoils of the robbery. I think Joe Junior told Brady and the two of them had the brilliant idea to blackmail two crooked cops. At first, they gave them a little cash just to shut them up. I think that's how Brady got his spending money. But maybe the boys pushed it too far and Guerlin got pissed."

"Then why didn't he kill Jaylene Boch?"

"Like Lennie said, maybe Guerlin had a soft spot for her." McAdams went silent as he drove up the ramp and out of the garage. "Maybe he thought she'd just die a natural death."

"Guerlin had no problem telling Lennie details about his part in the Levine robbery and murders, including getting Gregg Levine to commit perjury. Why was he so reticent to talk when she asked him about the murders of Neil and Boch?"

"Cut the rhetorical questions, Peter. I'm grumpy. It's late. Tell me what you're thinking."

"Maybe Guerlin didn't do the murders, but he knew who did."

McAdams didn't speak for a few moments. "You think he's protecting his sons."

"I could be way off base. But if my dad just got killed, and I had nothing to do with it, I'd certainly want to know what happened. Phil hasn't shown up for work in a couple of days. Shouldn't we talk to them to find out what they know? Shouldn't we at least see if they've been contacted?"

"And if they have been contacted?"

"Then I'll go home and go to bed and continue on with my musings tomorrow."

"And if they haven't been contacted?"

"Then I still have a little work to do."

Radar had deep bags under his eyes. His face was pasty and his lips were cracked. His white shirt, usually pressed to military degree, was wrinkled and dirty. All he wanted was to finish his paperwork and go to bed. What he didn't want was someone bringing up problems. His eyes swept over his desk and eventually landed on the faces of Decker and McAdams. "Guerlin admitted to the murders. It's Baccus's case. He's satisfied. Go home."

"Brady Neil is my case—"

"Go home!"

Decker said, "I'm just as tired as you are, Mike. Just call him up and ask if he's talked to Guerlin's sons."

"Baccus is with his daughter right now. I'm not about to disturb him. Go home."

Decker paused. "Yeah, you're right. He's probably not taking any phone calls. What about Wendell Tran? He should know if someone contacted the sons."

"Why is this so important to you?"

"Because Phil Guerlin hasn't shown up for work for days. I want to know where he is."

"Okay. You must think that Guerlin's sons had something to do with Neil's murder—even though Yves Guerlin admitted to killing Neil and Boch. And Brady Neil has been visiting his father for the last six months, so it's totally possible that Brandon told Brady everything about the robbery/murder. Blackmailing Yves Senior probably sounded like a sweet deal to Brady Neil."

"If Brandon told Brady all about the Levine murders, and Brady decided on a blackmail scheme, why would he drag Joe Junior into it?" McAdams said. "By all accounts, Joe was kind of an idiot and Brady was kind of a loner."

"You're not helping," Radar said.

"It's a good question," Decker said.

"This is what I think," Radar said. "Phil Guerlin overheard Boch and Neil talking about their blackmail plans and he told his dad about it. His dad offed them. End of story."

"That is completely logical," Decker said. "And I'd love to talk to Phil to verify that. But before I can, I'd like to know where he is. You're right about Baccus. He isn't going to talk to me. But how about if I make a call to Wendell Tran?"

"It's not your place to call."

"Then can you please make the call?"

Radar exhaled. "Since you said please. But the poor man is probably asleep."

"He's probably buried under a mound of paperwork. And if he's any kind of a detective, he's probably very busy trying to find Denny Mayhew," Decker said. "I think Guerlin and Mayhew had split up when they saw Gregg Levine go into Greenbury station house. I think the two of them knew that they had to split up. I bet at that point Mayhew wanted out and Guerlin was on his own. Please, can you call Tran?"

The captain's eyes were angry, but he nodded. "I'll see if Wendell Tran is answering his phone."

"Thank you very much."

"Wait outside," Radar said. "I don't want you listening to the conversation. You're making me nervous and mad at the same time." He paused. "How do you feel, Pete?"

"Horrible."

"After the phone call, you'll go home and get some rest?"

"Scout's honor."

"Get out of here." Radar picked up the phone. "Now."

Decker and McAdams waited in a dark, empty squad room shared by the detectives. A few minutes later, Radar came out and sat in a vacant chair. He held up his hands and let them drop by his side. "No word on the whereabouts of the boys or Mayhew. They've got an APB out for Denny."

"What about the boys?" McAdams said.

"What about them? They're not implicated in anything."

Decker said, "I think they—well, at least Phil— know something about the murders of Boxer and Brady. He worked with them and shortly after they were killed, he disappeared. That's not suspicious?"

"We don't know that Phil disappeared. All we know is that he's not home, he's not answering their phone."

"And we know he hasn't shown up for work," McAdams said.

"Maybe he took time off."

Decker said, "Can you put out an APB on him?"

Radar glared at him. "I asked Tran what he thought about that. It's his call. The Boch house murders are under his jurisdiction."

"You think he'll do it?"

"I don't know. He might. He does admire your persistence."

"Really?"

"That's what he said."

"Persistence is my middle name."

"No, that would be pain in the ass." Radar sighed. "Everything's being taken care of, Pete. Deal with the shit tomorrow—when you're more refreshed. Take him home, McAdams."

"Gladly."

Decker got up slowly. As he and Tyler reached the exit, Radar said, "Detectives?"

They both turned around.

"You made me look good. Excellent work."

He slept for fifteen hours. When he finally woke up, it was almost dinnertime and Rina was hovering over him, her face a mask of worry and concern. She placed a hand on his forehead. "You're hot."

"I'm okay," Decker answered. But clearly, he wasn't. He was stiff and in pain. His mouth was dry, and his pajamas were soaked in sweat. He smelled like a sewer.

"I think you're running a fever," she said. "I'll call the doctor—"

"No, please don't. Just bring me a couple of Advils and a couple of Tylenols. And a strong cup of coffee. I'll be fine."

She knew better than to argue. "You know, Peter, we moved here to get away from all the crime and the stress. Maybe it isn't working. Maybe you do need to retire."

"You might be right, but can we talk about this some other time?"

"Yes, of course. I'll get you that cup of coffee." Rina grimaced as she looked at him struggling to get up. "Need a hand?"

"No, no. I just need to feel like a human." He was finally on his feet. "I'll meet you in the kitchen as soon as I've washed off, shaved, and dressed."

"I'll get you a clean pair of pajamas."

"I need to go into work. I won't be long."

Rina laughed with incredulity. "It's after five in the afternoon. You're not going anywhere."

She was right. Decker sighed. "Okay. I won't argue."

His answer made Rina very concerned. "I'll go make coffee."

"Can you call Tyler for me? Ask him to drop by?"

Rina felt slightly better. Still obsessed with the case, but he'd pump McAdams from the comfort of home. "It's Shabbos, Peter."

Decker hit his head. "Of course. I'll do it. I'll make the coffee, too."

"No, I have instant and hot water. Don't worry about it. Go call Tyler."

An hour later, McAdams came waltzing through the front door. Decker had sponged himself off, washed his hair, shaved, and had put on a clean set of sweats. The medicine had also kicked in. He didn't feel good, but he did feel better. He envied McAdams's blithe spirit.

"Something smells good!" Tyler sang out.

Rina said, "Chicken vegetable soup."

"Yummy," Tyler said. "What else?"

"That's it. Chicken vegetable soup. Oh, I also bought a baguette. You're welcome to stay, but that's all there is."

"More than I have at home."

"What do you have at home?"

"A carton of milk, a can of instant coffee, and a bag of doughnut holes. You need help?"

"No, I can ladle soup."

"In that case . . ." McAdams pulled up a chair from the dining room table. He regarded Decker and clucked his tongue. "Boss."

"Hey." Decker took in a breath and let it out. It hurt. "What's happening with the Guerlin boys?"

"Still *ignotus*."

"Ignorant?"

"Unknown. Well, *they* aren't unknown, but their whereabouts are. How do you feel?"

"Never mind about me. What are the powers that be doing to find them?"

"Tran did put out an APB. Hamilton is doing what they can do."

484 · FAYE KELLERMAN

"Right."

"No, it's the truth, Decker. No one is sitting on their hands." McAdams leaned forward. "You might as well relax, because you can't get time to tick faster."

"I suppose that's true."

McAdams blew out air. "No easy way to say this, boss. Jaylene Boch died this morning of a massive heart attack. And before you even ask the question, yes, we had people on her day and night. No one went in or out without being screened. The upshot is she passed from natural causes, probably brought on by all the stress. But we both know she wasn't a well woman. Shit happens."

Decker bit his lip but said nothing. Although it hurt to talk, it didn't hurt to think. He spent a few moments taking in what the kid had told him.

McAdams filled in the silence. "Which means, or course, we'll never really know about the bloodbath at her house, the hidden pictures in her wheelchair, or the ins and outs of the Levine murders unless we get other people talking—like Brandon Gratz. And since he's not likely to talk, we are at an impasse. And maybe that's okay. It's a twenty-year-old case. If Guerlin Senior is to be believed, we basically know what happened. Maybe not every detail but . . ." He threw up his arms. "Boss, the Levine case is dead. Let's just say a few words and bury the body."

Decker didn't answer right away. Then he said, "I think you're right."

Tyler stared at him. "That's a first."

"When you're right, you're right."

"Why do I feel there's a *but*."

"I still have an open case with Brady Neil. I know you think that Phil Guerlin overheard Boxer and Neil talking about blackmail. I know you think that Phil told his father about the blackmail plot. And I know you think Yves killed them both, but it doesn't make sense. Why in the world would he and Mayhew stick around if they killed Boxer and Neil? The file was stolen *after* the murder, Harvard. The son, on the other hand, suddenly disappeared. The son. Not the dad. I mean, a seasoned cop murders two people, leaves a key witness alive, and then sticks around to steal a police file? Does that make any sense?"

"Not really," McAdams said. "What are your thoughts?"

"My thoughts are confused right now," Decker admitted. "I think we're working two different cases with different motives. I think we have Yves Guerlin and Denny Mayhew, who came to Hamilton to find out what we had on them regarding the Levine case when I started poking around. And I think we have the Phil Guerlin/Boxer/Neil case, which really didn't have anything to do with the Levine case."

"Okay, let's expand on your idea. Forget about Guerlin and Mayhew. Why would Phil Guerlin kill Boxer and Neil?"

"Let's look at the crime scene again, Harvard. Boxer's blood was all over the place. It spurted, it spattered, it dripped. Neil, on the other hand, was hit with a fatal blow to the back of his head."

"Boxer was the intended target. We always knew that."

"Right." A pause. "The one and only time I talked to Phil, he said he liked Neil. But it was clear he didn't like Boxer. Boxer and Neil were friends, although no one seems to know why. By all accounts, Neil was smarter than Boxer. Joe Junior was a dummy like his dad. And the two of them were ten years apart." Another pause. "Still, I'm sensing some kind of triangle here. No, not a lovers' triangle, but something."

McAdams said, "You are back to your original theory, then—that Neil was working some kind of electronic sales scam. Even though there are cameras all over the place."

"Cameras can't capture everything. We know that from experience, after looking at dozens of CCTV footage on the tollway. And if Neil worked there long enough, he might know where the cameras are."

"Maybe," McAdams said.

"Suppose . . ." Decker thought a moment. "Suppose that Neil was working the scam with Phil—who worked in the warehouse. Boxer found out about it and horned in."

"Or maybe Neil invited Boxer in because they were friends," McAdams said. "Phil didn't want it. The three of them argued and, boom, we have a bloodbath."

"Exactly."

"One thing, though. Why did Phil leave Jaylene alive?"

"Maybe the adrenaline had worn off and he didn't have the heart to kill an old lady. Or maybe she played dead."

"Why tie her up?"

"Just in case."

"Hmm, I don't know about that," McAdams said. "Anyway, when we find Phil, you can ask him yourself."

"If we find him. He may be long gone."

Rina brought in a tray of soup bowls. "Business is over."

"I'll eat to that," McAdams said.

"Are you hungry?" Rina asked her husband.

"Actually, I am."

"Then let's eat and talk about things other than unsolved cases and murder."

Which meant the three of them ate in silence.

Blessed silence.

Chapter 34

A week later, the small town still reeled in the aftermath. Lenora Baccus, adorned with honors and hailed as a heroine in service to her city, was given accolades as well as an extended leave of absence. She left Hamilton two days after it was over, without so much as a wave good-bye. Decker wasn't granted an opportunity to talk to her, but she did leave him a note—given to him by Wendell Tran—that included her warmest regards and her gratitude to him for being a true mentor. The phraseology didn't sound like her, and Decker suspected that someone in the office had penned it for her. He had thought about contacting her directly, but he had enough going on in his life without stirring up the pot.

Levine's Jewelry immediately posted a notice of indefinite closure. Going along with the same theme,

Yvonne Apple's house bore a For Sale sign that matched the sign sitting on Gregg Levine's front lawn. Both families moved out a few days after the incident. And both left no forwarding address.

Victor Baccus put in his papers for retirement: a good thing considering that the murder convictions of Brandon Gratz and Kyle Masterson were about to be overturned due to Gregg Levine's perjury. The felons knew that the wheels of justice grind slowly: red tape took a long time to advance through the system. The D.A. still had the option of retrial, but since the defendants had served almost twenty years and both were up for parole in a year, it was decided that the sentences would be commuted to time served. Within a couple of weeks, both men would be out—as free as yellowjackets, buzzing around some poor unsuspecting soul, waiting for their next meal of blood.

The dust was still settling when Philip Guerlin walked into Hamilton PD ten days after his father was murdered. By the time Decker arrived with McAdams in hand, Guerlin had been seated in an interview room. He had lost weight and muscle, and his inked arms sagged with loose flesh. His bald head had grown into a ginger crew cut now that his red mohawk was gone. His eyes were tired and his cheeks were all bone. He wore a black T-shirt over denim jeans, both items of apparel two sizes too big for him.

McAdams pulled out a laptop. His primary function was to take notes, although the interview was being recorded and videotaped. Tran and Decker would do the majority of the questioning. Tyler had no doubt that Decker would take the lead. He was not only a great detective, he was a great interrogator.

The men shook hands without enthusiasm. Guerlin took a sip of water. His voice was a quiet hollow. "I heard you were looking for me and my brother." He cleared his throat. "YJ isn't coming in. He's . . . I told him I'd find out what's going on for the both of us."

"Where is Yves Junior?"

"None of your business," Guerlin said. A beat. "What do you want?"

Tran opened a notepad. His dress included a white shirt, pink tie, black slacks, and black sneakers. "Initially, we wanted to contact you and your brother about your father's death."

"I think we're past that. Anything else? Your phone calls to me are menacing."

"That wasn't our purpose."

"What was your purpose?"

Decker said, "Thanks for coming in."

"Yeah, yeah. What do you want?"

Tran said, "Where have you been?"

"Anywhere but here. I don't want to talk to anyone."

"Must be hard for you," Decker said.

"Thank you, Detective Obvious."

"Press been hounding you?"

Guerlin fidgeted. "I don't talk to the press. And I really don't want to talk to the police."

"Yet here you are," Tran said.

"Like I said, the phone calls were threatening."

Decker said, "I'm sorry for your loss, Phil."

Guerlin's nostrils flared. "Right."

"I understand that your father was very dedicated to you and your brother."

"How would *you* know?"

"I don't know what he did behind closed doors, but that's what he showed to the public. Was it accurate?"

Guerlin stared into space. He didn't answer.

Decker continued. "When your father was in the jewelry store with Detective Baccus, he told her a lot of things." Guerlin's eyes returned to Decker's face. "We're wondering if he told you things about his life before he died—"

"Before he was murdered, you mean."

"Before he was killed," Decker said.

Guerlin shook his head. "If I were you, I wouldn't believe anything that the bitch said."

"We have their conversations recorded," Tran said.

"Right." Guerlin laughed without joy. "Play it for me."

"It's evidence," Tran told him. "There are things on it that you can't hear."

"I can't hear any of it because it doesn't exist. I know that the police are allowed to lie. I'm a cop's son." A pause. "I was a cop's son. You'd say anything to get . . ." His voice trailed off.

To get a confession. Decker said, "Baccus wore a wire."

"My dad would have found it. You're lying."

"It was very small and very hidden." Tran got up. "Let me see if we can key it up to something unimportant. Just so you can hear his voice."

"You can doctor in a voice."

"Then nothing we're saying will convince you that we taped your father before he died?" Tran said.

Guerlin didn't respond. Then he said, "I don't even know why you asked me here."

"Like Detective Tran said, we initially wanted to notify you," Decker said. "Now that you're here, you may have questions. Is there anything that you want to ask us?"

Guerlin was quiet. "Yeah, a big one. Why'd she have to kill him?"

"Detective Baccus went in unarmed," Tran said. "When SWAT came in, your father was attempting to kill her."

"Bullshit! She probably sprang first. My dad's a lot of things, but he's no murderer."

Tran looked at Decker, who said, "You know that your father killed the guard on duty at the jewelry store. You also must know that he confessed to two murders." Guerlin was silent. "Two men. Brady Neil and Joseph Boch. Your friends—"

"Not my friends," Guerlin said.

"You knew them," Tran said.

"Yeah, I knew them. We worked in the same big-ass store. So what? Lots of people work there."

"That's certainly true," Decker said. "But you happened to work in the warehouse with Joseph Boch. And you knew Brady Neil. As a matter of fact, when I first talked to you about Brady's death, you seemed to like him—Brady."

"Brady was okay." He looked down.

"Yeah, you seemed upset when you heard about his death."

"I was."

"What about Boxer?" Decker said.

"When you came in, I didn't know he was dead. He just didn't show up at work, remember?"

"Yes, you're right, Phil. I didn't even know who Boxer was. Later, I found out he was Brady's friend."

"He was an asshole."

"Yeah, I kind of remember that you didn't like him."

"No, I didn't like him. I don't like a lot of people, but they're all walking around. Not missing or dead."

Decker nodded. "Not many people liked Boxer."

"He was an asshole."

"Why do you think Brady liked him?" Decker asked.

Guerlin shrugged.

"More important, why do you think your dad killed them?" Tran said. "We've been looking for a motive, but we can't find one."

"So maybe he didn't kill them."

"Then why would he say he did?" Decker said. "I mean, how did he even know about them?"

Guerlin didn't answer. Finally, he said, "My father knew their fathers."

"Okay," Decker said. "We know they were all involved in the Levine murders."

Tran said, "You think he killed the sons to get revenge on the fathers?"

"Maybe."

"Anything is possible," Decker said. "But we're talking about a twenty-year-old crime. Why now?"

"Look, Detective, I don't know what was going on in my dad's final moments." Guerlin licked his lips. "If you have my dad on tape confessing to the murders, why all the questions?"

"He confessed to the murders," Decker told him. "He didn't say why. I don't understand why your dad would want to kill Neil and Boxer. What was in it for him?"

"This is getting boring. I think I should go."

"You can go," Decker said. "It's fine. But FYI, I'm not totally clueless. I have a few ideas that I'm working on. I'll call you when I get somewhere."

Guerlin tensed. "What ideas?"

"About why your dad would want Brady and Boxer dead. The thing is, Phil, I don't think he killed them—Brady and Boxer. Maybe your dad made a false confession to throw us off track or something like that. Why, I don't know. Do you have any ideas?"

"No."

The room went silent except for Guerlin's tapping foot. Then he spoke up. "Well, like I said, my dad knew their dads." Tap, tap. "Maybe they were trying to blackmail him—Brady and Boxer."

"Brady and Boxer were trying to blackmail your dad?" Decker said. "Over a twenty-year-old crime?"

Guerlin nodded. "I do remember something."

"Great," Decker said. "Tell me."

"He told me—my dad told me—that he took payoffs for the Levine robbery. Maybe Boxer and Neil found out about the payoffs and started blackmailing him."

"Did he tell you that?" Decker asked.

"Yeah, kinda."

"What did he tell you, Phil?"

"Just that," Guerlin said. "That he took payoffs and Boxer and Brady were blackmailing him."

Tran said, "How'd they find out about the payoffs?"

"Boxer's mom. She told them."

"Jaylene Boch told her son and Brady that your father made payoffs?"

"Yeah."

"Why would she want her son to know about her involvement in the crime?" Decker asked.

"Why do you think?" Phil said. "Money."

"Jaylene was in on the blackmail?"

"Maybe. I don't know everything." Guerlin became irritated. "You figure it out."

Tran said, "If you knew that Brady and Boxer were blackmailing your father, why were you friends with them?"

"Not Boxer. I hated him."

"Brady then," Decker said. "He was blackmailing your father, but you remained on friendly terms with him?"

"I didn't know Neil was blackmailing my dad until after he was dead. Then my father told me the whole story. That he was being blackmailed and he killed them."

"And knowing all this, you went to work the next day?"

"What else was I supposed to do?" Guerlin became agitated. "I wasn't going to rat him out. What kind of a son do you think I am?"

"I think you loved your dad."

"Damn straight." Guerlin looked at McAdams. "Do you talk?"

Tyler said, "I'm the tech guy."

Guerlin rolled his eyes.

"Let me wrap my head around this," Decker said. "Brady and Boxer started blackmailing your father. It was then that your father decided to kill them."

"No, he told me *after* he killed them."

"Then you'd be an accessory after the fact." That wasn't quite true, but Decker was on a roll. "Why would he put you in that position?"

Guerlin paused for a long time. "Maybe I got it wrong. Maybe he told me before he killed them."

"And you didn't think to say anything to Brady and Boxer about it?" Tran said. "That their lives might be in danger? You didn't think about contacting the police or trying to talk him out of it?"

"I didn't take him seriously. People spout off all the time."

"Yes, they do," Decker said. "But most people aren't being blackmailed. That's a very serious crime that pisses people off big-time."

"You maybe could have warned them to stop," Tran said. "Threatened to turn them in if they continued their scheme."

"Why should I?" Guerlin said. "Those two were always yapping with each other. Gossiping like little girls. What the fuck do I care about them?"

"Well, for one thing, their deaths immediately put the focus on you, Phil."

"Yeah, but I wasn't paying them off."

"I believe you," Decker said. "But frankly, Phil, we have no proof that your father was paying them off, either. Maybe you have proof. Do you have proof?"

"Check Brady's bank account. He always had spending money."

"Yeah, I know about that," Decker said. "His mother said the same thing. And I did check his bank account. He did have money, but not like a big score. I don't think he got that money by blackmail, Phil. But I do have other ideas about that money."

"Like what?"

"Later." Decker shook his head. "The thing is, Phil, your father was a seasoned cop. I can't see your father being scared into submission by a couple of punks with felons for fathers."

Guerlin's eyes looked on high alert. Then he said, "But it's true. They had this whole scheme that would have ruined my dad. I heard them talking about it. As a matter of fact, I told my dad about it."

"Okay." Decker was quiet. "Let me wrap my head around this. You told your father that Brady Neil and Joseph Boch were going to blackmail him over his participation in the Levine robbery/murder. And your father killed them to avoid being ruined."

"Yeah." Guerlin nodded his head. "Exactly."

"Then the money that Brady had in his bank account couldn't have been from blackmail because at that point, the scheme hadn't gone through yet, right?" When Guerlin was quiet, Decker said, "What did your father say when you told him about the blackmail scheme?"

Guerlin didn't answer.

"Phil?"

"He said . . . I told him, and he said he was going to kill the punks."

Using the same word *punks* that Decker had just used. "But you thought he was just spouting off."

"Yeah," Guerlin said. "But apparently he was serious."

"Didn't you say your father isn't a murderer?"

"Not without good reason."

Tran said, "Then your father does kill when there's a good reason?"

"When threatened, anyone can kill."

"True enough," Decker said. "So now you're telling me that your father killed Brady and Boxer because they threatened to blackmail him."

"For the hundredth time, yes." Guerlin took in a deep breath and let it out. "Boxer's old lady was in on the original plan. She was the one who told Boxer about my dad. And Boxer told Brady Neil and the two of them made these plans." He was breathing fast and didn't make eye contact. "I told my dad about it. He didn't go in with the intent to kill him—"

"Him?" Decker asked.

"Boxer. He was the main guy. Just another reason why I hated him."

"You're telling me now that your dad didn't go to Boxer's house with the intent to kill him."

"Yeah, right. He just wanted to scare him a little to get him to stop. You know, rough him up." He bit his lower lip. "I guess things got out of hand."

"I thought you just said he wanted to kill them," Decker said.

"I think that was a figure of speech," Guerlin said. "He just wanted to rough him up."

"Except that your father killed them."

"Like I said, maybe things got out of hand."

"That's how it sometimes happens." Decker waited a moment. "Okay. Let me wrap my head around this, Phil. You told your father about a blackmail scheme because you overheard Brady Neil and Boxer talking about it, right?"

Guerlin nodded.

"Can you say yes or no for our video recording?"

"Yes."

"Okay," Decker said. "Then your dad went to Boxer's house to get him to stop blackmailing him—or stop the scheme of blackmailing him. Because at this point, the blackmail hadn't gone through yet, right?"

"Right."

"But things got out of hand and your dad wound up killing Neil and Boxer."

"Yes."

"So Brady just happened to be there or . . ."

"I guess." Head down. "I wasn't there."

"Right," Decker said. "I do have a little question about what happened. Why did your father leave Brady's body in an open place to be easily discovered? And why would he bury Boxer where no one can find him?"

"How the hell do I know? We didn't talk about it—the killings. We certainly didn't talk about where he buried them."

"You have no idea where Boxer is buried, or if he's even dead?"

No eye contact. "No idea," Guerlin said.

But Decker had other ideas. After the murders, Phil called his father up in a panic, and the two of them took care of the bodies. They buried Boxer first and then dropped Brady Neil out in the open. Maybe Phil wanted him to be found. Or maybe, by that time, they were too exhausted to bury him properly. "And the crime scene," he continued. "Not much of Neil's blood. A shitload of Boxer's blood—"

"Boxer was a fucking idiot. I don't blame my dad for beating the shit out of him. That asshole can get under anyone's skin. It was probably his idea to do the blackmail in the first place. Brady probably just went along with it."

"Nah, I don't believe that," Decker said. "Boxer

wasn't smart enough to plan something that intricate. And in my opinion, Neil seemed too smart to try to blackmail a seasoned cop. He knows what a pissed-off cop is capable of doing. There must be some other reason why your father killed them."

Silence.

"Let's talk about other things, Phil," Decker said. "I got some interesting information from some teen-aged boys I interviewed a while back. This is what they told me, okay?"

No response.

"They told me that Brady was reselling electronics equipment at deep, discount prices. And whatever he got for them was pure profit because the electronics were stolen from Bigstore warehouses."

Guerlin's jaw was working overtime. His eyes were everywhere except on Decker's face. Finally, he said, "If Brady and Boxer had a side business going on, I didn't know about it."

"I don't think that's quite true, Phil, and here's why. To pull off this scheme, Brady needed someone way smarter than Boxer in the warehouse. You're a smart guy, Phil. I think that someone was you."

"You can think whatever shit you want to think, but it wasn't me."

"What happened, Phil? Did Boxer try to muscle in on your sweet deal?"

"I've heard enough." He got up from his chair and headed toward the door.

"Did things get out of hand at Boxer's house?" Decker called out. "Did you call in your father to help clean up the mess? Did your father give you a perfectly logical cover story in case the police questioned you?"

Phil turned the handle of a locked door. "Let me out of here!" Seething. "You can't keep me here."

"We just locked it for privacy, Phil."

"Then let me out of here. I know my rights! You have no fucking proof!"

His words were suspended in the air.

"Listen to what you just said, Phil," Decker said. "'I know my rights. You have no proof.'" A pause. "'You have no proof,' not 'I know my rights. I'm innocent.'"

"I am innocent! I'm fucking . . ." His eyes welled with tears. "My father was *murdered*. This is police harassment! I'm going to sue your asses off."

"You don't want to do that," Decker said. "Because once you do that, we are entitled to defend ourselves by examining every intricate detail of your life."

Phil wiped his wet face. "Let me *out* of here. I'm not talking to you anymore. I want a lawyer."

"If you're innocent, why do you need a lawyer?"

"You can't question me once I ask for a lawyer."

"I can do anything I want because you haven't been arrested."

"I'm not talking to you anymore." He dried his tears on his shirtsleeve. "Either let me go or arrest me and get me a lawyer. Which you can't do because you have no proof." He looked down. "And I'm innocent."

"Believe it or not, Phil, I'm not here to harass you. I just want to get to the bottom of everything because I don't believe your father killed Brady Neil and Joseph Boch Junior."

"I don't care what you believe. Open the fucking door."

"Sure," Decker got up. "Thanks for your help."

"Fuck you."

"Detective McAdams, can you kindly escort Mr. Guerlin out?"

Tyler got up. "You know what I think?"

"I don't give a shit what you think," Guerlin said.

McAdams looked him in the eye. "I think a guy who lets his daddy do his dirty work for him is a real *pussy.*"

Guerlin snapped. He went for the throat. Immediately Decker and Tran shot up, pulled him off Tyler, and slapped his arms behind his back.

Tran immediately snapped on the cuffs. "I'm arresting you for assaulting a police officer." Then he read Phil his rights. Guerlin responded with a resounding *fuck you.*

Decker said, "You're right about one thing, Phil. Detective McAdams doesn't say much. But when he does talk, he sure packs a punch."

Chapter 35

Guerlin spent a night in jail, pleaded no contest to the charge, and the judge gave him a suspended sentence with community service for six months. No other charges were filed against him. And Denny Mayhew was still at large. Since he lived in Arizona, rumor had it that he had crossed the border into Mexico, where he'd be lost for a while, if not forever.

Not everything was neatly wrapped up with a bow. Decker didn't feel a lot of satisfaction with the case. Two murderers were going to be released from prison, and Philip Guerlin, the man who was probably responsible for two deaths, was walking around town, cleaning up garbage on his weekends.

Two weeks later, Bergenshaw penitentiary announced the release date of Brandon Gratz and Kyle Masterson. Decker made the three-hour trip to the prison the day before the scheduled moment of freedom for the two felons. He was doubtful that Gratz would see him, but he was pleasantly surprised when he did agree.

Even with his liberty granted, the guard still chained Gratz to the bolted-down table in the windowless interview room. It was a move that Decker appreciated. He loosened the tie around his neck. It was hot inside.

He said, "Congratulations."

Gratz was relaxed. "I guess I have you to thank."

"The Bible asks, 'Does a leopard change its spots?' If it were up to me, I'd keep you here. But it's not up to me and there was a miscarriage of justice, and with that in mind, you're certainly entitled to what you're getting."

Gratz glared at him. "If you're pissed about my release, next time don't stick your nose where it doesn't belong."

"You're right about that." Decker took in a breath and let it out. "Yves Guerlin Senior confessed to killing your son."

"Not surprised," Gratz said. "And I'm glad Guerlin was killed. You think I'm a bastard? He was a monster."

"Not an honest man, that I'll give you. But I don't believe he murdered your son."

"No?" Gratz leaned forward. "Then who did it?"

"You figure it out," Decker said. "I'm not mentioning names. With you out of here, that's a death sentence."

Gratz grinned. "You're not stupid. I'll grant you that."

"You know your son was murdered along with another man."

"Yeah, Joe Boch's son."

"They were friends, although no one could figure it out. Joe Boch Junior—Boxer—was an idiot. Your son was a smart guy like his father. No telling taste, huh?"

Gratz was silent.

Decker said, "I keep thinking about why they were friends—ten years apart, different skill sets, different everything except they were both kind of small-ish guys." A pause. "As a matter of fact, they kind of looked alike."

Gratz smiled. "Maybe."

Decker said, "Did you tell your son that he and Joe were half brothers in one of his visits, or did he somehow figure it out?" No answer. "Jaylene's dead, you know."

Gratz shrugged. "Too bad for her."

"I think Guerlin Senior had a soft spot for her. I think that's why even though she was alive when he got to the house, he couldn't kill her. Did they have a thing as well?"

"Could be. Jaylene had a lot of things with a lot of people."

"Just like Margot Flint had lots of things with lots of people."

"Not me," Gratz said. "She went in for more . . . connected people. People who would do her good."

"Anyone in mind?"

"Like you just told me. You figure it out."

"Would this have anything to do with a certain detective with a chronically ill wife who was maybe after a little comfort himself?"

"You mean a certain up-and-coming detective who looked the other way when she and Mitch were about to be sentenced? I mean, someone fucked up with that, right?"

"Right," Decker said. He suddenly felt very depressed. All the good work that Victor Baccus did with the Levine children probably arose from guilt. Because he had to have known that Margot Flint, the woman he let go, was behind the murders. "Those pictures I showed you of Margot Flint. They were sewn into Jaylene's wheelchair. Looks to me like she kept them for insurance."

"Maybe."

"Insurance against Margot or insurance against Baccus?"

"Both probably." Gratz grinned. "You never can have too much insurance." He looked at the guard. "I'm done here."

Decker stood. "Thanks for your time."

"And thank you for getting me out of here."

"Right." Decker sighed.

A totally unsatisfactory case.

September came and Greenbury hummed with activity—students moving in for the next academic year. Tyler went back for his final year of law school and once again, Decker and Rina had the house to themselves. Although it took a few weeks for Decker to shake the blues, he soon became philosophical, which is the nature of survival in police work.

He never did hear from Lennie Baccus.

With the Jewish holidays approaching in a couple of weeks, Rina had begun to formulate her to-do lists. Lots of food and lots of cleaning, which meant lots of work. She was sitting at the dining room table, hair in her eyes because she wasn't wearing a ponytail holder or a hat. She was chewing on the back of a pencil.

Decker looked over her shoulder. Then he sat down. "Isn't there an easier way to do this?"

"Four married children and three grandchildren with another on the way, *baruch hashem*. And let's not

forget Gabe and Yasmine. You tell me how I'm supposed to relax."

"Can we do a potluck? Everyone bring their own
food?"

"No, we cannot do that," Rina said. "Actually, it'll
be easier this year. None of the gang is coming out
until Sukkoth. We're free for Rosh Hashanah and
Yom Kippur."

"Except you're hosting the Hillel lunches and the
Yom Kippur break-the-fast dinner, if I'm not mis-
taken."

Rina looked at her husband. With everything that
had happened over the summer, she never realized
how tired he looked. "You know, I haven't agreed to
anything. We can just keep it with the two of us."

"That won't work. You'll see all the meal-less students and feel guilty."

"You're probably right."

"But"—Decker lifted a finger—"if we were out of
town, that wouldn't be a problem, right?"

Rina looked up from her lists. "Right." She paused.
"What do you have in mind?"

He shrugged. "Anywhere but here. You choose."

"Wow." Rina put the pencil down. "Well, we can
visit our mothers again. Better weather and a little
more time?"

"You want us to spend Rosh Hashanah and Yom Kippur in Florida? At a nursing home?"

"I guess that is a little impractical." She thought for a second. "We can spend the holidays in Israel and then visit the mothers on the way back for a few days."

Decker thought a moment. "Spending the holidays in a country where I don't speak the language and don't know a soul except my soulmate. That sounds perfect! Let's do it."

"You're serious?" When he nodded, Rina grinned. "You're so funny. I adore you."

"Forever and ever?"

"Forever and ever."

About the Author

Faye Kellerman lives with her husband, *New York Times* bestselling author Jonathan Kellerman, in Los Angeles, California, and Santa Fe, New Mexico.